UNTIME

Kieran Marsh

Copyright © 2024 Kieran Marsh

All rights reserved.

ISBN:
ISBN-13:

Dedicated to anybody prepared to take time to read.

Reader Notes

First up: thanks! I really appreciate you taking time to read this book. Even if you don't make it through the first chapter, if you simply can't take it or you just don't have time, I still appreciate the fact that you have opened my book. Double appreciation if you do manage to finish, and triple if you can find some time to feed back to me.

A bit of background: in March 2020, I signed a contact with an agent in London for a previous novel. It was a very exciting time, she was enormously positive about selling the book. It needed some work but she predicted international sales. It went very sour very quickly. Covid arrived, and she was one of the first people in the UK to catch it. She seemed to take a long time to recover, and having to mind her young children took a lot out of her. Our edits, that should have taken three or four months, stretched on to eighteen months and by then her language had turned very negative: she had lost the passion for it. At the same time, the publishers were desperate for up-lit, and my novel was "very dark." In late 2021, she made an attempt to sell it, and in January 2022 she realised she could no longer give time to developing my work, and we ended the engagement.

I had seen it coming a long way out, and I tried to convince her to stick with me by passing a series of sketches of possible second novels by her. She chose the idea behind this novel because it was "high concept," i.e. it had a strong central concept that the publisher or reader could grasp. I threw together a first draft while I was waiting for her to finish her read through and try to sell it. It was a very bad first draft, even by first draft standards, and I honestly think that helped her make up her mind not to work any further with me, rather than convincing her to stick with me. Hey ho!

In 2023 I wrote a second draft which was much stronger, and since then I've been through several basic edits, aligning character voices, correcting the tone, etc. If I can use a building metaphor, the novel is at the end of first fix, but before plastering has begun. All the plumbing and wiring is in, but the finish has yet to be applied. Why am I giving it to you in this state? Because if there is heavy lifting to be done, if there is major structural work still required, now is the time to do it.

On the plus side, that means that you can make constructive comments and, if they ring true with me, you will have a chance to influence the development of this novel before I attempt to find a new agent. On the negative side, you will be exposed to a shocking level of finish, or lack of it. You will find punctuation, spelling and grammatical errors, but worse than that you'll find characters that are still weak, dialogue that is clunky, continuity errors, all kinds of things that would normally be sorted out in the many, many read throughs of the second fix. Please forgive those, and trust me that I can make the little details much better. Please look at the bigger picture.

So what am I looking for? I'm hoping you'll find most of the novel palatable, but some pieces will stick. Try to focus on the biggest things; try to be specific: "I couldn't believe in the Book because...", "I found the character of Jim didn't ring true because people accepted his behaviour too readily," "I found it too long." Whatever, give me two or three things that would go the furthest to make this book into something that you would recommend to a friend.

Here's some ideas to consider, but by no means are you limited to these:

- Title: is it apt? Compelling? Would you pick it off a bookshelf?
- Opening: does it grab you, make you want to keep reading? Should I leave out the Lorcan 1997 and dive straight into the doctor's office, or is it too important to have the *Book* front and centre?
- Pace: do you keep turning pages? How does the short chapter length work?
- Characters: particularly the two point-of-view characters: do they work? Do you see enough in them to want to read through and find out what happens?
- Sub plots: does Carlos have a place in the story or should he go? Is the Eamo arc satisfying or does it seem a little gratuitous? Does Mike become a real character? What about Rhia: you're not going to like her as a person, but can she hold her own as a character?

- Ending: do the events of the Sunday grab you and pull you through to the ending? Are you left with the sense that the story has been wound up? Do you have open questions? Were you left unmoved?

I will listen to all constructive feedback, take notes and take them away to ruminate. I won't agree with everything that's said, after all it is my novel, I need to write it as I want it, but it's likely that many of the points made will ring true to me. We often know what's wrong with our own writing, after all, we are all readers, but sometimes it takes somebody else to say it out loud before we can realise it's something that needs to be fixed.

I'll do a major edit to fix the things that do need to be fixed, then I'll read-read-read to get it polished and professional. I will try again to attract an agent, though at this point in my writing career, just having a novel that I am proud of and I know is good is a wonderful reward. Commercial success can be overrated.

Many thanks for being part of the creation of this work.

0: Beginning

Lorcan, 1997

It's like vomiting. Pressure builds to bursting in his head. Painful, desperate words are thrown onto the page. It won't stop. The past is explored, expunged, expelled.

'Help me!' he says out loud. His voice is sharp, his body shattered, exhausted.

Nobody answers. The writing continues compulsively as if the pen is pulling the hand.

Only snatches of it make sense:

"...out onto the street where the..."

"...in the back and my seatbelt..."

"...from the laneway..."

None of it is real; it is all too, too real. It spins and it swerves, nothing sticks.

And then, like a vast tidal bore-wave, it reaches the end, bends, breaks. The words are done. Lorcan is done. He falls over onto the bed and slips into sleep. He tosses in turbulent dreams, wakes later with a scream-shock.

He is gasping, panting. Fists clutch. He sits up suddenly. A dream. A nightmare, nothing more.

Ten years old, he trembles under the intensity. He is terrified. He goes to slide off the bed, to find Mam, but his hand falls on the *Book*.

His body shivers with sudden clear sight. No dream, the dreadful thing is real, is right here. Some old thing. Something ornate, antique. He touches it, is sickened by a familiarity. It's heavy; wooden covers with metal mountings, some weird temple thing. And the pages... not paper. But... what?

He opens it, pulls apart the stiff, suspicious leaves. There are many pages that have writing, all kinds of script, much of it he can't read. It's like hieroglyphs to start with, then something more like English. And there, the last thing written, is his handwriting. As he stares, a pain stabs his head. No! He doesn't want to read. Doesn't want to know. He slams the book closed.

As he does so, a small sheet falls out, a page torn from a school copy book with a scruffy scrawl, unfamiliar, roughly written:

> Listen bud. This buke is for you. I got it like when i was your age and all. Guess im not seeing you again so i guess you need to know some stuff about it.

It rambles on incomprehensibly, talking about the *Book* and something called *"Untime"*, until it is signed with the letter B. It makes no sense. Lorcan cannot take it in. What the hell is happening? He needs his Mam and his Dad. He drops the damned *Book* and walks backwards away from it.

On the landing outside his room, he meets Doircheas, two years younger. She is in her nightie, there are tracks of tears on her cheeks.

'It's Mam and Dad,' she says. 'They're broken.'

1: Falling

Alice, Tuesday, 11:13am

What will it take to stop him talking? Professor Bailey's voice booms, then descends to nasal drone, washing out of her grasp like soap. Her eyes are drawn to a carriage clock behind his shoulder with gold balls that spin one way, then the other, all fine wood filigree and gold leaf. Is it an antique? It fits with the oak panelling of the office, and the spin-stop-spin seems to counterpoint Bailey's jabber.

Her mind drifts from the room to the boys who will be out of school soon, to the pork in the fridge for dinner tonight, to the three hundred euro bill. Three hundred? Madness. Yes, her tiredness is taking a heavy toll, little illnesses haunt her, her energy feels like a battery that won't charge properly. Taking two young boys and a taxing job into account, she may be a bit rundown. Who wouldn't be? Why did the GP send her to this overpaid quack who can't even talk?

'...that there should be, ahem, the appropriate tests based on the presentation, that is, the symptoms as relayed...'

Bailey is old school, pompously professional but with a compassionate face, competent looking even if right now he is uttering nonsense, spilling a rolling noise, making no sense at all, nonsense. What will it take to stop him talking?

It's a frustrating fuss over nothing. She has fought colds and conquered flu; covid helped, all the mask wearing and hand washing, but it's left her exhausted with mouth ulcers and headaches, cold sweats at night. But stop, be sensible, no self-pity! A young mother needs one motto: just keep going.

Three hundred euros to sponsor this consultant and his mahogany bookshelves of massive medical tomes and his spinning balls. Worse, she was supposed to meet with the easy-smiling Eamo, a kid in her care with such a sweet spirit, but sorely exposed to the danger of his drug-dealing uncle, possibly now beyond hope because she has cancelled. Real remorse!

'…and so taking the two biopsies, that representing the anterior presentation, relative to the norm, as if to say…'

What will it take to stop him talking? She hears him but one end of his sentences have no connection with the other. Weird words pop out.

'…while the lymph nodes have normal indicators, the platelet counts show us a different story…'

He must have somebody else's notes, he's reading somebody else's illness. This would be hilarious if it wasn't infuriating. The tactile tap of his finger on the desk becomes a drumbeat, a kettle drum, a booming gong. She looks to Lorcan, expecting confusion but seeing soft concern.

'…though there's never full clarity at this stage in proceedings, it's difficult to raise any doubt…'

The professor is going on. The words start to fall coldly into place, dominoes placed end to end, snaking into something sinister.

'…and I'm very sorry to have to tell you that you have…'

It rings out through the room like a funeral bell across a still lake.

'…Leukaemia.'

Turns out that the bruising, battering rounds of flu symptoms, the hundred other tedious ailments are not just anxiety or long-Covid.

She's sick. Very sick. He mentions the five year survival rate and her heart stops. Twenty percent. He talks of paths and possibilities. Tests and then tests and then more tests. New drugs on trial, experimental therapies. Chemo. Very aggressive. Debilitating. All these words that are not her words.

Confused calm turns to clear panic. Nausea bursts over her. Waves of horror splash like thumps in her face, her belly, her groin. What will it take to stop him talking?

And then he stops. 'Have you any questions?'

The room spins too quickly. A voice, her voice, asks: 'Can I still work?' What a stupid, idiotic thing. She is reduced to blather.

'You can continue to work for now, but really you should be looking at winding down ahead of a lengthy period of absence.'

There is no office, no mahogany, no carriage-clock, no Bailey, no Lorcan. An ugly void has opened. She lets herself fall, feeling weightless, wasted, finished.

Lorcan, Tuesday, 11:19am

He holds her. Lorcan holds Alice in his arms as she unfolds, un-becomes a woman, becomes instead a broken child. Tears and trembling. He must keep memory of the doctor's words in his mind, Alice will not remember them. Lymph nodes, non-lymphocyte white blood cells, bone marrow. Chronic Myeloblastic Leukaemia.

There are tears, tight pain burning his eyes. He feels each shiver that runs through her; it forms a hum, a fundamental vibration from out of her core that seeps through him, scares him. This woman he has adored for twenty years, this woman is the world. He wants to fix her, untwist her, reform her back into the rock he relies on.

He can smell the freshness of the detergent from where his nose is pressed to her white tee-shirt. Her bra straps show through the fabric stretched over her taut and twisted back as she bends into him. There's a red stain on her shoulder, ketchup maybe? One of the boys must have smudged her.

It will be okay, it has to be. The doctor, the professor, he's good. His reassuring voice promises more tests, suggests treatments.

And, of course, there's the *Book*. That is the factor that will fix everything that medicine can't. He has never told her, not for want of trying. If she knew, she would realise: if the doctor does not undo the disease, *Untime* will remake these moments and turn the vicious illness into a blurry buckled memory fading from reality like a bad dream.

He knows it will be okay, and after that the only thing in his head, with immediate guilt, is whether they will still get out to the pub tonight like they had planned. It's an awful thought, but they have had awful news, after all. A drink: to mark the horror, to numb the pain? He closes his eyes, but the sound of her sobbing still hurts.

The professor is finished his monologue. He will give them a moment while he gets the wheels in motion.

'You're in good hands,' he says as he shuts the heavy wooden door behind him.

She is a mess. The shoulder of his nice new linen jacket is soaked through from her tears and snot. She is still trembling, deep tremors that seem to bubble up and burst like boiling mud, then collapse down again. A fit of sneezing overtakes her; there are tissues in a silver presentation box on the table, Bailey is clearly no stranger to trauma. Lorcan feeds her tissues as he has done for the last six months through one cold or flu after another.

He hates himself for thinking about beer, about drinking. What a bastard! If she could see into his head right now… But then if she could see into his head, she'd know about the *Book*. She'd laugh, and they'd head to the pub. Cancer, whah! He can feel a dryness in his mouth.

He's here for her. He is steadfast. He is her rock.

It takes twenty minutes for the subsonic vibrations to cease. Lorcan's arms grow sore from holding her, his spine cramped from immobility. He begins to unwind her, to unflex his own back. He is damp, she is a mess, mascara and lipstick smeared. He gets on his knees and with a tissue, slowly, gently, tidies her up as best he can.

'Where's the doctor?' she asks.

'I think we're done.'

'What? I have so many questions.'

'He's going to be available tomorrow, he said. We can talk to him then, we can call him, after we've had a night to let it sink in.'

'Tomorrow? What the hell is it with doctors?'

He takes her hand. There's still a fragility in it, her strength robbed by fear. Outside the perfection of the panelled office, the building shows signs of neglect. High up on the walls, in corners, paint peels, watermarks bloom. Carpets bump over floorboards that undulate like forest boardwalks. The secretary's office is more Scandi than Georgian. She's in her sixties, he thinks, grey hair judiciously darkened, conservative cardigan and skirt. He understands now the hushed tones and kind face she had greeted them with; she would have known. Now she has a look of *'I've been here before. I've seen you. I've known the sound of death approaching.'*

With gentle voice and frequent reassurance she tells them of what is to come. The business is mundane, but she fields Alice's repeated questions with grace. There are forms to sign for the insurance, she gives them a letter with all the appointments they'll have to make.

'I've added the numbers of the various managers,' she whispers conspiratorially. 'If you can get them on the phone, you know, if they have a voice to go with the name, well appointments can sometimes be got quicker.'

Alice carefully scans the sheet. Through her elbow, Lorcan feels a resurgence. The Alice he knows is a fighter, a little general. A flame lights somewhere, he cannot tell where, but he can smell the sodium smoke-flare of the match.

'I hear you,' says Alice. 'I will call these people; they will get to know me, whether they want to or not.'

The secretary's brief smile suggests she has sought this, to spark a fight. Motivation is a medicine. Alice is going to be one of the twenty-percenters, she's thinking, and Lorcan is pleased.

'Well, fuck,' he says as they make it out onto the street.

'Yes, fuck.'

'Jesus. I can't even talk about it. I mean…'

'Yeah, I know.'

'Maybe we should go somewhere, chat about it. You know, maybe go get a drink.' It sounds so horrible, suggesting drinking at this emotionally devastating time. There again, some shocks are so great that dissolving them in alcohol can be a positive move. When she doesn't initially freak out, he is encouraged. 'We could, you know, find somebody to pick the boys up.'

He knows immediately he has made a mistake. Her face becomes stark and solitary.

'No, Lorcan, sorry. I need my boys.' She checks her watch. 'Oh my goodness, it's after twelve, we have to go.'

'No, Alice, for goodness sake. We need some time, somebody else…'

Her eyes silence him. 'Come on,' she says simply, so he does.

Alice, Tuesday, 1:15pm

The world has turned into a fairground ride, one of the nauseating kind. She feels weightless, floating, then she's fountaining upwards, her stomach rioting, head reeling. In the car, as Lorcan drives, she panics so completely she can't breathe. Lorcan pulls in while she gasps and then pants. He suggests they call to her GP but she can only see her boys standing outside the school; nothing matters now, nothing matters except that she is there when they step out of class; a delicate hand, a delightful smile, an image complete with spatters of sunshine through leaves.

Looking outwards as they start driving again, unreality consumes her. The trees are caustic, the road twists in on itself, the people look grotesque. Passers-by carry on as if nothing has changed, they care nothing, they perceive no shift of the universe. She is nearly sick with the sensation of her news but these people keep milling past, running in front of the car as the lights change, talking on their phones. How can they not know?

The sea comes in sight, the choppy estuary. There's a car park jammed with Jaguars. The block of Clontarf boutiques sloping down to *the Yacht* pub, opposite the car park, attract a well-to-do clientele. Lorcan turns in and stops beside her car. They had met there at ten o'clock, a turbulent lifetime ago. Alice was coming from a meeting at an outreach centre, Lorcan had been reading mails at home, this was a handy midpoint.

'I... shouldn't leave you here,' says Lorcan.

'I'll be fine.'

'You probably shouldn't drive.'

A fire flashes in her and she only just catches it. She's not sick, not proper sick like... like she might soon be. Not an invalid. For now, she can look after herself. How can he suggest that? "Shouldn't drive?" She wants to belt him, blame him, tell him how irresponsible he can be. At times like this he can be so removed, so detached, so ignorant.

She stops, breathes deeply.

She can't blame him, he is what he is, a wonderful husband, her lover, her life partner. She smiles.

'No. I need this. I need time.'

'I'll come pick up the boys with you.'

'Go and work, Lorcan. I'll need you. There will be a thousand things I will have to ask you for in the…' She nearly said days, it's not just days. 'In the months ahead. Go work while you can. Or take the day off or whatever you need. I'll talk to you when I get home, this is something I have to do.'

His hand grips the gear lever, knuckles white. His nails have a tiny line of black dirt, a combination of him keeping them long — supposedly for his guitar — and a childish reluctance to shower regularly. If he would just take example from his well-brought-up sons. Infuriating, but Jesus, she loves him, needs him. She grips his broad fingers, feels strength, feels a tremble of foreboding.

'I love you, Lorcan,' she says, and means it.

Broad beams of light from the afternoon sun frame his face and there is a moment of surreality. Is he real? Is he a real thing, the man she says she loves, or has she imagined the last twenty years, the tenderness, the wild love, the soul-joy? His face flies apart, comes together again like a *Lego* man.

She reaches a finger to his chin. They have just been thrust into a battle and all they have is each other, the boys, and their love. She desperately hopes it will be enough.

He sucks in air and is suddenly crying. She holds his face in her hands while he regathers.

'I have to go,' she says once he is recomposed.

'Love you too,' he says, as Alice climbs out.

She has a cry herself when she gets in her car, a necessary let down. She bawls out curses at whatever deity might be listening. She thumps the dash. The black hole beneath her beckons, and she could let herself drop into it, but she has the boys to collect.

When she looks up, a man in his forties with a blue *Leinster* rugby hat and a fluffy white dog is watching, concern on his face, half stepping as if considering whether she needs help. She works up a smile and nods to him.

Should she wear a mask, she wonders as she drives? She has kept hers on long after others had stopped, had put Covid behind them. Flu after cold after illness has plagued her. Now she knows the cause, but also knows she is vulnerable. She should stay protected. There again, why care? If she is going to die… No, she is not. But she doesn't want to flag her predicament. But she's been wearing her mask anyway…

Oh God! There are too many things, too much to think about and thinking hurts. She starts driving but her heart keeps distorting, bending, until at one point she thinks she might pass out. She should stop. She doesn't. She breathes deep to keep the panic at bay.

She's too late for the good parking spots, close to the school. By the time she walks back, gangs of mothers have formed, cliques clicking with the competitive hum of the professional middle-class Clontarf set. Red jumpers are beginning to bounce around as the first of the boys and girls are let out into the sunshine. She does not want to be in the mix for the chats today; she tries to plot a course to the gate away from familiar faces.

'Alice,' says Mary O'Reilly, popping out of nowhere, 'how's things?' Mary with her big hair and big eyebrows, she's a lovely soul and Alice would normally stop to catch up with her, but not today.

'Ah, grand, you know yourself,' she nods, then "sees" somebody she has to talk to inside the gate and smiles her apologies to Mary.

Good. Her heart and head are in a good place. She has not panicked, not pandered to the disease. The future is fuzzy, but her present is solid. She finds a safe corner, beside the bike shed, just far enough away from the gate but with a good view and an escape path in case she is spotted. She waits.

There is a gratifying hum around the school, boys and girls are skittering out. Screams, yells, bold faces, beautiful joy broken into bite size pieces. All the passion of human life packaged in tiny bodies. Alice imagines the corruption of her illness amid this innocence. She almost panics yet again, breathes herself back to peace.

Darragh is out first, head down, flicking his speed-cube. He is only just seven and young for first class; a really smart kid who always gets "quiet in class" on school reports. He wears his beautiful brown hair long and scraggly so he can avoid eye contact when it suits. There's an edge of the spectrum about him, but he's content enough not to warrant going for medical assessment. As long as he's happy… But at some point in the future, maybe, she won't be around to make sure.

'Darragh,' she calls. He stops and looks about, not seeing her. 'Over here.' He runs to her, buries his head into her belly and hugs her. She had intended a hit and run: grab boys, hurry to car without interaction, get home. The moment he ducks in for a hug she is lost. She is on her knees and holding him so tight, heaving dry sobs as she grips him. For all that he is shy, he is never afraid of public displays of affection.

'Are you okay, Mam?' It is Cian, two years his brother's senior but a different brand of boy. Blond, tall for his age and with bright eyes that are always darting about. He is never without a ball in his hand; he is bouncing it now, and then hand-passing it off the wall. She reaches out and touches his head, and he ducks away from her.

'Listen guys, how about, instead of going home and doing our homework straight away, we go and get ice cream?'

'Yay!'

She had not seen that coming but, now that she's said it, it is exactly the right thing to do at this time, in this instant. No cataclysm here, no cause for tears. Sow joy in tiny heads and terrific love will grow. Make memories while you may.

She turns towards the gate but almost walks headlong into Rhia and her little weedy boy, Forry, short for Forest.

'Alice. Oh, I'm, you're...'

'Hi, Rhia, I...'

Rhia is a long time friend, mainly through Lorcan, and Alice still finds it hard to warm to the woman. She had been part of "The Gang" when Lorcan was in school, slim and pretty and headless, hippyish, like some naiad from a Shelley poem. But gorgeous, damn her, blessed with a head of scorching red hair that is to die for. No wonder Lorcan had a thing for her, had once burnt a candle that, Alice suspects, is still half-flickering today. But Rhia has only ever had eyes for the gombeen, Jim, the big waster. And who calls their child Forest and then sends him to an all boys school, for Christ's sake? Is it only jealousy that fuels Alice's antipathy, a lingering feeling she may have been the second choice? No, of course not.

'Are you okay?' Rhia asks. 'You look pale.'

'Just came from the doctor's.'

'Oh dear, nothing serious I hope.'

'No, well, look, I'm really sorry, Rhia, I need to run, but listen, I'll call you tomorrow.'

'If there's anything I can do? I have my homeopathy thing now, and I'm doing angel readings, you know you can come to me and I wouldn't charge you or anything.'

'You're a star, Rhia. Look, tomorrow, okay.' She does the thing wiggling her hand by her ear to indicate a phone while pushing the boys ahead of her as a shield against any other moms.

She usually lets the boys put their seat belts on themselves, but today she makes doubly sure that they are secured. It seems immensely important.

They chatter away about Minecraft and football in the back. Alice's head drifts away, dragged back again and again into darkness. Snatches of words the doctor used keep jumping out at her; she pushes each punch down, buries it in the noise of her brain, only for another punch to come swinging at her, catching her off guard. At one point she is very close to driving through a red light before she hits the brake.

'Mam!'

'Sorry, boys, I'm just a little... distracted.'

Distracted? Distraught, more like, and all the more so that she can say nothing. She does not want to lie to the boys; she wants them engaged, as much as boys of that age can be. That's near unthinkable; how can they be asked to bear this burden? Oh hell, she'll have to figure that out too, how to include them without breaking them.

The lights change and she pulls away taking greater care to focus.

And then there's her family. And Lorcan's family. Oh Jesus, so much to be faced.

Again, she needs to breathe deeply to stay in control. She tries chanting Hail Marys under her breath, a habit from her childhood which she reverts to in crisis, despite having lost her faith. The repeated prayer doesn't keep her from drifting to the darkness.

They get to the *Omni* shopping centre. She's been looking at *Emily's Amazing Ice Cream Emporium* since it opened a year or so back; it looks gaudy; cosmetic and brash. Nothing on the technicolour menu for less than a tenner and the thought of spending forty euro on ice cream has stopped her from darkening the doorway. Today is different.

Today is very different. The car seems to sink into a parking space like a stone in quicksand. For a moment, she has no idea what is happening, but then the car is stopped and the engine is off. The boys tumble out and she follows, dazed, dizzy, half-dreaming. She hopes to wake up, wipe out the doctor's visit, the diagnosis, the disease. It doesn't happen.

Cian won't take her hand as they navigate through traffic. She worries, but she's proud of his independence. The shop door plays a

Willie Wonka tune as they enter, and she feels like she's in *Oompa Loompa* land. Bright colours clash with stripes and slashes, great glass tubes rise to the ceilings filled with smarties and marshmallows and a dozen things she struggles to identify. Ordering turns out to be much more complicated than she had imagined. Not only do you have to choose between scoops or sundaes, brownies or bananas, but then there's sprinkles, sauces and whatever is in those tubes. The boys order directly from a girl who looks far too skinny to work here, Alice just points and nods till she ends up with something way more vulgar than she had intended.

They sit on round plastic seats at a round plastic table. The boy's faces are chocolated up in seconds.

'What do you want to be, boys?' The question tumbles out of her mouth while her brain is screaming no, don't do morose. Don't do the "I love you, always remember that." Her love will stay with them not because it is spoken, but because it is given, freely and frequently.

'I wanna be eight,' says Darragh.

'Don't be a gobbie,' Cian goads him. 'She means when you're older. Like I'm gonna play for Dublin.'

'I don't want to play football.'

'Just as well coz you can't.'

'Stop, Cian. Darragh, imagine you're really old, like as old as me, what would you like to be?'

'You mean like, would I be a daddy and married and all?'

'Would you?'

He shrugs, and the two of them are back in their ice cream. Serves her right for fishing. They're only boys. Life hasn't even begun properly for them, now that it's ending for her.

Or not, she has to remind herself; who knows, it's all in the lap of the gods of clinical testing, but the overwhelming feeling in her soul is of fishing lines being reeled in, timelines shortening, opportunities disappearing.

Speaking of opportunities, it's too late to get life assurance now, she'd always meant to. Nothing she can do about that one. She has her pension though, Lorcan could cash it in if he needed the money, or hold onto it and think of retiring early. In twenty years or so.

Twenty years. It cuts so sharply that she almost cries out. Twenty years that she will not see, may not see, might not see, oh, hell, she's going to die. It's so heavy that she's hyperventilating. Stop. Breathe. One step at a time. Don't look into the darkness.

She tries to eat the ice cream, but the sense of it is sour, bad to her taste, so she lets the boys at it and just watches them. They are so alike, so different. That little tweak in their noses, just like Lorcan, but Cian has broad cheekbones and Darragh has a pinched face. They both have their hair pushed back out of their faces as they eat; they get it done by the barber now. Apparently, these days, boys don't get their hair cut by their mothers. Their limbs thrust out at odd angles as their bones grow inside their skins, sharp elbows that they poke each other with, legs that splay across seats and sofas, teeth twisting loose. Boys under construction.

It has been a devastating day, but she has beautiful boys who need her, and she is damn well going to be needed as long as she can manage.

Lorcan, Tuesday, 1:20pm

It has been a devastating day. Lorcan had felt like he should wrap Alice in cotton wool, not let her out of his care, but he knew her face. He had watched her get into her car, then had driven away. A minute later, he had to park at the side of the road and let the emotion escape through a scream. 'Why? Why the fuck? Fucking leukaemia, are you fucking kidding?'

The sudden shock of it shakes something loose in his head, a half-memory half remembered. He reaches for it even as it evades him. The mind-fuck of moments that have been twisted and obfuscated but never quite erased. He sits panting, spent.

He pulls out a tissue, he had taken spares from the doctor's office, and wipes his wasted eyes. The rear view mirror shows a man not far off his forties. He imagines himself younger, but right now his face is good for every damn day of those years. The scar across his cheek shows faint white against the puffy pink, a scar that was living proof of the effectiveness of the *Book*, and the foolishness of ignoring its power. He wears a *V-for-Vendetta*-style moustache and beardlet, trimmed this morning, now looking grotesquely ridiculous. He had wanted to grow it for the Freebird-athon, for a laugh. Alice hates it, he should shave it when he gets home.

Home. The *Book*. He needs to get to the *Book*.

He pulls himself together and points the car home. There is a quickening in him now, a little shaft of excitement.

In the sitting room, where he works, he built a bookshelf, all wood and wax, an ugly thing but sturdy. Alice doesn't know, but there's a false panel on the base which, if you push it just so, swings away. He reaches inside, and pulls out the *Book*.

An object of fascination, almost worship, since he was ten. Since...

The event that had brought the thing into his life. It is a wasp, wisping at the back of his head, waggling away from his touch. He has the note, still, from somebody known as 'B', though he knew no B, not that he can remember. Memory is a harsh mistress, often absent, frequently misleading, sometimes punishing.

The *Book* is a wonderful, mysterious, magical, monstrous, magnificent thing. The cover is of wood, carved ornately with a curious figure sitting beneath a peaked pediment. Fine gilding picks out the detail, the twisted filigree that encloses the scene. Inside, the paper is... not paper. Some kind of parchment or papyrus. Or maybe skin. Not human skin, though. Surely, not human?

He expects, each time, to feel a frazzle, a shock, a zest, yet it is disappointing to touch, no different to any old hardback book in an antique bookshop. But open it, read the pages and his head swims. Maybe there's a hundred pages, maybe a thousand, maybe twenty, he can't grasp it. Only certain pages can be opened, the others shit-kick away from him like rats in a sewer.

He opens one, familiar scrawl:

3rd February 2003

We were on the ferry. On the deck. Smoking. Yeah, there was a smoking deck and Bob brought me up there. We watched the port coming up. Holyhead. We were coming into Wales. Bob looked so fucking cool, like he smoked every cigarette down till the filter caught and his hair all combed back, looked like that guy from Grease.

Oh God, he thinks. The memory of that day is both intolerable and intensely thrilling.

So anyway, we got into port and went to our bikes. 'Gonna be smooth,' he said to me. 'We're going to burn these bikes to hell and back.' He says that kind of crap, most of the time I laugh but, well, I've only had the bike a week. I don't even have a license. I was shit scared. 'Nothing to it, kid. It's like riding a bike.' Har har!

There was like a buzzing in my head. I shouldn't have had that pint, I know, and the second and third pints were a big mistake, but it was three hours since I stopped drinking, and it was gonna be like another hour till we got off the tub. I'd be fine.

I bought my Yamaha, bright yellow with chrome pipes and forks, 320 cc, a replica classic, with the money from stacking shelves. A lot of shelf-stacking, in the hope of earning more as a motorbike courier. Bob, not easily impressed, said we'll go to Wales, couple of turns around those hills and you'll sail through your test. We'll go to Wales, man, he said. Up till last week, I'd only ever been on a Honda 50.

Okay, so we were on our bikes for ages and they're letting off all the cars and trucks first. That was okay, it let me get my head clear. As soon as we were out of port, Bob was itching to get up to speed. The road was narrow and twisty so we were stuck behind traffic all the way to that big Menai bridge thing. As soon as we were across, the road started to open.

Wow! The power of the thing was immense.

What a fecking eejit that kid was, he thinks, yet he can still feel the throb of the thing between his legs and can't stop a smile.

Bob took mad risks overtaking but as soon as I pulled back on the throttle, my bike ripped past trucks and cars, what a fucking rush. I saw the needle hit 180 kmph on one nice stretch of dual carriageway.

We headed inland on the A5 through Snowdonia. The place was awesome, hairpin bends through hidden green valleys and then gush upwards again, the engine purring.

We took a bend at 120 but there was a tractor on the road and I'd no time to break so I overtook. There was a car coming the other way. I pointed myself at the crash barrier on the edge of the road. This is going to hurt, I thought.

It didn't. The crash barrier very effectively stopped the bike.

The crash barrier did not stop me. I continued, out over the cliffside. I sailed out, then over, then down. My legs hit first, they folded and rolled me so that my face was side-smacked into the cliff face. My last thought was Wow!

I was dead. For real. I was dead. I saw the scene from above. Bob was standing gazing down at me. He looked at my bike, thing was hardly damaged, bit of scuffing. He lit a cigarette, for fuck's sake. 'True,' he said. Standing on the side of the gorge looking down at his dead best friend, all he had to fricking say was 'True!'

He had died. He had died in some valley in Wales when he was eighteen and fuck what a thrill it had been, what a headscrew.

He can remember it, although memory is not the straight line for him that other people experience. His memories are full of knots and twists and blanks. Some of the things in the *Book* are gone from his head — totally — others are still lucid, some linger like a dream, just outside of comprehension. He can't go near that first incident, when he was ten years old, only knows that he got that *Book* and that it had broken the fabric of his family, left deep wounds that had never healed, that could never even be spoken of.

He remembers the bike well enough. Remembers a kind of out-of-body experience, watching Bob light a fag; he can even recall the way that Bob was holding the cigarette, fingers facing outward instead of his stylised clenched fist. Next thing, he was writing in the book, safe in his bedroom. It was the *previous* week, just before he bought the bike, before Bob had proposed the trip. He had never bought that ticket, never gone to Wales, never died. It was just... erased from everything except his own mind. And the *Book*.

This caused head-wrecking problems. He *had* bought his ticket, but he *hadn't*. He *had* boarded that ferry, but he *hadn't*. He *had* bought a bike and he *hadn't*. Both truths coexisted and conflicted. This was the source of the pain, of the difficulty talking to anybody else about it. How could you tell the truth when truth was two things?

The note is still tucked into the *Book*, still there from that first morning when he had woken. He pulls it out to read it, though he nearly knows it by heart.

> Listen bud. This buke is for you. I got it like when i was your age and all. Guess im not seeing you again so i guess you need to know some stuff about it.
>
> Look i dont know how it works. I wont pretend and all. But its a life saver. Like it saves your life for real. You die, see, and then you write it down and that, and you are not dead. You will see what I mean. In fact i guess you have already.

Right?

And not just dead, things like if youre in trouble or you done something bad or broke a leg and all. It does that too. Undoes it, i mean.

Only you cant make it do what you want, or when you want it. It decides. Sometimes it waits ages.

But come here, theres a thing, the bloke as gave me the buke called it UNTIME or something like that. You get to live it again. You go back in time, for real! And live the day or the week or the month again. No consequences. You get away with anything you do in Untime, see. CULE, huh? That sorted me for some good times, tell you that.

Last thing, you cant talk about the buke, kinda like that movie, ha ha. Well you can, only it does your head in really

> something rotten, you will see what I mean. Best just keep quiet and all.
> Best of luck
> B.

In his twenties, he had tried to figure the whole thing out, resolve the conflicts. He had tried to figure out who "B" might be, but never found any leads. Of course, he could not show anybody the note, that was too painful, too confusing to deal with.

He had read books, pounded the internet, tried to tease out some of the less readable pages, the ones that just blurred when he tried to look at them, or looked like indecipherable scribbles. It had messed his head up, brought on anxiety that was horrible, pulled him through periods of depression. He had been forced to back away.

And then there is *Untime* — those days or weeks that the book erases. That week between buying the bike and the crash that wasn't; all the cash he had spent was back in his pocket. As B's note had said, everything is undone, nothing has a consequence. If he knows he is in *Untime*, he can do what he likes and nobody will remember. Or very nearly so, as he once discovered.

The *Book* works, that much he is sure of, and he is not alone in that. Rhia knows also, from that night on Burrow Beach, though she could never fully grasp it. He knows, through her experience, that it's not just some psychosis, his own private hallucination.

Otherwise, he can't talk to anybody, not even Alice. Any attempt to even mention it and his head clogs up. Anxiety overwhelms him. Nobody knows. Not his friends, not his family. Him, and Rhia, and whoever "B" was.

The *Book* is real and will put this whole thing right, he is certain. He can feel an energy. A surety. Relax, steer clear of the anxiety, the *Book* will deal with Alice's illness.

In a moment, his head feels light. The awful truth is nothing of the sort. *This is Untime*. The *Book* will take away the illness, undo all the nonsense of this afternoon and, even better, it will give him a bit of time for a little self-indulgence. Not too much, of course, he still has to take Alice's illness seriously, but there is leeway.

He feels his insides untwist, a pain unravelling. He feels the absence, had not noticed the pain building since the diagnosis, but now feels relief.

He smiles, pushes the *Book* back into hiding — it will tell him when it's time — and checks his Guy Fawkes look in the hall mirror. No need to shave it just yet. He can have fun waiting for this time to be undone. And he can smoke, on the quiet, at least. Technically he is off them since Cian was born, but the habit has never quite died. If this time doesn't count, well, why not? Who will care once this time was erased?

Opportunity is king, and nobody will deny that an opportunity of this magnitude fully justifies a sneaky trip to the shops. He checks the Find-My app on his iPhone, Alice is showing up in the car-park of the Omni shopping centre. He's got at least an hour, he reckons.

Alice, Tuesday, 5pm

The smell of smoke assails her. Lorcan hustles to the door as soon as the kids burst in. He hugs them, then turns to her, face drawn with deep concern. That's when the odour hits her. He's been smoking. Some kind of curse forms but she swallows it.

'Are you okay?' he asks. 'You don't look... well.'

I don't look well? I'm diagnosed with cancer and I come home to find my husband sneaking cancer-sticks. Fuck-di-doo!

None of the anger emerges. It is swallowed by the void in her subconscious, a void that still roars loud so that nothing else can linger.

Lorcan dances about her, bringing her to the kitchen, sitting her down, getting a coffee brewing. It's a bit hollow, though. If he truly cared, he would not be smoking. She looks around her lovely kitchen. Two years ago, they had it converted and extended; when they moved in it had been a conservative-old-lady house, all striped wallpaper and good carpet with a dominant tone of beige. Now she had bright surfaces, a breakfast bar, space, light and somewhere to hang her mobiles, pieces she had created when she was pregnant with Darragh. She had three in the kitchen, each hanging several feet with little pieces of glass and colour ribbon to catch and refract the sunlight that streamed in on bright mornings.

Even on this day of death, it was a haven of hope.

'Are you okay?' he asks again.

'Never better. You?'

'Sheez, I don't know. It's mad like.'

'Yeah...' There is so much to say, so much they have to talk about. There is too much. More than they should ever have to talk about. Oh, God, where to start?

We are friends, she will say. *We're best friends. You're my rock. We need to fight this together*. All that. But why the hell can't he keep his lips off a cigarette for two fricking hours?

She needs her girl-friends. She will need Lorcan, yes, but Jackie and Beth: they will bring indignation at the unfairness, bring compassion and level-headedness; she wants to sink in the pool of their love. 'Look, I need to see Jackie and Beth tonight, you know. Girl thing.'

'Oh, I thought we were, you know…' She almost laughs at the slapped-puppy-dog look on his face. He can be so easy to wind up.

'Yeah, I know, we were going to do something together, date night. We will, look, I just need, you know, it's just…'

'You need the chats.'

She could slap him sometimes. The chats. *I have cancer, don't you get it?* But that void is still roaring. 'I need the chats. And so do you really. Would you think about going out with the lads?'

'Out with the lads?'

'Go get a couple of pints. Men talk, you know?' His face has a rare edge to it, sharpened by the run of his scar. When he smiles, the muscle on one side pulls up, the other side bends slightly down. He might not be conventionally handsome, but that face is her Apollo and her David and her Adonis. She loves him despite his tendency to childishness, despite the fact he could lose the plot and start smoking at a time like this. She takes his hand and holds it tight. 'I love you,' she says again.

'Oh, Alice!' He melts like snow in the sun, falls around her with hugs and she absorbs him.

'Don't worry,' she says. 'We'll get through it. As long as I can lean on you, I know we will.'

'It won't take long.'

'What?'

'I mean, it's like… We can push it back, make it un-happen.'

'No, Lorcan, no, we can't live in denial…'

'Not denial, I have a…' Something twists over his eyes, a wince. 'I can't say, but the cancer's not going to win, we can beat it.'

'Of course. Of course we can, Lorcan. But it's going to be a long road.'

'No, no, it's a…'

'Look,' she places a finger on his lips. 'I want to cook dinner. No, I *need* to cook dinner. Mad, I know, but listen. We'll talk, but, you know, I just need time, okay. Give your lads a shout, see if they're on for tonight. You need the self-care as much as me.'

And there's the mischievous spark in him, like Darragh being told he can stay up past his bed time for the Toy Show.

'Yeah, I guess.' He's trying to hide it, trying to pretend that her illness means too much for him to enjoy himself. 'I mean, we all have to stay well, to be there for you, like.'

'You got it.'

He scuttles off, already pulling his phone out.

She sends a *WhatsApp*, simply stated: 'My place, 9pm, need love, bring Prosecco', smothered with strings of smileys and hearts, to Jackie and Beth. They knew about the doctor's appointment, they would know something's up.

Time to cook dinner. She has no appetite. Twenty-percent five-year rate. She feels like she has her heels on porous rock, toes dangling over the blackness. If she looks down, the rock will crumble.

However, she has passion. Cooking for her boys, something they will love. Burgers. Mulching breadcrumbs into mince will keep the darkness down, and then she'll sit and smile at them as they stuff buns into their mouths, as if she's seeing them for the first time.

Lorcan, Tuesday, 8:30pm

The air is crisp and anointed as he walks out into the wind. On this late March evening, there is an almost autumnal breeze that creeps into corners, bending back branches just green with leaves. It reminds him of younger days when he first started heading out to meet the Gang, into the night air thick with the smog of smokey coal. The smell of coal and cigarettes continues to glow with warmth in his memories, even if coal is now banned from cities.

As soon as he's out of sight of his home, he lights up a cigarette and sucks in the smoke. The years fall away from him. Big Jim had been the cornerstone of the Gang, Rhia, Bob, a couple of others that have faded away now. They had brought about Lorcan's rite of passage from childhood to wild youth and, in truth, he has struggled to break from that notional wildness in the years since. Cans of beer on the slopes of Howth, bonfires burning into the nights, road-trips and binges, all with Jim as the Svengali — for better or worse. The buckle in Lorcan's brain as he breathes smoke out his nose carries him back. He can remember the thrill and the smell and the fire warming him, the long evenings, and the craving that he had felt, still feels in some ways, for Rhia.

He pulls out a hip flask and takes a small swig. It's an Irish single malt, good stuff; normally he'd just have vodka, still Jim's drink of least resistance, but tonight something a little special is justified. Tonight, he can play the victim, though he also knows that game won't last long. The Gang are good friends, but conversation is kept shallow, light hearted. They are none too far removed from those kids who swigged beer on the slopes of Howth.

It is *Untime*, though; anything he does or says tonight will be erased. He can have as good a time as he wants, and there will be no consequence.

The *Old Duke* pub is not by any means the nicest bar in the village but there's mercifully no music or pub quizzes, just the low drone of racing or golf from the telly, two or three quiet conversations and always plenty of seats. It is all polished wood, high wooden perches, filigreed mirrors, and a handful of drinkers. There's no having to elbow your way through crowds to the bar or shouting just to have a chat. It had been their watering hole on and off since school. As ever, there's maybe a dozen punters, mostly solitary. The lighting is dim, punctuated by the odd flashing as one telly or another goes to an ad break. The odour of the unwashed toilets floats on the air. Not particularly a pleasant place, but years of familiarity make it comfortable.

Bob is ahead of him, sitting in the corner with three pints of *Guinness* just settling. Bob was into bikes at a young age, hence that incident in Wales that still brings a half smile to Lorcan's face when they meet eyes. Somebody, had called him *Biker Bob* for fun and he'd taken the name to heart, adapting a persona halfway between the Fonz and Meatloaf, hair greased back, leather jacket and oil-stained jeans.

'Dude!' Bob embraces him in a swarthy man-hug, slapping his back with both hands but avoiding any contact that could be mistaken for affection. 'Respect. What's the emergency?'

'It's Alice,' says Lorcan, nodding. 'Jesus, it's bad, man.'

'Aw, hell. Spill it.'

'Leukaemia.'

Bob puts a heavy hand on Lorcan's shoulder, pulls him close. 'That sucks, my friend. Alice is almighty. Speak to me.'

It flows from Lorcan with quiet fury; with unusual honesty, he tells of the visit to the doctor, the diagnosis. He feels again the emotional distress that has been lingering despite the *Book*. He explains, with new-found wikipedia-authority, about chronic versus acute and lymphoblastic against myeloblastic. He speaks of red blood cells. They drink deep of the dark-ruby-red stout and let silence fall on the rage. Men are comfortable not talking, thinks Lorcan, though it's also common that Bob will close down if the conversation gets too emotive.

Eventually, Bob slaps his hands and gestures in mock surrender. 'I don't know what to say, man, I really don't. That's so cruel. What is the prognosis?'

'Five year survival rate is twenty percent, but, you know, it is what it is. Alice and I are too strong for this to break us.'

'True.'

'Yup.'

Although Bob buries any emotion in his childlike tough-guy image, Lorcan keeps faith. If he looks past the clichéd slang, there is a real heart beating. Bob is a friend.

As so many times in the past, Lorcan longs to talk about the *Book*, with Bob or with anybody. He's never managed; even with a few pints on him, any attempts to explain the mystery just come out as garbage, or else drive him into some kind of panic attack. All these years, there has been only one person he could share with, and even then only a couple of times across the decades.

So, he lets the subject peter out, and before they can decide on a new topic, Big Jim bursts in. Jim never just arrives, he happens. He is an event. It is a talent that Lorcan marvels at, and he has a voice on him would make a virgin cry. When he sings his songs there is silence, when he stops, his throat is killed with thirst. Jim has many dark facets, but the guy is a walking festival. He throws a quick glance at Bob and Lorcan before doing his rounds.

'Benny,' he grabs one old fellah sitting at the bar. 'How's the gout treating you? Looks like it's getting to your nose. Pedro, my man, my best wishes to the daughter, is she any better? Bart, those steaks you got me, they were heaven. Any more fall off a truck, yeh know where I am. William, bud,' he turns to the barman. 'My friends will be wanting another round, I feel sure, you may want to get it pouring.'

Billy the barman glances over at Lorcan. Jim is popular here, but there's nobody naive enough to believe he will ever pay for a pint. Lorcan gives the nod.

Jim strides over to them. He's a majestic figure, six-foot-six and broadly built with bit smiley head on him. He has been known to claim that the movie version of *Hagrid* was based on him after he went for an audition wearing his big Abercrombie coat and while he was still sporting his beard. Robbie Coltrane stole his look, though he could not carry off Jim's flair. So he says.

'Lads, yiz are looking glum.'

'S'bad news, Jim,' says Bob. 'Sit yourself down.'

'Jaysus, who's gone and died? Is that my pint?' He takes up the spare pint of *Guinness* and downs half of it in one slurp. 'Begob, I had a fierce thirst on me. So what's the badness?'

'It's Alice, she's been diagnosed with leukaemia.'

'Ah, Lorcan, like I'm gutted and all. Yeh must be busted, are yeh?'

'Yeah, pretty cut up.'

'When did yeh hear and all?'

'Just today.'

Silence settles. Bad news, delivered cold, is a curse. Leukaemia, it tickles the tongue, falls forward from Lorcan's mouth, lies twitching on the table. They stare, strong but solemn, silent for a man's moment.

Jim slams his heavy hand on the dying beast, destroys it. 'Jaysus, yeh must be hurting big time. Hey Billyer,' he calls to the barman. 'Hurry up with those pints now, this man's going through a world of pain, only one analgesic works on that kind of thing.'

Billy gives him a side-nod wink, happy to be part of the fun as long as somebody is paying.

'D'ye know what I was after thinking of,' Jim goes on, 'and this'd be the perfect thing to get yer mind off things. I was going to organise a day trip Holyhead, on the ferry, like. Do yiz remember, that used to be gas? Would do yeh good, Lorcan, get yer head out of the mess.'

Once, the Gang had taken the ferry to Wales, came back without debarking. It was an excuse to drink for the guts of twenty hours. By Jesus, Lorcan was wrecked, he remembers, but he also remembers a long chat with Rhia on the smoking deck, a deeply passionate chat. That was before Alice had strung along with them, before he had given up hope with Rhia, before… Another memory bounces into his head, but it was spiked with loss, and he lets it go.

He could go, if this was to be a forgotten time, a time of no consequences, then why not? Of course, Jim has no intention of organising anything. He might badger Lorcan into buying him tickets and booze, but just as likely he'll forget.

'Sounds like a gas,' says Bob.

'C'mere, Lorcan, she's going to be grand. I can feel it in the bones of me. Let's get another pint in to celebrate.'

It went without saying that it would be Bob's round again, but given the second pint had yet to be dropped to the table, Bob was in no hurry.

'How's Rhia?' Lorcan asks.

'Ah, yeh know,' says Jim. 'Women, huh? Jaysus, she's all over the place these days, doesn't know if she loves me or she's going to leave. Well leave then, I says to her, and see if I care. Course, she has no bleeding intent of doing such a thing, yeh know what I mean?'

'Right. You should go easy on her.'

'Easy? She should go easy on me, more like. Anyways, I'll tell her to give yer missus a bell, get the gossip from her on the leuko and all.'

'Yeah, let her know, will you. Alice asked me, she met Rhia today, you know, it was too raw to share.'

'I hear yeh, bro, say no more.'

'Smoke?' says Bob. The three of them shuffle out the door to the beer garden, actually a fire escape with a couple of ashtrays and a metal table for people to lean against. Lorcan proffers his cigarettes, Jim takes one.

As they light up, the chat drifts off into sports, the hope of Dublin GAA, the prospects for the summer rugby tour. Then it swings through several sci-fi box-sets running on Netflix. They speculate on what the turnout might be for the annual Lynard Skynard mass Freebird headbang in the park this year. By unspoken agreement, the conversation on Alice and her illness is done for tonight. From time to time, Lorcan wishes for friends that he could be close with emotionally, but most of the time, this is exactly what he wants: a pint, a smoke and a chat about boy stuff.

When they get back into the bar, Jim starts into his favourite monologue, *The Workman's Friend*, a famous Dublin-ese soliloquy on the spiritual compensation to be had from a Pint of Plain; the punters join in on the refrain. That done, he dives into the *Ould Triangle*, followed by *Come out yeh Black and Tans*. Lorcan lets himself join the mood, throws an arm around Jim's waist and helps belt out the lyrics. Even Bob has his pint and his voice raised in song.

It's all very familiar territory, but it brightens everybody in the pub, and by the time Bob's singing *Patricia the Stripper* the dozen-odd punters still there are standing and joining in. Lorcan and Bob oblige with the strip-mime.

Jim manages to wangle five pints out of them over the course of the evening, even though Lorcan and Bob stop at four, and then he talks himself into a freebie for the road from Billyer, on account of the entertainment. When they get outside, Lorcan produces his hip flask. The buzz from the pints is swimming round his head, and he feels great. This is exactly the escape he needed; tomorrow, unless the *Book* choses tonight to end this charade, there will be dark thoughts again, the anxieties, and the many tasks they must tackle, but tonight is about mindless, hedonistic friendship. He takes a good swig of the whiskey then passes it on. Bob takes a small sip and Jim guzzles.

The thought occurs to Lorcan, as Bob and Jim slap him in hugs and tell him to reach out to them, for anything, honest, that he might one day need to rely on this pair of socially-retarded friends.

Alice, Tuesday, 8:55pm

It's bedtime for the boys, her beautiful ritual. First there is the argument that Cian, being two years older, should not be 'forced' to bed at the same time as Darragh. It is so unfair! Then there was the separation of Cian from the Playstation: 'but there's just two minutes left in this match.' 'You said that five minutes ago.' 'That was a different match.' And the separation of Darragh from his speed-cube: 'I just want to show you this move, Mom, look at this, see the way the yellows are here and here and here, now watch this…' Flick-ticka-ticka-ticka-tack. 'See?' 'Great, now up to bed.' 'No, there's just this other combo I learned today…'

She helps Darragh with his electric toothbrush, 'you have to keep going till it buzzes four times.' 'I schngow!'

Cian will not let her into the bathroom any more. She knows he's not doing his full two minute's brushing but she's given him the lecture so often that he can quote it back at her now.

When they are bundled into bed, she pulls out the book. She's reading *The House At The Edge Of Magic,* part of her ongoing quest to spark an interest in reading in Cian, but he pulls out a football magazine. Darragh loves it, of course, and she's pretty sure that Cian is secretly tuned in; the pages in the magazine are not getting turned.

After two chapters, she closes it.

'More,' says Darragh.

'I'll read more, but I get to choose what.'

'Okay.'

'Right, *Where The Wild Things Are.*'

'Mom!' says Cian.

'What? I thought you were reading your comic.'

'It's not a comic, it's a magazine.'

'Well, excuse me.'

She reads, doing all her voices. Darragh is making claws, even Cian drops the pretence he isn't listening. When she's finished, she reaches for *Once There Were Giants*, a book she's never managed to get through without crying.

'Mom!' Both boys object this time, and she realises she may be veering towards maudlin.

'Goodnight,' she says, hugging Darragh as tight as she can without hurting him. 'I love you.'

'Love you, Mom.'

'Goodnight,' she says as she tucks Cian's sheet in tight and fluffs his pillow.

'Hrnk,' he says as he immerses again in his magazine, but she can see his eyelids are drooping.

She closes the door behind her, just as a small sob slips out.

She asked the girls not to come till ten, after the boys are settled, so she has time to make peace with her face. She still has her work makeup on, had made more of a point this morning ahead of the supposedly point*less* doctor's visit. Carefully, she clears it with cleanser and cotton wool.

She sees the surface of her face, sees dead skin. Images of corruption hang in her periphery, she fights hard to hold them off.

She strips off her work clothes, a matching light blue jacket and skirt with a white blouse, wondering what the right vibe for a cancer reveal might be. What's the colour of Leukaemia, pink or blue? First out of the wardrobe is a comfy beige jumper, but then she thinks *no, I need life affirming*. There's a figure-huggy red t-shirt that she loves, that she feels good in, and she matches with tight white jeans.

The mirror says only good things. She's done the tough job of losing the extra weight after the boys, but still everything curves in the right places. There's a small roll of belly but the t-shirt underplays it.

Is that good? Maybe she will need a bit of extra weight to deal with the chemo? Isn't there nausea and vomiting? Or is it the other way, might she bloat out?

Her heart is hammering. There is a gnawing black hole in her head, a thing that reaches out for her, trying to pull her in. What if, when, how, black, it's black. Stop! She does her breathing, pulling herself back, quelling the reaching tendrils.

She's calm again, and still looking good in the red t-shirt. She sits at her dresser to put a little makeup on, some foundation, a brush of blusher, nothing too serious, just take the paleness off. Of course, there's a sallowness to her skin that many Irish women covet, a gift from a father she's never met, she knows little more about him than his name. Spanish, her mother had told her; how, why, when, where? These questions were never properly addressed in their short years together. She had tried to find him once, in her twenties. Her Mammy had told her he was touring the world with Bruce Springsteen, she had told everybody that in school. He was playing the bass in the E-Street band or whatever, but her research did not show up any references to him on Wikipedia or album covers. Emails to agencies providing session musicians had found nothing.

Still, he has left her with a slightly hispanic look that Alice still feels very comfortable with. It has stopped with her, though, the boys are as pale as the middle panel of the tricolour.

Despite her natural colour, she feels pallid, pasty, exposed. A bit more blusher, a slip of lippie, then she can smile. She'd love to get her hair done, it's getting a little frizzy, she could do with a cut and shape. Maybe she'll book the beautician, just to show. There's nothing wrong here, nobody's dying, everything is good.

She is tired, ready for her bed, but fatigue has been her companion for some time. Now she knows why. She might make a gin and tonic while she's waiting, get out the good gin from the back of the press, but alcohol will only swell the soft buzz in her head and she won't last the evening. Instead, a hit of coffee lifts her.

Just before ten, Jackie and Beth arrive together. Beth is Alice's oldest friend; they met in school after Alice arrived from England, over her grieving but still alienated. She had grown up in London, knew little of Dublin.

Beth had pulled her out of her shell on that first foreign day and has not let her down since. She has the making of a model, sometimes a little too slim, but men admire, women wonder. She keeps her hair in a bob and tends to wear short dresses, a modern Mary Quant. Her smile warms Alice every time, her eyes invite trust. When she steps in to hug Alice, there is compassion in her embrace, confirmation she can sense what is coming.

Jackie is a bundle of joy, head often taken with the next big thing - right now it's touch therapy - but heart always in the right place. She brings happiness when she's about. She has no care for her looks, clothes are thrown on haphazardly with little consideration to colours or seasons, hair sticks out in ways hair really shouldn't. She lives for the moments that life brings.

Jackie comes in behind Beth so that it's a group hug. They will know, of course, that the news is bad, and Alice loses her calm. The warmth that her friends bring, from their bodies, from the years of friendship, helps her float back to the now and find the strength say: "Leukaemia!"

There is a collective gasp, then they cry together.

'Jesus Christ,' says Jackie, once they have heaved the horrors out. 'Could there be a mistake?'

They have moved to the kitchen, arrayed in Dutch armchairs set in a circle towards the garden end, out of earshot of the boys' bedroom; they are toting tumblers of Prosecco, having reckoned that this is not a night for gentility.

'Ah, Jackie, you can't say that to Alice. How can she deal if you're making her doubt?'

'Don't ever stop doubting, Beth, that's what keeps us human. How do we know this so-called doctor knows what he's saying?'

'You have to start by trusting him, though, right, Alice? You start at the worst and then anything after that just gets better.'

'Thanks, Beth, I don't have a fricking clue. I mean, it was less than an hour today, and horrible. What the hell could I take from it? My mind is a mess with questions now, and nobody to ask.'

'They'll give you a case manager. Your own personal contact. They always do that now with cancer.'

'Yeah, they *will* do this, they *will* do that. I'd like to know now.'

'Well, my friend Deirdre,' says Jackie. 'Her brother is an oncologist, I think, or something like that. Lives in Canada. I can call her, we can get him on the phone.'

'Ah no, like, what can I ask him. Sure he'd know nothing without all the charts and that. No, I'll find it all out and that, it's just... I'm a fucking shambles now.'

'Aw, babes!'

'There's all these things. Tests and meetings and I don't have my head around the half of it.'

'Yeah,' says Beth. 'You need to get your tests, and then ask the ears off everybody you meet, pin them down for information. We'll help. We'll pound on their doors for you.'

'I know, it's great to have friends like you guys.' She reaches out her hands and they each take one, squeeze tight. 'Leukaemia, though. Even the sound of it. It's like the worst horrible thing.'

'It's something to do with the blood and that, isn't it?' asks Jackie.

'Pretty much. There's a lot of complexity, but that's the root of it.'

'And it's, like…' Jackie stops, her mouth twisting to find the right words.

'It's terminal, yes. I will die of it, now they just need to find out how long.'

A silence descends, a silence of friendship, support, love; a silence of sadness. Hands squeeze tighter.

'You need to be thinking positive,' says Jackie at last. 'Not to be letting it get on top of you. Don't let it control you, you be in charge of it. Isn't that what they're always saying?'

'That's what they're always saying. Tonight though…'

'She's right,' says Beth, scooping a spill of bobbed hair out of her face. 'Tonight is just about tonight, nothing more.'

The horror of it washes over her yet again, and Alice cries. The three women come together, Beth hugging her, Jackie laying hands over Alice's chakras. Hands, arms, faces, bodies, the fierce intimacy without inhibition, a strong structure through which the women share, speak, survive.

When the emotion has eased, they settle in their chairs and slop out the rest of the Prosecco.

Jackie swallows a gulp of her wine and says: 'We need a bucket list.'

'It's terminal, Jackie, but I'm not dying yet.'

'Shut up, Jackie, for goodness' sake,' says Beth.

'God, don't jump down my throat, girls. All I'm saying, I mean, all those things you've always meant to do and life's just been too busy. Well fuck, let's do them. Let's grab this chance to get out there and… and… jump out of an airplane.'

'Jackie, for goodness sake. Alice needs our support here. She needs a shoulder to lean on, friends she can turn to, not a parachute jump. I mean, can you even do a parachute jump in your state?'

'What the hell are you two wittering on about? Parachute jumps?'

'Look, here's all I'm thinking: You've got tests coming up, you'll be in and out of doctors, clinics, maybe you'll be an inpatient, there might be surgery, whatever. That's what you're thinking, right? That's what you're seeing in your future?'

'Nice bit of sensitivity, Jackie.'

'Yeah, but, we put down on paper all the things that we, or should I say, Alice wanted to do all those years. I mean, there's New York, or sub-aqua diving, or the bazar in Marrakesh, or Christmas in Lapland, well, maybe not that because we'd have to take the kids. Then we just go and do it. Before the bad stuff kicks in, right. I mean, leave your kids with Lorcan, he can't say no. It's our sacred duty to do these things, it's our bucket list.'

'Jaysus, would you ever stop it, Jackie. Alice, you know we are here for you, whatever you need from us, we will always be by your side.'

'Thanks, Beth, and thanks, Jackie, I know what you're aiming at. Maybe a little early for that kind of thing.'

A fresh bottle is opened. Tumblers are refilled. Alice retells the story, re-experiences the frustration of not having the answers, reflects the fear and dread that dominates this day on her closest friends. Just saying the words is therapy. They ask again about the colds, flus and fatigue, the months of minor illnesses so that she can put voice to the whole message.

'Would it have made a difference? If I'd called it earlier?'

'You can't be regretting it though, Alice. You did absolutely the right thing at every point, the right thing for how you felt at the time.'

'But I don't know? Was there a point where I might have caught it early? Is there an early point for leukaemia? Should I have known?'

'What do any of us know?' says Jackie. 'I mean, I might have it now too? I've had terrible period pains the last two or three times, I should be past that kind of thing. Is that cancer? You know what I mean?'

'Jackie!' says Beth. 'Not the time!'

'But she's right,' says Alice. 'You go through life with a thousand different ailments and each day you think, oh my God, what if it's cancer, then you tell yourself you're being paranoid, but one day you're right. It is. Then you wonder if you should have…'

'Enough!' Beth slaps her palm down on the table top, nearly dropping her wine. 'No regrets, babes. You did the right thing. Say it after me. I did the right thing.'

'I did the right thing.'

'There is *no* point in looking back and regretting or questioning, you have to, must, look ahead. And we will be right there with you.'

'For once the skinny bitch is talking sense,' laughs Jackie.

It is exactly what Alice needs, the deep compassionate caring humour of friends. Genuine, heartfelt, a storehouse for whatever is ahead. As the soul's ease of the buzz of the wine washes over her, she allows herself to smile.

* * *

Later, she lies in bed, eyes wide. Lorcan came home singing, bleary eyed. He's snoring. Alice is still buzzing, the fuzz of fizzy wine fighting horrific thoughts that fleet around behind her eyes. Friendship brought support. Being alone leaves her exposed. She hears the noises of night, hot hatches graunching as they speed over the bumps, dogs barking, an alarm goes off, stops mercifully quickly. There's a high squawk, a heron maybe. Out there in the night, in the city, people are living, sleeping, loving, laughing, drinking. Out there in the city, people are dying. Right now, there are people passing up their last breaths.

Alice grieves for what she has lost, a life without care, without fear of death, fear of pain, fear of hospital. Gone.

Lights chase each other across the ceiling as the hot hatches keep on passing. Night slithers slowly by.

She reaches out a hand under the covers, slides it into Lorcan's, clutches tight.

'I need you,' she says, but Lorcan is still snoring.

Alice, Wednesday, 6:42am

What will it take to stop him talking? Professor Bailey's voice booms, then descends to nasal drone, washing out of her grasp like soap. Again and again, as the night grows black then grey with the dawn, she falls fitfully to spotty dreams that are punctuated by his compassionate face saying spiteful things, not medical, just mean. The pain of listening pushes her to wakefulness, but consciousness brings no relief from the nightmare.

Leukaemia... Look kaemia... Look Kim Mia... Look Killer Mine... The word dissolves and reforms and always, always carries poison, toxins that dissolve her. Her gut wrenches, her eyes explode.

As she meets the morning, she turns to Lorcan, now hopefully sober and sentient, and pulls him into her. He enfolds her, their limbs intertwine, heads touch. She drifts a finger over his scar, his cheek; she feels tears. She realises he has fears mirroring hers. She slides into his embrace, becoming him, melding two bodies. They absorb each other, and from that she draws a semblance of sanity, an edge of resilience. She breathes, unaware she had been holding her breath, paralysed by pure horror pushing heavily on her heart. She gets a head whoosh from the oxygen.

'Sorry I sent you out last night,' she says quietly to his shoulder. 'I mean, I needed it, to talk to my girls. But we should probably have been together.'

'I had a good night and all,' he says, 'but I missed you. You know, the lads...'

'You didn't get to talk?'

'They're like Olympic medalists in changing a difficult subject.'

'I thought you could do with some lightness, after the day.'

'We sang, we laughed, I mean that's all good, just...'

'We've so much to talk about.'

'They're my friends, but I can never bring feelings out. Not like you with your friends.'

'Not something you guys are good at. The Gang was always a bit of an emotional wasteland.'

Lorcan mumbles in agreement, still visibly upset.

His skin feels sensuous, strong; she wants to be close, so close. He doesn't have a hard-on. It makes her happy that this is simply love, not his lead-in to lust. She needs to spin about, have them orbit each other, coalesce, bind.

'Leukaemia,' she says.

'Yes.'

'Yesterday it was so alien, a word you hear about, read about. You hear somebody has it and, whatever, like, you go do a mini-marathon for some charity. You think: their poor kids; what would I do in that situation. Now it's here. It's my word. It's my world. It's my life, or death.'

'Don't say death. We need to stay positive.'

'I get that, but... The statistics don't tell a good story.'

'Statistics are what you measure after the fact, when everything is done. You're not a statistic. You are Alice, you're a fabulous, real-life and magnificent person, you will determine your own fate, or we will.' His mouth flops open like he's fishing for words. He's fighting to find some message, but after a few moments it seems to elude him.

'You were always the best thing about that Gang,' she says. 'I remember how much I needed you when we first started going out. I couldn't breathe without you.'

'I thought you were still pining after that guy, your summer heartthrob. Guy in a wheelchair, wasn't it?'

'I was not! He was a holiday romance. It was a difficult time. My mother had died.'

' I know. Sorry. I loved you, so deeply. I know what you mean about not being able to breathe.'

'It was a new start for me. A new life. I was a different person in England, with a mother, just the two of us, then bang. I was here, she was gone. I needed you and your love to make that journey.'

'I was your pupa.'

'My what? Pupa?'

'Yeah, like a chrysalis.'

'Eugh, nice image, insect boy!'

'Come on, it's a great metaphor, particularly the bit where you unfold your wings…'

She laughs, amazed she can find amusement in the pain of the moment. 'Okay, but, you know, that summer. The pain of it, and I had to make a new start. You were part of that. I kind of need that again, a new start. I need a new mindset to fight this, I want you here with me.' She pulls him close again, wraps her legs as tightly around his as she can.

'Have you been thinking about your mother?' he says.

'You mean Bella? Or Margaret?'

'I mean Margaret. The cancer…'

'Oh, yeah. I haven't even got my head to that space yet. Yeah. And of course how does that relate, like Bella, she helped me deal with her death, how do I help the boys to deal with mine?'

'Jesus. That's a dark place.'

'Well, I mean, it hit me hard. What can I do so that, live or die, I make the boys as strong as I can? Help them through whatever comes.'

'You need to look after here.' He taps her forehead.

'And you need to look after here.' She reciprocates.

They kiss. It is deep, so deep she feels her stomach swell. She smells his roughness, his manliness, she wants every part of him, even the spirit-smell of alcohol.

There they lie, a tangle, while the day begins and the noise of a world, untroubled by the drama going on in their home, rises towards morning commute levels. There is a momentum, a mandate to middle class norms that mere life-threatening illness cannot defuse. The boys have school. And then there's her mother — adoptive mother, aunt, Margaret — who must be told. And what about work?

Alice disengages and disrobes, checking her body in the mirror for signs. Nothing. No evil red marks, black patches, weight loss. She has a cold, more of an irritating companion than a real cold in truth, and one of her eyes is bloodshot; nothing new. Her hands ache. Is that the illness? Tension?

'Looking good, babes.' Through the sheet, she can see Lorcan has his hard-on now, and that too is right. She's not dead yet.

She showers and dresses, deciding against work-formal; a floral dress, hair flying loose, flat shoes. A stranger would look and say she seems happy, whole, ready. They would not say *but oh, how could this woman be dying of some fatal disorder?*

Her hand hesitates on the door handle. The beginning of a brand new day, a brand new life. *Let us bring joy, bring strength, build resilience.* She smiles, then goes in to wake her boys.

Lorcan, Wednesday, 8:15am

Morning light lingers on one of Alice's mobiles hanging in the bedroom. It's a spiral of wired cellophane in rainbow colours, with sparkling fronds snaking out like jellyfish tentacles. It rotates slowly, catching the sun on different surfaces, shimmering and shining.

He had dreamed that there was a serpent living in Alice, it would stick its head out of her mouth but, when he went to grab it, it would retreat back into her. The fright of it left a rank taste, a fetid foulness. For all that he had fixed his faith in the *Book*, the horror of Alice's illness was overwhelming and devastating. He had felt the tremble on her skin when they lay bound, had wanted to take her inside him and protect her. He wants to affix the world, make it immutable, undo this violent change. Their love can do that, the *Book* can help.

It has not helped today, at least. He had hoped after the drinking last night that he'd wake up this morning and it would be, what, some months back, before the illness took hold? That did not happen, but that's okay, there is time yet for time to be undone.

He hears Alice going in to wake the boys so swings out of bed and throws on his beige dressing gown. He wanders down to his work station in the front room and unlocks his laptop. There's a hundred unread mails, his penance for pissing off for most of yesterday, or a punishment for having a wife with cancer. He ponders his options; get back to work, or tell all and get sent away for a week. It made sense to keep working, he might need the time later. But later, well, later might never happen. This was *Untime*, after all, time that would be erased. Why should he do the work twice? He started a mail to his boss.

Boss, Alice has had a terrible diagnosis. I need to take a few days. I'll call. L.

Made sense, take advantage. Read a book, watch a movie. If he managed to hang on to his memories of this time, then he would retain those moments.

He thinks about taking the *Book* from its hidey-hole, but holding it while the others might walk in — that brought on anxiety and stress. It was autonomic, his heart would thump, muscles tense up, part of the Book's defence mechanism.

The sight of the dream stomach-serpent returns to him. What if he is wrong? What if the *Book* will not unwrap this wrongness. If this is real… It's unthinkable. No. It's beyond bearing. No. To be left alone? No. Alone with the boys to look after?

He is gripped by purest panic. His stomach screws up so tight he might spew. There is a balloon squeezing his belly, pressing into his heart, squashing it, slowing it. Pushing on his lungs so that he cannot breathe. Stop, he thinks, it's just hysteria…

A yelp escapes his throat. He pants as his breathing returns. He is dizzy, like he's been punched. The blood slowly returns to his face.

No. This is *Untime*, the storm before the calm. It must be. Nothing else is bearable. He will deal with what he needs to now, face what he must when he must. That will do for now.

He sees an insect, a minute black beetle with orange legs, crawl across the qwerty row of his keyboard. As he watches, it stops to wipe its tiny antennae. Insignificant. He could slam down the lid and end its brief existence. *We are all the playthings of forces we cannot comprehend*, he tells the bug, before blowing it off his laptop.

Alice, Wednesday, 8:25am

Fried breakfast is for the weekend, for soft Saturday mornings of family time. But what the hell! She throws sausages from the freezer onto the pan and croissants into the oven. The boys, all three of them, buzz with excitement when the plates are put down. It's funny how often she finds Lorcan's childishness endearing, how she loves his lust for life. His lack of responsibility still rankles: she needs him to walk with her on this. At the same time she cannot but enjoy his energy.

'I need a note for school,' says Cian as he wrestles with Darragh for the last sausage.

'What for?'

'Forgot to do me English.'

'And why should I give you a note for that?'

'Teacher says.'

'Teacher says don't do your English.'

'No, if I don't have me English, I have to have a note.'

'Cian, you know how important it is to get your homework done. I can't always be here to cover for you when you forget.'

'Owey-owey-owey,' sings Darragh, wagging a finger at him.

Immediately Alice regrets her sharp words when she sees the wounded look on Cian's face. She wonders how much he might be aware of the tension. He's a very smart kid despite hiding behind the sulky pre-teen image. How can she be terse with him?

At the same time, in the difficult days ahead, she doesn't want him using her illness as an excuse to doss. A gentle but firm hand, she thinks, a little bit like her own mother treated her. She reaches into his school bag and pulls out his journal, starts the note.

'I'm doing it today but I don't want to have to do this again this month, you hear me? I want your homework done and, if there's any issue, you tell me or your dad in the evening, not on your way to school. You understand?'

Cian just grunts his response.

Darragh holds out his journal. 'Can I have the day off then, if you're doing free journal signing?'

'Don't be smart, young man,' she says, but she moves in for a hug at the same time.

Lorcan offers to take them to school, but she's not going to let go of them one minute before she has to today. However she is running late so she slams the kids in the car, only two of them this time, and races to the school. The boys begin to dissolve into the melee in the yard when she feels a touch on her shoulder, turns to see Rhia who looks a little rough, with a red bruise on her left temple half hidden under crude foundation. 'Oh,' she says, 'I heard, I mean, Jim...'

'Sure, Rhia, look...' She turns to wave at the boys, but there is only the wasteland of heads. 'Has Forry gone in already? Have you time for a coffee?'

Rhia has faraway eyes. 'Jim was, well, he wasn't the most coherent last night when he got in,' says Rhia as they walk off towards the *Insomnia* coffee shop. 'But he said something about you.'

'Listen, Rhia, there's no easy way. I have Leukaemia.'

'Oh my God, are you serious? I was hoping he was just babbling. Oh, by all the angels, that's awful, Alice. My mother had it too, she was much older mind, it really tore her apart. She didn't die of it, like, but it weakened her so much that everything failed, all her organs and everything. She looked awful at the end.'

Rhia is a strange girl, distant and lacking in empathy. Much of what she says seems to only have one foot in reality. She also lacks the sense to keep bad news to herself at times like this, but Alice imagines she will get a lot of medical histories as the news spreads. People enjoy sharing misery with the miserable.

'When did you find out?'

'Yesterday. Not even twenty-four hours ago. I don't really know the half of it yet, I haven't even started hassling the hospital.'

'Which one?'

'Beaumont.'

'Oh, right. Jim used to be a porter there years ago. I wonder if he has any contacts that could help.'

Alice secretly sniggers at the notion; if she has to rely on Jim's contacts then she is in worse trouble than she already knows. She takes a seat in the café while Rhia is good enough to queue for the order.

'Are *you* okay, though,' she says as Rhia carried the coffees down.

'Me?'

'The...' Alice taps the side of her temple.

Rhia's fingers fly up defensively. 'Oh, no, it's nothing. I'm so clumsy, you know me, no coordination.'

Well that much is certainly true, but Alice can't let this pass. She reaches out and takes Rhia's hand. 'Please don't take this the wrong way. If there's anything, I mean anything you want to share...'

'You mean Jim, I mean, yes, I mean...' The words flood out in panic. 'Look, he's not a nasty man. You know Jim, he's a kind soul, just... The drinking, you know.'

'I know, Rhia, I remember him all the way back to the Gang, always sneaking drinks when you're not looking and thinking he's got away with it. But you don't have to put up with him. It's not your fault, he is the abuser.'

'Oh, no it's not abuse. Gosh, I know what I sound like, like all women will deny they're abused, but I'm really not. He gets drunk and he's effusive. He's dancing and there's arms everywhere and I'm pushing him into bed and next thing smack! He doesn't mean it.'

'They never do.'

A thin tear runs down Rhia's roughly rouged cheek. She folds her fingers through her passion-red curls and looks for a moment like a ginger Galadriel bemoaning the passing of the First Age. 'You know I have always loved Jim, don't you Alice. And I don't mean love, I mean everything. Everything. He is my everything. I'd like it if he eased back a bit on the drinking, yeah, you're right, he's always looking for the chance, but, you know, like would he still be Jim? If he stopped?'

'Yes, Rhia, yes he would. You don't have to burn yourself on his altar.'

'Oh. Oh.' Her hands start flapping in a fluster. 'Why are we talking about me? My God, Alice. Leukaemia?'

It was like two continents colliding. How could they dismiss Jim's violence? But she is not Rhia's mother, cannot tell the woman right from wrong, so instead she regurgitates the day, the hour, the professor's office. How many times, she wonders, will she have to walk this path? Already she can feel herself dissociating, floating above and watching as Rhia crumples like a crisp bag, tears flowing freely. As she wipes tears, she wipes blusher and her eye grows ugly and raw like a blue steak. The bruise is broader than her temple.

When Alice is done, Rhia squeezes her hands. 'You poor thing,' she sobs. 'And poor Lorcan.'

Lorcan, Wednsday, 8:50am

As soon as Alice is out the door with the boys, Lorcan is sucking down smoke in the back garden. He's flush with guilt, but also filled with the blood rush of the nicotine hit and loving it. It's a win either way, he reasons: this is *Untime,* and he's getting the kicks without the consequences of his indulgence.

Separated from the pretence of working, he sits in the kitchen and pulls out his iPad to browse. The news is all bad: wars and poverty and climate, so he thumbs through the tech news instead, always more rewarding. He checks *Find-My* on his iPad and sees that Alice is in the Insomnia near the school still, so he heads back to the garden for another fag.

He is just finishing the cigarette when his phone plays a tone he knows: *The Fairy Queen* by *Clannad*: Rhia! It must be a year since the last time that tune played. They hardly talk these days, after so much had been between them. His heart skips like a puppy, torn back to his teen years and the blind but overwhelming infatuation that nearly consumed him. For a moment she's with him, long curly hair clouding as she flies forward on the swing, back gracefully arched, silk skirt sailing, and Lorcan's heart bursting with bittersweet desire. That had been the passionate epicentre of his teen years, that special night. Until he met Alice, of course. Until he met Alice.

And Alice was his world now, so he had no cause to read the text that just came in. It would be best if he ignored it. She would understand. Even though it is *Untime…*

Ah hell. He heaves out his phone: *"Just spoke to Alice, omg, can't believe one of us lot is so sick. Can't believe it's not me, hur hur. I mean this honestly, if you wanna talk, just get it off your chest, I'm here. Just call me."*

Call her, it says. His finger hovers over the callback button, his heart loud. He stops: no! Cigarettes are one thing, reaching out to Rhia would be another level.

He sends a thumbs up, then pushes the phone back into his pocked and pulls out another cigarette.

Alice, Wednesday, 9:45am

Alice has calls to make. She is busy. She barely notices the aroma of tobacco wefting from Lorcan as he kisses the back of her neck. He fixes her an espresso but she's already pumped full of coffee as well as pumped full of things to do.

First there is work. Catherine, her boss in the Youth Protection team, picks up the phone on first ring.

'Hey, love, you okay?' Catherine is a caring boss, conscientious but also deeply empathic; she has a true vocation to help the kids that spills over onto the staff.

'No,' Alice manages before the tears burst through. She thought she had it in hand, she would deal with the ups and downs in a calm and professional manager. That dissolves instantly.

Catherine is the right person to talk to, good at listening, great at affirming. Alice mustn't think about coming in to work, she will redistribute Alice's casework straight away.

'Apart from Eamo,' says Alice. 'I need to talk to him.'

'You have to put it in perspective, Alice. Your troubles outweigh his right now. Focus on you.'

'I agree but… Eamo's different. We are so close with him, and at the same time almost losing him, so near to pulling him into something he could win with. Kid's got a heart of gold but a family of shit.'

'And I agree with you but, as of now, it's not your problem.'

'I just want to talk to him, Catherine. I'm so close, and he trusts me, and by the time somebody else builds that trust he's gonna be dead or in prison, believe me. He's due in Friday. I'll talk to him, then I'll hand over, okay?'

Catherine sucks air over teeth. 'Are you sure? Hey, how's about you do that, then we get lunch, just you and me?'

Alice thanks her and hangs up feeling a little better for the tears and the ear.

She realises, for the first time since her last maternity leave, she is effectively unemployed. The pressure of work is lifted. What might she fill her days with, so as not to become isolated and morose? She thinks again about Jackie's comment: a bucket list. What would she put on it? Live long enough to see my boys married? Live long enough for grandchildren?

Grandchildren. If she dies, they will never know her. Maybe she should make a memoir? If she dies, and the boys are young, what kind of memories will they have? Will they remember the warmth like she remembers about Mammy?

She closes the black curtain in the back of her consciousness. There's plenty of real roadblocks that need clearing before buckets become kickable.

Next up it's time for making fast friends in the health service. She has a list of clinics and the tests that she'll get or the consultants she'll see. Reception at Beaumont are a complete blank; they won't connect her to anybody. She should wait for a letter, the nice but clearly incompetent receptionist tells her.

The public website is not helpful, all queries are directed to reception, or to generic web forms that are only likely to be responded to the day after she wins the lottery.

On a mad whim, she gives Rhia a ring. Would Jim know anybody in MRI.

'Well, I, maybe, I, the thing is he's still asleep. Oh, but wait a moment.'

It turns out that Rhia had a copy of an internal phone number directory for Beaumont. Jim had written her a love poem on the back of it. Would Alice like it?

Ten minutes later, she has a scan of the document, including the handwritten piece of poetry Jim had gifted his wife:

"How do I love thee? Let em count the ways.
I love thee to the depth and breadth and height
My soul can reach."

Rhia was a tad ditsy, but could she really conceive that it was Jim's work, apart from the misspelling of me? No matter. The list was probably over ten years old, but why would they change the numbers? She tried one.

'Hello, Radiology.' Bingo!

'Hi, this is Alice Considine...' and she was off. Within a minute, the radiology nurse — Beibhín as it turns out and Alice carefully records — has Alice's life story, symptoms and knows all about the anxiety she is going through.

'Not a bother,' says Beibhín who has come out all sympathetic. 'But I can't arrange a thing till Professor Slevin has okayed it.'

'Ah, Professor Slevin,' says Alice with familiarity while she flits through the phone list. There's an office number, private number and page for a Mister Slevin. Must have had a promotion. 'Yes, I was just on to his PA,' she bluffs, 'now what was her name again?'

'Josie, was it?'

'Oh, yes it was Josie, I'll give her a quick call back.'

Two minutes later: 'Professor Slevin's office.'

'Hi, Josie, this is Alice Considine.'

And so, by a combination of stealth and schmoozing, Alice begins to bend the branches of the health service to her bidding.

Alice, Wednesday, 10:30am

Alice has five pages of notes, contacts, updates, references to online forms and information pages, but she has reached the end of the urgent list. There is much to do, but a start has been made.

Her stomach is acidy, sour and sore. There is an ache in her hands again. Are these symptoms of stress, or driven by her disease? Might she become hypochondriac, the horror of her diagnosis elevating minor aches to life threatening disorders? She vows she will not be a victim to imagination. She has carried head colds and headaches for a couple of years, she's not going to let them overwhelm her now. A time will come when it overcomes her, but not today.

She finds Lorcan at his workstation, diligently solving a Sudoku.

'We need to tell my family. And yours.'

Lorcan's look has something of the rabbit-in-headlights about it.

'It's too early. We don't want to… What if it, like, doesn't happen or that…'

'We don't have to wait till the second trimester, Lorcan, this illness is here and now.'

'What about the boys? We have to pick them up…'

'I have that covered. Cian has football. Mary O'Reilly will pick up Darragh and hold onto him, her Robby's on the same team.'

'Mary knows?'

'Not yet, but she's an astute woman. I'll have to tell her sooner rather than later.'

'Okay, but, I think maybe we need time, get our heads around it.'

'No. This is important, Lorcan. Our families are important. Come on.'

They climb into the car; she lets him drive.

'You know you don't have to tell them today,' he says as they merge onto the Malahide Road.

'I want to.'

'It's going to be very upsetting.'

'Really? I hadn't thought about that. It's not like I've just had to deal with the news myself.'

'But that's what I mean, wouldn't it be best to leave it for a day or two.'

'People know, Lorcan. That kind of word spreads, people know people. How would it be if Mam picked up the phone to one of her friends going "oh I'm so sorry" and she's saying "sorry for what?" That would really not be a nice situation for me to drop her in.'

'Granted, but you need to be thinking of you. You need to be putting yourself first, let other people look after their own opinions.'

'Okay, hows about this then: I'll sit in the car, you go in and tell her. Then I don't have to face it.'

There was a momentary flicker of fright on his face.

'Jeez!'

Five minutes later, they are parked outside. The mid-terrace house on Cloncarty road was barely big enough for the five of them when she arrived, though many people had raised bigger families around them. It had seemed so squat, so poor; now it shines.

'How are you going to broach it?'

'No idea.' She sits staring at the door. In her head, this is where she grew up. In fact, she was born in England and lived there till fifteen, just her and her mother. They had lived there until her mother died, slowly and painfully. When her aunt Margaret, who was now her "Mam," had brought her to Ireland, she was angry. It had taken that summer, spent mostly by the sea, in Enniscrone, in a caravan, to meld her into this family. When they had come back here after the summer, she had changed. England was like a bad dream, this was home.

'Okay, it's not going to get any easier just sitting here.'

She lets herself in through the front door and calls out: 'Mam, are you here? Mam, it's me?'

Margaret comes out of the kitchen, grinning, apron and hands floured, a vision of homeliness. The smile fades when she see's Alice's face.

'Mam, I...' And that's as much as she can manage. In a moment, Margaret has her wrapped in strong arms as if she might collapse. Alice cries, a vehemence, a violence overtakes her breathing. She cannot talk.

'Baby, baby, baby,' say Margaret. 'Oh, Jesus, what is it? Baby, oh there there…'

She feels Lorcan's hands on her elbows, supporting. Margaret and Lorcan manoeuvre her together into the kitchen, into a seat.

Like a voice echoing from a distant cave, she hears Lorcan begin. He tells Margaret of the weakness, the fatigue, the relentless illnesses. Of course, Margaret knows all this, had been telling her to see the GP. He tells her of the consultant, something she didn't know, Alice had not wanted to worry her. He brings out the brutal word: Leukaemia.

The horror weighs somehow heavier today, here in this place of supposed safety. She falls into dizzying flashbacks, those awful first days after Margaret had stayed with her in London, after they had buried her mother. There had been a black hole beneath her then. This is worse.

Lorcan, Wednesday, 12:15pm

Lorcan is flung into a flood of emotion and anxiety. He holds tight to the trembling frame of his wife, his lover, his other self. He has never seen her so broken, so shattered. In the office yesterday she was badly upset, today she is undone, unable to talk, incoherent. Her breathing seems a struggle; he almost wonders if she is actually ill, might need an ambulance, but in the arms of her adoptive mother she is in a safe place.

He is embarrassed, uncertain if he should even stay engaged, so intimate is this mother-daughter moment. Should he let go, back away, give them time?

He can see the detail of Margaret's brooch, twisted silver wire clinging to a gold crescent, silver apples of the moon, a gift from Frank. The close up view reminds him again of yesterday, less than twenty-four hours ago in Professor Bailey's office, of Alice curled up like this.

He lets go gently and stands up. Margaret is a small woman just turned sixty; she was older than her sister, Alice's birth mother Bella. You would not think Alice and Margaret are related. Alice is tall and gently sallow, Margaret is matronly and mild, strongly maternal looking. She has let her hair go grey though it still carries undertones of black.

There is a noise from the stairway, and Frank ambles down wrapped in a bathrobe. 'Jaysus,' he says. 'Didn't hear yeh come in.' He sees Alice bound up in Margaret's arms. 'Christ, what's wrong with the poor craytur?'

He's a lanky man, a sharp set to his face, big hands hardened from a life of labour. He came from a very poor background, old Dublin when people had nothing, was even poorer as a kid than Margaret and Bella, but he had an honesty and integrity that still shines in him and in his sons.

'It's bad, Frank,' says Margaret.

Frank makes the sign of the cross. He's not the most religious, but he and Margaret are regular churchgoers and rely on the daily rituals. Lorcan gives another telling of the tragic tale, briefer this time. Frank puts a hand on Alice's head. 'Jesus, would yeh not take me and leave the lassie alone?' he says.

Margaret taps messages into her phone with one free hand. 'Paul and Simon,' she says. 'They are on the way.'

These are Alice's cousins, only her brothers since her adoption but in truth much closer as siblings than he and Doircheas ever were. They are both hard working and successful in their own spheres, so dropping everything to come here is another sign of their closeness as a family.

Alice begins to calm, her breathing easing, the trembling tails off. Lorcan gets up to make tea, as much to leave the three of them alone as to actually share the beverage. Margaret looks so strong as she sits hugging her, Frank so concerned standing over them, holding her head.

Margaret gently but firmly starts to extracts truths. What tests? When? What specialists? What dates, times? They need the boys minded, she's there. They need dinners, she's there. She'll clean the house for them, but doesn't want to intrude. There is real warmth in her caring.

Simon arrives after fifteen minutes. He looks like a body builder, tight tee-shirt with extensive Maori tats up his arms, hair shaved to the scalp. Looks mean; you would never guess he was an accountant. Used to earn seven figures working for the big firms, saving billions for cash strapped multinationals, gave it up to work with charities, of which he is CFO for half a dozen of them. Complicated guy: skinhead, teddy-bear and bean-counter.

He's on is knees in front of Alice, holding her hands and crying while Margaret this time is the one to deliver the grim news. For Lorcan, whose only experience of simple affection came through Alice, this is a shocking sight.

When Lorcan answers the door to Paul, he notices the driver sitting in Paul's executive Audi just up the road. He's a tech CEO, has a company of over five thousand staff that delivers the latest AI-based anti-fraud systems to global banks. Paul loves his tech; he's always got the very latest of whatever kind of phone, watch, tablet, glasses, and

Darragh worships him. He is wearing a designer-scruffy silk suit and smells of something expensive.

Still, Paul is visibly moved at the news and joins in the Murphy family hug, arms tight about Alice and Simon. Lorcan stays making tea, flushing out the brew he's already made to make a fresh drop so that he doesn't feel like an ostracised baboon, excluded from the tribal grooming.

It is wonderful, it is magical, a magic that has been denied to him since something - was it the *Book* - tore his family apart when he was ten. He hopes, a vain hope, that Alice will not want to visit them. Not today.

Alice, Wednesday, 2:25pm

Alice cannot help smiling when they get back into the car. The absolute and unrelenting love of her family was expected, but the anticipation does not diminish the receiving. Her soul is lifted, suffused with light.

'I was wrong,' says Lorcan.

'Sorry?'

'You were right to tell them. They rally well, I'll give them that.'

'They were like a healing balm to me. I have a new strength, though how long that will last we'll see. At least I'm ready.'

'Ready for what?'

'Anything in the general sense. More specifically, let's call on your mother.'

'You want to go to my family?'

'Are you planning on keeping it a secret from them?'

Lorcan has to pull back from whatever he was intending to say. There is anguish inside him, she sees; she doesn't want to exacerbate it. However this isn't optional. For all his family are on the dysfunctional side, she still has affection for them, or at least for his mother, Helen, and his sister, Doircheas. They always made her welcome even if they have never come to visit. Still, she cannot overlook their concerns.

'Tomorrow,' he says.

'We're halfway there.'

'They're not expecting us.'

'You expect they'll be out.'

He shakes his head. He's unhappy, but still he's heading the car towards his childhood home.

The Considines own a detached five-bed on the Tonlegee road, madly over-sized for their needs, especially since Lorcan's father Patrick has lived in a shed in the back garden for the last thirty-odd years. Odd being the word. It is well enough kept, though; from outside you would not guess at the infirmities that sit behind the front door. They have a good pot of money from Patrick's time as a Principal Private Secretary in the Department of Defence, and Doircheas has little else to do with her time than to direct the handymen and gardeners that keep up appearances for them.

In the front garden stands a crocodile-barked cherry blossom tree as old as Lorcan, as Helen seems to enjoy reminding him. Leaf-bearing branches spring out to all corners. In the spring, for about a fortnight, it blooms and the morning sunlight makes a cerise blanket over the garden, a fabulous fairy-cave. For that short time, for whatever reason, the Considine house is happy.

Lorcan sticks his hands deep into his pockets as they approach the door. This isn't easy for him, she realises, though another voice in her head suggests she might expect a little more from him. He could park his immaturity and grow a pair just this once.

Dappled light from the afternoon sun plays on the path. The front door has been fresh-painted again, the same tone of mustard as before but the smell of emulsion is strong. She presses the doorbell.

Doircheas answers. She's three years younger than Lorcan but could be twenty years older. Her clothes are conservative grey, hair beaten tight to her head. After she dropped out of college she had considered a convent, explored a vocation, had spent three summers under their vows of silence. It turned out her vocation was to her mother and father, a harsher calling, Alice sometimes feels. A good thing for Helen and Patrick, since Lorcan would never give of himself like she has, and Alice, however much she might cherish his family, is not screaming for self-sacrifice.

'Hi, Doircheas.'

'Oh my, hi Alice, Lorcan. Mother,' she shouts behind her. 'Mother, it's Lorcan and Alice.'

'Hey, Doircheas.'

A shadow-play of expressions passes over her face, then she looks at her watch.

'I... But it's just...'

'I know,' says Alice. 'Maybe if we...'

Doircheas's lips purse apprehensively, but she steps aside to let them in.

Helen is in the front room, as she almost always is, sitting in a high-back orthopaedic chair, gazing at the window as if expecting the cherry blossom to bloom and not wanting to miss the moment. There is a peculiar aroma to the room, sweet but sour, sharp. There are flowers in vases about the room, mostly grown in the garden; perhaps the water needs changing.

Like Doircheas, she could be twenty years older than she is, hair shot grey but wild and wiry, looking like it's lost its zest. Despite Doircheas's urgings, she rarely changes out of her dressing gown, for she rarely goes out, rarely has visitors. She contents herself with gazing out, and with TV soaps once the sun goes down.

For all the seeming wreckage of her life, there is a light blazing in her head and there is no shortness of attention. She stands up, gathers a genuine smile and hugs Alice and then Lorcan.

'So lovely to see you both,' she says. 'Only, without the boys, and without your smiles. I'm going to guess it's not good news?'

'We were at the consultant yesterday.'

'You haven't been feeling well, is that why you went?' Doircheas's face has gone pale. She fumbles her hands as if longing to pray.

'Yes.'

'I thought you had been looking grey. I said a novena for you.'

'Oh, thank you, Doircheas.'

'Not that I'd believe those damn doctors,' says Helen, 'but what did he say?'

'I have Leukaemia.'

'Oh, Jesus, Mary and Joseph,' says Helen.

'And all his Holy Saints,' adds Doircheas as she stands by her mother and takes her hand, blessing herself repeatedly with the other hand.

The two women are genuinely distraught as Lorcan fills in the details, though neither of them cries. Alice has always struggled to understand the vibe in the house. Small things cause consternation, big things slip by. That's before she tries to get her head around the fact that Patrick, a senior civil servant of some renown, lives his life in the shed and barely has a friendly word for anybody.

The same questions come out. What tests and when? What doctors and where? The boys can be left here any time, she is assured, even though she's never felt comfortable leaving them here before, still she thanks them sincerely.

'I'm thinking,' says Lorcan, looking like there's a weight of pain hanging on his back, 'that maybe I should tell Dad. While you girls are chatting.'

'Do you want me to come?'

'How is he these days?' he asks Doircheas.

'Foul, I'm afraid. One of his Men's Shed buddies, Ray, passed away, God rest his soul. His face would sour the milk.'

Lorcan nods. 'Let me suss him out.'

Lorcan, Wednesday, 3:15pm

'Would you mind taking him his lunch?' says Doircheas, following him to the kitchen. She takes a plate of salad out of the fridge and pulls off the cling film.

'How is he doing? I mean, other than his friend dying.'

'Hard to tell. I hardly see him most days. Grabs the food from my hand, goes in and out by the laneway. He's even taking his dirty washing to the laundrette, poor man.'

'Poor man, indeed. It's his fault Mam's the way she is.'

'What way is she?'

'You know like, away with the fairies.'

'God forgive you, don't say such a thing.'

'It's true, though. She started with the depression as soon as he took it into his head to move to the shed.'

She scans him with a sour look, then whispers: 'She's not depressed and you're not to be saying that, may the good Lord forgive you.'

Doircheas had fought vehemently against medications for their mother, believing "those things fry your head" despite evidence to the contrary, but there were problems in this home that only a psychiatrist could resolve.

As if sensing his thoughts she added: 'Things are never as simple as they appear, Lorcan. Be gentle with him.'

When his father had first eschewed the family home, he had slept in what was then a large garden shed with a camp bed. It had been upgraded several times over the years and was now a sprawling garden-studio with French windows and a patio, set towards the rear of the half-acre of landscaped lawn, not exactly roughing it. There was a rear laneway, and the door in the garden-wall resembled a grand front entrance. Patrick did not even like to pass by the house, such was the depth of his revulsion.

The separation had never been explained, never spoken of. It dated back to that same dark void in Lorcan's head, when he was ten. Not that his father had ever been close, he had memories of a man who left early, came home late and often worked till midnight in his house-office, a man too busy for playing with his children, although kind to them on the odd times that he made time. Since then isolation, anger, unspoken harshness to his mother, and never a word of explanation.

Alice sometimes lectures him on respecting his own father, otherwise he would not now be carrying a plate of salad to him. Indeed, without her urgings, Lorcan would likely never visit this house of pain, why should he subject his head to the heartache?

Lorcan knocks on the door and waits, knowing it will be locked. A face appears at the small side window. He looks trim, well turned out, young, would pass for early fifties perhaps. There has been no question of decay, Patrick has built a separate life. There is even, Doircheas tells him, a small gym in the prefab. A look passes over his face when he sees Lorcan, as if he's just caught a bad odour. He disappears, then the door is opened

'Hello,' he says with little enthusiasm. 'Are you coming in?' He reaches for the salad.

'I have some news, Dad.'

'Is that so? You don't mind if I eat?' He doesn't wait for an answer but unwraps a fork and knife from the serviette supplied and starts lashing into his lettuce and boiled egg.

'It's Alice. She has Leukaemia.'

Lorcan is astonished when Patrick halts his progress and looks at him, though he can only guess if that look holds compassion or irritation.

'Blood cancer? Where's she being seen?'

'Beaumont.'

'Don't you have the money for private?'

'We don't need private, Dad, the public hospitals are great.'

'I can get her into the Mater Private today if you wish. I can make calls. I can pay.'

He looks to one side as if considering, then returns to his radishes. *Patrick is more concerned*, Lorcan thinks, *about sidestepping consequence than about Alice's health.* This is a charge that Alice has levelled at Lorcan more than once.

'No, we'll be fine.'

'Grand.'

'I wanted to let you know.'

'Grand. Thanks.'

'She'd come down and tell you herself but…'

'No, need. Sure don't I know now. Send her my condolences, tell her I hope for the best for her. Let her know what I said about the Mater.'

'Yes.'

He sits and watches his father eating, struggles for something to say. Kids, work, weather, all seems crass in the context.

'I'll be away so.'

'You wouldn't take the breakfast stuff up to the house.' He nods towards a tray by the door.

'Okay. I'll do that.'

Alice, Wednesday, 11:30pm

Alice is the cheese in the sandwich between the grossness of the illness that life has inflicted on her, and the unfettered love and support of her adoptive family. Tonight, the love part is uppermost, and her mood is mellow.

She is brushing her teeth, he slips into the bathroom and brackets her waist with his hands, gentle weight against her hips.

'I'm sorry,' he says.

'Shor whash?' she burbles through pasty teeth.

'I'm sorry this is happening. I'm… It's worse than that. This is the worst thing.'

Poor, poor boy, she thinks. Lost in incoherent utterances. Dealing with that thing, that black hole that looms beneath her feet, it takes all the maturity a man can muscle up, and poor Lorcan's supply is low, particularly following the painful visit to his father. Lorcan is a mad mix of man and child, strength and weakness, razor edge and marshmallow.

She lifts her hand to his face, brushes the rough stubble, skims over his scar. His hands tighten on her hips, turning her. She kisses him, ignoring the foam overflowing from her brushing. It's closed-mouth for a moment, then opens to full passion. She cannot help it, his touch undoes her. Her belly bends, heart skips, blood rushes full longing into her lips. What magic is this that he possesses, that can cut through any darkness, any disgust at his smoky smell, any sense that this is neither the time nor the place?

But oh, yes, oh, yes.

She tendrils her tongue into his mouth, sharing toothpaste. He brings his hands to her bum, lifting her, bringing her legs up around him.

They are seventeen again, exploring, seeking, wanting. Seventeen year olds don't have curious sons asleep, so she holds back, brings a finger round to his mouth, disengages. For a moment, he is disconsolate. She takes his hand, fingers interwoven, and leads him to their bedroom.

In cautious silence, they unwrap each other, disrobe from tee-shirts, jeans, then the delicate undoing of underwear, until the searing touch of his skin burns her from shoulder to thigh. They pull each other in, then tighter so that their bodies might merge and become a single creature, a living capsule of passion. His erection presses into to her and oh, she wants him now, but they mustn't. They must make it last, good couples take time with foreplay and… fuck it, she pulls him down on top of her on the bed so that nature can release its longing. She comes again and again as she bites into his neck wanting to taste, eat, absorb. She muffles her cries by pushing into his skin, nearly howling with the glory.

When they are done, they lie, slick with sweat, breathless, separate after the unity of sex.

'I love you,' he says, and it seems suddenly so apt, yet hopelessly honest.

'I love you too.'

'I… want you to know that I'm going to be here for you.'

'I know.'

'No, I mean… Hell, I don't know what I mean. I just feel, it's so crazy, like it's not real.'

She sniggers, snorts almost.

'What?' he asks, sounding slightly hurt.

'Sorry, it's like you've lost all power of English.'

'Zwam zping zpang!'

'Exactly. Look, Lorcan, I know you'll be there for me. I mean, sometimes, well, sometimes you can be a little bit childish…'

'Hey!'

'Sorry, but, like, the smoking thing.'

'Oh. You noticed?'

'Come on, of course. Not that I'm your keeper, if that's what you need to do, well, you know my feelings on it. But can you see how sometimes I wonder?'

'You wonder if I would stick by you?'

'No. Will you have the right… stuff… Jesus, I'm losing my own powers of speech. Listen. Everything about you is beautiful. Feeling you here, feeling your warmth, I couldn't care less about the disease. You liberate me. But I'm scared, and I'm scared of being hurt, and then I see the things you do, I see you denying the illness is real...'

'It's not the illness isn't real, it's just, I want to undo it, make everything right.'

'You see, that's it. That's it right there. I need you to stop trying to make it right and come with me. I need you to walk my journey. Don't you understand? You have to let go of this denial thing.'

'It's not denial.'

They lie again in silence for a while. She hangs her hand over him, feeling his ribcage strain out then sink back, the eternal time-signature of life. She says a quiet prayer for him, a humanist mantra she came across in a magazine, and in that prayer feels a peace descend over her that she has not felt since before the doctor's office.

'I will try to be there for you too,' she says. 'But please, come with me on this. I want you there with me.'

'Of course I will.'

Alice, Friday, 11:45am

Nelson Mandela House fails in its function as a monument to the great man unless you can honour with concrete. Built in the seventies using cheap slabs of pre-stressed concrete and a deficit of design, it resembles a World War Two bunker more than a modern office block.

Beyond reception, a coarse carpet worn threadbare with the passage of feet forms the path to the anonymous, open-plan desk-farm. Faces around her are unfamiliar as she sits at her day-booked hotdesk. She is glad; word will be getting out now that her work was being reassigned, there will be questions. Just now she wants to get in and out with minimal fuss.

Catherine, Alice's boss, signals her into the concrete cube that serves as her office. As soon as the door is closed, Catherine hugs her with a genuine warmth.

'I'm so sorry, Alice,' she says.

'Thanks.'

'I've not told anybody. Like you said. It's very difficult keeping it in.'

'I'm sorry to put that on you. I will tell them, just…'

'When you're ready, I understand, don't be worrying. If that's the hardest thing I had to do today, I'd be in good shape. You're sure you want to be here?'

'No. But it's Eamo, I feel I've made progress with him. If I let him drop now…'

'I will have one of the others take over.'

'You've put everything else out to the others. Just this one.'

'I don't want you putting too much faith in one miracle.'

'I know, you've said. Yet I want to try.'

Catherine looks at her long and hard, then nods. 'Okay, but anything I can do, you hear me?'

'Sure.'

'And... Look, I won't ask, about the illness. I know you'll be sick of talking about it, but I'm here and I'm a good listener. We're still going for lunch, right?'

'That will be great, so just give me twenty minutes...'

'Yeah.' She squeezes her hand, then opens the door for her.

Alice sorts out a bit of admin at her desk while she waits, sets her out of office notice, puts in her official application for *force majeure* leave. A message from reception pops up on her chat client, Eamo is in the waiting room.

There's three or four young men sitting in the sterile room, staring grimly at phones. Recovering junkies, mostly. Eamo is standing chatting to one of them, smiling, laughing, a beacon in the gloom. He always seems to know somebody here, and they all know him.

'How'r'ye, mizz Murphy?' he shouts. Alice uses her maiden name at work, feeling it distances her family from the hardness she encounters.

'Thanks for coming in to me,' she says as they settle into an interview cubicle. He's seventeen but you'd take him for ten years older. Well dressed in clean jeans and white tee-shirt, hair short but not intimidating despite a good showing of tattoos about his neck, always smiling, you'd be happy to recruit this kid, if you didn't know which family he came from.

'Only too happy, mizz Murphy. Sure it keeps me off the streets.' He gives her a big grin.

'And how's that going? Staying off the streets?'

Eamo shrugs. 'Ah, now, I can't be sitting inside, like, I'd be going nuts.'

'But staying away from Pluto?'

'He's me uncle. Yeh know, family.'

Pluto, nickname of Peter Shortall, is the consigliere of one of the most dangerous drugs gangs in the country. Eamo's brother, Jimmy Shortall, had been Pluto's right hand man and enforcer until he was shot earlier this year. The eyes of Pluto have turned on Eamo; Jimmy had been keeping him clear of the family business, and he made sure Eamo steered clear of the drugs.

'He's trying to pull you into the gang, Eamo. What kind of uncle would expose you to the same risks as your brother?'

'Now,' Eamo raises a hand to say stop. There's a tattoo on the heel of his palm, a tiny bird. 'We're here to talk about me, and I'm open to all that, but me family are off the table, right? All due respect, but, I can't stand by if you start dissing them.'

The smile has softened and an edge has entered his eyes. Family is always first on the streets of Darndale, blood trumps many sins. She could imagine that edge cutting men down; Eamo's a good guy, but he's a Shortall to the core.

'I'm sorry,' she says. 'We'll talk about you. How is the course going?'

'Meh, it wasn't for me.'

'You've left it?'

'Yeah.'

'I worked hard to get that for you.'

'And appreciated, mizz, don't be getting me wrong, like. And I would do it, the social work, only it was all essays and stuff, having to get up and do slides and shite. Just not me thing, yeh know. I gave it a lash and all.'

'Okay, you gave it a go.' Alice is nervous, she has to give Eamo something to work towards, something to empower him to say no to Pluto. 'Was there any other course you saw that might interest you?'

'Nah.'

'What about an apprenticeship?'

'Yeah maybe. I'd see myself in an office though. I'm not thick like.'

'Oh, I know you're not thick, Eamo, that I'm well aware of. But, why an office.'

'Well, not an office maybe, but, like, yeh know, what yeh're doing, nobody in my family's ever done that kind of thing. I'd like to do something like that.'

'Good, and that course would have brought you along that road. I can't get you a job like that unless you have the qualifications.'

'Ah, I know all that but Jaysus, writing and writing and writing and never doing anything. I couldn't hack it.'

'So, how do you put your days in at the moment.'

'Doing some deliveries.'

'Oh. Deliveries?'

'Yeah, now not drugs, like. Pluto wouldn't put me out there where I could get picked up by the pigs, he's got lads to do that. Nah, just like phones, watches, that kinda thing.'

'He's pulling you in, you know that.'

Eamo shrugs. 'Me uncle asks me to do a few favours, gives me money that I can help me Ma out with, I'm not gonna say no, am I?'

The signs are there. The battle is being lost. Alice scrapes for a solution.

'What if I got you into a respite centre? You know, a couple of weeks away from the city, chance to gather your thoughts.'

'Out of the city? Like in bogland?'

She laughs. 'Well, maybe not in the bog. You ever been to the west?'

'Leixlip,' he grins. These days Leixlip is almost a suburb of Dublin.

'Would you go, if I got you something?'

'Depends like, if there's something to do. But yeah, I mean, I see what yeh're doing and maybe yeh're right. Yeah okay, if yeh can get something and there's stuff to do, let me know.'

It is a total bluff. She has no idea if there are respite centres that would take a case like this, or how soon she could book him in, but by God she would give it a go. This could be this young man's last chance to escape prison, or worse.

As soon as she's left Eamo out of the building, she heads for Catherine's office.

Lorcan, Friday, 12:15pm

Lorcan takes a break from his iPad pinball game to slip outside for a cigarette. He doesn't mind giving them up, good for his lungs and his wallet, keeps Alice off his case, but it's lovely to have an odd relapse. The soft fog of smoke drawn in is an old friend, familiar and reassuring. "I've never been away," it seems to say, "nor will I ever again." The special satisfaction of blowing out a long stream through pursed lips, or twin pipes of smoke from his nostrils, is a joy that no non-smoker could hope to comprehend.

He loves, too, the crisp glow when the dull red turns to bright orange on the tip as he pulls, the tiny savage conflagration, all clean and self-contained as it burns back the watermark lines on the paper. Then the whoosh in his head as the nicotine hits and the blood spins around his eyes like a ball bearing in a race. Yes, he misses the pleasure, but it's the dearer for missing it.

And the sweeter too to know that the *Untime* will end and the smoking will subside again, gone as if it never existed. Except that's a lie; smoking is a psychological more than a physical addiction. Assuming he remembers this time after, and most times he does, then he'll remember the sweet taste and be tempted to re-experience. He will have to be disciplined, not something at which he tends to excel.

A part of him that is detached, that is looking down on this dickhead smoking his cigarette when his wife is going through cancer-hell, that part wonders how he can care so little about her.

Lorcan does not see things the way Alice sees them. They perceive differently. He has learned that over the years. It is not that they disagree about things, it's more that he's blind to things that are blindingly clear to her. *You have no empathy*, she has often said. It's not an insult, an attack, it's a simple statement, like *you have a sharp face*.

And like a sharp-faced man staring at himself in the mirror, Lorcan can only agree.

Last year, on a busy street, a woman fell over, tripped on a paving stone edge. She jumped straight back up again, embarrassed, flustered. Lorcan tried to sidle around, to not heap any more attention on the already clearly distressed woman. Alice went straight in. *Are you okay? Do you need to sit down? Can I get you a hot, sweet tea?*

The point is, she was there in the woman's head, straight away. Lorcan is trapped forever in his own head, staring out the same two eyeballs and, if he closes his eyes, seeing only the inside of the lids.

And here he is now, sucking the cigarette smoke down into the same lungs he was born with, and as far from feeling what she feels as he was that day on the street.

He has adopted a snap-close metal box as his ashtray. It stinks each time he opens it, but stops any smell after he stubs the butt and shuts it. It hides on a shelf in the garage where neither Alice nor the boys would ever look. He considers an espresso but he's already had two doubles and his stomach is beginning to cramp. The iPad game doesn't appeal; maybe he'll flick through the hundred odd TV channels. Sometimes the commercial presentations can be amusing, miracle machines that hone your fitness without effort.

In the front room, his workstation glares at him. He would be better to engage, get going with work again, but of course, when the *Book* kicks in, he will have to relive every email, rewrite every response, the thought is revolting.

Instead he pulls back the panel on the base and reaches for the *Book*. Immediately there is a twist in his stomach cramps, a peremptory anxiety, but he pushes past it.

'Hey,' he addresses the *Book*. 'Hey, is anybody… Listening? Is this… Can you, like, hear me?'

He knows this is nonsense.

'Listen, it's my wife, Alice. She's sick, like very sick. She needs to be cured. I know, it's not me, but in a way it is. I couldn't live without her.'

The words surprise him, but he knows how deep-down true they are. The thought of losing her, of living without her, is horrific. It overwhelms him, the very sense of it.

And the boys, without a mother? How would he manage, looking after them? Yes, he loves them both. With his life. But looking after them, well, it's not that it's Alice's job, but he relies on her. Maybe he lets her take more of the burden than is fair. When she's away, he's never quite sure what to give them for lunch.

The *Book* follows its own laws and hasn't got a how-to, unless you count the vague, semi-literate note from 'B'. The transition is vague, tenuous: he's writing something down, a story that did not happen, when suddenly it did happen, only it didn't. It's slippery, like soap. Probing his memory for that moment, the point where one becomes the other, is not only unclear but unpleasant to delve into. Trying too hard leaves him exhausted and anxious and, more than once, has tumbled him into a very dark mood.

So what does he know about triggering it? What does he know about the *Book*, full stop? He found a reference to it once in the bible, the book of Chronicles. Came across it by chance: "*Once more the Philistines raided the temple, and Zadok the priest drove them away. David sent for Zadok to ask how this came about. Zadok told David that the Philistines had struck him down, but God had blessed Zadok with a sacred book, and Zadok wrote down his death in the sacred book. When he was done, the Philistines had departed. David demanded the book be brought to him, but Zadok escaped from that place to the land of the Ammonites.*"

Not much to go on, the bible is perhaps not to be relied on, but the only possible historical reference he has discovered. True, the *Book's* cover is not contemporaneous with King David, perhaps it was re-bound at some point. It has the looks of something Byzantine, though again none of his google searches have turned up anything.

He had also researched into the ancient *Egyptian Book of the Dead*, admittedly not a book of itself but a set of writings designed to resurrect, could there be a connection?

Whatever, even if any of this is true, it gives him nothing. The *Book* protects itself. He isn't sure how or how he knows but there is something sacred or sentient in the artefact that cannot only turn back time but can turn people's minds. Look at the mess it had made of his family, his father. Lorcan knows if he takes a pen to it, if he tries to start trying to write in it, he will suffer headaches, dizziness, perhaps even fainting. All he can do was wait.

There is only one person he has ever spoken to about the *Book*: Rhia. She is bound in it.

He opens the *Book*, looking for that time. The thing is deceptive, does not let him see what he expects, turns up things he had forgotten. A bit like Facebook.

One page draws him in.

* * *

I am in Boston. It's summertime. So hot that you'd be wet from the sweat just trying to dry yourself down after a shower.

The warehouse has air con, at least, the only good thing about it. The boss buys in pallets of liquor salvage, piles of stale beer-infused boxes stuffed with broken bottle-glass and leaking cans, just a few cans or bottles still intact.

My job is to clean these down and make them good for sale. I have two buckets: filthy water and slightly less filthy water. I change them every half hour.

My clothes stink of rotten beer. My hands bleed from the glass splinters digging into them, tiny stilettos glued with beer to the bottles so that when I pick them up and they cut into me. Case after case, pallet after pallet. The boss never says a nice thing to me, only ever beats on me for not getting enough done, wasting my time refilling the buckets with fresh water too damn often.

Every night, I leave through the shop. Every night I buy something new to try out. I've been through most of the beers that the Dollar $aver Liquor Warehouse has to sell, I've been extending my alcoholic vocabulary into brandies, there's fifty different varieties on sale.

When I get home, sweating after the walk despite it being ten o'clock at night, there's a party on, some folks over from Dublin. I take out my latest brandy, gorgeous stuff. The bottle disappears fast, way too fast, I'm wondering if somebody else is drinking out of it. Jim puts together a punch, uses a couple of the bottles I've stashed in our room, doesn't bother asking me. I see him pull something out of his pocket, some kind of pill that he powders into the punch.

The party gets wilder, whatever that stuff is, it's given me a new lease of life. We are up on the roof dancing as the sun begins to pink up the sky.

I have work later so I throw my head down, I might get four hours if I'm lucky.

Whatever that stuff Jim threw in the punch sits red hot in my stomach, bubbles and froths and eventually spews up my throat into my mouth. I'm unconscious now, lying on my back. I splutter briefly, try to turn, but I'm too far gone and hypoxia has me before I can react.

At ten a.m., my alarm wakes Jim up and he goes to work. It's not until he comes home that night that he notices I'm still lying there, that there's dry vomit around my mouth and that I am not breathing.

Another death. The three of them, himself, Jim and Bob, had gone to Boston on a student visa and lived like pigs. How simple to slip from overindulgence to fatal intoxication, particularly with Jim being a dickhead. What a rotten job, a contender for worst jobs ever. He died, then he was writing that section down; he can remember it as he looks at the words, remember his pen tracing those letters out. Then he'd gone to work, gone to the party but thrown the punch down the sink. Then Jim punched him, literally. The man could not stand to see booze wasted, even if spiked. Especially if spiked. Lorcan broke a rib from the punch, but he lived. It did little to cut his alcohol consumption, though.

Another twisted fate avoided, but how did he avoid it. He doesn't know. He clutches his strange tome, torn by desire to see this terrible time ended and utter helplessness to trigger it. He feels like a little boy clutching at toys, unable to let go.

The *Book* will undo all of this mess, he is sure. It has to. Just hold true, he thinks. Have faith. Like Zadok the priest.

Lorcan, Sunday, 16:15pm

It has been an outstandingly ordinary weekend, given they have just been dumped into a private hell. They sat together and had some beers on Friday night after the boys were asleep, he had five or six smooth but strong IPAs, Alice had two lagers then had thrown up and gone to bed. It is not like her not to hold her drink, but the stress is exhausting her. She had kicked him out of bed to take the boys to the park on Saturday morning so she could rest.

Saturday afternoon had been shopping, she had got loads of outfits for the boys with plenty of growing room. Saturday evening, Lorcan had met Jim and Bob in the pub, bloody great night: Billy the Barman had got the karaoke machine out and they were singing well past closing. Sunday morning, when he could have done with a rest after two nights on the batter, Alice again asked him to get up with the boys. He was probably over the limit to drive still, so they sat watching *Disney+* together on the sofa. He did manage to catch up with a little sleep until they jumped on him for snoring.

The Sunday afternoon, Alice asks him to sort out something for dinner.

'I'm going to head to Mam's,' she says. 'I'll take the boys. If you don't fancy cooking anything then we can get a Chinese.'

He's quartered by that, pulled four different ways. Why is she leaving him? With all that's going on, shouldn't he be by her side? And why should he be left with the dinner? And why does she think he doesn't fancy it?

It lights a flame of indignation in the swirls of his brain. She's not trusting him, not listening to him. She's not keeping him close.

He tells her he loves her and watches them drive off. Then he bombs into the back garden and lights up. He gasps at the cigarette till his throat is throbbing, spitting out the smoke, letting his feelings ferment until they are something approaching anger.

You won't listen to me, he tells an imaginary Alice. *I know you're going to be okay, but you won't listen. You've got to put faith in me.* Not faith in the *Book* of course, he still can't talk to her about that, even if desperately wants to.

No matter how he words it he can see the weakness of his argument. It's not her, he realises. It's the spiteful buzz from the beer. It's the childish cry for help. It's the need to be at the centre of her life.

He wants to talk. He needs to talk. There is a pustule, a boil fit to burst and dammit he has no way to lance it. Last night, he had tried several times to bring up the conversation with the lads but Jim is the master of misdirection, a professional avoider of subjects that lose his interest. And the Gang are Lorcan's only real friends.

The *Book* is a freaky phenomenon, unreal and yet so, so real. But always stuck in some different world that cannot cross with this one, like a piece of a dream that has somehow become sown into the world.

With one exception: Rhia. He has not responded to her since she had texted him.

He pulls out his phone and sends: "Hey, are you free for me to call?"

As soon as he presses send he regrets it. No reply comes, and he is almost relieved. He pulled out another cigarette and lights up but halfway through it *The Fairy Queen* sounds: "sure."

He hits green. 'Hey, Lorcan,' says Rhia after a couple of rings.

'Sorry to call. You okay to talk?'

'Yeah, I'm here on my own, just doing my meditation.'

'Oh, sorry to disturb you...'

'No, no, it's really good to hear from you. I've been thinking about you a lot since I heard.'

'Yeah, well that's the thing, I guess.'

'Jesus, it's shit, Lorcan. I can't tell you how sorry I am.'

'I know.'

'And I feel really sorry for you. I mean, you must be going through hell, but she's the squeaking wheel.'

'Squeaking wheel?'

'You know, like the song: *the squeaking wheel always getting the grease.*' She sings it to him across the phone.

'*Shower the people you love with love.*' He can remember her singing it, back when they were still in school, up on the hill of Howth with a bonfire blazing.

'Yeah, that's the one. I've been looking to the angels. I've been asking them to look out for her.'

'Angels?'

'I'm doing a lot of research on angels, you wouldn't believe the power they have.'

'Oh, right.' Rhia rides from one alternative therapy to the next, the further from the mainstream, the better. When he had first fallen for her, she had believed she was a fairy who had been taken from Tír na n'Óg and she was trying to find her way back. Sex was a type of gateway, she had explained to him. He had been prepared to sign up to that one, but alas she never let him try his key in her lock.

'Listen, I...' The words stuck in his throat.

'What's wrong, Lorcan? I can sense your pain. Let it out, my sweet, don't hold it in.'

'I kinda need somebody to talk to.' The words come tumbling from his mouth and sit in there in the air, stabbing his eyes. He turns to check through the kitchen window just out of instinct, that Alice hasn't returned.

'Of course you do, you poor little boy. I'm on my way to an angel reading, but I could meet you tomorrow.'

Every straining stitch of Lorcan's being is screaming no, but he calmly arranges to meet her in a pub. He'll tell Alice he needs to drop into work.

He hits red.

Has he just murdered his marriage? *No*, he thinks, *first of all, I need to talk to somebody. Rhia is the only one with whom he can even mention the Book, right? So first, he needs to do it. He needs to figure out what's going on. Second, he can't tell Alice that he can't tell her about the Book because he can't tell her about the Book in the first place. Yeah. Besides, this is Untime, it will all be undone, no harm will come.*

No harm will come. And yet, he is deceiving her. Hiding his smoking - though she figured that one pretty quick. Will she figure his seeing Rhia just as easy? God, but that woman is intuitive.

No, hold your nerve. You need to talk to somebody.

It's still not settling him. He lights up another cigarette and sucks suffocating smoke into the listless energy.

Alice, Monday, 8:50am

The morning is dreary, so she ditches school.
'Eh, Mom,' says Cian. 'I think you're going the wrong way-ay!'
'Mom has gotten lo-ost,' sings Darragh.
'Nah, I'm ditching school. We're taking a duvet day, only we don't have our duvets.'
'Are you serious?'
'What's a duvet?'
Where to take them though? Where do dying moms take their kids?
'Mom, are you serious?'
'Yup.'
'Really?'
'Yup.'
'Where are we going?'
'Tayto Park.'
'Yay,' the two boys yell in the back. 'We're going to Tayto Park.'
She turns the car towards the M50, unsure of the route but hoping she can get into the signage boundary and guide herself in.
'Mom, are we allowed tell people?'
'People?'
'Yeh know, are we supposed to be…' Cian puts a finger to his lips and makes a shush.
Her instinct is no, don't tell, the school can't know, then realises *what the fuck*. She can turn the tables on any upstart teacher wanting to undermine her. Why did I do it? I'll tell you why, 'cause I'm dying. Hah!
'Is Dad coming?'
That stops her. He is on his way to the office, "squaring away" some stuff. She wants him with them. She could phone, but he'd have to get

home, they'd have to wait. If she wastes the energy of the moment, it will dissipate.

'Not today, boys, we'll come back again another time with Dad.'

A sense of control emerges as she cruises to the centre lane. So much time living by somebody else's rules, she could have done this any time. Why didn't she? Lost opportunities. This is a time of change, a coming to terms, a chance to live by her terms. She sees two bright boys thumping each other's shoulders in the rear-view and feels a deep warmth.

The surge of traffic ebbs and flows with a taste of its own, the price of crossing the city in school hours, but adventure is in the air. She switches the radio to Sunshine; normally she's on Newstalk, anxious about the latest crisis, today she's *Walking On Sunshine*. And at the top of her voice.

'Mom, you're embarrassing,' says Cian, but she needles them until they join in singing too.

The car park is quiet, the queues short. Well, it is a school day for most of the target audience. The layout is unfamiliar; they were here before, she's nearly certain. Perhaps there's been a big upgrade.

The boys point excitedly at the big map just inside. Darragh wants the roundabout and the zoo, Cian wants the scary thing that spins super fast. Alice's eyes slip immediately past the map to the actual roller coaster, a great wooden gantry that spirals into the sky with impossible slopes and twists.

They start easy. Alice persuades Cian that if they go on Darragh's preferences then he'll grow in daring. After they've been on the *Ladybird Loop*, then *Flight School*, Darragh agrees to the *Climbing Wall*. The boys are excited going in, but Alice can see them both biting their lips as they are strapped into harnesses. Neither of them gets more than three metres up, but once they learn to trust the ropes and fly back down the worry disappears.

The boys are both too young for the scary thing that spins super fast. They are brimming for burgers, but first Alice marches them to the *Cú Chullain Coaster*. Darragh's hand grips tight as they queue. 'I'll hold you, don't worry,' she whispers.

There is a mechanical fundamentalism to the roller coaster that scares her. Aroma of hewn timber and varnish, clunks and dings, the earthquake-rumble as the car goes overhead, the doppler screaming, the way the wooden structure sways. Alarming. For a moment, it is Darragh's hand that keeps her safe. For a moment it is another hand, a dark hand, a tall man. Daddy.

She jumps. There's a memory from deep in the vault.

'Are you okay, Mom?'

'You're not scared, are you?'

'Of course I'm scared,' she smiles. 'That's what it's for.'

Her head is wheeling. Was that a real memory? She had not thought she had an active memory of him, though she must have met him. Mammy said he was around on and off, though Margaret insists he was more or less gone since she was a baby, touring with his guitar. The sense of him in that moment though, a strong pillar of protection. She tries to reach for the sensation again, but it has slipped from her.

The queue truncates rapidly, the wagon trundles past them twice before they are waiting at the barrier. At the end of its run, the wagon pulls into the terminus with an artificial velocity as if it might at any moment rear up. Passengers with wind-brightened faces pull themselves up and watch each other excitedly, some wild secret has been shared, for a moment they are united in awe before the gantry stairs sweeps them back to their duller lives.

The barrier clicks open and they surge forward. The front carriage is taken but they get the second.

'I don't wanna sit at the front,' says Darragh, trepidation tightening his hand.

'It's worse in back,' says Cian with the wisdom of his age. 'It goes faster at the back.'

The lap bar is clunked into place and Darragh, in the middle, clutches her waist with casual desperation. The feel of the lap bar, the only thing preventing some fatal fallout, brings a moment of panic, indecision, then delicious appetite. Bring it on!

The beast kicks forward, stops, starts a gentle roll and slide that reels them round a bend onto the slope with its tractor chain. Chunk-chunk-chunk-chunk-chunk, they step-glide up the wooden ramp that cannot possibly hold them safely. The vanishing point creeps towards them with intent. Alice has one hand, literally white-knuckled, on the lap bar and one hand clenching Darragh's tee-shirt. She will never let him slip from her.

Then tick, tick, tick, ..., clack, and they're over. The track falls away at an impossible angle. Wind whips her hair. They grind fast, faster, wildly fast. The car rattles, it won't, can't stay on the rails. They plummet, plummet screaming. Cian has his hands held high. Alice grips the lap bar. Darragh burrows. Then swoosh, crunch, clatter and they're out the bottom of the slope and twisting sideways, upways, the sky on their right, ground to the left. Under the ramp, up, then down, then through a tunnel. Rattle, twist, bang, horrifying, terrifying, life affirming.

When they emerge, even Darragh has that bright look. She takes them both in her arms and pulls tight, Cian does not pull away. Hold this moment. Hold it tight. Put it into the zoetrope of happinesses for that long slide, that awful roller coaster that will await her when reality bites in.

Lorcan, Monday, 9:55am

Lorcan lurks. He has taken the small car, left the big one for Alice. It's a little grey runabout, unnoticeable, anonymous. He parks up the road and round the corner, on a cul-de-sac. Then he lurks, pretending to read. He's been here over an hour, the *Roundabout* opens at ten according to google. Nerves are needling him, an anxiety has settled at the base of his skull, paining him. He tries to lose himself in tech news, but can't concentrate, so he stares, and he lurks.

At last, it's close enough to ten to take the risk. He walks to the door. What if it's not open? He'll have to walk away. He might attract attention. No, it's open. He slips surreptitiously inside. It occurs to him, as he waits on a creamy pint to settle, that he probably drew more attention to himself being careful.

He's halfway down his pint before Rhia arrives. There are three crisply defined rings on the glass, sign of a good pint. Only in Ireland will you have the perfect pint poured for you at ten in the morning by a man who has devoted his whole adult life to pouring perfection.

'Hi,' she says, sweeping up. He stands and they do a double kiss; uncertain, he goes for a third and almost catches her on the lips. She shies away with a smile, and Lorcan's heart rate thumps up. Oh God, she still packs power.

'How are you?' he says, but the words tumble out.

'Totally in tune. The angel reading was, oh, I can't say how wonderful it was. Divine.'

'That's... great.'

Lorcan is in awe of Rhia's beauty. Her hair is divine, perhaps the influence of the angels. Fierce red curls race each other over her shoulders and down across her baby-blue linen dress, seeming alive like snakes. Her face, pale and freckled, is in danger of being swallowed in the red sea of swirls. Her smile is a soft panna cotta airbrushed with raspberry coolie.

'You should come to one. It would really open you up, Lorcan.'

'I... Yeah, maybe.'

He notices hairs on the back of her hand, coarse, and suddenly remembers her naked on Burrow Beach, lustily hirsute, glorious despite the horror.

'I saw Alice at the school. She looked powerful. Her aura showed so much inner strength, I can't believe she's as ill as she says.'

'Oh, no, it's not her who says, the doctors...'

'Ah, doctors, we'd all be dead if we believed doctors. There are some forces more powerful.'

Well, she's certainly right in one sense, he thinks.

'She's been ill. For a long time. Colds and headaches and, well, nothing ever specific, but she's never been well for longer than a week.'

'I never saw that. It's a pity you didn't tell me. I could have taught her how to live her life through angels. They can lift that illness straight off you.'

Lorcan can see there a risk that this conversation could get railroaded to Rhia's strange world. He lifts his pint and drains it.

'Rhia,' he says. 'I'm scared.'

She places a hand on his, a fragile hand like spiderweb. 'I will channel courage to you.'

'The *Book*,' he says.

Her face twitches; she looks odd for a moment, then nods.

'You remember the *Book*?'

'I've never seen this *Book*,' she says, 'nor do I want to. I remember that night. I...' Her mouth bends down, winces. She looks like she's tasted poison. 'I don't like to think about it. It hurts.'

'I know, I'm sorry but, I don't have anybody else. I literally can't talk to anybody. Even Jim, even when we're both pissed. It stops me.'

'There's something wrong with the thing, Lorcan. It's evil. You need to get away from it.'

'How can you say that? You wouldn't be here.'

'Would that be so bad?'

'What are you talking about? You want to be dead?'

Now the masque of her Greek drama turns to tragedy, her heavy eyebrows dip forlornly over her now dimmed eyes. 'Maybe. Perhaps I was never meant to live. Have you ever wondered?'

'Well, what about Forry?'

The seasons change again, eyes glisten as her face opens, mouth beams. 'Forry is beautiful. Forry is all the best bits of Jim, filtered, de-fuzzed. He is a dream come true.'

'But if you were dead, well, you wouldn't have had him.'

She nods. 'Oh. You're right of course. I must be grateful for life if only for Forry.'

'So you see then? I need to save Alice.'

'I can help.'

'No, no not angels. The *Book*. I have to use the *Book* to save her.'

'Now, you told me you don't know how it works, or how to trigger it at least.'

'No, I don't.'

'Shouldn't it have worked by now. I mean, that night, it was just that night, then, whatever, it was just gone. Only it wasn't, Lorcan. It's still in my head, and I can't get it out. It's still there and it's burning and it's screaming and it happened and it didn't and…'

He puts an arm around her, just to hold her, just to calm her. The barman, busy with beermats, is keeping a half eye in their direction. Lorcan waves his glass and he starts to pour another. Lorcan shouldn't really have two and drive, strictly speaking that's over the limit, but it is *Untime*.

'I don't really want to go there again,' says Rhia.

'I know but, I need to figure it out, like, I think I'm good, yeah, the Book, it'll help right? It helped you and all, so… Just why are we still here?'

She looks into his eyes, and he's suddenly conscious of how close they are. He's still holding her, her face inches from his. He can see the bruise Alice mentioned, bold on her temple. He almost feels like there's a spark of electricity linking their lips. He could, he knows, he could…

But, that is not it at all.

The barman places the pint on the table. He lets go of her shoulder and gently eases away.

'What if it doesn't?' she asks.

'What?'

'What if the *Book* won't work for her? If this is reality.'

'Then…'

'You need to get her to come to an angel reading, Lorcan, I really believe that's the best way.'

He can imagine the look on Alice's face if he told her about the angels, about Rhia suggesting it. It wouldn't be pretty!

'Okay. Hey, Alice told me about the bruise.' He points to her temple.

'Oh yes,' she puts up a hand over it. 'I can be so clumsy.'

'You said that Jim hit you.'

'Oh no, I mean, maybe, no. He's not a bad man, Lorcan. And I love him. More than life. More than you love…' She pauses over the next word, then smiles. 'Alice. You know that, don't you?'

'I do, but, I know he's a tough guy to deal with. Hell, I've had to deal with him a few times, once the drink takes him, and he takes the drink every day. And then there was that day…'

'Which we won't talk about.'

'Which we won't talk about but, Rhia, you have to look out for yourself. If there's anything we can do to help.'

'The angels will help,' she says, and she looks like she really believes it. 'Listen,' she says. 'I have to go now, I need to get my midday nap, but I'm here anytime, okay, just reach out. Only not tonight, though, I have naked yoga.'

Now there's a thing I could join, he thinks as she kisses him lightly on the cheek. Thankfully the words don't come out his mouth.

He finishes his pint and then, bathed in a warm glow, a combination of alcohol and infatuation, he orders a third. It's not too far to walk, he can say they took him out for a pint at work, pick the car up tomorrow.

He's surprised Alice is not there when he gets home, so he pulls another can from the fridge.

An hour later he gets a text. "Soz babes, took a doss day. Hope work's okay." It is accompanied by a photo, or a photo of a photo, one of those snaps you get coming off a fairground ride. Alice, hands and arms and hair flying, her mouth open in a scream as a roller coaster plummets. Cian, bright and ecstatic is on the other side, Darragh is holding tight to the lap bar.

Lorcan is suddenly heartsick. If he had been here, not sneaking off, she might have taken him with her. He has traded this moment, this magical flash, for a few drinks, for an empty and unresolved chat with Rhia. Stupidity is sucking out his soul. This thing needs to end, one way or another.

Alice, Thursday, 1:15pm

Alice's notebook bulges with names, numbers, appointments as she strives to close out all the tests she needs. She has learned all the shortcuts through the serpentine corridors of the sprawling Beaumont Hospital campus as she pushed herself into short notice cancellations and goodwill prioritisations, phone pressed to her ear lining up the next one. If this were a treasure hunt, she'd be taking home the trophy. She had two nights of fasting which left her exhausted though it lifted the heartburn that had been lodged in her gut.

She has been prodded and poked, punctured by needles that don't bear thinking about. She has seen all the big machines that rotate and spin and hover and buzz. She has had photographic plates pressed into various parts of her body and irradiated with X-rays. She has had samples of every conceivable bodily fluid and more than one solid scooped, bottled, labelled and sent to the labs. After a marathon of medical intrusion, she is done. Professor Bailey's PA, Gemma, to whom they had spoken on that first day, phoned her to express her astonishment. It normally took weeks, sometimes months to get all this done.

'You're a fighter,' Gemma said. 'That's the best way to be. Fight for every inch of ground.'

Alice feels affirmed by her call, and also by the ceaseless support from her family. Margaret and Frank, Simon and Paul have kept a constant conversation going on WhatsApp and have been sitting with her, dashing in with food or drinks to keep her going when she wasn't fasting. Lorcan has been picking the boys up, but they've been available as needed and they are dropping lunches for them. It's heartwarming.

Jackie and Beth have been tireless in entertaining and distracting her, calling in most evenings with books and magazines and a listening ear. Jackie has not brought the notion of a Bucket List up again, though it is beginning to get some traction. As Alice perused magazines while waiting for tests, she had half an eye on exotic islands and pampering spas. A break might just do her good.

She finds it oddly amusing looking back at the time when the Covid crisis had hit. They had all been terrified at work. The vulnerable kids they dealt with were particularly at risk, their immune systems dampened by drug abuse and exposure to needles. Healthcare professionals on the front line were dying. It was scary but, oh boy, how trivial all that seems now.

It's over a week since the diagnosis. The news is out there, she knows, and soon it will spread like a new Covid variant through the mothers at the school gate. It is only a matter of time before some kid overhears it from a parent and lets it slip to Cian and Darragh. They must not be left to deal with that unprepared. She has to tell them, at least tell them something if not the full truth. The idea appalls her, how do you break that to a child, but it must be done. Lorcan has been touchy on the topic. He seems to have some half-assed conviction that if they ignore the problem it will go away. That's always worked for him with laundry, but it's not going to work now. It is time to grasp the nettle.

She brings in a cup of espresso to Lorcan who is browsing through Facebook in the front room.

'I'm going to tell the boys today, after school,' she says.

'I don't think you should.'

'I have to, I can't bear it, the dishonesty.'

'It's not dishonest. It's just, it's not the right time yet. We need to know more. There's too many uncertainties.'

'Lorcan, there's one absolute certainty that I'm hiding from the people I love the most and it's hurting me.'

'You're not hiding it from me. Am I not in the group of people you love?'

'I didn't mean that and you know I didn't.'

His mouth moves like he's trying to speak without air in his lungs. He shakes his hands in apparent frustration.

'Listen, Alice, you love me, I love you, you trust me. I know you're going through the most horrible time in your whole life. You need to trust me now. This isn't going to be a big deal, you have to realise that.'

'What the almighty fuck? It already is a fucking big deal. I have

Leukaemia.'

'Yes, sorry, it's big, I know it is. But the outcome I mean. It's going to work out well.'

'You can't know that.'

'I do know it. No, sorry. I'm tripping myself up here. What I'm trying to say, like, we will get through this. And there's no point in telling the boys things like you're going to die or crap like that and then tell them later you're not. I mean, what's the point in that? Why put them through that?'

'Because it's real, Lorcan. You don't seem to accept that. I have to tell them, don't you see?'

'Okay, talk to them, yes, but don't break their hearts. You're ill but you're not dying.'

She wants to scream. She wants to take him by the hair and shake him. 'Why are you doing this? You make out that it's nothing. It's not nothing. I am dying.'

'You're not dying, the doctor never said that.'

'Twenty percent five-year survival rate. Just what do you think happens to the other eighty?'

'You're going to be in that twenty.'

'Jesus, I can't do this, Lorcan. I need to talk to my children. I need to be honest. In fact, I'm telling them today. As soon as I pick them up.'

'Don't you dare.'

'Again, what the almighty fuck are you saying?'

'I'm ordering you, for your own good.'

The words splash over her, searing. This is not her husband, not the man she loves. She can hear her heart thumping through the rush of blood to her ears. She finds her mouth doing the empty-air thing as she feels for a response.

'Fuck right off. I am leaving here in ten minutes to pick them up. I'm going to take them to the park and talk to them. You can come with me, or you can stay here.'

'I'm warning you...'

She is vibrating with anger. She had not realised that Lorcan had the capability for this level of, of what? Cruelty? Stupidity? She turns around and walks out of the room. He doesn't follow.

Lorcan, Thursday, 1:40pm

That went horribly wrong. He sits, barely able to catch breath. How did he say those things?

He tried, tried to push it out, tried to get the truth out there. She has to know about the *Book*, it makes common sense. But he can't say it. He feels dizzy, disoriented. The more he pushed, the more the sense turned to putty on his tongue, and what came out was nonsense.

If only she could trust him. The *Book*. If he could just tell her.

He finds it abhorrent to tell the boys about her illness. The tests; the doctors will surely find in the tests that there is nothing to worry about. In a couple of weeks they'll be done. If not, the *Book* will kick in. But the *Book* cannot erase everything. It leaves lingering trails with those impacted. What damage they might do to the boys, if they tell them this traumatic news. Will all that be undone? Can they ever undo the harm after she tells them? After all, something traumatic happened to him when he was ten, something that has left scars but no memories.

What he said was monumental stupidity. "I order you…" What was he thinking? He was a dick.

'I'm going,' she calls from the hallway, striding past with purpose, then the door slams and she's gone. He thinks he should go with her, even now, but he knows he can't. He watches through the window as the car pulls out.

Rage rises in his gut, rage against his impotence. He has to make this happen, make it work.

He lifts the *Book* out of its hidey-hole, clears the keyboard off his workspace and puts the *Book* onto it, opening it to the first blank page. There is a fountain pen on the bookshelf, a Christmas gift from Darragh. He twists the cap off and tries it on a slip of card, it flows.

'I am ready,' he says, but even saying it, he knows this is pointless. He lifts the pen up by his ear, closes his eyes, squeezes, holds his breath. *If I can hold long enough, I'll pass out, and then...* But it's stupidity. The *Book* does not respond to his whim, to his command.

There is a tremor in his hands, a half shake that feels weird, disembodied. He goes to the kitchen and pulls a beer from the fridge. The cold, hoppy foam refreshes, helps clear the fog. Out in the garden, he fumes a new fog of cigarette smoke.

It will come, he thinks. *I just need to have faith. Hold on.*

Alice, Thursday, 3:05pm

Alice's anger has eased but her anxiety is fierce. She has been wrong-footed, Lorcan's reticence has weakened her resolve, but this is too important to walk away from. A woman who has dragged herself through the hallways of hospitals begging for tests will not balk at this task, not when she knows in her soul how important it is.

And then there is that other thing, that butterfly in her heart that might grow to devour her. That fifteen-year-old Alice sitting in Walpole park in Ealing, watching the chickens, a dozen exotic breeds, roosting in the tree inside the fowl sanctuary, being told the awful news by... By a blank face, an empty space, a phantom. She remembers feelings, places, emotions, but not her Mammy's face. She is absent, has left Alice alone and frightened.

Mammy gave her strength, stoked her fire for life all through the illness and left her ready. Yes, when she had first come to Ireland she was numb, but that summer in Enniscrone, when she was sixteen, that is when she was reborn, and fire could flow again through her blood. Between, there is only an icy emptiness. She can barely remember her mother in that time, the time of starting to die, and that is what frightens her most. She remembers Aunt Margaret, wonderful, warm Aunt Margaret who dropped everything to nurse her sister. She has foggy memories of the death bed, the hospital, or the funeral in an empty Ealing church. It was a letting go, and by God has she gone. That is what she is afraid of; it's not the dying, it's the disappearing.

She is at the playground in St Annes Park, wondering if she has chosen this place because of the echoes of Walpole Park and the playground, children screaming while the cold news slipped out. It's not, though, it's simply that she cannot go home, not with Lorcan in his God-forsaken tantrum. Darragh is on a swing, spinning the layers on his speed cube one-handed. Cian is playing keepy-uppies with his ball. It will require a secret weapon.

'Chocolate doughnuts,' she calls, waving a bag, and half the children in the playground start staring hopefully at her.

She gets the boys seated at one of the picnic benches. If she rations the doughnuts, she might get five minutes of their attention. As they start to scoff, she hesitates. Need to dive in, like sea swimming, just do it.

'Boys, there's something I need to tell you.' Neither of them stops from their doughnuts. 'Cian, Darragh, I want you to hold my hand.' She gets one hand full of Boston Creme as Darragh reaches out without hesitation. Cian makes a face. 'Please, Cian.'

'Mom, people are looking,' he moans, but seeing her face he relents and takes her hand.

'Boys, I'm sick. I found out from the doctor a couple of weeks ago.'

'You don't look sick,' says Darragh.

'I've been, you see, I've had a lot of colds and flus and that, I've been tired…'

'You're just working too hard,' says Cian, mouth still full of doughnut.

'Well, it's not just that, it seems.' There's a numbness in her hands, a thumping reluctance inside. 'That's why I saw the doctor. There's something more. Have you heard of Leukaemia?'

They both shake their heads, faces looking puzzled.

'It's a disease in the blood.'

'Is it a virus?' asks Cian.

'No, but that's very smart, Cian. You can get viruses in the blood, but this is the blood itself.'

'What's wrong, Mom?' asks Darragh. His face is starting to turn sour, the chewing has stopped.

'I'm going to have to have a lot of treatment. I may get very sick.'

'You're not going to…' He has to stop and swallow. 'To d…?' The word catches in Darragh's throat and he starts to cry. She takes him in her arms, but still holds Cian's hand. She wants to say no, but she has to push on.

'We all die, Darragh.'

'No, Mom…' Now, Cian is crying. So proud and self-conscious but she's driven a nail into him so hard that he doesn't care who might see him.

'Eventually,' she says. 'We all die eventually. I may die of this illness.'

'But not yet, Mom?' says Cian with desperation.

'Not till we're grown up!' says Darragh, his face a mess of doughnut and snot. A big chocolate crumb sticks to his chin.

She is stung. This has gone too far and yet not far enough. She is the blank face of her own mother, her mother who didn't wait, who couldn't wait till she was grown. She had promised. She had lied. Alice will not lie. She mustn't. She can't.

She does.

'Not till you're grown up.'

'Promise?'

'I promise I'll do my best.'

'No, really promise.'

'I promise.'

Damage done. A promise made that cannot be kept. Another mother doomed to disappoint. Will her sons remember the day she spoke to them in the park but see only a blank space between the bag of doughnuts and the elephant-shaped climbing platform?

She doubles up on play, pushing Darragh on the swing until he soars, keeping goal for Cian as he scores the winner in the World Cup final. When she is satisfied that their restless minds have moved to other things, she takes them home.

Lorcan is drinking. She is neither surprised or upset, it's simply a thing that happens, like rain, or Leukaemia. No point getting annoyed.

She pulls from the bookshelf in the front room a photograph album. There is Mammy as a teenager, and there a woman, pale by comparison with Alice's skin. The woman loves her, cherishes her. The woman holds her. But what worth is the woman now that death has claimed her and Alice has had to grow up into a different life?

Lorcan, Thursday, 7:00pm

Lorcan enjoyed his beers until Alice got home. It wasn't that she objected, she could not have been more neutral, it was simply that the stupidity of it came home to him. Numbing out the moments he doesn't want to face is not answer. The buzz had begun to dull so he stopped.

The boys looked a little more gloomy than usual, but they said nothing. Cian did his homework, Darragh practiced a new move he was learning on the cube. A normal household, nothing to see here, nothing is wrong.

But everything is wrong. Alice's grey-man neutrality is a disconnection that he keenly feels. Each moment she is missing, that her soul is set away from his is like a slap. He lives for her, needs to feel her with him, on his side every moment. She's often told him he's too needy. So this cold shoulder is like a punishment.

If only he could get the *Book* to activate, undo the damage of this afternoon, wind back from the foolishness of his drinking. On the way to the bathroom he catches his reflection in the hall mirror. A fool looks back, a fool with a Guy Fawkes moustache and beard. Right, that is one thing he can fix right now!

Alice, Thursday, 9:55pm

The day is becoming debilitating. Dull pain has started to creep into her hips, a familiar, rusty pain. Her nose is bunged up, her sinuses screaming with the pressure of it. Her head feels as if it is she who was drinking. Are the symptoms getting worse? Or is it psychosomatic, now that she knows there's a deeper malaise, is she subconsciously exaggerating the little aches of the day into something bigger?

The boys are in bed. They are dealing well, as boys are won't to, though Darragh has been bargaining for extra stories and she is only too pleased to concede. Her back begins to bulge with soreness as she leans over the books but she refuses to let it win. It is another little battle, another little victory. Nothing to see here, nothing is wrong.

But that is wrong, she knows deep down. This is not just psychosomatic, but the beginning of a long and exhausting journey, one that she does not want to walk alone.

Downstairs, Lorcan is sitting at the breakfast bar in the kitchen. He stares at her with puppy dog eyes.

'You're not drinking?' she says.

'No, I... Sorry, I shouldn't have.'

She sits beside him, picks up the side-smell of stale beer and smoke. The flat odour of cigarettes is the norm now, and she is disappointed. It is his body, his life, but it hardly makes for walking the hard road beside her. She is too tired to question it now.

'It's up to you if you drink,' she says. 'Just maybe not so often.'

'Yeah.'

'I've seen it before, men losing their wives then lose themselves to the gargle.'

'I have not lost you, babe.'

'Exactly, you could have the decency to wait till I'm dead before you go to the bad.'

'Jesus, you can't say that, Alice. You're not dying.'

She takes his hand in hers, brings it up to her lips, kisses the light brown patch of nicotine flavoured skin.

Flawed. A fine man but with deep flaws that have forced themselves into her life. That had caught her eye, back in that summer. Lorcan was smart, he was funny, but his self-confidence was like a Russian doll, prone to disappearing behind shells. Her new family - Margaret and Frank had started the legal adoption process soon after they got back to Dublin - were perfect, strong, supportive; there for her at every turn. They picked her up, wiped her tears, set her straight. Hell, even Mike, the guy she had flirted with in Enniscrone had been a tonic for the soul, a crutch in troubled times.

When she spotted Lorcan, a gawky metal-head acting the mick with his boozy buddies, it was like she needed an antidote, somebody who embodied the kind of irresponsible fun that was more reminiscent of her Mammy before the illness. She attached herself to the Gang and unwrapped his protective shells. She found humour and humility, warmth and innocence. That was what she had signed up for, but the shell he wears now with the drinking and smoking, worst of all the denial, that she could do without.

Still she holds tight to his hand. She feels the warmth from it, the deep pulse of blood, the very beat of life. He is life, alive, aloof but — she knows in her heart and despite the evidence — loving, adrift on a reservoir of his own sillinesses and yet, by God, he is powerful. He possesses an inner potency that speaks right to her soul and brings her back from the tired, tedious, illness-bound place she has been sinking to.

She bites into his skin, not to draw blood, but to leave the white outline of her teeth, a dotted line to mark her man.

'Ow!'

'I love you, Lorcan.' And she does. In that moment she wants nothing more than to bite open his hand and climb inside, be protected under her man's skin.

Instead he wraps her into his arms, pulls her face into his chest. She is enclosed. She is contained, captured, cupped.

They drift, almost subliminally, to bed, losing their clothes like summer leaves and lie, spooning, as close as they can.

Alice, Saturday, 10:30am

Alice has another cup of coffee while waiting for Lorcan, then regrets it. Her stomach cramps up as she swallows the first slug of espresso and she has to run to the bathroom as she spasms.

She washes her face and feels a little better. *Curse this illness,* she thinks. Having to drop coffee from her life would hurt. That may be small potatoes in the bigger picture, but little luxuries lost could be disheartening. No, she must just moderate, the second cup was the problem.

Lorcan comes downstairs with something different about him. He stands grinning, but she can't put a finger on it.

'Well?' he grins, and does jazz hands either side of his clean shaven chin.

'The beard, you shaved?'

'It was time. I know you didn't like it.'

'Are we sure it's not that the boys at the Freebird-a-thon would have slagged you?'

'Well, it may be that too. Anyway, it's gone, that little adventure is over.' He looks aside as if reconsidering. 'Or possibly not.'

'Oh, please. Don't grow it again.'

'But what if...?' He stops mid-sentence and winces.

'You okay?'

'Yeah, I... I'm okay, just a little headache. Are we going?'

Cian is on the Playstation with some football game and Darragh is doing his cube with his eyes closed. They gather them into the car and head off.

Margaret has scones fresh from the oven when they arrive and opening the door the aroma is divine. Simon and Paul are there ahead of them, and Paul's wife Felicia. She's a diminutive woman who is usually slow to get chatting but is always smiling, so you would never feel her silence was stifling. Her daughter Adrienne is a little younger than Cian; she is a bright and friendly girl, always perfectly turned out, but a real girlie-girl so she and Cian have nearly nothing in common.

'How are my best boys?' Cian tolerates a hug, while Darragh dives onto his grandmother, adoptive grandmother, with real affection. 'Sit up at the table and I'll get the scones buttered.'

'We have fully leaded soft drinks, boys,' grins Simon. 'None of that diet stuff. Coke, Fanta, Sprite, you call it.'

Frank comes downstairs in a fluffy dressing gown, hair wet from the shower, brushed back so he looks like a bit like Michael Corleone.

'Look at them two boys,' he beams, scruffing their hair. 'Sure this is just like when me own young fellas were young fellas, yeh know what I mean, huh?'

Alice goes to put the kettle on and Margaret edges her into the utility.

'How are they doing since you told them?' she asks quietly.

'Very well, really, we had a bit of a cry in the park but they've not mentioned it to me since then. They are playing up a little, knowing I'm less likely to say no when they ask for stuff, but really they're just carrying on.'

'Aye. The poor little things. Well that's all they can do. Sure I remember a certain young lady facing the same thing.'

'I can't really remember. I mean, I do and I don't, you know. It's a bit of a blur at times.'

'You went through a lot of pain. I could hardly reach you at times. Of course we are looking back at, well… Let's hope they don't go through what you went through.'

'You mean let's hope I don't die?'

Margaret smiles, but there's struggle in the smile. 'Your mother loved you, you know.'

'Why do you say that?'

'I remember you after we brought you here. You were emotionally exhausted, we had no words that would cheer you. You kept saying there was nobody left who loved you, even though we kept telling you we did.'

'Really, I said that?'

'You did. And you were talking about your dad a lot, it kind of landed on you, that he wasn't there.'

There's a dark stain on the utility wall that suddenly catches Alice's eye. The shower had spilled over. Not long after she met Lorcan, they were alone in the house and nature had taken its course. Several times. Once when they were showering after a frisky escapade and she had not noticed the shower head fall outside the tray, drenching the ceiling below. The stain had been painted over, but always resurfaced.

'I had a weird flashback the other day,' she says. 'When I took them to Tayto world. I had a sudden memory of being with Dad, I assume it was Dad, I was little and he was holding my hand. In an amusement park. But you said he was gone after I was a baby? Touring?'

'As far as I knew, but then I was never sure if that man was coming or going. Oh, he could make me angry, and sorry to say this in front of you. Ah, he was charming as you like. You know these musicians, lovely to your face, but gone as soon as he can get away. Always something better going on. Sometimes when I visited your mother he'd be there, sometimes all there would be was excuses.'

'You're saying he was there after I as born?'

She frowns. 'I'm not sure. I'd say I did see him once or twice, does that count as him being there?'

'You don't even know?'

'It wasn't up to me. I was there for my sister and anybody who wasn't putting her first didn't deserve my attention. I know she loved him. She was passionate, maybe too much so at times. I don't know if he was the best type for her, but she wouldn't have anybody else. Anyway, I don't want to be too down on him, he's your father. I wish I could give you more.'

'I wish he could give me more.'

'Exactly. Now I think there's two boys that need a bit of attention.'

'Or maybe four,' says Alice.

When they emerge from the utility, there are indeed four boys at the table, Cian and Darragh have coke while Lorcan and Frank are happily laying into some fancy looking IPA. Adrienne, Felicia and Paul are sitting opposite them. Simon is buttering scones.

'I was telling the boys I'd take them down to Enniscrone, teach them to surf.'

'Oh, that's a lovely idea. Although, we'll have to see how things are going. I'm not sure how long I'll be able to face a journey like that.'

Simon puts an arm around her. 'Maybe we should go now? Next week?'

'Up to my neck in tests.'

'Yeah. Look, the offer's there. No hurries. There will be time.'

She makes a pot of tea and they all sit at the table. Cian, on best behaviour, doesn't take his Nintendo Switch out at the table, but he looks impatient to escape. Darragh is effusing about one of his new algorithms for speed-solving, and Paul is trading tips with him. Lorcan looks really happy sitting between them, and Alice hopes it's about being with them rather than the beer.

For now, everything is warm and the blackness has receded in her head. In it's place, a little slideshow of images plays: her mother, the great big beautiful head on her as the laugh together; her father holding her hand; a summer in a caravan in Enniscrone and gleeful adolescent joy of it overwhelming the grief; the love that she and Lorcan found in the year after. They swirl together into the vortex of tea and talking and she can only smile as she starts to cry.

Lorcan, Sunday, 8:30am

It's mad to imagine that Jim will actually be out of bed, unless he's still up since last night. Lorcan parks outside his house, an ex-council maisonette with tiny windows. The garden is a jungle overgrown with buddleja and bamboo. Lorcan has to duck through them, picking up a patina of spider web as he goes.

Rhia answers the door wearing only a red silk dressing gown. Lorcan has to struggle to keep his eyes on her face.

'Lorcan, hi,' she welcomes him with a smile that wants to melt him.

'I'm guessing he's in bed?'

She shakes her head, the long red waves of hair washing over her shoulders. 'He's up.'

Lorcan is about to laugh at her humour when Jim appears behind her.

'Morning, good man yerself. Grab that for me, will yeh.' He pulls his amp, a monster with antique batteries that weigh a ton, to the door and leaves it there. Lorcan ignores it and walks to the car to open the boot, but has to run back when he sees Rhia hefting it. He helps her lift it into the boot, catching an inadvertent glimpse of a delicate breast that he has been coveting for as long as he can remember.

'Oh, good Jesus,' he says, as soon as she's gone back inside. His hard-on makes it difficult to sit into the car.

Jim emerges after several minutes, throws the rest of his stuff on the back seat, sits in the front and cracks open a can of Guinness.

'Fancy a slug?'

'Maybe not while I'm actually driving.'

'Fair 'nuff. How's the missus doing?'

This is not Jim asking, of course, Rhia has prompted him. Lorcan is warmed in a weird little way that Jim respects her enough to make that little effort.

'Ah you know, it's not easy.'

'Tell me about it, bro. My ould one keeps talking about leaving. I mean, come on, how many years I been looking after her and now she's gone and got some mad notions. I told her to go and get checked for early onset menopause, yeh get me?'

There are times when Lorcan would like to punch Jim. Instead he reaches into the glovebox when they're stopped at the traffic lights and hands him a naggin of vodka.

'Yeh're me guardian angel, cheers, bro.'

It only takes a few minutes to get to St Anne's park in the light traffic. Bob is chaining up his Yamaha as they pull in behind.

'Cool,' says Bob, pulling off his helmet to reveal a thick black wig that wefts down to his waist.

'Yeh're looking sexy,' says Jim.

'I like to please,' says Bob, adding a pair of black sunglasses.

They lug the monster amp between them up the main avenue, nearly a mile long. Every so often they stop and slip a beer out of Bob's stash, share it between them.

The park once belonged to Lord Iveagh of the Guinness dynasty, bequeathed to the state. The avenue led up to one of the most glorious stately houses on the island, which was burnt down with supreme carelessness by Dublin Corporation who could think of nothing else to do with this embarrassing reminder of England's imperial heritage than to use it as a store for flammable solvents. The remains were bulldozed and buried under a mound from which the view is as wonderful as the Lords and Ladies Iveagh would have commanded.

This morning, the mound has been mounted by rockers of all ages. There are children and pensioners and every age between, men and women, although considerably more men, many of whom would have twenty or thirty year's seniority on Lorcan. Tee-shirts, jeans and cool hats are everywhere, and hair, lots and lots of hair, much of it real. This is a serious crowd.

A van has been driven to the front of the mound with a big screen. Cecil the DJ, a local hero, is just setting up when they arrive. *Sweet Home Alabama* issues from the massive speakers on the van, and a concert of *Lynard Skynyrd* from the seventies plays on the screen.

Jim gets his amp set up. He is one of the few people who have the full rig, a few have guitars, acoustic or electric without amps, but most are armed with nothing more dangerous than an air-guitar. Jim warms his Stratocaster up with a few riffs, playing along with the southern US rock outfit. Bob hands Lorcan another beer.

'Okay, folks,' Cecil breaks in once *Alabama* starts to fade. 'We've got a whole morning of heavy rock hits for you this morning, but first of all, we're gonna have our main act. We'll be counting the rockers on the mound, y'all get up there now. After we'll be coming around with a bucket, remember today's record breaking attempt is in aid of brain damage. Now, what song is it you want to hear?'

A feeble shout of *Freebird* rigs out.

'I said what song is it you want to hear?' Cecil roars.

This time the *Freebird* is universal and boisterous.

The first chords rings out. Rockers everywhere dip heads, hold their left hands out to imaginary guitar necks and hang their right hands poised to strum.

Then the riff kicks in and Lorcan, head beginning to buzz from the beer, is in heaven. Jim plays along note perfect. Bob leans into him and, shoulder to shoulder, they give themselves to the winding guitar lick.

He had wondered if it was appropriate to come here this morning, but now, as he feels at one with close on two hundred fellow overgrown rockers, he is overwhelmed by a near euphoria. He hopes the memory of this moment will stay with him after the *Book* has undone this *Untime*.

Alice, Sunday, 5:30pm

Jackie has the table held at the back of Insomnia. She stands to hug Alice, wrapping her up in the warmth of her arms.
'Sit down there, I'll get your coffee in.'
'Jesus, Jackie, I'm not a cripple yet. I'll get my own.'
Alice gets a flat white and treats herself to a white chocolate and lemon muffin. She gets a second coffee when she sees Beth arriving in.
'Babe,' says Beth as Alice carries the drinks down. 'Are you okay?'
'Still alive, if that's what you mean.'
'Hah,' says Jackie. 'Now you're the one who doesn't have any tact instead of me for once.'
'Jackie, shush,' says Beth.
'Shush yourself, we need to have a bit of fun, is what we need. Brighten up Alice's day.'
'Thanks, I could do with it. I had to go and pick up Lorcan from the park, would you believe. Went to that bloody Freebird yoke, and next thing I get a call. "Hey Alice, I love you but I'm too drunk to drive."'
'Oh my God, you're kidding. What a dick!'
'And the worst thing was I had to give Jim a lift home, him sitting in the back perched between Cian and Darragh like a big grown up kid.'
'Jesus, you should have told him to walk home.'
'Didn't he have his guitar and his amp. I'll say one thing though, he got the boys singing along. Whatever kind of creep Jim is, he has a gift when it comes to bringing people out of themselves.'
'I think we'd all have that talent if we were roaring alcoholics like him. I read somewhere that drunks are great manipulators because they spend their lives trying to set up the next excuse for drinking.'
'Well, whatever, I was none too pleased with Lorcan. Is it just me or

is he twice as childish since I was diagnosed?'

'Any word back on the tests yet?'

'Nah, it might be weeks. Depends on what shows up, I guess, and I may end up getting sent for more.'

'And there's nothing you have to do now? You're not on any meds or anything?'

'Not a thing. It's weird, I had to get myself ready for all these crazy treatments, I take leave from work, now I'm just twiddling my thumbs. I jump at every phone call, you know, just in case it's the doctor, but otherwise, well, life goes on.'

'We are wasting good bucket-list time, if you ask me.'

'Jackie! I warned you not to start going on about that. Alice, don't listen to her.'

'Ah, don't be worrying, Jackie's right, we should be light hearted. There's no point in being morose. I'm just not jumping out of a plane or heading to Everest.'

'What would you do then?'

'I've been half thinking of Enniscrone.'

'Ah Jaysus, yeh wild thing yeh. Enniscrone? Sligo? Wild Western Way and all? Like your mother's caravan?'

'It's a mobile home now, but yeah, that's what I mean.'

'Would you not even go to Torremolinos, for goodness sake. We could make it a Bucket-Break.'

'Jackie, shush, will you! Why Enniscrone, Alice? I mean, I know you used to go there for the summers and that, but why now?'

The glossy table surface has a fine sprinkling of sugar, some of it stuck, glued by moisture to make a sandpaper texture.

'I don't know,' she says. 'I've been thinking a lot about my mother. What she went through. And what I went through. It's bringing it home.'

'Ah, I'm so sorry,' says Beth, taking her hand and squeezing, feeding affirmation through her finger tips, using her skills as a Touch Therapist. 'And what about London? You used to live in Ealing? We could go over there.'

'Yeah, I've been back a few times but it's not the same really. We rented and moved about a bit. Home was whereever Mammy was more than a location. And I've no family there. I would like to find out a bit more about my father, but I don't have any leads. Mammy said he was touring with Bruce Springsteen but that's a dead end, I don't think he was ever with them. I do an odd search on google and that but there's millions of Carlos Garcia's, none of them bass guitarists.'

'So Enniscrone?'

'Ah, don't be minding me, I'm just getting nostalgic.'

'And,' says Jackie with a sly grin, 'perhaps a touch of nostalgia for a certain Mike, wasn't that his name?'

'Oh,' says Beth. 'Tell me more about Mike.'

'Jesus, that's all I need, my first boyfriend. He was a lovely guy, I mean you couldn't meet a nicer bloke. Disabled, like in a wheelchair, but so full of energy, great pianist.'

'Great what?' the two women ask in unison.

'Pi-an-ist, I said.'

'Oh, sorry, though I notice you're not denying it.'

'Jackie!'

'No, nothing happened between us, but he was lovely, he was a part of the journey, I guess.'

'If he was that nice, why did you dump him for Lorcan?'

'Jackie, I will strangle you one of these days,' says Beth.

'Different attractions,' says Alice, remembering that water stain on her mother's utility ceiling. 'Different needs.'

'Okay, well, I can cancel clients no problem, just let me know and I'll be there.'

'Oh, me too,' says Jackie. 'Easter's coming up so the kids will be off school but that should be an issue.'

'And there's Simon, he said he'd teach the boys to surf.'

'There you go, all makes sense.'

'Maybe. We'll see. I'm just not sure which way to go at the moment, and I'm tired so much of the time.'

'Two weeks in Torremolinos and you won't know what tired means, I tell you,' says Jackie.

Jackie lets out a belly laugh throwing goodwill across the table, her short hair flicking into her eyes, while Beth's beautiful hands hold hers with tenderness. She is so lucky to be enclosed by such people, her friends, her fabulous family. If only that was all she needed, if she could survive on the support, sustain herself on their love. But the dark hole in her heart is brimming and heaving with malice and nothing, not this love nor any solace, can contain it if it bursts.

Lorcan, Tuesday, 8:25am

Alice is asleep. Lorcan sneaks up with tea. She doesn't stir. It is the first time since the fateful day that she has not been wide awake, staring at the ceiling, or stepping straight into the shower stupid early. He is glad. She needs rest, God knows. He puts the tea quietly on the bedside table.

She is on her back, head tilted toward him, mouth slightly gaping. Perfectly still. Peaceful. He has a sudden fright. What if... But no, he sees her draw in breath.

What if one day he is looking at her, standing over her in bed? What if she is dying, or already dead? Is this how she would look, pale, peaceful, still? No, much more emaciated, drawn, skeletal. For a moment he sees death, a hollow husk, silent, mute, lifeless. The awful truth of it is so real, so right in front of him, his head spins, he gasps...

She moves, sighs. Lorcan backs out carefully, not wanting to disturb her. He stops on the stair, takes deep breaths. That was intense. A waking nightmare. He must avoid being made morose, being dragged too far into *Untime*.

The boys eat breakfast. Cian has a ball in one hand he's trying to spin on a finger. Darragh is solving a cube in one hand. Their other hands spoon sugar puffs. The blessings of boyhood, that the immediate, the physical, the *now* can overplay what disasters might be unfolding. Lorcan envies them; a little more immaturity would do him good.

'Ha!' he says.

'What?' says Cian.

'Oh, sorry. My mind was miles away.'

The irony is not lost. A dearth of childishness is not his problem. Particularly during *Untime*, letting himself drink and smoke, sneaking out to talk to Rhia. What was he thinking? He had his *Book*, he had his out, his escape clause. Why then did he not feel relaxed and relishing the day like his sons?

'Right, boys, time for school.'

'I need a note,' says Cian.

'What for?'

'I didn't do my history.'

'Why do I have to give you a note because you didn't do your homework?'

'I'll be suspended if you don't.'

'What?'

'That's what Mr. Farren says.'

'Why didn't you do your history?'

'Dunno. I was upset, cause of Mam and all that.'

Lorcan looks into his face, innocent but insightful. Is he harbouring deep pain? Or is he smart enough to know he can get away with things? Either way, now is not the time to test him.

'Give me your journal so.'

'O-M-G, that is *so* unfair,' says Darragh.

The traffic is tedious, but he is happy to be with the boys. He is aware of how little time he has spent with them, since the diagnosis. Some of that is deliberate, seeking excuses to drink and smoke without exposing them. Some of it is incidental, such as visits to her family where the boys are sucked away and smothered with love. After *Untime*, they won't remember, but he will, most likely.

'We should do something, boys. Together. Father and son stuff.'

'Can we got to Tayto Park?'

'Maybe at the weekend.'

'We could go now. Mam took us last week.'

Thoughts rumble through his head like a deck of cards riffling. He could go. Just go. Alice had done so last week. She hadn't taken him. But he was with Rhia. He had lied. It wasn't payback. He couldn't leave her out. He could go back for her. But the boys had to stay in school. God forbid, he might be left in charge. Keeping discipline might fall on him. No, the *Book* will be his certainty, his salvation.

'Dad, the light's green.'

'Whoa, sorry,' he has to rush through the lights on amber. 'Look, we'll do it again, guys.'

'Aw, Dad.'

He understands it's the right thing, but he knows he's not spending enough time with them. Normally he's too busy with work; he is full time, after all, Alice only part time, and when the pressure's on he could do fifty, sometimes sixty hour weeks. Alice naturally takes the lead on nurturing, but the consequence is that Lorcan is excluding himself.

It's not normal times though, and he's not bothering with either work or parenting.

He imagines a shed in the back garden. He sees himself sitting in it, watching the house. He sees the boys, distant phantoms, with their mother. Is that what his father saw, all those years? Two children growing up isolated, removed. Did he have regrets? Were there moments like this when he might have reached out?

No. He is not his father. He will not renege on his children. As soon as *Untime* is over, then he will take them on a whim to Tayto Park. Yes, he will.

Alice, Tuesday, 12:15pm

It has been a torrid two weeks since the diagnosis, since that dreadful day staring at the professors carriage clock. She can still see the balls spin.

Alice has a case worker. Jane is lovely, she has tons of time to talk and no subject is off the table. They talked for two hours on her first appointment, there was tears, tissues, tea; consolation, affirmation. Jane was her friend.

Jane might wish that was not the case. Alice's number came up on her phone at least twice every day, and sometimes on weekends. Jane was never anything but gracious, greeting her with good will even when it was clearly outside her working time. Jane could talk consultants and clinical meetings, referrals and opinions, but the key, the outcome, was outside of her remit. Results would be analysed, experts consulted, then Bailey would call.

Bailey was calling. His landline was in her contacts.

'Hello,' snatching at the phone, almost accidentally dropping the call. Then she accidentally puts it on hold and has to click another button to bring it back. 'Hello?'

'Oh, hello, is that Alice Considine?' It was Bailey's PA.

'Hi, yes, Gemma isn't it?'

'Yes, this is Gemma from Professor Bailey's surgery.'

'Can I talk to him, Gemma?'

'Em…' She seemed a little taken aback at Alice's forthrightness. 'I'm calling to try and make an appointment for you…'

'Oh, I'm free now.'

'Eh, I was hoping for maybe Thursday.'

'Oh, Gemma, please. I need to know. I can't sleep at night for not knowing what the outcome is. Does he have all the tests?'

'Um, I really don't...'

'Please, Gemma, I'm really desperate to know. Would he be able to come to the phone?'

'I...'

'Please!'

There is a pause. She likes the pause, she has pushed past business and she has reached compassion.

'Please?'

'I shouldn't but... He's probably busy... Let me see if I can talk to him.'

A tinny, tip-tap-tacky version of *Edelweiss* begins twisting her ear. She wonders what kind of idiot decided that was a suitable tune for people waiting to hear whether they will live or die.

The song is on its fourth iteration when it clicks off.

'Alice,' says Professor Bailey, and she cannot help but feel there is a book, a whole volume, hard bound and leather backed, tight-spaced typeface, in that single word. It's not good. Her heart takes up a thumping that she can actually hear.

'We've been looking through...'

'Just tell me!'

He pauses for a moment. 'Are you sure this is a good time for us to talk? Is Lorcan around?'

'Please Professor, I need to know. It's not good news, is it?'

He sighs. 'No, it's not good news. There's a lot of detail in here, and I'd like you to come in. We found an epidural metastasis, basically a tumour on your spine. It hasn't begun to destroy the bone yet but it is beginning to press against the nerve. It's quite uncommon for Leukaemia, but, well, it's very clear on the MRI. We'll have to do a biopsy but I believe it's a formality.'

He unleashes a universe of detail, she scribbles and scratches in her notepad: treatment options, palliative care, attacking the symptoms. With this cancer, a cure is not a realistic option. Nerve damage. Paralysis. Death.

He stops. Has she any questions? Can he fill any gaps. There are no gaps. The fight is over even before it has begun. She waits for an ice-cold grip in her guts, a dizziness, some sign that her body has entered fight-or-flight mode, but there is nothing. The news is bad. She will die. Amen.

She is passed back to Gemma. Calmly, she makes her appointment, carefully she writes the date, time, address in her notebook even though it's the same office. She thanks Gemma very carefully, assures her she will be good to herself, and hangs up.

She drops her bum against the kitchen cabinet, slides to the floor. How weird the world looks, looking up. Familiar features from a fresh angle. Strange the things that show up, stains normally unseen beneath the worktop, that drawer is not quite sliding home, crumbs lingering in the gap under the fridge. Is this really her kitchen? Is this really her? What is "her?" So many things she has never got around to wondering about and now, now there is no time. Life has been a constantly spinning plate but very soon, it will slow, wobble, topple, smash.

Still no tears. Why not? Because it's not her, not her world, not her truth. Instead, she is a new set of requirements: she has to tell Lorcan when he comes back from the shops; she has to tell Margaret and Frank and Simon and Paul; shit, she has to tell Jackie and Beth. Invite them round? No, she can't face that just yet. Work. Eamo; what about Eamo? Why the hell is she worrying about Eamo?

Stop. Breathe. Calm. Mindfulness, why didn't she learn to do that?

Death. Oh, Jesus.

No. Not death. Dying yes. It's just one more thing to cope with. No silly twenty percent thing now. Just a winding down, a natural order. It was always coming, it's just come on a little sooner than she hoped.

And Enniscrone. It had been rattling around, becoming a belief, a thing. Was it a real thing now? Was there even time now? There had been suggestions of surgery. Urgently. What did that mean?

Still, no tears.

A vague relief, that she had told the boys. Yes, there was the promise not to die before the grew up. She would break that promise. But they would forgive her, wouldn't they?

A searing pain slips up from her back into her neck, her spine twisted recklessly. She does not have time for such triviality. She pulls herself up, legs burning with pins and needles, her back no better.

Time to start making lists. Maybe start with the Bucket-Break, hah, only there's nothing else she really wants to do. So. Enniscrone, then.

Lorcan, Tuesday, 1:13pm

Lorcan grabs his groceries fast, the shopping trip being a thin excuse for some time out. He drives to the sea front. There is a pump station, a grim concrete blockhouse that sluices sewage under the bay to the treatment plant in Ringsend. 'The only thing the Northside of Dublin gives to the Southside,' Jim is fond of intoning, 'is a pipe full o' shit.'

The building itself looks innocent, and the council have pimped it out with a plaza that has views and seats. Lorcan likes to stand hidden by the pump house, enjoying the vista while he smokes. A salt marsh game reserve stretches across at low tide to the grass and sandy reaches of Bull Island dotted with waders and gulls. The horizon beyond is a dark sea castellated with ferries and freight ships.

It's just over a week since he met Rhia. There is a lingering longing in him, despite his self-disgust. He wanted to see her again, not for... Well, nothing sinister. Just talking. He still has a compulsion to talk about the *Book*, to scratch the unbearable itch between his ears, and still she is the only person he can even mention it to. He pulls out his phone, flips up her number, flicks it away again. No. Yes. No.

Not now, he decides. Too soon. Later. Or if something changes. Yes. Leave it for now.

He smokes to the end of his third cigarette, flips the butt into the sea, then walks across the road back to the car.

Back home, he does not notice Alice reclining against the kitchen cupboards, throws his groceries in the fridge, and is heading to the coffee machine when he nearly steps on her.

'Jesus, what the hell? Are you hurt?'

'I am oddly okay.'

'What's wrong?'

'Bailey phoned.'

'Oh. Oh. That's good right?'

'Good that he phoned, I guess. Not good what he said.' There is a sing-song tone to her voice, and artificial cheeriness that chills him.

'He gave you results?'

'They found a tumour. On my spine.'

'What? What the hell?'

'They can look at surgery, but it's... Palliative, I guess.'

'Are you sure that's what he said?' he asks.

'Jesus, of course I am. Do you think I made it up?'

'No, there must be some mistake.'

'There's no mistake, Lorcan. There's an appointment to see him Thursday but this is what he's going to tell us.'

'Look you're upset, you may have misheard him.'

'Fucking right I'm upset but I wasn't before you came in.'

'What's upsetting you?'

'You, with this freaking deny-everything attitude.'

'You can't blame me for this, Alice. I'm trying to stay positive. Trying to have faith.'

'I'm not blaming you...' She is almost shouting now as her voice escalated with her anger; she stops, lowers her voice. 'Sorry, I'm not blaming you. Look, I have it here, I wrote it down as soon as he said it.'

'Did you write it down as he was saying it.'

'For fuck's sake it's there in black and white.'

'We need a second opinion. That's it. My father was talking about the Mater Private, he can get you in...'

'We don't need a fucking second opinion. One person telling me I'm going to die is quite enough.'

'You can't just give up like that.'

'I'm not fucking...'

Her face crumples, closes up with washed strain. Her hands form fists, she shakes them in the air as if fighting something off, then pushes herself to her feet. He watches her walk past him, hears her stamp upstairs and lock the bathroom door.

Lorcan slaps a hand hard against the fridge. What an eejit he can be. There was no need to question her but... But it has to be wrong. The diagnosis is getting worse? No.

He pulls his phone out. He needs to talk to Rhia. He puts it away again.

He walks to the front room, flips open the slot on the bottom of the bookshelf, pulls out the *Book*. It looks so alien, an ancient artefact in the mundane middle class setting of the sitting room. He knows it's pointless. He has to try.

He locks the front room door. It is rarely locked, the key is stiff. He slides the keyboard off his workspace, lays the *Book* out as if exalting it. He opens it to an early page. It slaps his head. There are languages, scripts even, that slip past his senses like water through a sieve. A piercing sound pushes through his ears, fizzy flashes in his fingers like holding an electric eel. He pushes through, through centuries? Who knows how long, to sections that are in English, then to his own handwriting. Some of these he can read. Other pages are like trying to push his eyes into a liquidiser.

Enough. He finds a blank page. Lays it flat. On his shelf is a box, a gift, a fountain pen. It is dry, he spins off the barrel, replaces the cartridge. Quick now, she'll be down.

He hovers the pen on the page, nib hovering. Mark it. Make a date. Do it.

He cannot.

Make a date, note a name, just do it.

He cannot.

It will happen. It needs no thought, his pen will write it down. From Professor Bailey. He'll write that scene in the office. Every moment since, it will pulse from his fingers like mercury twisting into tangible shapes on the page as all of the world is rolled up like a magic carpet.

Just make a date.

He cannot.

A staggering spasm grasps his hand. He has to drop the pen. A stitch, a cramp, a warning?

Pick the pen up.

Bring it down.

Bring it slowly down.

Make a mark.

Make it.

The nib descends, a tulip drop of ink poised on the nib. It need only touch the page, parchment, skin.

Just push...

Where is he? Something urgent, something impinging... a banging. There is a hammering at the door. Alice is yelling, slapping the wood.

Where is he? Lying under his workstation. The pen is beside him on the floor. Smashed. Ink in a blob like a clot of blood. He leaps to his feet, shocked. Steps towards the door but turns. The *Book* must go away. It is closed. He lifts it into the hidey-hole, pushes home the panel.

'Are you okay?' Alice grabs him by the arms.

'Yeah... Fine... I...'

'The door was locked?'

'I...'

'What the hell have you written on your forehead?'

'What?'

She points to his forehead. He goes to the hall mirror. The word 'NO' is scrawled in blue ink.

'Okay, I...'

'What the fuck is going on, Lorcan? You're freaking me out. You're not on some kind of drugs, are you?'

'Drugs?'

'You're not like in there snorting or injecting or something? Has Jim fixed you up with something? Why did you have the door locked?'

'I'm just... It upset me. I got lost in myself, I'm okay. No, no drugs, I'm not that stupid.'

'Really? I sometimes wonder. I really fucking wonder. Jesus. And what the hell is that?' She points to his forehead again. 'I mean talk about living in fucking denial. I'm going to get the boys. Wash that the fuck off before I get back.'

As he watches her storm out the door he notices that set to her shoulders. She had been slumped when he came in. She has a fire again. It's a shame that it's his shameful actions that have inflamed the fight in her.

He sees no clue at his workstation. Did he just fall? Faint? Did he write on his forehead? A message from the *Book*. Ah hell!

He wipes up the ink and pen splinters off the floor, then goes into the bathroom and scrubs his face. Who knew that fountain pen ink could be so hard to wash off?

There is a deep dizziness stuck at the back of his skull, a soft void into which he cannot see, as if something has scooped out a memory. The *Book* messes with his head. What damage might it have done this time. The booze battering his brain cells is bad enough, the end of *Untime* should undo that, but the harm from the *Book* is for life. What has he lost?

Lorcan, Thursday, 12pm

The fresh slash of polish plays havoc with Lorcan's sinuses. Professor Bailey is somber. There is a yellowing of skin under his eyes that Lorcan had not noticed before. It fascinates him almost as much as the news horrifies him.

Alice has an Epidural Metastasis. It is unusual, but is a recognised element of the wider syndrome. Particularly unusual where the disease is not yet advanced, a further cause for concern. The fact that Alice is not suffering significant back pain is a plus, but the MRI - he turns his screen to show them something out of an Alien movie - shows that it is already impinging on the spinal column. Chemotherapy and steroids are an option, radiotherapy could reduce its size. Surgery is also an option, though rarely a first step.

It is a balance, Bailey explains. The degree of invasiveness suggests urgency, the lack of pain suggests caution. An injection of a corticosteroid - Bailey drops the word in as if they should know what this particular piece of magic is about - directly into the tumour is the best short term action. Significant reduction of the tumour is common. With her permission, he will send her straight to the clinic.

Lorcan's head is shaking back and forth of its own accord. This is not the right story. Not the plan.

Last time they were here, Alice had dissolved, decayed under the dreadful revelation. Today, her face is flat, lips sharp with cold determination. Her hand sits in his, listless, lifeless, disinterested. He notices a tremble, a tiny thing like a fluttering hummingbird, in her left eyelid.

This scares him more than anything that has happened. There is deep down trauma here. Can the *Book* really undo all of this? She will remember. Rhia remembers part of her experience, perhaps not with complete coherence, but some of it stays. The pain was so consuming that some of it stuck in her head. Surely, once the Book undoes this *Untime*, some of the agony must stay with Alice. Can she ever be the same?

Alice pulls out her notebook; it bulges now, so many pages filled, pamphlets, cards, referral letters pushing in between. With a voice that would slice an eyeball, she calmly has Bailey repeat key points, therapies, treatments, options. She writes everything down.

Bailey does not mention survival rates. Alice does not ask.

When she has scribbled enough, Bailey calls Gemma on the intercom.

'Did you get the injection set up?' he asks.

'They are ready for Alice now, if she can go.'

Alice knows where she must go when Gemma explains the wing of the hospital and the room.

'I was there for the marrow biopsy.'

As they walk the corridors, following Alice's prodigious knowledge of linking corridors and stairs, they say nothing. It feels like there is nothing to be said. If Lorcan tries to be positive, she may actually hit him. He knows from the tension in her shoulders that she's barely holding it together. How do you chat about tumours?

They get to a check in area and they are expected. Still there is ten minutes of bureaucracy; forms have to be filled in. Her date of birth is checked four times. Has she allergies, heart complaints, has she recently had surgery, any symptoms of Covid?

They are passed to the care of a doctor called Mary who walks them to a private room and then checks all the same information again. Lorcan holds onto Alice's shoulder while Mary presses into her neck, feeling for the tumour. Confident she has it, the needle she delivers into the skin, entering with a pop, is horrifyingly large. He flashes back, he is holding her, angled forward over the bump, the anaesthetist delivering the epidural lumbar needle into her spine. That was Darragh. Or was it Cian?

Today is a different medicine. That time led on to love, today drives her deeper into disease. A frightful judder runs through Alice's frame, but she does not make the slightest sound.

Alice, Thursday, 12:55pm

The world is hard and made of cardboard. It tastes of dry ice and Dettol. It is a process, she tells herself. Get through it. She's had worse in her two weeks of tests. She is too strong to buckle, not yet. The pain when the needle goes in is horrific, but she bites down, and then it has passed, leaving only a lingering ache. The doctor gives her paracetamol before they leave.

'The car's this way,' says Lorcan.

'Sorry, I forgot to tell you. I need to call into work.'

'Jesus, work, you're kidding?'

'It's important.'

Lorcan looks dubious, but perhaps he knows he will be walking on glass if he tries to object.

Nelson Mandela House is only a short walk from the hospital. Normally, security would get obstreperous about her bringing Lorcan into the building without the appropriate visitor forms and authorisation. The deferential looks and whispered tones from Charlie, a forty year veteran of door minding, friend to everybody working there and only a month from retirement, tell her that her illness is general news, and also that it has bought her some privileges.

Catherine comes straight out of her office.

'Lorcan, lovely to see you again. Come on the pair of you, into my office.'

She shows them in. 'Will you have tea?'

'Ah, no, thanks, Catherine, I want to be getting off home. I've got a royal headache building, I'm afraid.'

'Oh Jesus, I'm sorry.'

'Ah don't be worrying, all part of the package.'

'She tells me not to be worrying yet here she is in my office when she should be looking after herself.'

'Yeah. Just one last thing though. Eamo.'

'I know you asked about respite, I've been going through the forms. I think we should be good. I was kind of thinking out in the Burren, there's an adventure centre, and it's a good distance from Dublin.'

'That's great, thanks Catherine. Look, here's what I'm thinking. I'm probably, actually no, I'm definitely taking a break down in Sligo, you know, Enniscrone, the caravan my mother has.'

'Excuse me,' says Lorcan, as if just tuning back in. 'You're doing what now?'

'Sorry, should have said. I've been thinking about it. Jackie calls it a Bucket-Break, just to get my head straight. We've a couple of weeks before they start anything, to see if the steroids work. There's never going to be a better time.'

'Really? You think a caravan is the best place for you right now? In your condition?'

'Well it's actually a mobile home, and a damn good one. It's warm and it's dry. *In my condition* be damned.'

'But it's hours from the hospital.'

'Lorcan, please. Leave it for now, okay. Catherine, if there was a centre somewhere nearby, I could look in on him. Make sure he was settling in, type of thing.'

'Jesus, Alice, you're taking your work on holiday now, are you mad?' Despite this, Catherine turns to her computer and begins to type. She goes down through a few layers and comes up with a spreadsheet. 'Well, there you go: Enniscrone. Twelve beds for under-eighteens. Run by Bernardos. There's another one in Sligo town, Childline, only six beds and it's mostly younger kids. Hmm. After that you're probably looking at Castlebar. Leave it with me, babe. I will turn this town over to fight for a place for him.'

The pain is back. It has risen to the point of blurring her vision as they walk back to the car. It has crept like an acid burn down her spine and into her hips, making each step cringing agony. She has to hold tight to Lorcan's arm and hope she can get there before losing heart.

'Am I supposed to be going to Sligo too?' asks Lorcan.

'Yes. Yes of course you are. I need my family.'

'You might have told me.'

She does not have the strength to respond. Her head is red with torment. Lorcan's grip, solid but gentle, steadying her, is gold.

Lorcan, Saturday, 9:55pm

Lorcan's on his third pint but it's not settling well in his stomach. He has heartburn, but he's bravely battling through it. It stresses him, the situation with Alice. He has tried a couple of times to coerce the *Book*, but it's messing with him, like he can feel pieces of himself dissolving under its glare. Now she has everybody set up to spend a week, maybe longer, in a damned caravan on the west coast of Ireland. Does he bring the *Book* with him? How can he keep it hidden in the confined space? Will it just mess even worse with his head? The whole thing is twisting his stomach tight.

'Brian O'Driscoll, right, yeh know what I mean. Brian O'Driscoll!' Jim is wafting his opinions with much waving of the hands. As ever, he's managed to get a couple of pints ahead of them without putting his hand into his pocket.

'True,' says Bob. He has his special leather jacket on, the one with the patches for the biker gang that he is a member of. This is apparently to honour Alice, though Lorcan won't be relaying that particular honour to her.

'Brian O'Driscoll, now ask anybody in the pub,' Jim waves around at the half dozen locals who are staring alternately at the half pints in front of them and the golf on the telly. 'Ask anybody and they'll say he's the best Irish rugby player of all time, right? Wrong! Peter Clohessy. The Claw!'

'What?' Lorcan is roused from his reverie. You never quite know what will come out of Jim's mouth. 'A Munster prop? You're saying he had more tries than Brian O'Driscoll?'

'Ah, yeh know what they say. The forwards win the match, how much they win by depends on the backs. That was mister B.O.D. all over, keeping his hairstyle all nice and clean and flashing his

Southsider teeth at the girls in the crowd while the Claw was digging the ball out of the ruck and setting him off. That's how he scored so many tries, the Claw opened the way for him. Vastly underestimated player.'

'He's from Clontarf though, Brian O'Driscoll, a Northsider.'

'Listen to me, he may have been born there, may have played for the club more than once, but that man is a much a D-4 Ladyboy as any of his mates in *Black-rawk Caw-lege*.'

'True,' says Bob.

'Don't be mad,' says Lorcan. 'I mean, yeah, the Claw was a great prop and all, but you can't be comparing him to Briano.'

'I fecking can. And that comparison doesn't come out well in O'Driscoll's favour, but listen, hold that thought. I'll pop out to the bog, then maybe one of yiz would be so kind as to lend me a fag.'

They watch him head off towards the bathroom, swapping a laugh, as ever, with a few regulars along the way.

'How are things with your fine lady?' asks Bob.

'Ah, good and bad. I mean, the doctors are telling us it's getting worse. She has some kind of tumour now, this thing on her spine, it seems, and like it could end up pressing into her nerves and all.'

Bob screws up his face in a look of pain. 'Sounds rough beyond words, my friend.'

'I know, it's rotten. I mean, it's just so bloody unfair. And yet, she's in better health both physically and mentally than she's been for months. The whole thing of having illness after illness without knowing why seems to have taken more out of her than this awful news. There's a, how can I put it, a kind of cold calmness to her now.'

'She is strong, you know. She is stronger than that sickness.'

'And she's in such good mood. She's going everywhere with the boys, trying to be with them, you know it's almost as if she's giving them something to remember her by.'

'It can be a tonic, feeling like you're leaving a legacy, you know.'

'Maybe. I guess it's just nice to see her, like, so buoyant when maybe some people would be torn apart by it.'

'True.'

'Latest thing now is she's talking about going down and staying in the caravan in Enniscrone.'

'Where's that, brother?'

'Sligo, like right out on the Atlantic. Lovely resort when the weather's good and all but, you know, this time of year.'

'Why a caravan?'

'Ah, her family have been going down there forever. They have a mobile home, she used to go after her real mother died and it's, I don't know, taken on some kind of nostalgic significance now. So we all have to go down with her, and she wants her mother, and her brothers and their wives. And she's inviting all her friends, you know Beth and Jackie…'

'Inviting friends where?' asks Jim who has just arrived back from the bathroom.

'This caravan her family have in Enniscrone. At least, we're not all going to fit in the one mobile home, like, people will have to book hotels or other caravans or whatever.'

'That sounds like mad crack.'

'Well, it's…'

'Jaysus but Rhia's going to be excited by that. Maybe we'll book our own caravan, take Forry with us, like. Yiz're bringing yer kids, I presume?'

'Yeah, but…'

'Man, that'll be a gas.'

'Are you sure you're invited, Jim?' Bob puts in, spotting Lorcan's discomfort.

'Ah, don't be worrying, biker boy, there'll be a bed in the caravan for yeh and all, if yeh wanna go halves on it like.'

'Generous, man.'

'Right, ciggie time, come on.' Jim stands up and leads the way to the smoking area. Lorcan is left gaping for a moment. Jim's just invited himself, Alice will be livid. A hot wash flushes through him: typical of Jim, just takes what he wants.

As the heat eases, the upsides come to the fore. There won't be much drinking going on with Alice's family; Frank is the only one that enjoys a pint and he's generally a two-will-do kind of guy. With his mates there, he can slip out in the evenings.

And Rhia. He finds himself drawn to her, thinking about her hair and her face and that faraway look in her eyes. He has arranged to meet her on Monday in the pub again and that is beckoning his thoughts like moths to a candle. To have her there, in the same place for a week…

Ah, what's he worrying about? Jim will never get off his arse to organise it. Probably won't even remember tomorrow. He follows the others out for a smoke.

Alice, Monday, 10:30am

There is a ferocious fatefulness in her days. She is putting the pieces in place. She can see the coming week or two, beyond that is a black space. Do not think of the black space. It will fill out with procedures and surgery and more tests and heaven knows what else, for now leave it blank.

She lets her mind rest on one of the messages on her phone from Doircheas, Lorcan's sister. It shows a radiant Virgin Mary standing on a cloud with a face of pure compassion. Doircheas has been sending daily pictures and prayers and, while Alice has mostly let go of her childhood faith, there is a soft affection to these daily offerings. She feels guilty she is not spending more time with Lorcan's family, but they are not an easy bunch to deal with and right now she must show self-care.

Her list is mostly crossed out. Just a few items need focus. She lifts her phone and dials.

'How'r'ye, mizz Murphy?' Eamo answers.

'Hi Eamo, sorry to bother you. Can you talk for a moment?'

'Giz a minute.' There is a murmur of muffled voices, then a door closing. 'Go on, I'm in the bog.'

'Thanks for sharing.'

'Ah no, I'm not like going or that.'

'I know, I was joking. Listen, you remember we were talking about a respite centre? You getting away for a bit, out of the way.'

'Yeah, yeh said it and all, but like I'd be understanding if yeh couldn't get a place and that. Sure there's never resources when they hear Darndale, yeh know what I'm saying?'

'No, I did get you a place, if you can go.'

'Really, like a holiday?'

'Exactly like a holiday, and away from... Well, away from bad influences.'

'Ha, I know what yeh mean.' He lowers his voice. 'Me uncle Pluto's coming down the heavy on me, took me shooting and all.'

'Shooting? What?'

'Don't be making a fuss, mizz, Jaysus, ye'll get us all in the shits.'

'But, what does that involve?'

'We went up the mountains, this lad he knows has this barn like miles from anybody. Had me shooting a Glock, it was cool. Excepting, he wasn't doing it for the fun, know what I mean?'

She sees a spider just outside the kitchen window, a tiny thing, sitting on a web so fine it can only be perceived by the minute carcasses silk-wrapped into it. A fly is caught, struggles to break free as this tiny eight-legged thing scuttles voraciously. A bite, then more silk-wrapping and it is done.

'Okay, I really want you to do this thing, Eamo, yeah? We have a train ticket for you, and some spending money to get lunch on the train or whatever. You just need a couple of changes of clothes, they have washing facilities.'

'Ah, wait, mizz, what is this place all about?'

'It's in Sligo, a place called Enniscrone. It's right by the sea, so bring your togs.'

'Togs? Yeh're fucking joking. I never had no togs, go swimming in me jocks.'

'Okay, I'll get you togs. Thing is, I'll be nearby. I won't be working, but I'll be about. I hope maybe I can show you a few places, get you settled in. I've got two full weeks lined up for you.'

'Right, well, okay. I'm probably gonna have to sneak away, like. Don't think Pluto would be thinking too much of this holiday camp thing. Where is Sligo, that's out west or something?'

'You'll get a train to Sligo town and somebody will pick you up in a van, you'll be there in no time. And because it's a respite centre they won't let anybody in. You switch your phone off and you'll be in another world. You're going to love it, honestly.'

'Right.'

She tells him how to pick up the ticket from the office, then wishes him well. As she hangs up, she says a little prayer to holy saint Doircheas, Lorcan's sister, since praying to a God tends to feel a little hypocritical. She can hear the uncertainty in Eamo's voice, knows that she's in a battle with his uncle Pluto. He can still be swayed either way.

The spider is still sitting on the silk threads.

Stop overthinking. Tick, another task completed.

She has Jackie and Beth lined up. Paul and Simon are coming. Margaret is sorting out accommodation for everybody. Everything is in place for whatever this trip is supposed to be.

Nothing can go wrong now.

Lorcan, Monday, 11am

Lorcan props up the bar at the *Roundabout*, a silky smooth pint settling in front of him. He is calm, his mind a pale soft surface like the head on the *Guinness*. He watches the waves of nitrogen micro-bubbles in their intoxicating dance, verging upwards away from the void of ruby-black stout.

He sees a swathe of red in the mirror, a halo of flame as Rhia approaches. He cannot help but smile as he turns.

'Are you okay?' she asks, moving for a kiss, leaving her cheek lingering against his just a moment too long for propriety. He is immediately flustered, flushed

'Yeah, I'm, well, you know.' He is suddenly a tongue-tied teenager. 'I'm okay, all things considered. It's very hard. It's horrible knowing that there's nothing I can do, or anything I try to do doesn't work.'

'I'm so sorry, Lorcan. Let's sit.'

'You want a drink?'

'No, I'm fine.'

He watches her lithe body in that step-dance she has, the sunlight from the windows shining through her flowing Indian skirt so that he can see the skinniness of her legs. Oh God, that child in him, that teenage Lorcan is still alive and still lusting after her. The pull of her perfume coaxes his nose as he sits down, like the aroma of fresh baked scones.

'Sounds like you had a good time Saturday,' she says.

'Ah, you know, it's great to get out, let the worries go and all that. I'll say one thing about Jim, he knows how to get a room going. He had the ould blokes in the bar doing the Macarena, albeit that they wouldn't get off their barstools, still, it was impressive to see.'

'He came home talking about some kind of caravan holiday.'

'Down in Sligo, yeah. Alice wants her family down there.'

'He asked me to look up the prices today. Seems to have taken his imagination.'

'Oh, I, well...' He had assumed that the idea would have dissolved in the copious volumes of alcohol Jim managed to swill. Why did this one idea have to stick? 'Maybe you shouldn't...' Or maybe she should. He remembered the hedonistic little thrill that had taken him when Jim grasped the wrong end of that stick with both hands and his teeth. Having Rhia down there for a week or two mightn't be a bad thing.

'Oh, is Alice okay with that? I hope he didn't push himself into it?'

'Oh no. No. No she's grand, you know, the more the merrier and all. Weather's supposed to be good, I heard.' He feels like an imbecile again, barely coherent.

'Alice didn't expect us, did she?' Rhia smiles.

'Well, she was a little surprised...'

'I thought not.' She gives a little laugh, a gorgeous giggle that folds the skin on her face in a fascinating way. 'Well, don't worry, if we do end up going, I'll try and keep him out of her way.'

'It's not that she doesn't like Jim.'

'I know. He can be a bit of a handful.'

'And she was saying...'

'What?' There is a cheese-wire edge to her voice.

'Well, the bruise.' He points to his temple. 'And it's not the first.'

'What the hell are you saying?'

'I'm not saying anything...'

'Does Alice think he beats me up, is that it?'

'Rhia, I know what you've been through.'

'Oh, that's it? It's all about you? You still think you can get him to leave me? You think my love isn't strong enough?'

'Rhia, stop. You know that's not true. I know how much you feel for Jim, hell you broke my heart over it.'

'You don't own me, Lorcan. It's not my fucking fault your heart was broken. You chose that.'

'I did, you're right. Look, all I'm saying is that if she knew what was going on...'

'What is going on, Lorcan?'

Some of her sharpness has eased, her vulnerability is visible again. Her eyes are down on the floor, not laced with rage as a moment before.

'Do you remember...?' He struggles to put words around it. His mind is bending, breaking, but he pushes out. 'Do you remember the night on Burrow beach, when you died?'

'What are you talking about?'

'You killed yourself, Rhia.' He has to choke his voice, in case the barman overhears. 'You went into the sea, you remember that?'

'I remember a dream...'

'And we talked about it the next day. We talked about it a week ago. You said you remembered.'

'I just remember feeling sick, what you said sickened me.'

'No, remembering it made you feel sick, because the *Book* erased it.'

Her head cocks, her eyes clear as if she sees, then she shakes her luscious hair. 'Give me a cigarette.'

'I... Okay. There's a smoking area at the back.'

He follows her to a covered concrete yard with perspex roof, a Covid beer garden. They are alone. He hands her a fag, takes one himself, lights them both.

'How did you know I was smoking?'

'You never stopped.'

'I did. I haven't smoked properly for years.'

'And yet...' she smiles.

They smoke in silence for a while. He watches her lips, the loop they form as she raises the cigarette, the wrinkling of skin when she sucks on it, the sleek sensual cone of smoke she exhales.

'And you don't remember where you got this *Book*?'

'No. The thing is, the *Book* fucks with your head. Sometimes I remember stuff, sometimes not, and it just messes with you and you can't think straight. Or sometimes I can't remember at all but I can read what I wrote, like. And some of the stuff I wrote I can't read.' He shrugs. 'I don't remember where I got it. Something happened, something bad, like, really bad. Maybe. I don't know.'

'Fuck. You don't know a lot.' She puffs a perfect smoke ring that pushes up against the perspex roof, then dwindles. 'So, let's say I believe you.'

'Then you know that I know. About Jim. How bad it gets.'

'So I know you know.'

'But it's a secret. Even Alice doesn't know about the *Book*, never mind that night.'

'Nobody knows about the *Book* except me?'

'I can't talk to people, literally can't physically talk. I tried to use the *Book*, to cure Alice, but... I don't know, I just can't.'

'Yet it saved me.'

'Yes.'

She turns her eyes on him. The deep greens grab his whole heart, pull him in. He remembers, when they were kids, when there was still a hope. He hears his heart whumping in his ears, feels cheeks flush. The woman is gorgeous.

She reaches out her arms. She takes his face between her hands. She pulls him close. Her lips push hard into his. Her tongue brushes. He opens his mouth. She pulls away and lets him go.

A surge of blood floods his limbs, searing. His ears go deaf with pressure, his eyes blur with moisture. A sea-swim shiver overwhelms him.

'I love you, Lorcan.'

'And I love you,' he says desperately. 'I always have.'

'But Jim is my heart. You must know that.'

'Oh Jesus, Rhiannon, of course I know that. I know it every day of my life. I'm so glad the *Book* was able to save you. And despite everything that Jim does, despite what I saw that night, he's still my oldest mate.'

She nods. 'I better be getting back. Forry will be waking from his nap.' She starts to head back out to the bar, Lorcan follows.

'Isn't he at school?'

'He was nervous, didn't want to get up. I kept him home.'

'Wouldn't he be a bit old for a nap.'

'No, it does him good to replenish.'

'Okay, and Jim's with him.'

'No, I've locked him in the bedroom.'

'Forry, or Jim?'

'Forry of course. No point locking Jim in, he'd kick his way out.'

'You locked your son into his bedroom?'

'He feels safer that way.'

'Right. Okay then. So anyway, you're coming down to Enniscrone?'

'Do you want me to?'

She stops on her way to the door. She looks at him again, and he sees echos of the kiss. No. He has to say no, that it's not right, that this is Alice's week.

'Yes,' he says.

Alice, Monday, 1:10pm

'You what the fuck now?' Alice could not believe what she was hearing.

'I know, not what we wanted but…'

'Really? Not what *we* wanted? You don't even want to go.'

'Hey, that's not fair. I never said I didn't.'

'No, you didn't. You whinged and you moaned but you never actually said you didn't want to go. And then you roll in, on a Monday morning, stinking of drink and fags, fuck knows why you're drinking on a Monday morning, and tell me you've invited your boozehound friends along. Why the hell didn't you even tell me this on Saturday?'

There is a *Guinness* stain the size of a golf ball on his tea shirt. There's a tuft of hair sticking up, wild, over his ear. Thank goodness the Guy Faulks goatee is gone.

'I… didn't think they'd actually want to come.'

'But now you do?'

'Well…'

'What changed your mind? Were you drinking with big man Jim?'

'Em… yeah, just a couple.'

'Jesus!'

'Babe, sorry, I didn't mean… It's just, like, I know it's your gig and all.'

'My gig?'

'Yeah, like your family, your friends, all that.'

'And? Did you want to invite your family?'

'No, I… Look, sorry. If I wasn't all over it, it wasn't deliberate. I'm here for you babe. You know that. It's just…'

'You just thought you'd invite your drinking buddies and your ex-girlfriend. Whoop-ti-do. Way to support me.'

'I'm sorry. I was wrong to do it without asking you, Alice, I know. But they won't be anywhere near us. I mean, I've told them the name of the campsite but they won't be anywhere near your mother's mobile home, right? And they're our friends. They want to support you too.'

'*Our* friends? Really?'

'You were part of the Gang too.'

'Really?'

'Come on. You can't deny, you were all over us. That was the same summer, wasn't it. You started hanging around with us just after you got back from Enniscrone that year, the one you keep remembering, what did you call it, your halcyon summer?'

'Okay, yes, I did. There was a reason.'

'And what was that?'

'What the fuck do you think, mister Lorcan H. Considine?'

'Jesus, I don't know. 'Because we were fun, I assume? That was what had pulled me in. Jim was always a gas man. Before I started hanging around with him, I never got invited to the parties and all that. I mean, we were out every second night. It was brilliant. It was kinda my halcyon summer too, I think.'

'Okay, I'll give you that. When Jim was about there was always somebody singing, people laughing. He was great for that. That wasn't why I was hanging around with them, though.'

'Why then?'

'God, you can be awful thick, you know.'

The *Guinness* stain, the tuft of hair, the eyes, empty but expecting, the child. She loves him deeply, and loves that little boy innocence. Look at him, like a puppy, waiting. His ingenuousness is seductive, but his immaturity can be infuriating. Her stomach is sour, spitting, upset by her anger. She needs to let go, for her own health. She needs his love.

She reaches out her arms. She takes his face between her hands. She pulls him close, pushes lips against his, kisses out the love and the anger that are pulsing in her. 'It was you, you fecking eejit. That party we were at, d'you remember? Was it Emily Harte's party? Just before school started. You were there with the Gang and you were dancing, and you read that poem, you remember you used to be a poet? That was all it took. Jesus, I was smitten.'

He is grinning. He is the puppy who got the treat. He doesn't deserve this, but she needs peace in her soul, and she needs her love to flow.

'I love you,' he says.

'I know you do. I need you to. I need you with me. I need your support every hour of the day. I mean, I'll have the others, but...' A tear trails down her cheek. 'It's hard, Lorcan. This journey. I can't do this alone. Be there for me, okay?'

'You got it, babe. I love you.'

2: Travelling

Alice, Saturday, 3:05pm

The trip is dismal. Alice is nauseous nearly as soon as Lorcan navigates onto the N4 heading west. They stop at the Enfield services to get lunch. The boys, including Lorcan, munch into *Happy Meals*.

Back on the road, she rolls her neck while napping and it cramps up, stinging her to tears. Cian complains that caravans are uncool and Darragh chimes in. They wail and whinge but she cannot turn her head to shush them.

They have to stop again twice so she can unwind the twist in her spine. Each time the boys are hungry. It is warming in one way as she watches Lorcan scoff into yet another burger with the same relish as Cian and Darragh; she can see how his seeming immaturity may work in building bonds with his boys. She imagines them in a year, maybe two, if her fight has been fought, communing silently over mince beef patties and tasteless potato fries. Meanwhile, she can barely tolerate buttered toast from the cafe next door.

They leave the N4 at Collooney and slide onto a single-lane, twisting, winding, roller-coaster of a road. Seized by nausea and neck pain, she grips to the door handle painfully tight. Each tiny detail of the trim, the contour and the chrome strip highlighting the handle, become her intimate acquaintances as she battles to stabilise the swinging motion. It is only as they slow on the outskirts of Enniscrone that she can ease off.

'My God,' says Lorcan, as they pass the *Out Of Town* hotel. 'Was that there last time we were here?'

My God, thinks Alice, *that trip was horrific, and all he can talk about is some fricking hotel.*

Her neck has eased enough for her to turn and take in the facade. It is immense, a long low barn like some kind of demented data centre. It must stretch along the coast for two hundred metres, and beyond are lines of holiday cottages, a whole suburb of hospitality. The heads of sand dunes try to rise above the roofs but are almost lost to this temple of tourism.

'It's been that way for a few years, maybe not since you were down.'

'So much for small seaside village.'

'Yeah, a bit of sprawl, but I think the town still has its charm.'

'We haven't been down for a good while.'

'No, not really since Cian got boisterous.'

'Hey,' says Cian. 'I'm not boisterous.'

'Ha, sure you're not. You don't remember that time it was raining all day and you started playing football inside the mobile home?'

'I never did.'

'Broke a vase, you did. Besides, you were never a big fan, Lorcan.'

'Well, I was and I wasn't. I mean being so close, cooked up all day. You might have come down by yourself, though, with Margaret, like.'

'What would I be going without you guys for? Mind you, being away from the moods on the lot of you might have been a holiday in itself.'

'Well thanks!'

'And on that note, you will try and fit in, won't you, Lorcan? I mean, I know you don't like being clammed up in a tin can, but, you know, this is important to me. Just try and get on. Join in.'

Lorcan takes a deep breath. The request has irked him, and he's edgy anyway, but he forces himself to relax. 'I promise I'll do my best.'

'I might let you out to play with your friends if you're on your best behaviour. Look this is it here.'

They are coming up to the campsite, a broad stretch of sand and maram grass that winds away to the dunes and has been solidly settled with caravans, mobile home and cabins. When Margaret had first brought her here it had been little more than a field with no fixtures. Now it is a well organised and sprawling setup with a wooden palisade at the entrance bearing the sign *Atlantic Caravan Park*, and a custom built reception building. They drive in and take a right and then a left, but she realises they've missed a turn.

'The place keeps changing,' she says.

'Shifting sands.

On the second attempt, they find the stub road that leads to the tight little neighbourhood of mostly fixed mobile homes where her mother's place sits. It was all caravans once, but there is something of a mobile home arms race in progress. Without an elevated decking and barbecue patio you can't hold your head up around here.

It isn't the nearly-new chrome-and-green mobile home with bay windows and roof lights that nudges her nostalgia as they pull up, but the memory of the old, crappy, yellow caravan, the trudge to the pump with the ten gallon water keg, the days spent running wild, climbing the dunes just behind that gave onto the beach. It is as if somebody had bottled that summer, that coming of age, after her grief was gone, and just uncorked it now, letting the aroma drift. She breathes deeply on its draft, spiced by the tang of salt and seaweed.

She swings herself stiffly out of the car and a gusty wind whips at her hair, an old friend patting her head in greeting. Cian is already out and doing keepy-uppies with his brand new ball, a bribe to get him down here. Darragh stays in the car, eyes shut, doing a blind *Rubik's* cube solve.

'Alice!' Margaret runs down the steps from the decking. Normally she'd be all over her grandchildren first, today Alice gets her focus.

'Are you alright, pet. You look peaky.'

It is too much after the hours of aching. A wave washes over her and she breaks into tears. She heaves her head onto Margaret's shoulders hoping to stifle the sobs, not to frighten the boys. She is wrapped in love and hustled into the mobile home, supplied with tissues and hot tea poured by Frank.

'What is it, pet?' says Margaret.

'Ah it's nothing. It's everything. I was uncomfortable in the car, and then we got here, I mean, this, what, a holiday? I've made it into something bigger in my head, you know, like a bucket list thing. A final fling, almost. And now we're here.'

There is a simple warmth in Margaret's embrace, a motherly compassion that draws out pain like salt drawing out water. There is a deeper wound, a gash of loss, a lingering grief from her mother —her birth mother — still within her. She overcame it, that year, but lacks words to shape it, lacks emotion to express it, so it resides inside. It breaks out in odd moments like a dropped egg.

'Y'alright?' says Lorcan stepping in sideways, burdened with baggage. 'Hey, what's wrong?'

'She's a bit screwed from the journey,' says Frank. 'Took it out of her.'

'Ah, you should have said, we could have stopped. Wow, this place is huge. Have you made it bigger since I was down?'

'Jaysus, yeah, guess it's a few years since yiz both came down, what with the Covid and all. The first mobile we had was second-hand, the one we upgraded to from the caravan, but that was leaking like a bleeding sponge so we went the whole hog, got the de-luxe. Gorgeous, isn't it?'

'It's something else alright. This is the living room? It's probably larger than our one at home, huh Alice? And the kitchen's got everything.'

'Your bedroom's down the far end on the right,' says Margaret. 'It's a double.'

'Fantastic, I'll just pop the bags down. I hope we're not putting you out?'

'Not a bit of it.'

'Where are the boys?' asks Alice, as the sobbing starts to soften.

'Simon popped up from nowhere, he's out kicking a ball with them.'

'Even Darragh?'

'Yeah, Simon's got some game that involves prime numbers and kicking, don't quite get it but it seems to have captured both of them.'

She walks across the room to the bay window, sees them playing. Simon is there, passing the ball back and forth between the boys, shouting and pointing as he goes. They look happy. Why isn't Lorcan out there with them? He hasn't really been engaged with them much of late.

The kettle is boiled and tea is put on to draw. Margaret made sandwiches and baked fresh choux cream buns. There was never such a thing as baking, back in the caravan days. Had there even been an oven? They had a gas hob, no electricity, the simplicity brings a smile to Alice's face.

Margaret mentions each of the neighbours, the mobile home-ees that form a fast community in this corner of the campsite. Alice can put a face to several names. They have all rallied, offering their mobile homes so that Simon, Paul and his family, and Beth and Jackie will all have guest-homes to themselves. Alice, Lorcan and the boys will get the two big bedrooms at the end, with Margaret and Frank taking the smaller room amidships.

'We should let you have the big room,' says Alice.

'Not a bit of it.' says Frank. 'Sure at our age, it's no harm being nearer the loo in the middle of the night.' He gives her a big wink.

A car cruises to a stop outside the broad bay window, a space-grey Tesla, sleek if somewhat soulless.

'Fancy car,' says Frank.

'That'll be Jackie now,' says Alice. 'She likes her electric cars. And Beth with her, I hope.' Such a privilege and a pleasure to share this time with her two confidantes, as well as her fine family. Despite the ongoing neck pain and the settling nausea, Alice is in a good place.

Jackie and Beth bustle in burdened with gifts: toys for the boys, a Foxford blanket for Margaret to say thanks for having them; wine, cheese, crackers.

'Bloody hell, Mrs M,' says Jackie as she stuffs a choux bun in. 'This place is roomier than my house.'

'That's what I said,' says Lorcan, returning from the bedroom. Hopefully he's been unpacking rather than smoking out the window. He sprawls himself across the generous couch-space.

'It's lovely,' says Beth. 'Maybe we could throw a couple of sleeping bags down on these sofas, if that's not in anybody's way?'

'Don't be silly,' says Margaret. 'Our friend Bernie Tory has the place two doors up, we go way back, she was only too delighted to let us use it for the week, and she has a cleaner that comes in once you're gone so you can be as messy as you like.'

'Ah, she's great, but she'll want paying for it.'

'Not at all. Everybody just wants to pitch in what they can, and it's lovely that you girls could afford the time off work just to be with Alice.'

'I have a trainee,' says Beth. 'She's a bit useless, but she'll hold up the fort. Anybody doesn't want to see her, I'll just refund them.'

'A trainee touch therapist?'

'Yeah, you can do a diploma in it now, and they send you out for hands-on experience. Literally, in this case.'

'I just fecked off, didn't bother telling them,' laughs Jackie. 'Sure if they miss me, then they'll just value me the more when I'm back.'

'Remind me what you do, dear?' said Margaret.

'Me? I'm a restaurant buyer. For a chain of hotels. Hell, those chefs are paid enough they can do re-orders themselves if I'm not around.'

'Sounds like you have a good number there.'

'Well, let's just say some of the wine and cheese we brought may have been purloined from the premium menus. I'm going to call it taste testing. Should be nice stuff though.'

'You didn't bring the boys down?'

'They're doing rugby camp, couldn't tear them away, and John was happy to stay behind and ferry them back and forth.'

'What age are they now?'

'Fiachra is fifteen and Ben is fourteen.'

'God, don't the years fly.'

'Tell me about it. On a different note, do you have electric charging anywhere near?'

'Are you kidding me,' says Margaret. 'Sure this is darkest Sligo. You'll probably have to take that thing to Collooney to charge.'

Spirits are high: her mother, her girlfriends, ebullient with anticipation, like the start of a holiday. Even Lorcan seems relaxed, though she expects he is still anxious about being in close quarters. There's an edge of the spectrum in his personality, she has always felt, and not having space of his own brings it out.

Alice feels a strength rise in her. Doubts that had dented her confidence in the car are diminished. A week, maybe a few days longer depending on medical appointments that have to be worked out. That is what she must focus on, and keep the darkness down.

Her brother Paul arrives then with his wife, Felicia. She has a bunch of flowers so big it nearly doesn't make it through the door.

They know Jackie and Beth quite well but haven't seen them for a while, so there is a round of air kisses and best wishes.

'Where's your daughter?' asks Jackie. 'Adrianne, isn't it?'

'She's outside giving Cian a run for his money with the football. I think he may have the upper hand though.'

'I'll just check that Darragh's okay,' says Alice.

'He's just fine, don't be worrying,' says Felicia, but Alice goes anyway.

Felicia is right. Darragh's in the middle of the melee. Simon has upped the stakes in the game and now, every time the ball is kicked, everybody has to run to a different spot according to some kind of complex pattern that Alice can't even guess at. Darragh is loving it; it's as close to sports as she's seen him since the short-lived cricket enthusiasm last year. Simon kicks the ball and Darragh runs into him as they swap places. The two of them go down laughing.

As the initial excitement fades, she starts to feel foul again; nausea and neck pain still pang. She wants to have a shower and put on fresh clothes, but she also wants to be young again, fifteen and free. The sound of the sea calls to her. She drifts to the dunes, letting the smell of the salt air and the whoosh of the waves assail her. She is transported to a time when Simon and Paul had played ball with her. It had started with her as the sulky cousin, girdled with grief and self-pity.

There are two memories here, sandwiched together by that summer. A devastated, distraught child, riven by loss, torn from home and dumped in this dark backwater town, feeling half dead. A spiky smiling teen, fresh with discovery, bursting with ebullience, desperate for life. How could such a sea change have happened? Did it only need the soft splash of the ocean air?

She sees the streets of Ealing, her school, the cafe where she and Mammy went for hot chocolate, that funny smell of cinnamon and lemongrass. She can conjure the flat, the last flat they had rented, heavy with the burnished brass ornaments that Mammy loved, dark from building-shadowed windows but brilliant with love. The sounds of the tube starting up at five am, the grind and clang of metal wheels on rattling tracks. The streets in autumn thick with golden leaves that clogged drains and left their prints on parked cars. The rain clattering off roof tiles so close overhead, the drip from the leak into the bucket in the corner. The warm-warm-warmth of Mammy's hands, her arms, her breasts as she would wrap herself around Alice's head.

This is a precious zoo full of weird and wild animals that she has locked in cages since that year, since that month she and Aunty Margaret went back to the empty flat, clearing it out, selling off the brass gewgaws and handing back the keys. Then she brought her here to Sligo, to the yellow caravan in Enniscrone. Out of England into deepest Ireland to become something else.

And then there is Mike. Gosh, a name from a foreign place. Mike was there at the very cusp, the turning point where the change that had seemed impossible became a reality. Mike is muted memory, present but left out of sight. Before Mike, she cried. Margaret and Frank, Paul and Simon danced their tender Tarantellas about her to cheer her but their firm joy fell from her like shed skin from a snake. Whatever it was Mike did to her, he changed her course, set her sailing to what she has now become, then faded into her past, like Mammy.

It is her grief-shroud that she has wrapped around Mike, around those early grief-ridden day, a textile of self protection.

She crests the dune to be greeted by the Atlantic wind, mild but cold, forever blustery but gently familiar. A mile of sandy beach that steals its colour from the sky, dun today under the greying clouds with flashes of gold mirroring the small splashes of sun. And there, stretching to the cerulean horizon, is an ocean, the majestic Atlantic, the vastness of it echoed in the mile long breakers spatting onto the sand.

There's maybe a few hundred hardy souls, a weekend crowd on a windy day. Most are walking, there's surfers and a few sea swimmers. It's a delicate sight, gentle and calming.

A small river flows to one side of the campsite and slides over the sand down to the sea, splitting the beach in two. The far side, stretching to her right, reaches towards the old harbour wall and the stone edifice of the seaweed baths five hundred metres away. To her left is a seeming infinity of dunes closing on - but never touching - the sea, until the weird shapes of Bartragh island's sandy slopes bring her eyes back to earth.

'Mammy,' she says aloud, intoning a prayer she had said every day at the start of that long ago summer. She had despised Margaret for hauling her here. Oh, there was bleakness in those days, and hatred, the things she said to them... But Margaret had persisted with soft love. Then Alice broke.

She does not know, to this day, what changed. Was it the daily ordeal of the water and the earwigs and the little gas stove and the condensation on the card-thin windows? Was it Mike, with his wheelchair love and his smoothing voice? Was it being physically close to four other people in a small space? Or was it simply the track of time letting her grief run its course? Everybody lives a different mourning; afterwards she didn't feel guilt at letting go of Mammy so soon.

Although, perhaps, she never truly did let go?

'Mammy,' she says again, the word being swallowed by the wind.

Lorcan, Saturday, 3:40pm

Lorcan watches from the bay window as Alice wanders away. He is feeling a little like a sixth toe. The boys are being bombarded with love by Simon, Alice has all the affirmation she needs from the girl's gang in here. Lorcan is left on one side, alone, not excluded per se, by unneeded. This could be a long week.

At least the mobile home is luxurious. Alice was right in saying that he wasn't looking forward to being sardined with Margaret and Frank; unable to fart at night without sharing the experience. The unit they had upgraded to seemed to offer a better outcome. It was big, but also solid. The living room was particularly generous, with bench sofas around a sizeable dining table that were more comfortable than their living room back home.

He is sorry now that he had not been more supportive to Alice with the discomfort she was going through. He had been aware, but perhaps had not realised how severe it was. Now he feels crass wolfing down burgers with the boys.

He steps outside. The weather is warm, clouds white and bubbling under a blue sky, not at all like the last time he can remember being here, and that had been high summer. Maybe three, four years ago, baleful black clouds had emptied waves of rain, day after day, barely a gap long enough for a beach walk without getting wet. Not surprising given the full force of the Atlantic Ocean that bore down on the beach below them; these clouds came in from the Azores, saturated by two thousand kilometres of sea haze and brought to a state of bursting by slackening temperatures as they travelled north.

He has been wondering why she wants to return here. It seems an odd choice after the impact of the diagnoses. This is where she let go of the grief, she's told him that before. And yes, she must see parallels with her mother's battle. Yet it seems to have grown into something bigger.

He never saw her grieving; didn't meet her till after. He wasn't aware of her when she started in their school, just after that summer. The first time he noticed her was when she started hanging around with the Gang, but he'd naturally thought she fancied Jim. Lorcan was going through a grunge phase, hating the world, writing bleak poetry, feeling sorry for himself. Rhia had been his object of desperate desire, and the occasional almost-sexual encounter she had shared with him had only twisted his thirst for her more.

Then, one night, there was Alice, beautiful, smiling, eyes on him and him alone. It was at a party, they were playing Joni Mitchell. They danced, they kissed, they became one. For a while he had feared that Jim would take her away from him too, but she had no time for him, any more than she does now.

The passion and energy she had brought were a lifetime away from the broody, grieving teenager that she supposedly was before the summer. Perhaps she was hoping for an injection of some of the same energy.

He sees her standing at the top of the dune behind the mobile home, and thinks to follow her, but at that moment his phone buzzes with *The Fairy Queen*, a text from Rhia.

"Just arrived at camp site."

He responds: "Where are you."

Almost immediately he gets "At reception".

He sticks his head back inside.

'Hey guys, Jim and Rhia just arrived. I'm going to nip across to reception to make sure they're okay.'

'Oh, right,' says Margaret. 'They made it then, Alice will be pleased. And your friend Bob?'

'Haven't heard. He may be with them.'

'Okay, well tell them we have places booked for them at dinner tonight, eight o'clock in the Diamond Coast, you know that big hotel on the edge of town.'

'Great.'

'And tell them we have a table for the children so she can bring Woody,' says Frank.

'Woody?'

'Her son, what's his name again?'

'Forry.'

'Ah, yeah, I knew it were something timber related.'

'Right, okay, see you in a bit.'

Lorcan is not sure if they're making fun of him, a sense that's exacerbated when a few seconds later a burst of laughter breaks out from behind.

He tries to take a short-cut between the roadways delineating the park but quickly gets confused and has to double back.

Rhia's little yellow Mini is parked outside the reception, and he notices Forry is in the back, head lolling, sleeping. She emerges in a stunning yellow dress, bright in the sunshine, almost the same shade as the car. He has a sudden flutter of butterflies, remembers the kiss. Should he even be seen alone with her?

'Hey, sweetie,' she says.

'Hiya, you all checked in?'

'Good to go, first left turn and third cabin on the left, apparently.'

'Where's Jim?'

'In the pub. We passed a place on the high street he liked the look of so I let him off.'

'Jeez, he doesn't hang around, does he?' He watches her face, wondering, as he often has, how complicit she is in his drinking. Does she prefer him drinking because he's out of her face, or does she dread him arriving home drunk? 'How's he going to get the locals to buy him a drink, do you reckon?'

'I gave him enough for two pints to get him started, if he hasn't charmed his way into the barman's pants by the third then he'll be crawling back. Unless, of course, you fancy joining him?'

'Fancy paying for him, you mean?'

'Well, there's that. I'm just going to settle in.'

'Did Bob come with you?'

She nods to her left and Lorcan sees Bob's Harley poking from behind the reception building.

'He took a tent, apparently. You want to come with?'

He climbs awkwardly into the yellow mini, the *snuffbox* as Jim calls it. Forry wakes up and squints at him. 'Ah, hey, Forry, what's up.'

'S'alright,' says the boy, pulling out his tablet.

'Enjoy the journey?'

'S'alright.'

'Looking forward to going swimming?'

'S'alright,'

'Alright, good for you.'

The cabin really isn't that far from reception.

'Ah,' says Rhia, pulling up. 'This must be it. *Tír na n'Óg.*'

The cabin holding the sign is even flashier and larger than Margarets mobile home. Teak timbered wings and bays poke out between splashes of decking and patio, there's even a rooftop viewing platform complete with a brass telescope.

'You didn't go for the bargain basement then?'

'What?'

'This place, must have set you back a few pennies?'

'Oh, I suppose. I just booked the first thing I saw.'

Rhia's father is something big in the world of jam, apparently. She grew up in a ten bedroom mansion on top of the hill of Howth. Her father has concerns about Jim, not without good reason, and regularly cuts her off. When the credit cards are maxed out and the mortgage is in arrears, he relents and bails her out. Where Lorcan buries the consequences of life in his *Book*, Rhia and Jim are kept afloat by jam.

He helps her carry her baggage in, and then she begins her Feng Shui to bring the cabin to the correct spiritual pitch. Lorcan tells her about the dinner.

'We should be heading there for about eightish, I think. Hey, do you want to come over and meet Alice's family?'

'Thanks, but Forry will need his nap. Are you going over to have a drink with Jim?'

'I wouldn't mind, but family first, I suppose.'

'Well, if you could let him know about the dinner.'

Rhia closes her eyes and brings her hand to prayer position, humming a deep guttural throat-tone. Lorcan stands gazing, the light catching her hair, the delicacy of her pale nose. He could reach out and touch her...

Even as the thought teases him, he blushes. There is a shame in his longing, his looking. Yes, this is *Untime*, no consequence will follow, but still.

Her eyes flick open and she catches his leer, smiles impishly.

'Sorry,' he mumbles. 'I'd better...'

He makes an embarrassed exit.

As he winds his way back, balanced between wishing he had stayed and wishing he had never gone in, Bob pulls up beside him on his Harley, engine cracking and firing in a way that only expressively maintained bikes can sustain. The matt black paint, flush chrome, swept back handlebars look so out of place here in this windswept western campsite.

'Dude,' he says after peeling off his helmet. They hug, slapping backs in a manful way. 'I hear Jim's in the pub already.'

'So it seems. And I have to tell him about dinner tonight, according to Rhia.'

'Dinner?'

'Eightish, up at that hotel, you know the one you passed coming in.'

'Grand. Heading across now?'

'I'd better show my face back home. I'll get over when I can.'

'Righteous. I'll get my tent pitched, give you a shout.'

Lorcan watches him ride away, imperious, glorifying in an image that is somewhat foolish but seems to make him happy.

Alice, Saturday, 4:00pm

Alice stands staring at the sea, letting tears surge, caught between the sadness of memory and the delicious release.

'Hey, Sis, we're heading down for ice-cream, want to come?' Simon has ascended the dune like a Pied Piper with three happy children in tow. 'There's a van down by the surf school.'

Alice goes to wipe away her tears but finds her eyes dried by wind.

'Sure,' she says, deciding now is not a time to be overwhelmed by nostalgia.

They trail along the dunes to where the river splits the beach. Just a little inland from the strand, there's a metal footbridge that they cross. The surf school is situated in a concrete blockhouse just on the other side, a building that used to be a lifeguard centre many years ago.

'You ever gone surfing guys?' Simon asks the kids. Cian and Adrianne are excited; Darragh holds his peace but, Alice notices, doesn't look too frightened. Maybe the mood is taking him.

'Could we get them lessons?'

'Man, are you kidding?' says Simon, making some kind of cool hand gestures. 'I am the surfing king.'

'I didn't know you surfed.'

'Yeah, weird, never surfed here, couple of years back I had a boyfriend was really into it. You remember Pete? Pete's gone, but surfing's still a thing for me. Every so often I'll go camping on beaches in the remotest corners, and it turns out Sligo has some of the best surf beaches in Europe.'

'Wow.'

'We'll rent some suits and boards tomorrow, how about it kids.'

This time even Darragh is cheering. A smile finds its way across Alice's face. This is what it should be about.

'Ice-cream?' she says, spying a van behind the surf school. She gets them each a '99.

Five minutes later, she is regretting it. As Simon leads his merry crew down to paddle their feet in the sea, which is way out on low tide, she rushes back to the caravan. The rich ice-cream just gagged with her, her stomach is churning. She just wants to sit down.

Margaret is on her own, putting away groceries.

'I showed your friends to their mobile, I think they're just getting a bit of rest.'

'Oh, great.'

'What's wrong? Are you okay, you look peaky?'

'The ice-cream just turned my...'

She doesn't get to finish the sentence. Her stomach turns over and she runs for the loo, but doesn't make it. She vomits down the side of the door.

'Oh shit, sorry.'

Margaret bursts into action. She gets a bowl to put under Alices face and leads her into the big bedroom at the back.

'I'm really sorry,' says Alice.

'You poor thing, lie down there, I'll get a towel for you.'

'But your carpet...'

'Oh don't be worrying, I'll get that soaking in a moment. The carpet can be replaced. It's you I'm worried about.'

Alice's head is suddenly pounding with pain. Her stomach is cramped something rotten. She curls up on the bed.

Margaret returns with a wet towel and starts wiping her face. She pulls the curtains closed; the dimness helps settle the pain in Alice's head.

'Do you have a hot water bottle?'

'I think I have one, give me a minute.'

Lorcan, Saturday, 4:15pm

There's a sour odour when Lorcan goes in the door of the mobile home. Margaret is pouring from a kettle into a hot water bottle.

'Hi, what's up?'

'She got sick,' says Margaret. She nods towards the toilet.

Lorcan sees a trail of pale vomit down the door.

'Oh, God, is she okay? Can I help?'

'Here, bring this down to her, I'll start cleaning.'

'Thanks.'

Lorcan brings the hot water bottle down to their bedroom. Alice is lying on the bed, the curtains closed.

'Babe, are you okay?'

'I'm fine, just something came over me. It's easing up now.' She slips the bottle across her stomach.

'What happened?'

'Don't know. Can I… I just need a little time. Some quiet.' There is strain in her voice.

'Okay.'

He sits down silently on a stool by the bed. Perhaps she doesn't notice, at least she doesn't react. His eyes adapt to the dimness. He sees her laboured breathing, hears Margaret's brushing. He knows he should help her, hell, he should be much more engaged. This is part of the problem. Through the long months of her minor illnesses, Lorcan stood by her every step. It was their private bother, their bubble. He cooked and cleaned whenever she was weakened, brought her breakfast, got the boys out to the park to giver her space.

Since the dreadful diagnosis, others who knew passing details of the little colds are now descending like angels of compassion while Lorcan is locked in the conviction that this cannot be allowed to happen, that the *Book* must, absolutely has to intervene. *Untime* must unwind, it has to, but in the meantime the pressure is increasing and the pleasure growing thin.

His eyes find the outline of his suitcase. The *Book* is within. There are few places of concealment in the cramped quarters of the caravan, but he could not come without it. His gut feel is that he needs the *Book* beside him for it to wield its weird power.

Yet, of course, if *Untime* is pushed back to before the diagnosis, then he will be, or rather he *was*, at home. Before the visit to the doctor, he was at home and had the *Book* there. And is that enough? After all, it isn't the diagnosis that's the problem but the illness itself and that could predate the diagnosis by months, maybe years. It hurts his head to even think of it.

The deciding factor is the US trip, his student work visa. He had taken the *Book* and it had saved his life, when Jim put together a "punch" that included ground up caffeine pills. He had partied till dawn then fallen unconscious and choked on his own vomit, then woken up that same morning In Boston writing it all down. Second time around he avoided the punch.

Alice twists in the bed and he leaps to his feet, but it's just a passing spasm. He puts a hand to her forehead; it's not unduly warm. She rolls slightly, her face now relaxed, mouth half open. She is asleep; he knows that look from years of marriage. She is beautiful, even at her most vulnerable, her most exposed. The delicate sallow complexion, hair like a wild storm in tight curls twisted under, the pencil shade of eyebrows edged in black. He wants to fix her.

He kisses the tips of his fingers and places them gently to her cheek, then backs silently out, pulling the plywood door closed quietly.

Margaret has cleaned up the mess. There is a strong smell of disinfectant. She is mopping the carpet with a towel.

'Thanks so much for that, Margaret, sorry for the mess.'

'Will you get off with your apologies. I'd do anything for my poor Alice, no more than yourself. And it's not the first time I've been on my knees wiping up a mess from one of them.' She gives him a big grin.

'Where are my boys?'

'Simon has them down on the beach, I think they're grand. Where are your friends?'

'Off in the pub already.'

'Should have known,' she chuckles. She has finished the cleaning and is washing her hands. 'Since Alice first picked up with your gang,

Jim's been a demon for the drink, God love him. I suppose you'll be heading for a quick one before the dinner yourself? You might take Frank with you, he's moping around like a lost soul.'

'What's that?' says Frank from the living room.

'I was just saying you and Lorcan should go over to the pub and meet Lorcan's friends.'

'Could be a plan.'

'I... well, Alice...'

'Only don't be late now, that dinner is important to her. I know her, she's not going to let a little wobble upset the evening.'

'But I suppose I should be here.'

'Mind you, it'll take us some time to get her feeling good enough to go. I'll let her sleep it out a little then I'll call in Jackie and Beth.'

'I suppose I could...'

'Just don't be late. And of course get the other lads over to the hotel on time, they're invited too, though Lord knows why.'

Lorcan is conflicted and confused. His place is here, Alice isn't well. He's been there through all her illnesses. Walking away feels like betrayal, a loss of faith, a failure of his love.

Yet Margaret's right. Alice has her family around her, she's safe, and it seems the nausea is passed. The kids are being well looked after. Why can't he go and have a good time in the pub. He's put the hours in over the months, it's his turn for some time off, and of course the moment it was suggested he could taste the beer in his throat.

'Are you sure?' he asks warily. 'I wouldn't like to impose.'

'Come on with yeh,' says Frank, pulling his coat on. 'Sure Margaret has her here. She'll give yeh a yell if yeh're needed.'

'Well, if you're sure...'

'Go on. You mightn't get the chance again.'

Alice, Saturday, 5:15pm

'Is Lorcan here?' Alice is groggy, but the nausea and head pain has receded. Margaret is sitting beside her.

'He came back but I sent him off to play with his friends.'

'Play with his friends?' It takes a few moments to realise Margaret is talking about her husband and not her children. 'I thought he came in to me. Did I dream that?'

'No, he was with you for a few minutes while I was cleaning up. His buddies went to the pub so I figured he may as well be off with them.'

'Good to know where his priorities lie, I guess. Hey, sorry for the mess.'

'Take that apology back, young lady. You will not be sorry about your illness, under strict orders. You are to rejoice in any moment you feel well, and fall back on us when you don't. There's plenty of us here. Beth and Jackie are waiting on you but I wanted to keep it quiet.'

'Thanks, Mam.'

'Should I call Lorcan? Get him back?'

'Nah, what the hell. He may as well go out with his friends, as long as he's there in time for dinner.'

Margaret gives her a smile, holds her hand. When Alice was fifteen, Margaret had spent a lot of time with her just like this. There were no proper bedrooms then, no privacy. Her bed was actually the bench seat in the dining area, with Paul on the other side and Simon on the floor in between. She had cried herself dry to start with. Margaret had never weakened in her determination. She had used the same words, brought the same compassion.

'The thing that scares me most,' she says, 'is that she's dead. My Mammy. Like really dead. I don't know, maybe I thought I'd feel her again, coming here, closing that gap, but I don't. She's dead.'

Margaret closes her eyes, shakes her head. The early wrinkles around the edge of her eyes stand out, as if some artist shaded them in, using charcoal for the harshness of life that has formed her face.

'I have been able to deal with a lot, Alice. But that one is still beyond me. Your mother was the most beautiful sister, the most beautiful woman. And so daring, so adventurous. I was lost when she up and went to London. The second time, that is. I told you about the first time?'

'I'm not sure.'

'When she was fifteen?'

'What? Do remember that one.'

'Yeah, mad story, she took all her money out of her Post Office account and ran away to London.'

'No?'

'She got to Euston and ran out of money, had just enough to phone home. Your poor granny had to borrow money and she sent muggins here over to fetch her home. Bella didn't even have a passport.'

'You're kidding me?'

'No, that's just the kind of girl she was, anxious to be off. Always wanted to see what was on the other side of the hill. Then when she hit nineteen she got a job on some Soho music newspaper, can't remember the name of it. Paid damn all but nothing was going to stop her. God I missed her. None of us had much cash in those days so I hardly saw her, we couldn't travel much. After Mammy died she rarely came home. Then you were born and I made sure I got over every year at least twice. And then…' She stops. An opaque look falls over her eyes. 'And then she called and said she had cancer.'

'You came over, didn't you? You were with us from the start, is what I remember.'

'On and off. I couldn't leave the boys for too long. Frank was taking on extra jobs to pay for me to fly over. But by damn it was hard. I'd lost Mammy, now I was losing Bella.'

Memories like ghosts dance into Alice's mind-sight. Taking the train to Luton Airport to meet Margaret, when her Mammy was still mobile. Frank, Paul and Simon sitting in their tiny apartment one time. Kew Gardens on an unbearably warm summer afternoon, Margaret holding Alice in the loos while they listened to the retching of her Mammy getting sick.

'I… never really valued that.'

'Valued what?'

'What you and Frank did for us back then. Like, before you brought me here. That was real sacrifice.'

'It was hard, yes, but I had to be there for Bella. And for you.'

'I remember you at the funeral, you saying to me I had to go with you and I thought you meant home but you took me to the airport. I remember that, it stands out like…'

'Oh. Was it too soon? I was all over the place. But I had to get home. I was balancing my love. It was a horrible time.'

Alice rubs her thumb in Margaret's palm. 'I remember she was like the sun. My bright Mammy. She was all heat and light and energy. She was so strong. She was everything. And then she was broken. She tried to make it fun but it was awful, those days in bed, the pills that made her sleep, the vomiting, not being able to get off the toilet all day and me bringing her water and pills. It became a nightmare.'

'You poor chicken.'

'I'm not even sure how long it lasted.'

'Over a year, can you believe?' There is a tear swelling in Margaret's eye. There is a tension in her hands. Alice can feel the surge of loss that has pumped her, knows this is hurting. Margaret is sandwiched between grief for her sister and fear for her adopted daughter.

'She left me.'

'She left us both.'

'I needed her. Right then I needed her and she wasn't there.'

'No. She wasn't.'

'And when the time comes, I won't be there for Cian and Darragh.'

'Lorcan will be.'

It's shocking that Margaret has affirmed her likely death, not denied it. She has been through it before. She will not hide from the truth. *You'll be dead*, she is saying, *but at least the boys will have a father.*

A father.

'Tell me about Carlos,' she says.

'I'm not sure I have much to tell. I didn't get over much when she first met him, and he would be gone playing with bands more often than not. Very attractive man. He had a charisma; your eyes would follow him across the street, across a room. When he smiled, you smiled. Bella fell for him, like woah! She was just bonkers for him. So charming whenever I met him, he'd be dressed in a linen suit, you felt like he was somebody special. Of course, the two of them were, how would you put it? Fiery? You remember Bella, happy and sweet and smiling and next thing she'd throw a cup at the wall in wild anger.'

'God, yes, she did go off the handle. But five minutes later it would be gone and she'd be sorry.'

'Well, not always, sometimes she could hold a grudge. And Carlos was the same, it seems. He'd go nuts over little things. There was a pair of them in it.'

'You told me he was playing with Bruce Springsteen.'

'Did I? Sorry, I never really paid that much attention. He was a very good musician but I don't think his bands ever did well so he spent most of his time as a session musician is what I understand. Damned if I can remember who he was with, but he was good. It might have been Bruce.'

'No it wasn't. I checked online, Springsteen's band lineups, album lineups, I couldn't find any mention.'

'Sorry, then, babe, I can't remember. But he did do some big gigs. Course that meant he was away most of the time.'

'I can remember him being there. I might have been eight or ten.'

'You said that, but I've no idea. I thought he was gone when you were a baby. He was probably back now and again and maybe she forgot to mention it to me.'

'What happened to them? Mammy and Daddy?'

'Didn't your mother tell you?'

'She didn't say very much. She cursed him for not being about to help, I remember that.'

'Yes, she was angry at him being away, sometimes. But at the same time she loved the whole scene, loved being a free spirit.'

'But he didn't come back. When she was sick. He didn't come back for me.'

'I think something must have happened. Between them. They must have had a bust up is all I can think that he wouldn't have come for you. I never had any contact details for him. I took Bella's phone but there was no Carlos or anything like that. I wouldn't be surprised if she deleted it in anger one day. I don't know if you remember but I was asking everybody at the funeral, nobody had a contact for him. Also, you don't know this but I kept the phone under contract for a couple of years, in case he called.'

'Might he have died?'

Margaret squeezes her hand again. 'I wouldn't think so, but who knows. I'm really sorry there's a blank space where your father should be, but I don't think I can do anything about it. Let's try and keep our focus on what we can affect.'

'Like dinner tonight?'

'How can you even think about dinner?'

'I'm fine now. It's weird. After the ice-cream, I thought I was dying, it was horrible. Five minutes nap and I'm absolutely fine. Mind you, I'll be going easy on the food.'

'You're sure you still want to go?'

'Positive.'

'Right.' Margaret calls out the door. 'Beth, any chance of a cup of tea for the patient?'

In a moment, Jackie and Beth are with her. Beth gives her a reiki neck massage that helps ease the last of the pain while Jackie runs for tea.

Lorcan, Saturday, 5:25pm

He had been hit by a lingering guilt on leaving the mobile home, a sense that he should stay and see to Alice. Frank's chatter helped.

'Don't be worrying, Lorcan. Best hands in the world, I'm telling yeh, that Mags has on her. She'll see to her something rotten.'

'I know, still I haven't really been there for her all day.'

'I'm telling yeh, the girls will sort her out. This is a celebration, and all, let's make the night of it, yeah?'

'Yeah, I know.'

'That's the spirit!'

At the same time, he cannot suppress a mild zing of excitement, getting a few beers in to take the edge off the day, and a nice dinner out after. Paul and Simon don't really drink much, but Frank doesn't mind a few pints, and of course there will be the irreverent wildness of Jim and the Gang, it could be a good night yet.

They walk out of the park and cross the road to McGinty's pub.

'They're in the Music Bar,' he says. 'According to the text from Bob.'

'Right, that's just down the laneway, in behind the main bar.'

It's early yet but the place is busy. There's music playing; a couple of young lads with a guitar and a fiddle are giving it plenty of passion, many people are just sitting listening to them.

Jim is at the bar and seems to have found his crowd. Three young men in Sligo GAA jerseys are standing around him, with Bob sitting on a barstool nodding sagely.

'Now yeh see, the problem with Sligo football,' he is saying as Lorcan and Frank get to them, 'is it's handpass-handpass-handpass. It's too bleeding predictable. Now look at Dublin, or Kerry. They vary it up, long balls, short balls, a bit of passing, then a bomb.'

'Well now,' one of the poor young lads says, 'I'm not sure you're right about that. Sure, the new coach, he's got them doing all kinds of exercises…'

'There yeh are,' Jim stabs him in the chest with a finger. 'Exercises. They need to know that stuff in their bones, yeh see, yeh can't learn it to a man, yeh gotta teach the boy. Ah, my man Lorcan, just in time. And would this be the sound man, Frank?'

'Howarya, Jim.'

'At me best. Alison,' he turns to the woman tending the bar. 'Another round of yer creamy pints, one each for me buddies, Lorcan and Frank.'

'Ah now, c'mere,' says another of the young lads who clearly is just figuring out Jim's strategy. 'We've already bought yiz three pints.'

'Don't worry, lads,' says Lorcan. 'Let me buy you one back.'

As he sits waiting for Alison to let the pints settle so that he can pay, Lorcan ponders his own hypocrisy. Two hours earlier, he had been thinking Rhia was complicit, driving Jim down here then dropping him straight to the pub, and now it's himself who's enabling the toxic behaviour. Why does he do this, when he knows it's wrong?

But of course he knows the answer to this. Rhia holds a power over him. His obsession with her, his adoration of her beauty, keeps him here. He knows how much she loves this man, even if the drunk doesn't deserve it, and Lorcan has little choice but to look out for him.

The other factor, he imagines as he taps his card, the bill including nine pints by the time all Jim's benefactors have been satisfied, is the party thing. Even at his age, Jim can bring a room alive. The young lads, pissed off a moment ago at his stuckering for pints, are now roaring with laughter as Jim starts belting out *The Green And Red of Mayo* during a gap in the music. Next thing there are half a dozen boys singing with him, and another dozen trying to drown them out with *My Old Sligo Home*.

'He's settled in, I see,' Lorcan says to Bob.

'True!'

A glass is placed in front of him, swimming in the slops on the bar top. He places it onto a beer mat to mop the drips. A deep, billow sweeps through the dark drink, liquid light separating out, drawing itself upwards, caught from moment to moment in reverse eddies only to resume its rise. At last, there is only black and white, a sharp line delineating. If only life were so simple.

He takes a deep slug, pushing through the creamy head to the half bitter elixir. It evokes a thirst: the taste of *Guinness* opens a gap in his gut that only the booze can abate.

'Amen,' he says, plonking the glass back down.

'Hallelujah,' says Bob.

'Right back at yeh,' says Frank, slapping his glass down with a good glug gone.

The bar is at one end of a long room with the music focussed at the other end. There's a small stage that's equipped with a big electric piano and a full set of drums as well as amplifiers. The two lads who were playing have now quit the stage, taking the chairs they were on.

A man in a wheelchair is hooshed up a ramp to one side then propels himself towards the piano. He pulls himself into place to play and shifts a microphone, giving it the mandatory thump to ensure it's on.

'How is he going to play that without pedals?'

'I didn't think an electric piano had pedals, dude.'

'Oh, yeah.'

A bit of hush whispers over the crowd; the player is known. He riffles his fingers together, then turns them out to crack them. He could be lampooning the cat from Tom and Jerry. He hesitates, fingers poised over the keyboard. Lorcan is waiting for Chopin or Debussy.

The fingers flood down into a massive opening chord then twist into intricate slide. The melody is instantly familiar, *A Remembrance of Nothing*. It had been a big hit for Beyoncé or Kylie or somebody a few years previously. The performer pulls finely on the lonely lyrics while maintaining a jaunty right hand rhythm. He has skill.

'Who is this guy?' Lorcan asks Bob.

'They were saying it's the McGinty guy. He owns the pub, made money on his music or something like that.'

'He's got a good ear for that song.'

The player doesn't end the song but whips it up into a rhapsody, fingering fine arpeggios and complex chords until he brings it down into another karaoke classic, *Your Eyes Are Mine*.

'That guy can tinkle them ivories,' says Jim. 'That baby is mine.' He sets off before Lorcan can grab his arm and advise discretion.

Jim pounds through the crowd and arrives beside the disabled pianist just as he's finishing the song. Lorcan is horrified to see him shouting into the disabled man's ear. To his surprise, the performer nods then slaps into a full blown Jerry Lee Lewis. Jim grabs a microphone and starts belting out *Great Balls Of Fire*. It's early evening, but McGinty's comes alive.

'How does he do that?' Lorcan asks.

'He has the gift of a golden voice, man,' says Bob.

'He has the gall to assume he can do what he wants, more like,' says Frank.

Jim covers *Summer in Dublin,* and then the two young lads come back on stage. Jim has a long chat with the pianist before rejoining them at the bar.

'Lovely guy,' says Jim. 'Great on the keyboard, right? Told me to come in tomorrow early and we'll do a few tunes together.'

Three more pints arrive at the bar. 'Mike sent them over to you,' says Alison.

'Mike?' says Lorcan.

'Yer man on the piano. Bloody decent of him. Cheers.' Jim swigs down half the pint in one go. 'Thirsty work all this singing. Now there you go,' he ostentatiously places the other two pints in front of Lorcan and Bob. 'Never say I don't get me round in!'

Alice, Saturday, 7:15pm

'Are you certain now?' Margaret asks yet again. 'It's only a dinner. We can get a booking again tomorrow, I'm sure.'

'No, Mam, thanks but I really want this. I want the family together. Did you hear from Lorcan?'

'He's not answering his phone,' says Beth. 'I've sent texts to remind him.'

'Don't be worrying. I'm betting they're still up in McGinty's. We'll send Simon to collect them.'

Lorcan's ongoing absence is upsetting Alice, but maybe she's letting it get to her more than it should. She's aware the meal has acquired a significance that is beyond the context. It's almost become a sort of last supper. The pain and nausea have left her with a sense of vulnerability. It is not just passing symptoms, she knows, but the beginning of a long road.

She just wants to keep her head clear and buoyant, to celebrate life.

Beth helps her doing her make up, the contact is warm and affirming. Beth's hands are scary thin, the veins painting a roadmap across her sharply defined tendons that twist and dance as she skims on layers of blusher and mascara. Hands that carry such care, that radiate health into her patients. Perhaps the years of healing have left her brittle.

The blood drains from Alice's head. A cold flush floods her belly. *What will it take to stop him talking?* Like an icy splash, Alice is plunged back into Professor Bailey's office. He is reading out a death sentence. She is a prisoner, doomed to die. She stops breathing.

'What? What's wrong? Alice, talk to me.'

The air floods back to her lungs, the world spins.

'Right,' says Beth. 'That's it, you're not well. We'll cancel.'

'No. No, I'm fine. Panic attack, that's all. No, Beth, please. Tonight is very important.'

'Hey, babes,' says Jackie, arriving into the mobile home in an elegant black dress, her hair pulled back from her face. 'You're not looking too bad for somebody who's just puked their guts up.'

'Jackie!' says Beth. 'For God's sake.'

'What? She does look good.'

'Yes but she looks good not because she… Oh, never mind.'

'Are we going dancing after?' says Jackie.

'Let's just deal with dinner first,' says Alice.

'I don't know, five Pornstar Martinis and you'll be singing a different song.'

'Five Pornstar Martinis and I'll be back to puking my guts up.'

Jackie belts out the chorus of *Dancing Queen*, arms spinning in the air, and Alice can't help but join in.

The boys come bouncing in.

'Nan, it was great, the beach is brill.' Darragh runs to Margaret and gives her a long hug.

'We went swimming and everything,' Cian adds, keeping his distance from the hug zone.

'Uncle Simon got us wet suits and we put them on over our underpants.'

'He bought you wet suits?' Alice asks.

'Nah, they were rented.'

'You were in the sea?'

'Yeah.'

'Without togs?'

'We just kept our pants and tee shirts on.'

'And then put your trousers back on over them?'

'Yeah!'

'Aw, Lord. Go into your rooms and change and leave all your clothes out to wash, put on something nice.'

'Ah Mom!'

Margaret wrangles the boys into their going-to-the-restaurant clothes. The girls finish their work on Alice and help her pick something she feels good in, a dark red dress with a matching black and red bolero.

'Right,' she says. 'All we're missing is Lorcan.' She checks her phone, he hasn't responded to the text she sent half an hour back.

'Ah, don't be worrying,' says Margaret. 'Simon will haul them in.'

Is it too much to ask, Alice wonders, that Lorcan make an effort for this one evening?

They bundle into Paul's car, with Jackie and Beth travelling separately, though it only takes five minutes to get to the restaurant.

In the reception, Rhia is curled up in a large luxurious easy chair, barefooted, beaming beatifically as only she can while cradling Forry, an icon of divine motherhood.

'Alice, you're looking great,' Rhia beams. 'Come and sit down, we're still waiting on the boys, I think.'

Alice does the introductions. Rhia has met her family before but typically only in passing and not for some years.

'Do you know where they are now?'

'Lord knows. Jim headed to that place, McGinty's I think it was, the one just beside the camp site, but he could be anywhere within a hundred miles now.'

'We thought as much.'

'Don't worry, Sis,' says Paul holding up his phone. 'Message from Simon, they have been sighted.'

'Tell him to watch out,' laughs Rhia, 'or Jim will have him sucking down pints.'

'No worries there, he's not had a drink for over ten years,' says Margaret.

'I respect that, it takes a lot of courage,' says Rhia, but Alice can't tell if she means it or is mocking.

Jackie steps in. 'I, on the other hand,' she says with a smile, 'have not had a drink for over ten days. I want a gin and tonic in a glass that's bigger than my head. Alice?'

'Bigger than your head? Go on then.'

Lorcan, Saturday, 8:10pm

Initially his intentions were good, one pint, maybe two, keep himself composed for the dinner, knowing it is an important night for Alice. A third and a fourth came uninvited, and now the fifth is flowing smoothly down. Remorse peaked at the second and has since fallen away. Banter and the bawdy jokes with their new buddies, the singing and shouting, he's having too good a time to worry.

Frank is settling in too, not keeping up with the pace of the drinking but he's happy enough, gets chatting with the lads at the bar who are glad of a break from Jim.

Lorcan has just come back from smoking out the back when he gets a tap on the shoulder.

'Lorcan!'

It takes him a moment to figure it's Simon, and his heart sinks.

'Hey Simon, is it time…?' He glances at his phone and sees missed messages and calls. More time has passed than he realised. 'Ah shit, sorry. We better go, I guess.'

'Jaysus, awful sorry,' says Frank. 'Didn't the time only get away from us.'

'Yup, got the car outside. Dinner's waiting. Jim, Bob, if you guys are ready I can give you both a lift.'

'Hey, Alice's brother, right?' says Jim, who is a good few pints further on. 'Simon, isn't it? Just in time to get the round in.'

'Sorry, Jim, it's actually time to go. I'm on a mission.'

'Time for one more, though,' says Jim.

Simon looks at him. There is nothing judgemental to his gaze, he is unfazed. 'You can stay if you want, Jim. Lorcan, I'm sorry but my sister will string me up if I don't get you there pronto.'

'No worries, I'm on the way.'

Bob is tipping the last of his pint down his throat so Jim has little choice but to acquiesce.

The salt air outside the pub hits Lorcan with a slap and suddenly his head is spinning. The crisp air makes a caustic cocktail with the beer that shuts down his brain, barely leaving the pilot light running. He is drunk, he realises, and he is sunk. He had hoped he might let on he was only the two pints in, Alice might not be so upset. He is sloppy and slurry, thick tongued and heavy footed; this is not going to be good.

It worries him. Even now as he sits beside Simon: he's drinking a lot since the diagnosis. The rules of *Untime* say that he can do this. There's no come-back, no consequence. But *Untime* is supposed to be a day, a week. It should not drag on. It did one time, yeah, but the anxiety is growing, nevertheless. What if…? What if he's fooling himself and acting like a dick, no better than Jim's petty self-excuses for one more drink?

The buzz has been burned from him by the time they park outside the hotel. He feels like a condemned criminal approaching the gallows as they walk towards the front entrance.

Everybody's there ahead of them mingling in a cosy corner of the lobby, chatting. Alice is with Margaret, Jackie and Beth. Rhia is nearby, curled up in a circular easy chair in orange and pink print pyjamas, her bright red hair cascading about her, Forry tucked up like a toddler in her arms. She looks to Lorcan like some Celtic fertility goddess. Paul and Felicia hover over her talking with her as she smiles serenely.

'Baby Cheeks!' Jim pushes roughly in to kiss Rhia, ignoring the others. 'McGinty's was lovely, yeh must come, so yeh must. We'll go and have breakfast in the morning.'

'Oh, okay.'

'What about yeh, Paul, Felicia, yeh up for an early fry and a pint?'

'Ah, you're good, I think we may be busy.'

Lorcan is tempted by the sound of breakfast pints, but best keep schtum for now, play it by ear depending on how much trouble he finds himself in.

'Well, look what the cat dragged in,' says Alice, as if she's overheard his thoughts. 'Did you enjoy your drinks?'

'Oh, yeah, thanks.'

It's an innocent question, but there's a mountain of meaning in her face.

'You'll take it easy, won't you?' she says quietly in his ear. 'I want to enjoy this and not be minding you.'

'Uh, yeah, sure.' Maybe he's managed to dodge the worst of it.

Rhia is going to the bar to get a pint for Jim who settles into the seat she vacates. Forry, climbs out from under him and quietly follows his mother. She asks Lorcan if he fancies anything.

'Just a water,' he says. His throat is dry for another pint but maybe best to moderate for now.

They are led to a private dining room. It looks fabulous, a long oaken table with ornate place settings, cascading candelabras, crystal decanters and shining silver service. Fine filigrees of glitter are spilled in spiral patterns over the dark oak giving a magical glow about the room.

Alice sits at one end of the table and immediately Margaret is on one side, Jackie and Beth on the other. Simon and Paul and Felicia get the next seats with the kids; Paul brought some kind of prototype mini-game consoles that link together to play a racing game.

Lorcan is damned to the dunces end of the table with Frank, Jim and Bob. He wants to be beside Alice, close to her. On the flip side, down here he might sneak a glass of wine without getting a glare.

Rhia turns up with Jim's pint and another for Bob. She ends up opposite Lorcan. He smiles at her, unbidden. She tilts her head slightly to one side, red hair dipping over her chin.

'Are you okay, Lorcan?' she asks.

'Grand, yeah.'

'It must be very hard on you, all this? You know, like, making a special time for Alice, and all she's going through. And who's looking out for you?'

'Me? I'm fine.'

'You're very brave. The partner never gets the nourishing, and they often need it just as much.'

He finds himself flushing. The words touch him but he knows it's undeserved. He's evaded bravery with self-indulgence. The words bring him warmth, a good feeling of support, and a bad feeling of anxiety. He knows he should be more engaged with Alice, drop this sense of *Untime*, but the *Book* is too powerful, too present.

He feels her foot brush onto his leg under the table. Instinctively, he pulls back his leg, but her foot follows. The warmth washes fresh over him; she is playing footsie with him. She turns her gaze demurely to the menu in front of her, but there's a teasing twist to her smile.

When a waiter offers him wine, he asks for red and gulps it greedily.

Alice, Saturday, 10:00pm

There is rancour in her belly again, though a lesser venom than had hit her earlier. She is surprised how much Lorcan's disappearance bothered her. She is oddly happy to have him left him the sloppy end of the table.

Everyone is smiling, everyone is laughing, Jackie is knocking back the gins, Cian and Darragh are showing speed-cube finger tricks to Adrienne and Frank and even Forry is joining in the chatter for once. Barring the banishment of her husband, this is the evening she had envisaged, a cherry on the cake of her life.

'It's lovely to see everybody looking so well,' Margaret says, holding up a glass of wine in salute.

'We do scrub up nicely,' says Jackie, clinking her glass with Margaret's.

'It's such a lovely town,' says Beth. 'We had a quick walk down the high street, it's still so old fashioned, it hasn't been ruined by tourism.'

'It's changed though, since we first brought a young lady called Alice down. The caravan park was just that, very humble, this hotel was tiny, and there were half as many houses on the road in.'

'But you wouldn't see that in the shops, I mean it's not pouring with souvenir stalls or tattoo parlours or whatever.'

'Tattoo parlours, God preserve us.'

'That's an idea,' says Jackie, 'how about a group tattoo!'

'The only tattoo I'm getting involves no pain in applying it and washes off in water,' laughs Beth.

'Do you like Enniscrone, Felicia,' says Alice across them. She hasn't had a chance to talk to Paul's wife yet and she's always enjoyed her wit.

'Love it to bits, Paul and I come down all the time, sometimes he flies into Knock airport and I meet him here. The walks are amazing, if you're prepared to drive a bit.'

'Up and down the beach isn't too bad.'

'Great if you want a quick stretch of the legs, maybe a bit flat for my taste.'

Paul is keeping an eye on the hosting, orders another white and red for the table. The bottles seem to make their way fairly quickly to the naughty end of the table where Jim was holding forth: 'And when I saw Paul O'Connell rising ten feet off the ground in the line out, towering above the heads of the English that day in Croke Park, I says to me mates, it's our day, lads, it's our day.' He waves his full wine glass gleefully. She has to admit, Jim is a powerhouse of energy when he's at his boisterous best, he can be the life and soul. However, she knows well his dark side, his insidious influence on Lorcan, his insatiable drinking, and the worrying bruises that Rhia develops from time to time. She claims Jim is just clumsy, but that's surely dangerous nonsense.

Her langoustine main arrives with dauphinoise potatoes and a rich and deep bisque with a heady aroma and complex layers of flavour. She might have expected farmer food, given the location, but this is fine dining. There are appreciative noises from around the table. She loves the flavours but she's very careful just to pick at it. Take too much and the night could end too soon.

'I still think we should be doing something more like a bucket list,' says Jackie, voice getting louder as she also enjoys the aromatic white wine. 'You know like, ballooning over Everest.'

'Jackie,' says Beth. 'For goodness sake, it's not time for bucket lists.'

'When is it going to be time, Beth? You tell me that.'

Beth tries to shush her, making eyes at Alice.

'Are you saying you can't talk bucket lists in front of the invalid,' Alice says, keeping her voice low in case the kids overhear, 'or that I won't have time now to tick the boxes?'

Jackie guffaws but Beth is abashed.

'I'm so sorry, Alice.'

'Don't let it get to you, Beth. This is a celebration. Call it a bucket list or whatever you want, this is what I chose, and thank you all for coming.'

The table is raucous by the time the desserts arrive. Still more wine is sent for. Alice skips dessert, but even the little bit she's eaten is sitting like acid on her belly.

'Are you okay?' Margaret leans over to her. 'You've hardly eaten.'
'Ah, you know.'
'Do you need to go back?'
'Not yet. This is too nice.'

Margaret smiles, and slides a soft hand onto her wrist. There was no more that could be said.

Cian runs around the table and taps her shoulder. 'Can we have a second dessert, Mom?'

'Second? Did you eat your dinner?'

'Ah, yeah, like mostly.'

She is almost minded to say yes, it's the night that's in it, but sense prevails. 'No, not a second dessert. They have hot chocolate, you can have that when the adults are having coffee.'

'Aw, Mom!'

'Come on, I'll come down with you and see what's happening.'

She follows him back to the children's ghetto. She touches Lorcan's shoulder swiftly as she passes; he catches her eye, looks startled, unsure if he's in trouble, but she gives him a smile and he relaxes. She sits with the kids. Adrienne is quite precocious and begins to tell to her what everybody ate or didn't and what was said. Darragh drops his cube and wraps himself warmly around her arm. Forry has climbed back onto Rhia's lap. Cian is draping himself awkwardly backwards around his chair because he's just so bored!

She tells them a rude joke, and then Frank tells them an even ruder one, and soon the kids are joining in, 'bum' and 'fart' and other words flying. Adrienne looks a little wary at first, but it turns out she knows the rudest ones. They end up telling their favourite *Horrible Histories* episodes.

With everybody grinning, she gathers her boys into her and, for a moment, among the noise and the cheer and the clatter of cutlery, they come together. There is warmth. There is joy.

This is it, she thinks. *This is the moment I will hold onto when that curtain in my head drops and darkness overwhelms me. This is the point in time I will come back to, to know that life is good. And I dearly hope that this is also a memory they will cherish.*

And then Cian wriggles out of her grip.

She notices Paul slipping away discretely to pay. She should really go fight him, if she leaves it till later he won't take money from her, but the emotion in her mind is powerful, and money's only money.

She looks at Lorcan, his side lip stained red but smiling. One last task to top off the evening.

'Will you walk back with me?' she says to him.

'Woho,' shouts Jim. 'I think your luck's in, me boy. Hey, how's about Rhia and me join yiz, we can do a foursome, huh?'

'Shut up, Jim,' says Lorcan, an unusual display of backbone. 'I'd love to.'

'Simon…?'

'I can take the boys,' says Simon. 'There's a really good ice-cream shop down the town, five minute walk. If you don't mind?'

'That would be brilliant.'

She thanks everybody for making the night so enjoyable, so fine. 'It was truly wonderful, and Paul, thanks for organising. I'll settle it with you later.'

'A privilege, Sis.'

She gives Darragh a big hug, and Cian gets a sense of the moment and hugs the two of them. There are tears in her eyes as she leaves the crowd behind, and walks out the front door with Lorcan.

'Sorry,' he says. 'I should have been here.'

'Well, fuck yes, you should have been here.'

'Sorry.'

She lets him stew in it for a moment, then reaches out and pulls each side of his mouth with her thumbs into a fake smile.

'Cheer up. I'm not going to eat you.'

'You're confusing me.'

'Maybe you're easily confused. The booze'll do that. Come on, this way.'

She leads him away from the road and towards the back of the hotel, towards the beach. There is a phalanx of parallel holiday cottages marching across the dunes, but she finds a path beyond them. They skirt the edge of a golf course and climb a mountain of marram grass over the monster dunes. They run laughing like children.

It is an evening of elements. Atlantic wind whips up turbulence on the undulating sea waves. Gulls scream their greed. A lustrous moon shines cobweb curls over the shore as the last lustrous orange of the setting sun clings. Despite the dimness, a single surfer still seeks the rolling wave, but falls from a half-hearted breaker.

'The last evening of the world,' she says.

'That's a little fatalistic.'

'I don't see it as fatalistic, it's more… This is a real thing, Lorcan, this is…' She holds up a hand as he draws breath. 'I know, I know you think you can fix it all and, godammit Lorcan, I have no idea where you came up with that but I have to live with this. Or not. Or die, if and when that comes about. This is real, Lorcan. I am coming to terms. One journey is starting but another is coming to an end.'

'Please, Alice,' Lorcan is almost in tears. 'Please don't say that. I can't lose you. I will fix all this.'

'No. No you won't but that's okay. I'm feeling my way through this, I mean, Mammy must have gone through this. She had to say goodbye and I never knew what she was saying and I still don't but, Jesus, I'm rambling.'

Alice is crying now. She throws her head into his shoulders, he wraps his arms around her.

'Look at us,' she says. 'Two fools standing on a beach crying. It doesn't seem like too many years since you would have been dragging me into those dunes for a shag.'

'Is that what you—?'

'No. No, sorry. But Lorcan, what a ride it has been. I took the boys out to Tayto Park and we went on that roller coaster, hah!' She laughs. 'Thanks for being there. I love you.'

'Ah, fucks sake. I love you, Alice, please stop. You're not going to die.'

'Maybe I am, maybe I'm not. But I need to ask this of you now, Lorcan, as I've asked nothing of you before. Please, walk the path with me. Whatever comes, please, be there.'

'Oh, Jesus.'

She kisses him. She opens her head, sets out her spirit on the sands for him to see. She absorbs him, takes him body and soul inside her. The stars leap out of the twilight and touch the lovers, linger on their bodies.

'Let's dance,' she says. She takes his left hand out into a pose and he accedes, pulls her close around the waist. He starts a waltz step but she twists him into a tango. On the soft sandy grass they dance, they swing about, he tilts her. There is no music except in their souls. They live, they are both alive.

'You will be there, Lorcan?'

'I will of course. You know that, Alice.'

'Say it. Say it and mean it.'

'I will be there, Alice. I made my vows and I meant them. In sickness and in health.'

She lets herself lean into him. *This moment*, she thinks, *and this. And this. May it stay with me.*

Lorcan, Sunday, 10:20am

Lorcan wakes when his phone pings. His work team always start the week with a one hour catch up, a level-setter. He's missed two; his boss, Gerry, told him take his time, but the supportive mails have been getting steadily more solicitous. Lorcan is ignoring them. *Untime* should have no consequences, why the hell waste it working. Still, there is an increasing unease.

He rolls over to find the bed empty. Living in such cramped conditions - relative to home - he is surprised that he did not notice her get up. Might she have been ill again? He pulls on his clothes to go and check but finds the women: Alice and Margaret, Jackie and Beth, bumping into each other in the galley kitchen while the boys are eating a fry at the table. Alice looks beautiful and strong, as if there was nothing wrong with her.

'We'll have something ready for you in five minutes,' says Margaret. 'Fried egg or boiled?'

'Eh, fried would be good, thanks. I think I'll pop out for a minute, get some sea air.'

He heads out and finds a spot in the dunes between the camp site and the sea where he won't be seen. He lights a cigarette and pulls deep. He has got very used to having his fags now, it may be a challenge to drop them again when this is over. The physical addiction shouldn't be a problem, but the psychological addiction, the habit of having the fag between his fingers, that is insidious.

The sky is blue and the morning is warm. The sun is savage already, searing down through a sky that is untainted by city pollution. Out here on the edge of the Atlantic, when the sun does come out, it will burn the unwary in minutes. Alice won't let Cian or Darragh out the door without slathering on the sun cream.

Out over the ocean, thick clouds are gathering, a dark bank like furrowed eyebrows disapproving of a bright day, threatening to blanket the land and dim the daylight. The weather just seems to churn overhead, pulling two or three seasons through every day.

There's a churn across his head as he stands pulling smoke into his lungs. How long can he maintain his faith in the *Book*?

He rubs a finger along the scar that serrates his cheek. Alice had said it made him look mysterious, half laughing; she never grasped the real truth.

He was twenty-three when it happened, not long out of college. Alice announced she was going inter-railing with Jackie and Beth. Lorcan took umbrage, first at the notion of spending two weeks on a train, his vision of living hell. Then he was informed that he wasn't, in any case, invited. Feeling belligerent, he booked a forest trekking holiday on the Congo river, an impulsive idea he immediately regretted but then could not retract. He did not have time for inoculations; Jim had just got the job working in the hospital and was able to "find" a fake certificate.

The heat and the flies had been ferocious, the pace menacing and the terrain tortuous. On the third day, he fell and rolled into a ravine, cutting himself up badly and breaking his right leg. They managed to port him to a village with a modern hospital, a legacy of Belgian colonialism, but no real doctors and very little medicine. The trekkers left promising to send help.

Nobody in the hospital spoke English and Lorcan's school French could not cope with the local accent, so that as the pain in his leg grew piercing, nobody seemed to realise that it was badly infected. They pumped whatever kind of opiates they had into him, but when he emerged from one hallucinatory journey he found that the leg had been amputated below the knee. It should have been the most horrific moment of his life, but he was awash with drugs.

He lay for days, sweating and screaming, the pain getting obscene, waiting for the *Book* to kick in. The other leg began to swell and turn an appalling shade of purple.

He lost faith. He decided that the *Book* had failed him, he had to escape. Probably fuelled by the opiates, he made an attempt to get out of the hospital intending to hitch a lift back to civilisation. He found an emergency exit, but realised too late it was ten feet above the car park and the emergency staircase had been removed. He plummeted onto pavement.

That was when he ripped his face open. He nearly died, losing blood. From his limited grasp of their French it seemed his blood pressure was impossibly low. He remembered being torn apart, the pain of them stitching his face, both legs screaming, and the weird whirling from the drugs.

Then he was writing it down in the *Book*, struggling to find superlatives to describe the agony, the anxiety, the awful sense of loss that the *Book* had abandoned him. He was back before his departure date. It was done, his leg was still where his leg should be, the swelling gone. The pain a ghost memory.

Except, that is, the pain in his cheek. He rushed to the bathroom mirror; there were crude, careless stitches. His face was like a roughly repaired potato sack. In the hospital they asked him repeatedly where he had come across such bad surgery that in the end he pretended it was a drunken mate after he'd taken a drunken fall. The doctor did miracles with him but his cheek is still puffy to this day, with a stark white scar running across it.

This had been the beginning of one of the worst phases of agitation and angst. Not only was there nearly two weeks of time to live through again, but he could not reconcile in his head how one injury - the leg - had now not happened, while the other - the face - was still all too evident. Only, it had not happened, he had never gone to Africa in this reset time, so how was the scar still there?

He had dreams, over and over, where his legs were both gone, then his head had been removed and his legs were back. He cried aloud frequently, post traumatic tension twisting him so that he needed extended sick leave.

The scar has no sensation. The skin below is nerveless. He can feel it with his finger, but there is no sense of his finger on his cheek. The *Book* had punished him. That was the only conclusion he could reach to after a week in bed with the curtain closed. He had doubted it. He had tried to fix it himself so the *Book* had left him with that scar. It was to remind him that it was the *Book*, not him, who could choose his fate.

That was nonsense, of course. There was no indication the *Book* had any thought, any motivation, it just was. But he could neither dismiss nor explain it. There was a great scar on his cheek that proved the whole episode was real, while much greater wounds had been wiped away. No matter how he threw it about, whenever his finger strayed to the numb space in the middle of his face, he was gripped by a fear of doubting the power of the *Book*.

At the time, Alice had laughed at him when she saw his wound, the day she got back from inter-railing. He tried to explain it to her but of course he couldn't. He had ended up blustering out some nonsense about Jim and a window smashing. If only he could explain it. The *Book* would decide the outcome of this horrible disease, and if he tries too hard to influence it, the outcome could be worse. Couldn't it?

He sucks on the end of his cigarette and flicks it into the sand. He can smell the sausages cooking, and he'd love to sit with his boys and enjoy a good breakfast.

By the time he gets back to the mobile home, Cian and Darragh have left with their uncle Simon.

Alice, Monday, 12:20pm

Simon has lived up to his promises, taking Cian, Darragh and Adrienne down to the sea straight after breakfast each day to learn to surf. She's never seen Darragh so keen on physical activities and he's taking to it. He looks so sturdy once Simon helps him stand on the board in the water, but he's still not confident enough to get up by himself. Cian on the other hand is fighting to stand but falling straight in. They are all having a ball.

She left Lorcan sleeping to come down and watch them. *I will be there*, he had said, but he isn't here. He was out with his buddies last night, drinking till the small hours. Jim has taken quite a shine to Mike McGinty, the wheelchair-bound pianist in the music bar. Seemingly they did a set together last night; Jim must be delighted to have an independent supply of beer coming in, not solely reliant on Bob and Lorcan.

She has not shared with Lorcan that this is *the* Mike, the kid with whom she had a brief romance that summer, the year after her mother died. At least it has to be; how many disabled musical prodigies named Mike McGinty can Enniscrone host, after all? She's curious; he was a lovely guy, not long term boyfriend material, but very sensitive, kind, compassionate. Just what she needed at that fragile moment in time. She had kissed him a few times but really the romance had been about words, about meeting spiritually.

A different experience to Lorcan. The desire as soon as she saw Lorcan had been physical, visceral, lustful. With Mike, it had been more numinous. She might just head out with them one of these evenings. Mike is framed in her head as a plain total nice guy, a sixteen year old kid with a cracking sense of humour, she would love to see what he has turned into, and what has him apparently running and owning a bar.

It is other business, though, that walks her away from her boys splashing in the surf. She strides up from the sea, past the amusement arcade and onto the main street of the town.

There is a cafe called Munnelly's. It has been there since that first summer. She used to sit for long hours with Mike. When trying to think of a good rendezvous it just leaped out at her.

Eamo is standing outside looking wary, glancing up and down the street every few seconds, a boy not comfortable with being so exposed. He is probably feeling edgy without a phone, one of the rules of the respite is he surrender it to break contact and remain out of sight.

'Mizz Murphy,' he shouts when he sees her, and his face takes on that childish glee that so endears him. He's had his hair tonsured even tighter and he could be fourteen, if you ignore the dangerous look that lingers.

'Great to see you, Eamo. You got here okay?'

'Not a bov. Got the train and they met me off it.'

'Can I buy you breakfast.'

'Ah, yeh're a star, mizz.'

'Please call me Alice.'

They take a table inside. The menu is nearly identical to what she remembers, she decides to go for a crepe. Eamo shifts about like a nervous dog, checking the menu while keeping two eyes on the door.

'You seem unsettled?'

'Can't get used to it, Mizz. So bleedin' quiet, like. Yeh know what I mean?'

'You've been out of Dublin before, though?'

'Ah yeah, Leixlip, Willow, that kinda thing. Told yeh.'

'Right. I thought you were joking, maybe. You enjoying it?'

'Yeah, but, like...' He screws up his face. 'Not sure how to say it. Like, everybody in the hostel is great and all and the food's great and there's crack, they have pool tables and that, but...'

'How are yee,' the waitress, a girl in her late teens with a happy smile and a vacant look, comes to the table. 'Lovely day out there, huh?'

'It's beautiful.'

'Are you down on holidays, is it?'

'Yes, we're in the camp site.'

'Ah that's lovely, so it is. Is it Dublin yee're from?'

'How'd yeh guess,' laughs Eamo with his charming smile. They give their orders, Eamo goes for the full Irish and a glass of milk, she gets tea and toast.

'But you're missing home?' says Alice once they're alone again.

'Missing me family, yeah, and like, there's nothing to do here.'

'You swim?'

'No.'

'I can get you togs if you want. You could go for walks.'

'Bleedin' Jaysus, Mizz, what are yeh trying to turn me into?'

'What would you be doing at home?'

'Off out with me mates, me brothers and all.'

'And your uncle Pluto.'

'Jasus, Mizz, he's going spare, so he is. "Where the fuck are yeh?" he kept texting me before they took me phone. "I'll send a lad to get yeh," he says. I'd say he's loco now. It's weird not knowing nothing.'

Alice cringes at the ironic phrase. She knows she's close to losing this battle. 'Good. You didn't tell him?'

'Ah, no, but…'

'But what?'

'I'm off me tits with boredom, know what I mean?'

'You've been here three days.'

'I know, but.'

'What about a job? For a few days, try something out.'

'Ye mean like I should look for one? Who the hell's gonna trust a Dublin scumbag with no bleedin' qualifications or experience, know what I mean?'

A job. Might that be something that could keep him here? She could probably get him an extension in the hostel if he had work. Maybe the hostel might have casual work for him, she could check that. Or maybe Simon or Paul might have contacts. 'I'll see if I can get you something. Just… Just don't give up. Not yet.'

He gives her that sweet smile again. 'Well, I owe yeh, I guess. I'll give it another couple'a days.'

'Listen, don't leave, please, not without talking to me. Right? I know if you go back that he'll have you front and centre. You remember what happened to your brother? It'll be you next.'

'Yeah, but family like. I'll do that. I won't go without talking to yeh, I owe yeh that.'

'Thanks.'

Lorcan, Tuesday, 1:00pm

Lorcan is feeling foul. The near constant drinking over the last few weeks, and the last few days in particular is taking a toll on his body. His sleep is either comatose or fitful and his stomach is crampy and bloated. He had been sincere in saying he would join Alice on her journey, even if he still believed — had to believe — it was bogus, a blip that the *Book* would erase. Yet he had failed, finding himself separated from his family, the boys being monopolised by Simon's surfing and Paul's tech toys, and Alice being constantly bathed in the compassion of Margaret, Beth and Jackie, sometimes up and gone before he's awake and then asleep before he gets back from the evening trip to McGinty's. Lorcan spends more time with his buddies and that inevitably means even more drinking.

This afternoon, Paul has organised a lunch barbecue. He's hired a monster metal appliance that sits in the middle of the sandy space between the cluster of caravans and mobile homes. He's also brought in a professional cook. Paul is not ostentatious, but he's wealthy and uninclined to underdo things. Half the campsite has been invited. Lorcan had half hoped this might be a quiet family activity and give him a chance to show his dedication to Alice and the boys. Instead there's over a hundred people here. Alice knows some guests from her occasional trips down here and she's mingling and chatting.

Jim and Bob turn up and pull beers out of the ice buckets that Paul has arranged, and the drinking begins again. *I need a day off*, thinks Lorcan, but the thought is synchronous with him popping the lid on a lager.

'Mackerel,' says Paul, coming around with plates. 'Straight in off the sea this morning.' There are fillets of scorched fish, finely filleted, skin near burnt but still dripping and fresh.

'Fish?' says Jim. 'Sure where's the burgers?'

'They'll be up in a minute, the fish cooks quicker.'

'I'll hold off so,' laughs Jim. 'Though maybe hold onto one for Mike, he says he's a pescamaniac or something like that.'

'Pescatarian?'

'That's the one.'

'Wait,' says Lorcan. 'You invited Mike from the pub here?'

'Ah, sure, couldn't keep him away. He's all agog to be meeting with the patient, don't yiz know.'

'Patient?'

'Yer missus. Ah, don't be minding me calling her a patient, but he's all ears whenever her name comes up.'

Lorcan wonders if he should intervene. If pub-mates start turning up, he's not sure what Alice will think. On the flip side, Mike's a nice enough guy, from the little that Lorcan has seen of him, not the usual bawdy bar-fly that Lorcan more often turns up with.

He takes a plate of mackerel just to see what it's like, he's not a big fan of fish but this is stunning, succulent, well seared, sweet and deeply umami.

'Wow,' he says as Paul returns with more plates.

'Lobster anybody?' he says.

'Oh, I'll grab a lobster,' says Jim.

'I thought you were waiting on the burgers?'

'Ah, needs must. C'mere,' he says, pointing inland. 'Is that an airport over there.'

Paul laughs. 'Not a bit. Glamping.'

'You are fucking kidding me?'

'No, well, he hasn't opened the place yet, but there's going to be train carriages and busses and the likes.'

'What are we talking about?' asks Lorcan.

'The bleedin' plane. Didn't yeh see it? Come over here.'

Jim pulls Lorcan to a spot that's slightly higher, and where a gap in the mobile homes leaves a view towards the hills. There, the other side of the main road, through a gap in the hedges, Lorcan sees a plane, a full size passenger jet, or at least the tail of it sticking up in the air.

'That is mad!'

'C'mere, Paul, bud, how did they get that bugger in there?'

'Sailed it into the harbour on a barge, I believe. Took the wings off after it landed on Shannon Airport, then they had to barge it up here and wheel it up through the town. Middle of the night, I heard, to catch the tides, whole town was out to watch it.'

'Now wouldn't that be a fecking thing to see. I'll drink a toast to that man's daring,' Jim says, grabbing another can from the ice buckets.

The lobster looks expensive. Each plate has a half lobster shell with chunks of tail seared and smoked. Very tasty, though Lorcan is finding himself drawn back to the mackerel.

A taxi turns up.

'Ah, here's me mate,' says Jim.

The door of the taxi slides open and a ramp sweeps out. Mike is inside; he undoes the safety strap and pushes his chair down the ramp.

'How'r'ye, bud,' shouts Jim. 'Come here and let us get yeh some lobster, bloody good.'

Jim heads off to the barbecue stand with Mike. Lorcan is left nursing his beer. He spots Rhia on the far side of the crowd. She's just brought Forry in and seems to be putting him in Simon's care. He watches her as she makes her way through the mobile homes and off into the dunes towards the hotel.

Alice, Tuesday, 1:20pm

Alice is feeling foul. She has the ghost of a headache. She has loaded up with paracetamol and ibuprofen, but stopped short of the stuff with the codeine. She is nauseous from the stink of burger and can't stomach the mackerel. She slaps on a smile and carries on, there are too many old acquaintances that need renewing.

She hears Jim's voice about the crowd shouting "Mike" and turns to see a man in a wheelchair pushing himself towards them. With the potholed sandy grass the chair keeps bucking, but there's strength in his arms. It has been more than twenty years, but she knows him immediately. A smile makes its way onto her face, betraying the child within who once had a mad crush on him.

She is in mid-flow of conversation with Amanda Clarke, another mobile-homer from Laois who has a superb singing voice, as Alice remembers from that summer when a barbecue would be born from campfire lit on a bundle of driftwood and any spare sausages that were hanging about, and the near neighbours would sing into the small hours. While Amanda rambles on, she keeps a half eye on Mike as Jim bundles him to the barbecue grill then tries to push beer on him, which he refuses.

At one point, their eyes meet. There is a moment, a mutual recognition, and then Jim steps in the way.

Amanda introduces her to another two ladies who are veterans, that Alice would know from that same happy summer, and she's half tempted to ask if they remember him. She is just turning to replenish her water and nearly trips over him.

'Hi,' he says.

And there he is. Out of nowhere, a little flutter heaves in her heart, a misplaced memory of teen infatuation replayed over this fine fettled man. He looks good, well groomed, clearly not wanting for money by the cut of his linen suit and shirt. His hair has the same wild quality that she used to wonder about, though it is not a stranger to a good hairdresser, she thinks. There is power in his torso and in the upright posture.

'You look good.' The words slip out.

'You look better.'

'Did I look that bad back then?'

He opens his mouth and laughs with that tinkling tone that she loved in him. 'Oh, that's the Alice I remember. How the hell are you?'

She is flushed with a feeling from long ago and nearly goes to hug him. She smiles at him.

'Great. Thanks. It's really nice to see you. You… own a pub now?'

'I own a lot of things. You lost the chance to be a very wealthy WAG.'

'Glad to hear it, but…?'

'Turns out I do have a talent for music. Will we… Take a little roll maybe?'

'Sure. The surface here is fairly rough. Do you need me to push you?'

'Nope. You also lost the chance to be the WAG of a pretty pumped cripple, pardon my lack of political correctness.'

They start wandering back up the track, away from the crowd.

'Jesus, political correctness is the last thing I would ever expect of you. You always called a spade a fucking shovel. Or maybe a baby beating stick, I think that's one of yours?'

'Yeah, probably.'

'So I missed out?'

'You sure did, although, and please don't take this as a personal statement, I realised I was gay shortly after our brief time together.'

'Right. A month with me and you were gay, then?'

He treats her to that tinkling laugh again. 'I'm afraid I was gay all along, I just hadn't figured it.'

'Same with my brother, Simon, as it happens.'

'Oh yeah? Hey, maybe it was he who missed out then. Jeez, that could have been some summer.'

'Did you find me so repulsive that I pushed you that last one percent?'

'I found you beautiful, Alice.' He stops and looks up at her, that rugged strop of hair drooping into his eyes. 'Would I have gone straight? To keep you? Not a fricking chance, sorry. But, there was something special in our relationship. It helped me find myself.'

'Ha. That summer was a total life changer for me.'

'Your mother had just died?'

'I was pretty cut up over it.'

'Pretty cut up? You were in bits, I remember. First couple of times we went to that cafe, Munnelly's, you just cried.'

They have come to the corner of the campsite, to the footbridge over the river. Alice remembers many days spent just sitting here, throwing stones into the water.

'I changed here, Mike. Became a different person. I left something behind. I mean, that was a good thing, yeah, but... Maybe I'm trying to find that thing I left behind now.' She is about to talk about her illness, but then pulls back. He might be Mike, the guy she dated and was hugely fond of, but he's a near stranger now. 'So you're gay?'

'Very gay and very proud. It was a bit of a thing, coming out in Enniscrone back then, but there's loads of us now.'

'Well done, finding that part of yourself, I guess. I'm very proud of you. It's not a gay bar that you run?' She gives him a smile as she asks.

'Good Jesus, no. Traditional pub, but the music bar was what I was after. It used to be a trad place, like a little shebeen out the back with banjos. Now we have all kinds of music all day. I just love it. You should call in.'

'Glad you're still into your music.'

'Still into it? So, you don't know, then?'

'Sorry?'

'The thing you set off in me, other than realising I was gay, was a passion for songwriting. Alice, I've sold dozens of songs. I'm a freaking millionaire, would you believe.'

'Really? Anything I'd have heard of?'

'Well, you might have come across *A Remembrance of Nothing?*'

'The Beyoncé song?'

'Well her and a dozen other A-listers who have covered it. Cha-ching,' he laughs. 'And *Your Eyes Are Mine*. And *Seven Times That Sing*. All mine.'

'My God, wow. That's amazing.'

'And prepare yourself for this. Do you remember *Sweet Summer Something*? David Bowie covered it but it was originally Chris Rea.'

'Yeah, I loved that song. Wasn't big into Chris Rea at the time, but I loved that one. That was yours?'

'Not only was that mine, but I wrote it for you.'

'Holy God. For me?'

'Yeah, it was my homage to that summer. *For you freed me from the ties that bind,*' he sings. '*You opened my eyes, cleared the clouds from my skies, when you took my hand and sang.*'

'And that *you* is me?'

'Sure is.'

'Wowser's. So you must owe me millions in royalties.'

He laughs again, a joyous rejuvenating sound that takes her back to when she had held his hand, when she had sung to him. Joni Mitchel mostly, from what she can recall.

'Seriously, though. I'm so damn rich I could give you millions. I mean, sorry, that sounds rotten. What I mean is if you are ever in need, just ask. Honestly.'

The time seems right.

'I am in need, Mike, but nothing that money could fix, I'm afraid.'

'Oh, sorry to hear that.'

'I have Leukaemia.'

He stops and turns the chair towards her. 'Jim told me some of it,' he says. 'Though I wasn't sure if I could believe him.'

'Diagnosed three weeks ago, about to start my therapies.'

'I'm so sorry, God, Alice. I mean what I said, if you need money, you know, second opinion, some foreign doctor or treatment. I literally have money coming out my arse. Well, not literally, thank God.'

'Thanks, Mike. Unfortunately this is a problem you can't just throw money at. You can't just fix this thing.'

He places a hand onto her elbow, a strangely intimate touch, lets it linger for a little while. 'Oh, Alice.' Fingers of sorrow rasp his voice. 'When I knew you first, cancer had poisoned your life.'

'Yes.'

'You found the strength to overcome the grief, that's what I felt. I really admired you for that.'

'It's true, I got over it damn fast. Only now it's opening up again, an old wound that never really healed. That's kind of why I'm here. I mean, the main reason I'm here is to just be with my family, away from everything, just have this time. But there's also a sense of going back, you know? Trying to remember what Mammy meant to me then, how she dealt with it. I've got two young boys.'

'I know. I asked Jim about you, he told me a good bit of stuff.'

'Great to know he respects my privacy. Good friend.'

'I'm getting that impression, big on noise, maybe a little light on empathy.' He lets his hand drop from her arm, she feels the warmth of his touch remain.

He starts to push himself along again and she follows. It's a nice day, not sunny but warm enough. There's plenty of people pottering about the park, heading to the beach with towels or walking up to the town. Everybody seems happy, enjoying the brightness.

'You never knew your father, I seem to remember? A bass guitarist, you said.'

'No. I have a vague memory of him, but I'm not even completely sure it was him. He was away touring with different bands. I don't know why he didn't come back when she died.'

'And you still have no contact with him?'

'None. No address or anything, just a name. I was told he was with Bruce Springsteen's band but I couldn't find any record of it.'

'Maybe that's somewhere I could help?'

'How so?'

'I've got a manager in the UK, Bob, makes a damn fortune from me for doing next to nothing. I'm sure he'd know who to talk to, knows everybody in the damn industry. You know any bands he was definitely with?'

'Anything I thought I knew turned into a dead end.'

'He was Spanish, right?'

'So I was told. Jesus, I don't even know that for sure. We have his name, Carlos Garcia. That's about all I know.'

'Bob will dig him out. Maybe give me your last address in England, or any you remember. I presume he lived there with your mother? He was probably registered there, you know social insurance, driving license, that kind of thing.'

'You can't just go asking for those details. There's privacy and all that.'

Mike shrugs. 'It's funny how much privacy a shed load of money can buy.' He treats her to his tinkly laugh again. 'Look, I'm probably talking crap. Do you mind if I call Bob, have him look into it? I mean, it can't hurt, right?'

Alice finds herself smiling. Mike has always been a kind soul, considerate in ways that Lorcan never was. Two different men in so many ways.

There is a sudden cacophony of screeching, a coven of gulls are crowding round a rogue sandwich on the sand below. She watches the vicious swoops as they each seek advantage. The harder they fight, the more the sandwich is dispersed and destroyed. A life lesson they are failing to learn.

'What are the chances on the Leukaemia?' he asks.

'We don't talk about chances, we talk about opportunities to enhance our life experiences. Like taking a holiday in Enniscrone.'

'I see. I wish I could fix it.'

'So does Lorcan. My husband.'

'There you go. He's a lucky man, you're a beautiful person.'

'Thank you.'

Mike stops again. He spins his wheels back and forth, pointing himself left, then right, like a nervous fidget. 'Do you remember the whale?'

'Whale?'

'You remember we used to go walking up the coast, up there beyond the harbour. A dead whale washed up on shore and they couldn't get rid of it.'

'God, yeah, the thing stank.'

'I remember that stink, it used to fascinate me.'

'I hated the stink but I loved drawing it.'

'Yeah, you were really good at gothic noir. The skin splitting and the backbone sticking out. And then the ribcage starting to appear.'

'I had a penchant for the macabre. Went with the grieving teen image.'

'Did you go on to do art?'

'Social work. Work with a lot of socially disadvantaged young people, trying to keep them off the street. Or worked, I guess.'

'Wow, well done. You must feel very proud.'

'I feel more frustrated than proud. Although, yes, when I stop and think about it, it's lovely to feel I've made some kind of contribution here and there.'

'That whale. It stays in my head. It has become a symbol for me, a metaphor. I've tried to write the song a dozen times but it eludes me. I can't quite tie it down, at least not in words that are lyrical. All of that summer, something grew. Something grew for both of us. You found your feet, found your head. I could see that. Each day you felt firmer, more at home with your family, less weighted down by your past. And me, I was having the beginnings of the realisations that changed my life: my sexuality and my music.

'And all the while, that thing sank and soured, and got stinkier and more putrid, until at last it was a loose bag of bones under a few strips of skin. I felt, I know this sounds mad, Alice, I felt that whale gave up its being for us, dissolved itself out of everything that it was while we watched, so that we could dissolve our own pasts and become something new.'

'Jesus. No wonder you're the music millionaire.'

'Hey, way to go with pissing on my beautiful artistic metaphor, doll!'

'Sorry.'

He laughs again, and she remembers why she almost, oh so almost, fell in love with him. Just as well she didn't, it would seem.

'Only kidding,' he says. 'I think you can see why I never got that into a song.'

'Yeah, but I do see what you mean. And I agree. I changed, and it sounds like you changed.'

'Hey, why don't you come across to the music bar tonight? I'd love to sing your song for you.'

'I will not sit there humiliated while you croon at me.'

'I won't say anything, I'll just sing it, how about that?'

'Maybe. And maybe we could get coffee in Munnelly's.'

'It's a date.'

'I guess I should be getting back and chatting to folks.'

'Yup, it's unfair of me to monopolise you.'

He starts to push his chair back the way they had come, Alice walks alongside him.

'One other thing,' she says. 'You wouldn't have a job for a very capable if somewhat inexperienced young man?'

Lorcan, Tuesday, 1:45pm

Lorcan is literally scratching his head watching Alice wander off chatting to Mike. At first, he thought she had ejected him, was walking him away, but it's clear they are chatting, talking.

Mike. The name transforms, at one moment a musical barfly, then whisked into a hazy memory. There was a Mike, a guy who had been her summer romance. Did she say he was disabled? Yes. He had a wheelchair. And he was a musician. This is Mike. *The* Mike. What are the chances of that? Enniscrone is not a big town, but even still, the first pub they walk into is owned by the guy that used to be her crush.

He sought her out, Lorcan realises. That's why he jumped on Jim's invitation, he wanted to see her again. Alice is happy to see him. A worm of jealousy wriggles through him, but Mike is barely even an old flame.

As he stands watching her stroll away, his eyes flick to the dunes, to where Rhia recently retreated. Cian and Darragh are playing a complicated game involving pretend surfing, mental arithmetic and chasing with Adrienne and Forry and a couple of other kids from the site. With an inside shrug, he walks toward the dunes.

The sandy hollow hosting the barbecue sits in a wind shadow, warded by dunes from the freshness of the breeze. As he climbs, he sees a path that weaves as the dunes duck and dive. Walking quickly, his legs are pinpricked by maram grass. He is mesmerised by the sand and sea and the sweep of the wind, the ever present ear-churn of waves washing ashore, a white noise whoosh punctuated by the harsh cawing of gulls bobbing for beach-treats. As he reaches the ridge of the first peaks, he spots Rhia fifty metres further on, leaning over to look at the local flora.

She has not moved by the time he gains the spot. He stops to survey for a moment, but his shadow betrays him.

'Hey,' she says, looking up and shielding her eyes from the sun with her hand. 'I found orchids.'

He walks down from the high sand to stand beside her. She is cradling and small green stem with a round pink fluorescence.

'That's an orchid?'

'Yeah. Look close. Come in close, I don't want to pick it.'

He hunkers down beside her, and she shuffles closer. The pressure of her outer thigh against him catches his breath. He leans in to see the shape of the blossoms; tiny trefoil pink petals role out from little mouths, ripe with pollen for any insect attracted to it.

'Wow, yeah, it is an orchid.'

'They're indigenous to the local area.'

'Really?'

She stands up and stretches lazily.

'Were you bored by the barbecue too?'

'Yeah, though... I guess I kind of wanted to talk to you too.'

'That's nice. Wow, it's hot here.' They are in another wind shade, a dip in the dunes with shining sand on all side reflecting the meagre sunlight, magnifying the heat. She heaves off her jumper, and Lorcan catches a glimpse of pale midriff.

'I need to talk to you about the *Book*.'

'You're always on about that bloody *Book*. Why do you harp on so much?'

'Because you're the only one I can talk to. Literally. You're the only one who remembered something from what happened, everybody else ends up confused and I end up with horrible headaches if I even try to mention it.'

'I don't remember it, Lorcan. You keep talking about it but there's nothing here.' She taps her forehead.

'But you do remember. We've talked about it before. That evening on Burrow beach. Remember, you called me and you were all upset over Jim. He was abusing you at the time.'

'I... I called you...'

'And we met on the beach. And you were all upset, like hysterical. And you pulled your clothes off and...' Lorcan has to pause to catch his breath; despite the horror of the memory, that vision of her naked in the twilight on that beach, framed by dunes on the far shore, still haunts him. 'And you had all these bruises on you and you said Jim was hitting you.'

'He was hitting me.'

'And then you ran into the sea and you just kept running and I ran after you and we were down under the water and the waves took us and I tried to hold onto you but my head hit something…'

'Oh, God, oh hell…'

'You drowned, Rhia. You drowned on the beach. I was clinging to you but I couldn't pull you out.'

'But then… I didn't.'

'Right. That's it. You didn't. You died, I woke up but it was that morning and I was writing it down in the *Book*, but I didn't wait for your call, I went right round to you, you brought me into your house…'

'And we made love.'

'We did?' His head is spinning, the heat is searing, he can't breathe. He stumbles and falls on his bum. Rhia is standing, shaking her head, looking dazed. 'I don't remember that…'

'Poor baby.' She fixes him with a ferocious smile.

Could it be true? Was he unfaithful to Alice. She had only been his girlfriend but they were already having sex, had already exchanged promises. He is at once horrified and elated, excited.

But it could be just a side effect of the *Book's* actions, the thing does crazy things to your memories. 'I remember we talked about Jim. And you made me swear not to do anything, not to say anything.'

'Yes.'

'And like a fool I agreed.'

'Not a fool. You loved me.'

'I loved you.' *I still love you*, he nearly says, but doesn't. 'And you love him.'

'Oh, Lorcan, you don't know how much.' A moist glow illuminates her face as she says this. Rhia's love for Jim, lifelong and soul-deep, has a spiritual wing.

Sweat beads trace lines down Lorcan's forehead as the sun continues to cook him in this makeshift microwave oven of a dune-hole.

'So, you remember?'

'Yes. But no. No, it's not true.' She closes her eyes, screws up her face as if trying to push out a baby, a child of unwanted memories. 'I don't know, it's like a dream when you wake up and you know exactly what it was about, then a moment later it's all fragmented and fading.'

'I know what you mean. The *Book* fucks with your head. It's impossible to keep something in focus, the *Untime* I call it. It's something that happens, but doesn't happen. It sort of screws with you.'

'Why? Why are you doing this to me?'

He is passionately conscious of her closeness. He's aware of her bare skin beneath her top, the lack of a bra. The intoxicating thought of them making love is overwhelming him. 'Can we walk? It's too hot here?'

She shrugs, still shaking her head, red rivers of hair waving about in confusion, then she stands and starts to climb the dune out of the reflection oven.

'You know how head wrecking this is,' he says. 'I've got that problem squared. Alice is ill, I mean really ill. She's throwing up and sucking down pain killers. I know she doesn't look bad but she's trying to hide it. She's got this notion that this trip is some kind of, I don't, last chance for happiness or something. Like she's putting her affairs in order.'

'And you think the *Book* will fix her?'

'I just need to figure out how. The *Book*, it's a black hole, a mystery. I don't even know where I got it, for Christ's sake. I know I didn't have it when I was a kid then...' Even just thinking about it sends a spasm of anxiety across his head, makes his bowel rumble, his neck tense up, like his memory is fighting back. 'Something happened when I was ten. I think... I think I need to find out what it was.'

'What do you mean something happened?'

'I can't say. It's like, you know when you have somebody's name on the tip of your tongue, but the harder you try to say it the more it fights back, and it just won't come out until maybe two hours later and it suddenly comes to you unbidden. Something bad happened to me, and I think to my family, like my mother and father. Except, no matter how long I wait, it never comes back to me. All I know for sure is I had the *Book* after that. I think the first entry I wrote was that time, but I can't read the damn thing, it fights back.'

'So go ask them.'

'They're all nuts, though. I mean my dad lives in the shed, for God's sake. I think that started shortly after.'

'But you haven't asked them?'

'No.'

'Maybe you should.'

'Maybe I should. Or maybe I should just figure out how to trigger the fucking *Book*.'

'How did it work with my thing? We both drowned. Is that it, you both got to kill yourselves?'

'That's not even funny.'

'Funny?' She turns to him with tears touching her eyes. 'What the hell is funny about you giving me these hallucinations of suicide?'

'It's not hallucinations…'

'Look, stop! You're freaking me out. I need to get my head out of this space. I don't know what to tell you about your *Book*. I know you made that vow.' She stops at the top of the dune ridge and reaches out a hand to his face, strokes his cheek. 'You're beautiful, Lorcan. I wish I could love you, I really do, but my heart's not free to give.'

She leans over him, since she's slightly above him on the slope, throws arms and fronds of hair about him, kisses him savagely, passionately. She pulls away, leaving his heart screaming, his nose tingling with the earthy sweat of her.

'I gotta go and talk to my angels, okay. Maybe you'd go back and make sure Forry's okay? Thanks.'

She walks away back towards the campsite. He stands watching her red tresses flowing until she disappears.

Alice, Thursday, 8:20am

Nights are becoming a nuisance. Nausea is a frequent visitor, though Alice has become adept at not losing her dinner. She often lies, sometimes three or four times in a night, as the world whirls around, her eyes go funny and her stomach cramps up like a thumbscrew. Dark pain haunts her head, extending tendrils down her back. She thinks about the tumour that is sitting there, sometimes thinks she can feel it throbbing. The soreness grows to peaks that are barely sustainable despite sucking down the paracetamol and ibuprofen. She wakes feeling exhausted, legs aching as if she's walked miles. How she would love to be out stomping the beaches, climbing the nearby hills, but that is beyond her.

She wonders if she will last till next week before looking for help, but she will not be defeated until she has to. She sets an alarm and is up and out before the rest of them are up. She heads to the hostel, aware that she should not really intrude in this space but Eamo doesn't have a mobile phone, or at least not one he's prepared to confess to, and she hasn't been able to get through to the caretakers.

She's not surprised to find he's also up and about when she gets there; he's that kind of kid, energetic and, weirdly enough for a family neck deep in drug dealing and inter-gang violence, clean living.

'How'r'ye, Mizz Murphy.'

'Great, thanks Eamo,' she lies. 'How is the place treating you?'

'Ah, they're great here, not a word of complaint, but, yeh know, nothing to do and all.'

'I might have a solution to that. Have you ever worked as a barman?'

It turns out he has, or at least as a lounge boy, though he's familiar enough with the pouring of a pint of Guinness.

'I did a few weeks in the *Horse Breaker's* pub, you know that one there in Stamullen. Then me uncle Pluto pulls me out, says our family are too good for the likes of that, and if I'm wanting money, I'm to work for him and he'll see me right. And in fairness, there isn't much dosh in bartending compared to drugs, know'm saying?'

'This isn't about money, though. You're bored, I'm thinking this place could be good for you. I know you're not a drinker, so I'm not worried about that side. And I know Mike, he's a good guy, caring.'

'I'll tell yeh what, Mizz Murphy, yeh've been a star. I'll stick me nose in the door, like, have a look and all, if I think the place looks any good, I'll ask for Mike.'

'That's great. Thanks for that. McGinty's pub, anyone you ask will know it, you can't miss it. Go to the music bar round the back. He said that would be more suitable for you. The bar on the main street is a bit spit-and-sawdust, I'm told.'

She leaves him in the hostel. He is an honest lad, if you overlook his occasional involvement in the family business which in fairness is purely family pressure. She is confident he will at least look in on Mike who assured her there was a great buzz in the music bar. She can only hope that might be enough to catch his interest; she has no other cards up her sleeve.

She gets fresh bread from a bakery on the way back. Margaret is sitting alone having a cup of tea in the broad picture window of the mobile home. Alice hears a sonorous snoring from the bedrooms.

'Lorcan's not up yet, then?'

'What was the giveaway?'

'What about the boys?'

'I swear to God, Alice, they've fallen in love with the sea. And Simon is great of course, he's not had any time to himself, but if I'd known that Darragh — Darragh of all people — would turn into a mini-surfer I'd have had them down here every week since they were born.'

'Ah it's great, and Simon's a total star. Shame their dad can't be quite so keen and eager.'

'Don't be too harsh now, you get a taste for the sea when you're young, they tell me, and if you don't have it, you don't have it.'

Alice has more to say about Lorcan's lack of involvement in the family holiday, his constant drinking and stinking of fags, but she doesn't want to be all the time demeaning him. She doesn't need that.

'I have fresh baked bread if you want a slice?'

She pours herself tea then cuts and butters some bread, but at once the delicious aroma is a stomach turner and she has to run for the bathroom. She doesn't vomit, but threads of spume force their wicked way up her throat and out her mouth. She wipes herself down, dries her eyes.

'Should I take you to the hospital?' says Margaret.

'It's not time yet.'

'You're not well.'

'Do you think?' She puts her arms around Margaret and her mother-in-all-but-birth holds her, soothes her. 'I don't want to break the spell,' she says. 'And besides, what will the doctors say. You have Leukaemia, go talk to your consultant, and he'll just say he's sorting it out, getting the dates lined up.'

'But still...'

'Shhh...!' She puts a finger to Margaret's lips. 'I'm fine. I'll let you know when I'm not.'

Margaret pauses, a mini-drama plays out across her face, ending with a smile. 'You were always so strong,' she says. 'Just like your mother.'

'Ha, I wish.'

'No, you are. I mean look at you. We both know you're not well, you need help, but there you are pushing your finger to my lips in case I spoil the party. You're like her. You are her, my Bella.'

There is a tremble in Margaret's jaw, a juddering energy shakes her spine. Alice pulls her tighter.

'I'm not, though. I'm just, I don't know, I'm hiding here. My little calm before the storm, and I don't want that storm to ever hit.'

'And that was her all over. Live for today. Live for what's in front of you, don't be dwelling on what might happen or mightn't happen.'

'Carpe Diem.'

'Exactly.'

'Not escapism?'

'Another word for the same thing.'

'And what about my dad?'

'Worse, I guess. I mean, he left. So intent on Carpe-bloody-Diem that he didn't stay around to see what became of his beautiful daughter. Where is he now, eh?'

'Funny you should ask. I met Mike.'

'I talked to him at the barbecue, turned into a lovely man. Perfect boy for a summer romance.'

'He's gay.'

'All the more reason.'

'Anyway, he said he's going to look into Dad, try and work out what happened to him.'

'How's he going to do that?'

'He's a big noise in the music industry, pardon the pun. He's got an agent in London who's going to ask around.'

'Oh, I don't know if that's such a good idea.'

'Why the hell not?'

'Look, the man left you and your mother. What's the point in digging up past pain?'

'I just want to know about him, what the hell's wrong with that? All I have is a few old photographs we took from Mammy's and a half a memory from my childhood.'

'There's many people don't even get that. You should just accept and move on.'

'I can't believe you're even saying that. Christ, I might be dying here, it might be my last chance to find out about my own father. About my boys' grandfather. I mean, it's not like the other grandfather is a shining example of a good father or anything, you know, Lorcan's dad-in-the-shed.'

'I'm sorry, don't be minding me. I'm just a bitter old woman. I closed my mind to him after what he did to you and Bella. He wasn't even there for her. And she never blamed or cursed him. She died with her head held high. That was so important to her. She never compromised.'

'What use is that, she's still dead?'

The skin around Margaret's lips pulls back, taut and white. There are years of stress twisted in that look, losing her sister was not easy, perhaps hearing her niece-now-daughter dismissing the memory of that beautiful woman is too much to take. Or perhaps it's the knowledge she will have to go through it all again. No words emerge.

'Sorry,' says Alice. 'I didn't mean...'

'No, don't be apologising again. There shouldn't be a need to apologise, whatever's said.'

'Sor... God, I can't say that to you any more.'

'Proper order.'

'All I want... All I want is to make sure my family are okay. Cian and Darragh, to lose a mother so young...'

'As did you.'

'I wasn't that young.'

'No, but you survived. And the boys have a father.'

'Well, as long as he can stay sober and stop being a child himself.'

'Stop!' Now it's Margaret's turn to put a finger to Alice's lips. 'Stop. Your boys are beautiful and they have the same strength that powers you. And Lorcan is a fine man, he's thrown by what's happening. Alice, you may have years, decades left. Whatever it is, take your joy. Let it fly while you can. But look after yourself, okay?'

Alice wants to agree, to let the anxieties loose and just live while she can live, but the dark place will not go away. It lingers at the back of her head. 'I want to thank you, Mam. I want to say that, make sure it doesn't go unsaid. Thanks for being there, for taking care of me when Mammy died.'

'I'll do it again if I need to.'

Lorcan, Friday, 6:20pm

The west is wet: soaked, saturated, sopping, sodden. Chalk-brushed clouds spill sprawls of pastel rain that wash across the campsite. Glistening spreels of drizzle scatter colours over a grey afternoon. The wind is sharp, not cold but prone to gusts that spread chill fingers down the necks of wetted beach-walkers. It is Good Friday, and nature is lamenting the death of the saviour by dampening the spirits of those taking advantage of the Easter school holiday.

Cian and Darragh have been immune to the communal mourning as they have spent much of the morning and afternoon splashing in the sea with Simon. When Alice announced that she was going to the Easter vigil with Margaret and Frank in the nearby church of Our Lady Assumed into Heaven, Lorcan considered going out to replace Simon, who would normally go to the vigil too, but it was damn cold out there.

He nursed himself instead with an aged whiskey he had brought with him, letting the mellowness take the edge off the undermining anxiety that plagued him these days. His lethargy and self indulgence could only be justified by the notion — no, by the absolute necessity — that this was *Untime*, and that the *Book* would soon resolve all of his problems. But the longer it rolled on, the less likely this seemed. He was not yet ready to face that. The dark peatyness of the whiskey, combined with trips into the dunes for a quick smoke, took the edge off it.

Once the churchgoers return, Cian and Darragh are called home shivering, teeth chattering. Alice and Margaret jump to it with towels, and Lorcan is left lounging on the sofa in the main room, listening idly to Jackie and Beth talking about how moving the vigil was and speculating that they might go back to mass more often. The radio is playing MidWest, the "Death-Has-Ocurred" notices are being read out in a morbid voice.

As the whiskey clears, a fuzzy frizz of excitement starts to set in. The gang are going to the pub. Alice, who's been in great spirits so far today, is keen to go. Jackie and Beth won't be left behind, Simon is coming too.

Despite the growing sense of unease, Lorcan has been enjoying the booze, the nights out with no notion of consequences, smoking and singing. Arriving home to this little haven of good behaviours, where even Frank has been keeping his head down, is building his sense of wrongdoing and leading to remorse.

With the guys all going, it lends a legitimacy. Tonight he can let go and not have any doubts.

Once the boys have been warmed up and Margaret is heating spaghetti hoops and fish fingers for them, the ladies retreat to the bedroom for communal pampering.

It is past nine before they are ready to go, a full hour after they had intended. Lorcan is biting his tongue; his throat has acquired an unnatural dryness. It's still bright as they start their walk, though the ink-wash rain is still spreading the damp across the campsite, and through their coats. It doesn't seem wet, when they look at it, but once they're out in it, the heavy drops soak in. They are all shivering when they get to the pub.

The place is packed, the Friday crowd is in. A trio of young red-haired women are singing something like an upbeat sean-nós and in fairness there are plenty of folks staying quiet, listening, so it's far from the deafening din you can get in here.

He stands on tip-toes to look around, afraid they may have to stand, when the new barman, a Dubliner with heavy neck tattoos, pops his head out of the crowd.

'How'r'yeh,' he bellows. 'I have yer table held.'

'Eamo?' says Alice.

'How'r'ye, Mizz Murphy. I knew it was you so didn't I keep the best table, and I been beating people off with a stick.'

'You took the job then.'

'Fucking right, excuse me French and all. Mike's a superstar, best bloody queer I met, like. Worked last night, isn't the right Jimbo, yeh big scab?'

'Eamo, me man, best damn virgin pint pourer I ever put me eyes on. Do yeh know he only started yesterday, Alice?'

'I do Jim, thanks.'

'Follow me, folks.' Eamo channels a hole through the crown and takes them up towards the stage.

'Wait a sec,' says Lorcan. 'This is the kid you're helping out? From your work, like.'

'It is. He was looking likely to leave and Mike said he'd give him a job. Didn't think he'd take quiet so enthusiastically.'

'Jaysus, you should have told me. If I'd known that was the guy I'd have tipped him big.'

'Yeah, I kind of think he doesn't really need the tips. Besides, if you were around a bit more I'd keep you better informed.'

The comment cuts Lorcan, leaving him flapping, but they've arrived at a top table within spitting distance of the performers.

'First round's on me, folks, on account'a Mizz Murphy here putting me in the way of this place. It's fucking gear so it is.'

They object but he insists. Pints for the lads, even Simon, G-and-Ts for the ladies. Eamo gives a wild wail and scrambles up onto the top of the partition separating them from the next table, then tightropes across the interlocking partitions as far as the bar, getting yelps from the audience.

'Go'wan Eamo!'

'Well,' says Beth, 'think you might have a bit of a success story on your hands there.'

'Need to wait and see. How long will bartending keep him going?'

'I think you can afford to give yourself a pat on the back with that one.'

Lorcan is amazed too. He has heard horror stories about Eamo's family. His uncle Pluto is one of the most feared criminals in Dublin. People who push up against that family tend to end up buried. And here's this kid bouncing around a country pub like he owns the place. 'Yeah, fair play to you, Alice.'

'Thanks,' she says. 'It's nice you say that. You don't often compliment me on my work.'

'Oh. Sorry, I...'

'Ah, stop worrying and drink up.' She laughs.

The drinks are coming down by a human chain with Eamo standing on the bar and directing where they are to go. People are cheering him, clapping a rhythm and telling him to dance, which he duly does, throwing a mad impression of a jig on the bar top.

'Is the place always this lively?' Alice asks.

'Yeah, well, Eamo adds an extra dimension to proceedings, but it's always loud and good natured. The singing will start in a bit. There'll be a few proper bands on like those girls, but loads of people will do a party piece. Your best buddy Jim included, I don't doubt.'

'Well I can see now why you're down here every night.'

The words warm him. There might be a lingering tail of sarcasm in there but there's just enough sincerity for Lorcan to take home with him. Just enough approval to take the edge off his conscience.

One nice thing: it's not his night with his friends, or her night with hers, they are out with shared friends and family. It seems so rare these days that they can do that. Alice has her friends and her brother, Lorcan has his buddies, even Rhia has joined them having managed to offload Forry on Paul and Felicia. There's laughter everywhere, and singing. Alice has a smile sitting softly on her face, there's a gentle ease to her he has not seen in some weeks. This is great. He takes Alice's hand under the table and she squeezes him back.

The three girls have finished their set and there are a few minutes of relative quiet as their second pints arrive.

'C'mere,' says Eamo, arriving back to them by the more conventional route of walking the floor. 'Will one of youz get up and do a song?'

'I would,' shouts Jim. 'Only I need to wet me whistle before I start. Yeh start singing dry and who knows what damage yeh might do.'

'Right,' says Eamo. 'I better get the party rolling then.' He jumps up on the stage. 'C'mere, youz, proper song, this.'

He starts belting out *Dublin in the Rare Ould Times*, only it's a mad version, more shouted than sung as he leaps around the stage. The crowd stops to watch, enthusiastic if a little nervous of his energy.

He's only stopped when another cheer goes up, and Mike appears from the back of the stage.

'I'm not paying you to sing, Eamo,' he says with a smile. 'Get back to the bar.'

'You're hardly paying me at all, Mr. McGinty.'

The audience howls with laughter as Mike makes his way to the piano, but falls to soft silence as he lays hands on the keys. He starts with a cascade of chords that tumble in turns, then slows into the tidy tinkling that is clearly the intro to *Sweet Summer Something*.

'*For you feed me from the ties that bind,*' he sings. '*You opened my eyes, cleared the clouds from my skies, when you took my hand and sang.*'

'Apparently he wrote that song,' Lorcan says to Alice. 'Can you imagine? This guy.'

'Really?' she says, though there is a curious curl in her smile.

The whole place joins in at the chorus, '*Sweet Summer Something, it all ends too soon, it lingers long after, after the glorious summer.*'

'One of my biggest hits, that one,' says Mike when the chorus has been through six repetitions and he crashes it to it's closing chords. 'Written for somebody very special.'

Lorcan looks at Alice's face again. This guy knew her, back then, that summer. He started writing music. He wrote that song for somebody. *It lingers long after.*

Alice's mouth has a curious smile, as if tasting a jelly baby. Did Mike write this for her? She never really talked about him, dismissed him as a summer fling whenever it had come up but it sounds like he's something more than that. For a moment his mind runs down a rat hole: could she be… No surely not, she'd never…

It doesn't last long. Alice is solid, Mike is gay. He takes a deep glug of his pint and laughs. How could he even think it. His anxieties are taking him over.

'So I've been hearing a couple of things,' says Mike to the crowd, 'like maybe we have a few veterans of the Annual Lynyrd Skynyrd Freebird-a-thon, and I was thinking,' he effortlessly sweeps into a piano rendition of the fabulous opening arpeggios of Freebird. Eamo appears carrying an electric guitar, plugs it to the amp that lives at the back of the stage and holds it in Jim's direction.

'Come on, guys, we got this,' says Jim, slurping the end of his pint, then dragging Lorcan and Bob to the stage, dragging them by the coat sleeves.

Jim takes the guitar and picks up the arpeggio from Mike, Bob walks to the microphone begins the soft opening verse. Lorcan stands on the stage like a spare sock, the eyes of the room burning him red. Young folks are standing open-mouthed, but there's plenty of oldies waving hands, joining in with Bob. What the hell, he thinks. He grabs his invisible guitar neck, mentally plays the opening chords, sticks his face into the microphone beside Bob and joins in. In that moment, his is as free as a raucous and fairly drunken bird.

3: Rising

Alice, Sunday, 7:50am

There are dark, dirty bruises on Alice's skinny shins. She notices them while pulling on her shoes, black abstract patches mottling her sallow skin. She looks as if she's been kicked by a tiny football team. 'Fuck,' she says quietly, then checks Lorcan, but he hasn't moved, is still deep in his dreams. Probably still head-banging.

The signs are ominous: the headaches, the nausea, the deep drawn out pain that runs through her neck down to her groin. Margaret has given her some Tramadol as the paracetamol just isn't cutting it. She's getting close now, she knows. Has this holiday been enough? What was it she needed from it? To revisit that special summer? To meet her mother on equal terms? To understand death, perhaps?

These are grand themes, the stuff of epic novels by verbose Russians, whereas her week here in Sligo has been barely a short story. There is so much she must explore but time is short.

She's up early. It's Easter Sunday. She had heard Margaret and Frank get up for the eight o'clock mass. They asked last night if she had wanted to go. She was tempted for a moment. Mammy had raised her as an atheist, of course, but the deep faith of her adoptive family had always impressed her. Paul and his family will be there; even Simon, despite the fact that gays have never had a proper home in the church. Perhaps, with her illness marching forward, now would be a good time to explore her options.

But she had already made an arrangement with Mike and she wasn't minded to move it. The boys are still in bed; she pokes her head into the room. Cian is still sleeping, Darragh is awake. She kisses his forehead.

'Are you going out?' he whispers.

'Just going for a coffee. I'll be back in an hour.'

'Can we have our Easter Eggs?'
'Not till after breakfast.'
'Can I have breakfast now?'
'Not till your granny and grandad are back from mass.'
'I'm starving.'
'Starving for chocolate, I'll bet. I'll be back before you know it and then you can make yourself sick on chocolate.'
'I can't though coz Uncle Simon is renting us paddle boards and we can't eat before we swim.'

She has to laugh to hear her little nerdy boy all concerned about swimming. She kisses his head and pulls him in tight.

'I love you, Mom.'
'Love you too.' And she does. In that moment kneeling on the floor of the mobile home, clinging to Darragh, her heart does not have room for so much love.

She is late by the time she drags herself away. The morning is fresh, a fine mist spritzes her face, wetting her clothes more than she would expect but washing away the fog of sleep. Clouds hang low quashing the traffic sounds, leaving a low hum. The sun is a dim disk through the mist, she can stare straight at it.

Mike is on his own in a nearly empty Munnelley's cafe when she gets there. He's checking down the menu, though he must be well familiar with it.

'Hey,' he says. 'Great night on Friday, huh?'
'It was indeed a Good Friday. You certainly know how to get a crowd going.'
'I live for that, Alice. It's my life. Well, that and Brady.'
'Brady?'
'My partner. He was there last night, guy with the red shirt.'
'Ah right, I think I saw him. He was a looker. You are a lucky man.'
'I am.'
'I'm glad.'
'Glad of what?'
'Glad you found yourself, your sexuality. It means, well, I don't have to feel guilty about sitting here talking to you.' She smiles.
'Oh, intriguing. And if I were straight, this would be shameful?' He gives her a gushing grin, all white teeth and innuendo.
'No, but… You were my boyfriend, here I am alone with you again.'
'The horror!'
'I know! So, would you take me?'

'What, here in the cafe, in front of poor young Bridgie there,' he nods at the young kid who is sitting behind the counter waiting for custom to show up. 'How are yeh, Bridgie.'

She nods at him, smiles. 'How are yeh doing, Mike?'

'Can I get a tea and a croissant, when you have a minute. What about you, Alice?'

'A croissant sounds good, and a cappuccino.'

'Sorry, missus,' says Bridgie. 'We don't have a machine. Instant okay?'

'Grand,' she says, stomach turning at the thought.

He turns back to Alice. 'So, I think I'm going to say no, sorry, I won't take you.'

'Ah well, I guess I've lost out on that one.'

'You certainly have. Apart from the old legs not being up to much, I'm a very good lover. And I sing as I go.'

'I'm jealous.'

'But you found your love, your life partner, and from what I've hear from *The Gang*,' he puts on a Dublin accent for that, 'you met him not long after you dumped me.'

'I didn't dump you.'

'Oh,' he puts the back of his hand to his forehead and leans over sideways in mock pain. 'How you broke my heart. But seriously, you left a very deep emotion in my soul. Those lyrics in *Sweet Summer Something*, heartfelt, I kid you not. But it was a beautiful heartache, and, you know, sexuality aside, I still have that joy-pain right here,' he grabs his chest over his heart, 'whenever I think about it.'

'Really?'

'Oh, very much so.'

'You old romantic.' She mocks, but her own heart resonates. *Sweet Summer Something* is a beautiful breakup song. If there's even a chance that it relates to her... Wow, to be immortalised in such a gorgeous creation!

'I was hoping for a *me too*,' he grins.

Alice reaches to his hand, the fingers soft, nails manicured. 'It was a beautiful summer for me, the latter half at least. And you were front and centre. I...'

'Don't worry, Alice. I wasn't fishing for compliments.'

'No, sorry, it's just... My head spins when I think about that time. I came to this place bereft and alienated. I was a London girl, I mean, I was English. I had known nothing but London and Mammy and our beautiful closeted little life. Hell, I didn't even know my father. And look where I ended up. Jesus, I'm gobsmacked now. This place. My family. You. Something happened. My grief dried up. I still don't understand. The badness flowed out of me. And you were part of it.'

'Well. I'm so pleased. I'm glad I helped in some small way.'

'No, it was huge, that's what I'm trying to say.'

'And do you think you're looking for that again? Because of the, you know...'

'The Leukaemia? It's okay, you can say it. I don't know, something brought me back. Maybe I needed to touch that time again, the grief, the sense of loss. Maybe I need to look back...' She stops to take a drink of the coffee, regrets it when she gets the insipid milky taste of the instant. She has to rip a chunk of croissant to cover the taste. 'I remember looking at her one day, like, she had told me and I understood, but you're young, you think it's all going to go on forever. The bubble we lived in, she and I, ah, it was lovely. We were struggling, God knows, but she made everything warm, she filled my life with love. But then I looked at her one day and her face had changed. It was thin, not slim, the way she had always been, but thin, and her eyes had these dark patches around them, and suddenly I knew...' She has to stop and take in a breath as a deep emotion rolls over her. She doesn't cry, but it hits her hard. 'I remember tiny details, the green coral necklace she used to wear, and it went missing after... We never found it. But she died. She died and she died and she died.'

They sit in silence for a few minutes. She can remember talking like that when they first met, when she first sat in here with him. She waits for the feelings to come flooding back, but they don't. Old Alice does not return. Her mother's memory is still distant, still more full of the warm weekends than the cold final days.

'I think I'm ready to move on,' she says at last. 'My battle is different to hers, and I need to find my own strength. Maybe that's what I needed to find out here.'

'Amen to that. I hope you will find it. Oh, speaking of finding things, I've got my boy in London working feverishly on tracing your father.'

'Your boy?'

'Bob, my agent. A grand gentleman in his late fifties, educated at Eton and Cambridge, so I call him my boy just to annoy him. He's recruited his own super-spy, an old Etonian who runs a private detective agency or some nonsense like that.'

'You shouldn't be doing that. You're throwing money into a hole.'

'Ah, one of my favourite pastimes. I've had a big hole dug in my back garden just so I can shovel money into it whenever the mood takes me. Look, it's probably all a big waste of time and maybe it's not even wise, but it's something I can do, a gift I can give. And who knows, maybe something will come of it.'

She finds her mind drifting now, trying to picture them that summer. What would he have seen in her? She had a vague notion that she might have resembled a goth, though it was not a lifestyle choice. Well it was, of course, though she had justified it as a tribute for Mammy. Somehow, Mike had coaxed her out of black and into bright, out of dour and into delight. They had kissed but no more than that. Probably Mike's sexuality was beginning to assert itself, maybe that's why they took it no further.

Also likely that was part of what attracted her to Lorcan. He was sensitive in his own way with his poetry and his vulnerability, but he had an unambiguous masculinity to him; strong but also flawed, foolish at times. She had not expected those flaws might still be featuring at this stage, but perhaps that is just the way life goes. Mike's straightforward sincerity and pure soul had taken her one step, and the rough edges of Lorcan were the fire for her future. Perhaps Mike's honesty was a little too close to her brothers, or cousins as they were at the time; she needed something different to realise herself.

'What was I like?' she asks him.

'You were... Beautiful.'

'No, I mean, well, thanks that's lovely, but my mood. I must have been a pain in the arse, moping around.'

'You were very distracted. You would drift off while I was talking and not know what I said. A bit like you did just a moment ago.' He gives her a broad smile. 'You'd cry for no reason. And you wouldn't talk about it, the loss or the loneliness. You kept saying you needed to get away from thinking about that past. I found that very hard, I have to say, I thought at first you didn't trust me. But I think it was deeper than that. You needed to escape your mother's death.'

'It sounds bad that I wouldn't talk, but I kind of think I was done with it. I think my grief had run its course.'

'It was only a few months.'

'Maybe Mammy had prepared me for it in some way. My grief sank beneath the sea, into that ocean out there, and I've sometimes felt, like, it's there waiting for me. That's what's there at the back of my head, the dark space you know, but it isn't. It's me. I'm afraid I won't be able to bring my kids through it.'

'Wow.'

'Wow, indeed. Jesus, I don't know where that came from.'

'You're just worried about your kids?'

She turns and looks out the window. The business of life is going on, cars driving up and down, families stopping to read the menu, an old man stands outside the newsagents across the road chatting to somebody inside. And here she is sitting with her ex-boyfriend talking intimately about her children and how they would deal with her death. 'Yeah,' she says, turning back to him. 'That's a huge part of it. And I'm worried about Lorcan.'

'Why?'

'He's just, like, he's living in denial. I know he can be a bit of an eejit sometimes, hell, that's half of why I love him, but he will normally snap out of it, see sense. He's still telling me I shouldn't even speak to the boys about it.'

'That's not good.' He takes a bite from his untouched croissant. 'But you know, it can't be too easy on him. Somebody said to me that it can be the partner who suffers more psychologically, the patient gets the care and compassion.'

'And have you heard that the partners often heavily self-medicate with booze?' She regrets the sharpness of the tone. Mike doesn't need to hear her woes.

'Ah,' he says. 'And I guess my pub serving him isn't helping, I suppose.'

'You? Don't be silly, you're not the cause of it.'

'Nor the solution. I'll keep an eye on him.'

'No, don't. He's a grown man. He's not your responsibility. And he's smoking again, was supposed to be stopped years ago. And I don't know what the hell he does during the day. Sometimes I'm glad he comes home smelling of beer and fags, at least I know where he was, even if I don't know with whom.'

Mike sucks in air over his teeth. 'Not my place, doll, but sounds like you and him need to take some time out.'

'That's what we are supposed to be doing here, only…'

'Only he's drinking too much. And around we go. But you need to talk to him.'

She pulls a corner off his croissant and chews on it. 'Ah, I should stop, you didn't come here to hear me gripe about my husband.'

'If there's anything I can do, Alice, just let me know.'

Lorcan, Sunday, 9:10am

Lorcan wakes with a woozy head and stumbles to the tiny toilet. He checks the living room but everybody is out. He slips back to the bedroom and pulls out a naughty naggin, a little bottle of whiskey he bought in *Mike's* last night. His love-hate relationship with constant drinking is slipping more and more into day-drinking; the punishment he is meting on his body leaves him waking with jitters that can only be calmed with another snifter.

The pleasure of *Untime* is gone, or almost so, and the anxiety that the lack of resolution is stoking in him is becoming unbearable. He stubs out his cigarette and stomps inside, feeling like he must confront the *Book*. He opens it, hoping for something, anything.

He comes upon a page from when he was in his twenties. He and Alice had just moved into a flat in a lovely leafy street in Ranelagh, a beautiful Georgian house with three stories over a basement, they had the first floor flat. It was whitewashed, bay-windowed with a crawl-on balcony that Lorcan took advantage of for smoking. It was a great space and a great time. First of all he got out from under the heavy atmosphere of home, his father spiteful and grim in the shed, his mother barely able to find the energy to get out of bed some days. He got to spend all his time with Alice, and this was before the responsibility of children. They both worked hard, but evenings were about people and parties.

That night, Bob had come around. Even then, Alice was not a big fan of Jim, despite the nights round the bonfires in their teens with Jim belting out *Summer in Dublin* and Alice, happy on cider, singing her heart out, but she always had a bit of a soft spot for Biker Bob. They invited him to "warm" the flat and stay over in the spare room. They went out for pizza, had a few pints in the pub and came back to the flat to break into the stash of home-brew bottles in the fridge. They did their own bit of singing even without Jim.

He reads:

Bob came around last night, our first visitor. We went out to eat. There's a bistro just up the street great pizza. The menus are all hand written, and every one of them is slightly different so the food you can order depends on which menu you're handed, and there's a scat-poet-singer who gets everybody up to do their turn. Really fun, we were swapping menus and writing our own. Called in at McGovern's and they had a new craft beer, strong stuff.

We were all fairly ratty when we got back and Alice went to bed. Bob and I pulled up the sash window and sat out on the tiny little balcony having a fag. There has been scaffolding all up the front of the building since before we moved in. There's something wrong with the roof or the chimneys or something. Bob and I were still drinking, I have some home brew. In truth, it's probably not ready for drinking yet but needs must.

So we were sitting there looking up at the scaffolding, next thing he's hanging out of one of the horizontal bars, his feet hanging over the gap. Then I was hanging out of the bar, then we were climbing up, and climbing down. We got onto the roof, swung across in front of the next door flats, and back again.

We were standing on the roof, in the darkness. 'Dare you to jump for that bar,' says Bob, pointing at a scaffolding bar that's maybe three feet out from the roof. It was just about doable so I jumped.

I was half way across when the thought suddenly hit me. It was like a light came on, I could suddenly see the truth. It did not matter if I made the leap or not. It did not matter if I held that bar or I fell. I would not die this night, or tomorrow night or next month or next year. The Book will see to that.

So I pulled my hands in. I closed my eyes and rolled into a ball and let the air scream past me until...

Until I woke, and picked up my pen, and started to write.

Had he deliberately fallen? Let himself die, believing he would wake and be scribbling that into the *Book*?

And here's the real question: did he trigger it?

Had he really intended to fall? It cannot be told; the book tinkers with his mind. Remembering can be like recalling a dream in the middle of a migraine. On top of that, he was totalled on home-brew. Yet it was there in the *Book*, and still a trace of it tracking round his head. Fallen, or leapt to near certain death?

Because if it was an act of volition, then could he find a way to waken the *Book* again? What if he walked into the sea? Jumped out of the top window of the hotel? Drove Bob's bike off a cliff?

He feels at first a little thrill, a sharp excitement. Maybe he has found a path to escape this cycle of painful and endless waiting. To others he might appear as a prick, drinking and smoking to celebrate her sickness. He can say nothing, explain nothing, talk to nobody but Rhia whose winds swing with wild delight to any compass corner that suits her on a given day.

Once *Untime* ends, all of this stupid cycle of drinking and smoking and self-centred disarray will be wiped and, once the illness is erased, they can be happy together. Just one act. The *Book* will save him, of course it will, and in doing so, it will take away this pathetic dream of Leukaemia. Just one small act of selflessness.

One act, one brief act. To fill the pockets of his jacket with stones and walk out into the sea, not stopping till the waves tip him face first into the foam and the weight pulls him down. But he will stop, of course, the cold water-shock shocking his legs, driving him back.

Or he could stand above a cliff looking down at the sea and, with one mighty heave, throw himself into a hover and then a fall. Yet he cannot walk within a metre if a cliff edge without the belly burrowing out of him.

Or to take Bob's bike and race at a riotous speed along the twisted highways of Sligo until that one bend that the bike could not take and…

And he is a fool to even think it. There is no way he can bring himself to take his own life, at least not without a skinful on him. He's like some farce version of Hamlet, muttering about ghosts and books but unable to act.

He takes another deep draft of the naggin, nearly finishing it. His body is booze-adapted, even this whiskey will not be enough to render him insensible, or capable of self harm. If he cannot draw a conclusion to this *Untime*, and the fun is largely finished, he can at least benumb himself to get through it.

Alice, Sunday, 9:50am

Alice is walking back to the mobile home when a text comes in. It's from Mike, and she wonders if she's sent some wrong signal by having coffee, but it's unrelated.

"A. Word from Bob, first trace of father. Was signed in eighties to MISTER MUSIC agents, session musician, reaching out to contacts. More soonest xx M."

She stops at the gate of the campsite. Sligo's skies are a phenomenon, a cloudscape that changes with each moment. It can be blue, then white, then black, all within an hour. Radiant puffballs shine out in front of ominous monsters. Cracks pass glorious fans of light as if God himself were just hiding, so that you stand tall and say yes, yes the world is a beautiful place, and then in a minute it is gone and the mist washes the joy from you.

Thoughts of her father leave her with trepidation. If he were still alive, if they could talk, even meet, what might she learn about those years, about her mother? But what could he say that would make him into anything other than a man who put his own music career in front of his wife and his daughter, left his lover to die alone? Part of her hoped it would be an empty lead. Another side is excited to see what will turn up.

Despite the morning light, the wetting mist still washes her face, makes her feel vital. The pain in her neck is throbbing, her stomach is acid. Still she feels bright and alive. On a gentle whim she turns left just inside the campsite gate instead of the normal path towards the sea. She will explore other corners.

She is strolling down an avenue that features fashionable homes and cabins, the higher cost end of the site, when she sees Jim and Rhia through the window of an ostentatious cabin. She is about to lift a hand to wave when she realises Jim is holding Rhia by he hair, twisting it to the side so her head is bent.

It is a violent scene, vicious. Alice feels a gut fear rising, flooding her eyes. A man, primal and angry. A woman, weak and twisted. Alice is frozen, wanting to scream, wanting to run in and stop it, wanting to run away.

Jim throws Rhia roughly, her head nearly hitting a cupboard. Rhia runs out the door. Jim turns and sees Alice through the window, puts on a broad smile, then waves, takes a swig from a can.

Rhia emerges, panicked.

'Rhia,' says Alice.

'Oh,' Rhia is flustered, face flushed, eyes puffed. There is a red rash on her temple near where she had her bruise. 'Oh.' With one hand, she sweeps hair back over her face, then becomes, like a magic trick, a different person. 'Hi, Alice.'

'Are you okay?'

'I'm fine, don't be worrying.'

The bruise-to-be is still pulsing, otherwise she might think she had misunderstood what she saw.

'No. You're not fine, Rhia. You are a victim of domestic violence.'

'It's not his fault.'

'It's never the man's fault, but it's always the woman's face. Rhia, you have to stop this.'

'No.'

'You must. I… I can't stand aside any more. I've known, kind of known, but always let it ride. That ends here. He can't be let get away with it.'

'Alice, no, you don't understand. This is my love, and my losing, to love is to lose. I would lose my life to save my soul, lose my face to give my all. Do you understand? It's that deep. I would bare my veins if he needed my blood. This is how I live, it's not simple. I love, I love before darkness and after the dawn, I love through the pain and the pity.'

Alice is stunned. The words, though jumbled and lost to her senses, carry the emotion. She can see that Rhia believes, honestly believes, that what she is experiencing is love. And she can believe that what Rhia feels is more powerful than any emotion that Alice has encountered.

'I can't do it. Can't turn my back.'

'No, no, you don't understand. You can't understand. It's not like you think.'

'It's exactly like I think.'

'Jesus, Alice. This is hard enough. All I ask is that you keep out of it. I know what you think you see but you're wrong. Just… Just don't interfere.'

She stops and shivers, her hands wrench in a funny gesture that Alice can't read, then she turns and walks back to the cabin.

Alice stands shaking, stupefied, barely able to contain the anger. She saw his heavy hand, her hair in his fist. Could her love become so obsessive? Could love ever be reduced to such dust, dirt and shame?

Through the window, she watches Rhia stand while Jim hugs her, kisses her hair, rocks her gently. Sickening. How can she do that?

She has to go in, tell it like it is. It's not right that Rhia accepts this awful excuse for tenderness from a drunken dope.

She takes a step towards the door but suddenly the skin of her stomach explodes with pain, a violent urgency seizes her bowel, she has to squeeze her bum to prevent an accident and, woozy with agony, she runs in the direction of Margaret's mobile home.

Alice, Sunday, 10:10am

Alice only just makes it to the bathroom, and then has to make a call on which end first. The next few minutes are deeply unpleasant and not a little sore. She's conscious of the close confines of the mobile home, not the best isolator of sound or smell. She has been through many bouts of illness but this is worse. There can be no doubt her symptoms are getting much worse. How long can she let this go on?

Margaret hands her towels and sends her to the shower.

'It's a mess,' Alice says.

'If that's the worst mess I have to deal with, the life's letting me off easy, now go and get yourself fresh.'

Ten minutes later, wrapped in a freshly laundered bathrobe, she feels much better. The nausea is all but gone, the ache has bubbled down the level of general unpleasantness. Margaret is warming chicken broth on the hob.

There's a little electric coal-effect fire that's pumping out heat; Alice crumbles beside it, wraps herself against her shivers. Margaret sits down beside her, chicken soup at the ready.

'Do you want me to feed you?'

'I'm not dead yet.'

'Jesus, it's only soup, don't bite the hand off me.'

'Sorry. And sorry for saying sorry.' She takes the bowl, sips some of the warm broth, but a burning wash spreads through her and she puts it down.

'You need to go to the doctor, or the hospital maybe.'

'I'm not quite done here.'

'What the hell does that mean? You're not well, it's obvious.'

'I'm not ready. I'm not... Empty. I think I came here for something and I haven't got it yet.'

'I don't know what that means.'

'Neither do I.'

She stares at the swirling surface of her soup, thick with noodles. The ebbs and eddies speak to warmth and wholesomeness.

'I remember Mammy in the good times. I remember how close we were, in our little flat, no, in half a dozen flats getting smaller each time but I never cared. It just meant we were closer. I don't remember her being ill. There's, like, some mugginess that hides her from me. I remember that summer, but not the year before. I needed life, needed to breathe, but I never meant to negate her, to neutralise her in my mind. I don't want to fade, like she did.'

'Oh, Alice.'

'I thought I would find her here, but I've found... Strange things, odd things, some bad, some good. But not her.'

'Do you remember her braiding your hair?'

'Yes. Tiny little string braids. My neck would ache from holding still.'

'Do you remember the stall she ran for a while, Camden market, she made those mobiles with feathers and sticks and found things?'

'Yes, of course. I still make mobiles. I got that from her.'

'Do you remember *Tenderly's*?'

'The cafe in Ealing? Just beside our flat, the last one. Big steaming mugs of hot chocolate. We used to go there every Saturday morning and we'd sit for hours reading.'

'Isn't that enough?'

'Yes. No. No, it's not enough. I want more. And I want my boys to have more than *Emily's Amazing Ice Cream Emporium*.'

'What's that?'

'You don't want to know.'

'You are so much more. You always will be.'

'I'm not ready yet, not ready to fail.'

'And that's why you have to get help for your health.'

'I will. I will go to the hospital tomorrow. No, Tuesday, Monday's a holiday, there won't be any proper doctors. I just want this one last weekend.'

Margaret sighs, unconvinced. 'Will you make it to Tuesday? If you can't even eat soup?'

She takes the spoon up, tastes the soft chicken flavour. No burn this time, the soup has cooled, her stomach has eased.

'I'll eat this,' she says. 'Or you can drive me there now.'

She does manage a few spoonfuls. She's wound up with anxiety, but not nauseous.

'Wait a minute, the boys, the Easter Eggs…'

'Don't be worrying. We gave them breakfast when we got back from mass. Lorcan was up and gave them their eggs, then I had eggs for them, Simon had eggs for them, Paul had eggs for them, Beth and Jackie had eggs for them. They did not go short, and then they were too excited to wait for you, couldn't wait to go paddle boarding. But don't be worrying, they'll be back for lunch, or you can pop down the beach and see them at it.'

'God, of all the times to miss Easter morning.'

Her phone rings. She pulls it out. 'It's my boss. That's weird.' She answers. 'Catherine? What's up?'

'Sorry to call Alice, I hate to upset you. It's nothing serious, at least I hope not.'

'Okay.'

'It's about Eamo. His uncle Pluto. Apparently the guy is going around knocking on doors looking for Eamo.'

'No surprise there. I'm just hoping Eamo's still keeping his head low. We got him a job in a bar, like, a music bar, and he loves it. Adores it, I mean I really think we've turned a corner.'

'That's brilliant, but Pluto's boys pushed their way into the methadone clinic this morning. They had your name.'

'How would they know my name?'

'Who knows? I've always said our consultancy rooms are too open. Anybody in the waiting room will see you. Course, it could also be that Eamo was talking to his family about you. He's always thought the world of you. Anyway, nobody on duty knew anything, so no crisis, but they're serious. One of the porters was taken in a neck hold. A window got smashed. And they threatened to come back, so I've got onto the security agency to get some serious beef in here for tomorrow and ongoing.'

'Jesus. That's the last thing we need.'

'I'm thinking, if they did find out. You know, if they got the address of the hostel he's in…'

'Yeah, I might see if I can get him somewhere to stay. The guy, Mike, who gave him the job. Maybe he's got a spare room or something.'

'That might be no harm, though to be honest, I'm more concerned about you. If he found out where you were…'

'He won't, I'm safe.'

'Just stay safe. How are you doing anyway? Is the holiday helping?'
'Well…'

Lorcan, Sunday, 2:30pm

'You see the thing is,' says Jim, pausing to empty a third of his pint into his gullet. 'Women are their own worst enemy, yeh get me. They don't know what they want. They only think they know.'

Lorcan is holding back. One on one, in the mostly empty bar in the afternoon, Jim is hard work. The man can sing, and get the excitement going in a gang, but he is an objectionable bastard on his own. He is racist, sexist, pretty much anything-ist that is going, as long as you give him he opportunity to rant on.

Worst of all is his disregard — too weak a word — his misogyny towards Rhia. Lorcan knows the inside story. He has seen the bruises on her naked body. Twenty years he has kept his oath, sworn in sincerity to Rhia after she came back from death. He tells nobody, not that the *Book* would let him; it would spin his head and scramble his intent. Worse, he treats Jim as a friend, stays close to him, rescues him from his own stupidity, sees him into taxis, diverts him away from all-nighters insofar as anybody can. There are times, not infrequently, when he feels like hitting the man, not that he's ever hit anybody, but the frustration is fierce. Jim's charisma is a vehicle, it lets Lorcan overlook the loathsome side, lets him ease into the hedonism. Left alone to listen to this hot air and blather, Lorcan wonders why he is prepared to tolerate it. Is it only his oath to Rhia?

He had finished his naggin. He was still largely sober after it, but just got an edge of buzz from the last glug. He had decided to slip out before Alice got back, maybe find an off-license, but then he'd seen the bar was open, and indeed the music bar round the back, so he slipped in for one.

His head was heaving. He hates this dilemma. He does not want to accept the Leukaemia. The thought is too horrifying. But rejecting it is turning him into a total prick. Worse than Jim.

He was halfway through his second when Jim arrived in, "just checking how young Eamo's getting on." He sat down and called up a pint, not even pretending he was going to pay.

Lorcan is on his fourth now, Jim has caught up with him. Eamo is mopping the floor with a zest that seems unwarranted, whistling some tune as he goes, popping behind the bar whenever a fresh round is ordered. There's three or four others sitting around with newspapers or laptops. And Jim's voice thundering as he trots out every high-horse that takes his fancy.

'I mean, women's lib, yeh know, I'm a big fan and all. Women have had a rough time of it. Why shouldn't they get the chance to work, it's only right. Rhia loves her job, and look at me, can't get a job. We'd be right screwed if Rhia didn't work, so it's great and all that they can work now and earn as much as the men. But that doesn't mean the man's place in the home is usurped, like. Am I right now, Lorco?'

'It's great to hear you're so modern in your thinking.'

Mike appears from the back of the bar and calls: 'hey, Eamo, can you come in the back, I need a word.'

He turns and sees them sitting at the bar. 'Lorcan,' he says, 'didn't expect you in so early.'

'Ah, you know, on my holidays.'

'Holidays? Okay, good stuff. How'r'ye, Jim. Come on, Eamo.' The two of them disappear into the back.

'So anyways,' Jim goes on, 'poor ould Rhia, she gets herself so confused. Can't tell up from down some time. That's when a man comes into his own, guide and support, yeh know what I mean. Keep her on the straight and narrow.'

'Who do you think is going to be up for the Six Nations this year,' says Lorcan, unable to bear any more of the man's toxic talk.

'Well now France, yeh see, everybody thinks they're gonna be on top, but if they lose Dupont now, I think they will be screwed.'

A few minutes later, Eamo emerges again, followed by Mike.

'See yiz in a bit, lads,' he says, and walks out the door.

'Everything alright, Mike?' asks Jim.

'Ah yeah, not a bother, just going to put Eamo up in my spare room upstairs for a few days. It was Alice was on the phone to me, Lorcan, she was asking me to give him a place. She was a bit surprised to hear you were here. I think it might be best of you toddled on home.'

A flush of anger spurs up Lorcan's neck. He has to pull himself back from responding, asking why the hell a barman is telling his wife where he is, and what business is it of his anyway. He decides against saying anything and stands up.

'You wouldn't lend us a tenner?' asks Jim.

Outside, he nearly stumbles and has to grab a railing to steady himself. He had thought the beer wasn't really going to his head, despite the whiskey earlier, but he feels well woozy now. He takes extra care crossing the road, realising his judgement is likely impaired. He has to focus on walking straight, particularly as the mobile home comes in sight.

He wonders momentarily if it's a good idea to go back at all. The whole thing is a crock. He's supposed to be just having a go, enjoying himself with no consequences, but he's actually just feeling shit the whole time. Alice is going to be pissed off, would it really be any worse if he just didn't go back to her till tonight. He could go back to the bar.

Back to the bar and listen to Jim talking crap for another few hours, on the other hand, maybe going home would be better. Maybe, a few drinks in, he can tell her how he feels. Maybe he can slip out something about the *Book*, not that being drunk has ever helped before.

'Oh well,' he says to himself as he gets to the door. 'I'll go in and tell her I love her. It's time to knuckle down.'

Alice, Sunday, 3:20pm

A deep unsettlement shifts Alice's gut when she hears that Lorcan is in the pub in the middle of the afternoon. She has asked him to stand with her, though God knows she should never have to ask. She has tolerated so much; he is drinking nightly, has spent no time with his children, hell, Simon has been a better dad to them. And he has given her no love.

Now, he's drinking in the day, not for the first time. She can barely hold the bile back as she politely asks Mike to encourage Lorcan to come home. When Mike texts back a couple of minutes later to say he's on the way, she asks Margaret if she could go and check on the boys. Margaret can clearly see the situation and leaves.

'Just look after yourself, won't you,' she says as she closes the door.

Alice sits and takes long slow breaths. She does not want to react in anger. Words must be had, rules laid down. This cannot be tolerated, but if her temper rules then she will say things she may regret.

Why should I regret? she thinks. The fault is all his, entirely his. He's never been the most empathic of people, but he's always been loving and caring. Since the diagnosis, he's fallen more and more into miserable habits, drinking and smoking and looking after himself. No, there's nothing to regret here. It's time to take stock.

She hears him at the door, he has to scrabble a couple of times before he can grasp the handle. He pulls the door open and falls in onto the floor, landing heavily.

'Jesus!'

'Uh, sorry, I tripped.'

She runs to help him up. The odour of booze and cigarette smoke is choking. He is slurring his words. He has to take three goes before he can get his legs under him.

'You're pissed. How much have you been drinking?'

'I'm just on holidays…'

'Fuck's sake, Lorcan, you're totally fucking stocious. It's the middle of the afternoon. What the hell?'

'Why can't I have a little drink with my friends?'

The black hole at the back of her head bursts. A pressure that has been building rages forth. The site of Jim beating Rhia. Pulling her by the hair. Smacking her face to the table. Rhia's silent acceptance. That savage is the friend. Hot sparks spray through her head bouncing, burning.

'Friend. That fucking wife-beating drunk is not your friend, he's a fucking monster. And I don't know why the hell you ever kept him in our lives except that you're still sniffing after Rhia. What is it? You think she might take you back once your wife croaks, is that it?'

'God, Alice, I don't… It's not that.'

'What the fuck is it then?'

'It's the *Book*?'

'What fucking book? What the fuck are you talking about?'

'I… I said it.' There's a visage of surprise over the twisted drunkenness on his face, as if he's just figured something out. 'I just told you about the *Book*. I was able to.'

'I don't believe this. Listen, Lorcan, I have fucking had enough of this. You've gone too far this time.'

'No you have to listen, this is important.'

'No you listen. Listen to me. I've had enough. Don't you get that? Can't you get that into that thick head of yours?'

'No, you see Rhia died —'

'Stop. Stop now. This is just shite.'

'But she —'

'No just fucking stop.' The hate has risen too high now. She slaps, she spits, she shouts. She has managed so much, it is larger than life. It is no longer containable. All the ineffable energy built by the illness speeds out of her with such force and ferocity that spins as she smacks out again and again.

'Jesus, stop for God's sake, I'm trying to fucking tell you something.' He puts his hands over his head in defence.

'Tell me hole.'

'Fuck. Stop.'

But she doesn't. She goes on and on, the rain, the thunder, the cacophony, the energy, the violence. It grows like a volcanic pyroclastic flow, spewing and spurting and outside of any control. There is pain in her hands from hitting, in her arms now, in her shoulders from the effort of it, but it's clearing. The pent up rage has drained from her and she is slowing down.

Lorcan takes the opportunity to run to the door and out, slamming it hard behind him.

And then she's done. Spent. Exhausted. Empty.

She stands, panting, unable to comprehend what has happened, an elemental force has overcome her and left her dehumanised, diminished.

Than the pain. Hard hitting, raw, penalising, penetrating. It sears from her neck to her bum, burning fiercely. She cries out as she bends double. She cannot straighten, but is brought low, to the floor, to hands and knees.

'Lorcan,' she shouts. The agony is beyond anything, belittling childbirth. To move is to drive a spike in her head, to stay still is worse. She crawls, excruciatingly towards the door. She has to climb the door, pulling herself handhold by handhold.

She gets the door open. Lorcan is not there. The car is not there.

Lorcan, Sunday, 3:30pm

Her words drove him to humiliation. He was two inches tall. A scolded dog with his nose pressed in pee. He could hardly breathe from the effort. But out of it he lifted a new strength. He called the *Book* by name, gave it voice for the first time since he met her. He could have told her. If she would listen.

She did not. She beat him. Alice. His love. His life. His divinity and his presence and his all. She hit him.

Thoughts swirl. His blood is high. There is a now or never in the air.

The moment. That moment on the scaffolding, the world landscaped below, his fingers failing to find a hold.

The car keys are in his pocket. Habit. He opens it, sits into it. Will somebody stop him?

The controls are curious, different. He presses Start. Has to remember to push down the clutch. It starts. He moves slowly, slowly between the mobile homes. As his blood pounds, his vision leaps.

He makes it to the road, turns right, avoid the town.

He speeds up, remembering the bike, the thrill, the flying.

There is somewhere he needs to go. There's a ridge. The road falls away. He will go there. Where? It's this way, or is it?

The road bends and he nearly doesn't. He has to spin both hands to pull back onto the left. Through narrow country road tight lined with hedgerow he heaves, skirting past passing cars, their drivers' eyes wide.

He gets to the main road and turns left. Much wider here. He brings the needle up to one hundred, one-twenty, one-forty, was he going this fast on the bike? What was that number he got to? One-eighty? He has it written down in his *Book* — but was it miles or kilometres —

The truck, when it comes, is almost incidental. The road is clear. He checks his speed. The road is not clear.

The car spins straight under the high bumper of the oncoming truck. There is a monstrous noise: SKREEEEESHKAWWWWWWPHLUNK!!....

Lorcan, Sunday, 9:10am

There is a pen in his hand and he is writing. There is no choice in it, no volition. His hand moves, words appear.

I was drunk. Very drunk. Rotten drunk. I have been a shit-head since Alice was diagnosed. I hate the thing that I have become. I don't know why. I couldn't stop.

I was in the pub with Jim. Mike said I should go home. I could barely stagger home. Alice went mental. I don't blame her, the state of me falling in the door in the middle of the afternoon. Her family are all so good, her brothers, and there's me out of my tree. She went completely off on one and next thing she was hitting me and slapping me and I couldn't say anything except that I could nearly talk about the Book, for the first time, words started to come out of me but it was too late and she wouldn't listen and I ran. Like a coward I ran.

I got into the car. There was this mad notion going through my head. I could trigger the Book. That's all I wanted. Trigger the Book, undo the Untime, get back to where this fucking nightmare all started. That is what I wanted. I didn't want to hurt anybody. I just wanted the nightmare to end. I wanted it to end.

So I drove like a fucking lunatic. I was off my head, no concentration. It was only a matter of time. And it happened. I slammed into a truck. I went right under the truck, saw its axle through the shattering glass.

I saw the scene, like I was a fucking drone hovering. Nobody was hurt. The truck driver was hysterical, but unharmed. Thank God. If there is a God, thank You.

He stops. He breathes. Was he breathing at all a moment ago?

A moment ago. What is a moment? Time is a tacky thing, plastic.

Memories of memories, none of them real. *Now* is unreal, fluid, ungraspable. The drunkenness is still in his head, but not the drink.

The image of the truck, its underside, its axle inches from his nose, is active at the centre of his head.

But it's not, because it never happened. It simply never happened. If he drove now, a little woozy but basically sober because he has not started day on the whiskey in his naggin, he would find no crash, no shattered glass, no tyre marks, no wreckage. It did not happen, and unless he chooses it, it will not happen.

No mater how many times he has been through this, it is still incomprehensible. It has happened. It has not happened. That is all.

He looks at the *Book*, sitting innocently on his lap as he lies in bed. The writing is fresh, the ink still not dried into the dense skin. Flicking back, other pages, younger handwriting, each event chosen by the Book, not by him.

He has waited for this, burned bridges with his family, for this moment. But it's not right. The diagnosis has not been wiped out. That did happen. He is still in Sligo, in the mobile home in Enniscrone. The Book has not unwound all that *Unime*. It was never *Untime*.

'Shit!'

All the drinking, the smoking. Hell, Alice hates him. That last freak out, beaten bitterly into his brain, has not happened, will not happen, but the emotion that drove it is still there, still unrequited. He must repair the damage he has done. How can he do that? He has sailed too far, knew he was sailing too far. Convinced himself it would come good but there had always been a voice, a doubt, an undoing that he failed to heed.

Tears come to him, brutal burning tears that sting his eyes. He might well have broken his marriage, broken his family.

Fuck. Fuck all that. Alice is dying.

It is there. It rushes back into his head, a flood of badness. The doctors office, the word Leukaemia wafted by the doctors clipped voice, the awful tearing void, a vast hole. Stomach sickening. He had bridged the void with the *Book*, but that now is exposed as the sham, a shameless crutch, a tattered parachute.

Unless —

Could the *Book* repeat? Could it work again, covering this time but going back further? He has triggered it, his action has set off this chain. He flicks through, ignoring the stabbing head pains that smack him as his eyes graze each page, searching for something that might be a sense of how to proceed. Back through violent illnesses, through the bike accident, the fall from the roof, the impact from the bus, back to…

Back to the first entry he had made. Could it be? The previous page, illegible but strong, not his handwriting, flicks back. Yes, this is it.

I am playing in my room. Mam and Dad are fighting. It's really loud and I'm closing my ears so I don't hear. I push

He can read it. That has never happened before. His head is tormented, something is unwinding his mind like a spiderweb collapsing. The next bit blurs, he can't see it, then he can read:

and he's there with Mam in the hall and Dad is shouting at him get out get out and he's using bad words. I shouldn't write them.
  Mam takes us

Again his mind is pulled sideways, like popping a childproof medicine bottle. He skips a few lines:

putting Doircheas and me into the back seat and Dad is banging on the roof. Doircheas is crying and I'm holding her but she's screaming. Mam yells to shut up and now she's using bad words. He drives off

He loses it again, then:

out of a laneway or something cause he's right there and he jumps onto the bonnet of the car and we're still driving only we're not cause he can't control it with Dad on there and the car goes funny. We're not on the road. The road is above and below and above and Doircheas slips and

And he woke up with the *Book*. Flashes of it are falling into place. There was another man. Who was he?

It must have been on the main road, near the house. There's a laneway, he remembers, his father could have run through that from the house and cut them off. But why?

Questions and no answers. He has visibility into the murk, the mire of his childhood that has always been blinded to him. He tries again to read, but the words fade from him as if a net curtain has been drawn over them. He tries to remember more, push his mind back but again the gap is closing.

That was the time when the *Book* came to him, when his life changed. Can he dig into this information? Get closer to the source? Why did his family never talk about this? And who is the man? Did the *Book* come from him? Could he be of help?

Lorcan's hands shake. For the first time in his life he has a lead. He needs to talk to his mother, his father. How long would it take to drive back?

A shiver runs through him when he thinks of driving, remembering the wreckage, but he's not drunk and he's not going to drink. He walks into the bathroom, runs the water, and pours the naggin of whiskey into the drain. Enough of this. It's has become time, it is time to become.

Alice, Sunday, 9:50am

She sees Jim and Rhia through the window. Jim is holding Rhia by he hair, twisting it to the side so her head is bent.

It is a violent scene, vicious. Alice feels a gut fear rising and filling the universe. It floods her eyes. A man, primal and angry. A woman, weak and twisted. Alice is frozen, wanting to scream, wanting to run in and stop it, wanting to run away.

Jim throws Rhia roughly, her head nearly hitting a cupboard. Rhia runs out the door. Jim turns and sees Alice through the window, puts on a broad smile, then waves, takes a swig from a can.

Rhia emerges, panicked.

'Rhia,' says Alice.

'Oh,' Rhia is flustered, face flushed, eyes puffed. There is a red rash on her temple near where she had her bruise. 'Oh.' With one hand, she sweeps hair back over her face, then emerges, a magic trick, a different person. 'Hi, Alice.'

'Hi, I...' *Say something, for fuck's sake say something.* 'I was just out walking.'

'Okay. I was just putting something in the bin, I, oh, I must have forgotten it.'

She turns to go back inside. *Say something. You have to.*

But she doesn't. She stands open mouthed, amazed at her own emptiness.

Then she vomits, a spume of instant coffee and croissant splats the sandy grass. She turns to run and only just makes it to the mobile home before the other end opens.

Lorcan, Sunday, 1:50pm

Lorcan's memories are a mess. Strong swells of thoughts wash in and back, shifting the same sand over and over. He must go, it is an inescapable compulsion, he is so close to the truth. He may solve the puzzle, right now. Then: what the hell is he thinking? For the first time, he has clarity on his own stupidity and selfishness and what does he do but jump in the car and abandon Alice and the boys. Back and forth, over and over. He has to make himself drive well below the speed limit as he's struggling to pay full attention, the sight of the truck's axle so close to his face still swirling around his head.

Stupid, stupid, stupid, he berates himself continuously, but keeps driving.

He had stopped into the *Circle K* in Dromore West shortly after leaving Enniscrone, realising he was low on fuel. He had looked at the lonely sandwiches there but felt too queasy. By the time he gets to Dublin, he's starving, he hasn't eaten anything today. At least, not today since the *Book* apparently wound back part of the *Untime*. It's not helping his driving. He thinks about stopping into roadside services but elects to keep going.

He pulls up outside his house, there's a few Tesco Finest pizzas in the freezer, he'll grab one before heading to his folks. He reaches for his phone to check for messages. He'd sent a text before he left, very curt, asking for trust. He's surprised his phone hasn't been hopping with messages from her.

It hasn't been hopping because it's not there. He checks the floor, the glovebox, pockets, door pockets, the floor again, the boot. Nowhere. Where the hell is it? Could he have left it behind? No, he had it when he got into the car, sent the message to Alice.

'How'r'ye, Lorcan.' A voice comes from behind him as he's

rummaging in the boot. He turns to find a short man with a bald head and a muscle-taut tee-shirt despite the cool afternoon. His hands are flexed by his side, as if he's used to holding something. He has a familiar look to his face, but Lorcan can't place him. Must be a neighbour; he's terrible at remembering the neighbours, barely knows the people living across from them to say hello to. He's probably talked to this man at some local funeral after a few beers.

'Ah, hi, how are you?' he says, feigning recognition.

'Alice in?' the man says, nodding in the direction of the house. 'Not seen her about, was just wondering and all.'

'Ah, no, we've been away.'

'Right, somewhere good I hope. And yiz're back?'

'Eh, no, I just popped back for something.' Should he say something about Alice's illness? It's not a secret, but how many neighbours know he can't say. 'She's, eh, she's still down there.'

'Now, isn't that nice, that she gets to get away, at a time like this and all.'

'It is, yeah, it's great. Her mother has the mobile home down there so we're staying with her.'

'Fab-you-lus, bud. We used to go to me Ma's mobile up in Skerries, lovely days them were. She's not in Skerries is she? I mean, small world and all, like, isn't it?'

'Ah no, out the west, it is. Enniscrone, you know, Sligo.'

'Sligo? Aren't yiz the lucky duckers and all, Sligo, sure I'd love to stay there. Listen, good catching up, right, I'll see yiz around. Give me love to Alice, won't yeh.'

He strides off up the road, arms swinging with gym-built stiffness. Weird man, thinks Lorcan. He watches him, hoping to catch sight of which house he lives in but he climbs into a car, an black Audi that Lorcan doesn't recognise, and drives away.

Right, he thinks, where the hell is that phone. There's a mobile in the house, a brick phone with a pay-as-you-go SIM card, he bought it last year as a stop-gap for Alice when she lost hers. They kept it in case they ever wanted to give Cian a phone, in case they needed him to stay in touch on a sleepover or something. He goes inside and gets it, turns it on. Fifty percent battery. He dials his own number and sticks his head in the car while it rings but there's no sound, not even the buzz you might hear if it's on silent.

Could he have left it when he stopped for petrol? Must be. He will call in on the way back.

He gets a pizza into the oven and calls Alice but it rings out. He doesn't have Margaret's number, or the brothers. He sends Alice a message: "Got to Dublin. Need to see my folks. Lost my phone somewhere, using this number for now. Will be right back. Love you. Trust me."

Trust me, indeed. What right has he to talk of trust? Cheap words washing down cheap deeds. He pulls his cigarettes out of his pocket. He wants one, here in the kitchen, not skulking in the garden. Funny how he got do Dublin with fags but no phone, a statement of intent, maybe.

There has been no *Untime*. All that nonsense, drink as much as he like, smoke as much as he like, act in whatever way he wanted, all of it now is carved in reality, will not be erased by the *Book*. He was sneaking off to meet Rhia, secretly. She kissed him. He was drinking and kissing in secret in the middle of the day. Jesus!

Enough! Deep damage has been done, bridges have been burned. The first rule of holes, fool: stop digging!

He may yet be wrong, there may be another way, if he can just get some more information. He has his first lead in his life, he needs to grab it.

However, some things need to change.

He pulls the fags from the packs, rips them and rips them again so that there is a hash of tobacco and torn paper which he flings in the bin. Step one.

He eats the pizza quickly, burning the top of his mouth with tomato sauce, then runs out the door. He should probably phone ahead, always does before visiting, but today is different.

Doircheas answers the door and gives him a quizzical look.

'You're back early?' she says.

'Hello, Doircheas, and yes, well, no, actually, I… Look, long story. I need to talk to Mam. And Dad too, probably. But Mam first.'

'Lorcan, you can't just—'

'I'm sorry. Sorry for bursting in, but this is really important. Life and death important.'

'Mam isn't great.' She lowers her voice. 'She hasn't really been sleeping. She's in an awful state. I don't want you upsetting her.'

He's never seen Doircheas so ruffled, and so assertive. She's normally a model of calm and quietude. Is his presence here upsetting her, or does she have some inkling of his purpose. He remembers the words he wrote in the *Book*, Mam putting Doircheas into the back seat. She was there. What does she remember? What might she not want to remember.

His mother, as ever, is in the front room on her orthopaedic chair, but she is slumped, her back bent like she's aged another ten years. The change is so stark that he fears for her; she is too young to look so old. The white hair and wine-stained skin of her face could mark her as eighty.

The television is on, probably the Coronation Street Omnibus, but her eyes, still bright despite all, stare out the window.

'Hi, Mam,' he says as he pulls up a chair to sit beside her.

She starts at his voice, looks on him like he was an intruder.

'It's Lorcan, Mam,' he says.

'I know it's you. Do you think I'm gone gaga?'

'Sorry, no,' he laughs. 'Just you looked a bit… Taken aback.'

'No grandchildren again?'

'No sorry. They're still in Sligo. I'll bring them round. I will. Next week.'

She nods, and her eyes edge back to the window.

'I'll make the tea, so,' says Doircheas. 'I'll leave you to it.' She leaves the door open as she goes to the kitchen.

'It's wonderful, isn't it,' says Helen, an edge of awe in her voice.

He looks at the window, and realises the apple blossom tree is in full bloom, its blossoms diffusing a mystical luminosity into the room, making it brighter than the daylight outside. He had not noticed, so intent on truth. Her eyes are sprinkled with light like icing sugar. Smiles suffuse her cheeks.

How many times has she gazed upon this tree, commanding the front garden since he was a child, since… Since when? He cannot quite remember when it came to be here. Was it there before the incident he has come to question?

There were happy times when the apple light shone. Sadness would lift from her, all through his teens as her solidity melted into this soft cheese of mental muddle. The tree matured, becoming broader, brighter, bolder, while she became smaller, less significant in its glow.

'Yes. Yes, it's wonderful. I always liked that tree.'

'I miss him, you know.'

'Who? Dad?'

'No.'

'Who do you miss, Mam?'

'Every year, when this time comes around. I feel the warmth off the tree and it's like he's here.'

'Who's here, Mam?'

'What?' Her eyes flick back to him, obfuscated in shadow as the shine from the apple blossom fades from them. She looks like she has just woken from a dream.

'You were talking about somebody. You said you missed him. The tree, it reminds you?'

'Did I? I'm not sure. Was there…? Was it… Barry? He planted it.'

She seems to be losing the thread again. 'Barry? I don't remember any Barry?'

'He planted the tree, you see. That's why it reminds me.'

He looks out at the glowing tree. He has a half memory, a gardener, somebody working in the garden. 'And it's him you miss?'

But she has left the room, following her eyes into the divinity of light. She starts to hum, *Raglin Road* he thinks it is.

'Mam?'

She takes no notice of him, but turns instead to *Coronation Street*. He goes out to the kitchen where Doircheas is stirring the teapot.

'I've never seen her so bad,' he says, voice lowered.

'It's that bloody tree,' she says. 'Excuse my language, but it wrecks her every year.'

'She's worse, though.'

'Yes, she is declining. She won't go for her walk any more, hardly does her physio, she's breaking my heart just to keep her going most days.'

'Sorry, Doircheas.'

'Sorry for what?'

'I know it's a lot of work for you. I know I should be here more.'

'Hah,' she smiles, shrugs. 'It's not me you should say sorry to. She's the one you should be visiting more often.'

'She hardly knows if I'm here or not.'

'She knows more than you think. What did you want to talk to her about?'

'Well, I think that might be it, this Barry fellow. Do you know who he is?'

'No. I've heard the name often enough but it's only when she's in this mood, I don't pay any attention to the blather she comes out with while that tree is in bloom.'

'You don't remember a man? You would have been seven. Do you remember anything? An accident? Do you remember being in the car, and Dad chased after us?'

Doircheas is slowly shaking her head. 'I had nightmares. When I was eight or nine. You remember, I had to sleep in Mam's bed for a couple of years, I was terrified. But it was only a nightmare. Is that what you're thinking of?'

'You don't remember a man?'

'A man?'

'It might be Barry. You don't remember?'

'Like I said, she uses the name each time that thing blossoms. Would he have been a gardener?' A look flashes on her face. 'Hang on a sec.' She goes out to the telephone console-seat in the hall and returns with the battered address book that has served as the family telephone list since as long as Lorcan can remember. She opens it on one of the tabbed letters, gazes down, flicks, flicks again, then: 'Got it. Gardener, Barry. Right here. Has a number too, a mobile. From the fading of the ink, you would think it's too long ago for a mobile. Don't remember her ever having him here, but there you go. She misses the guy who planted a tree. It's a shame she doesn't miss our Dad instead. Mind you, I don't take anything she says in this mood with any weight. It's like she goes moonblind, staring at that bloody tree, may God forgive me.'

She's worked herself up into quite a state of upset. Lorcan puts his arm around her, maybe the first time in two decades he's shown her any affection. She flinches at the touch, but does not pull away.

'Sorry, Doircheas.'

He holds her for a minute, feeling awkward, then lets her go.

'I'll go down and talk to himself.'

'Better bring some tea,' she says, getting a tray out. While she preps the tea, he takes a note of the number in the phone book.

The shed door is locked so he knocks. His Dad's face appears at the little window, grimaces, then the door is unlocked and pulled open.

'You're back so?' says his father.

'I came back to ask about something.'

'Oh? Leave that tray down there. Two cups I see. I suppose I should offer you a cup, then?'

'No, I'm grand. Who is Barry?'

Patrick pulls his hand back sharply, as if he's been shot with static shock from the teapot. His face flushes rage, and Lorcan expects to be told to feck off out as has happened too often in the past. Patrick regathers himself though, looks Lorcan up and down as if weighing up a draft policy document from some junior bureaucrat.

'Maybe not tea, then.' He opens a press behind him and pulls out a bottle of whiskey. He pops two glasses on the table, pours a splash into each. Momentarily, Lorcan wonders why he would have two glasses here, did he have occasional visitors through the gate into the back alleyway, so that Doircheas and Helen would be unaware. Patrick puts one glass in front of Lorcan, indicating the chair opposite while he sits on his own, drawing a draft of whiskey over his tongue. 'Barry, so. What do you know about him?'

'Nothing. Mam just mentioned him.'

'Just now?'

'Yes.'

'And you never heard her mention him before?'

'I don't know, maybe. Maybe I didn't pay attention or something.'

'Hmph. You didn't pay attention?'

'I don't know. I don't recognise the name but it's important.'

'Maybe, but why should I be telling you anything?'

'Because I'm your son, perhaps.'

'What's that supposed to mean? Drink that whiskey.'

Lorcan doesn't want to. He wants to stay clean, purge the pain of the last few weeks. He takes a small sip; it's good, single malt Irish, very peaty. He nods his approval.

'Barry was the fucking gardener. Your mother started to *employ* him before you were born. Oh, he did the gardens for all the ladies round here, the ones whose husbands were out working. It was still a thing, back then, for women to stay at home, not like now when all the flossies are out looking for jobs. I didn't see the point in her working, we didn't need the money, she didn't like her work. So she saw to the garden. Or he saw to her.'

'Are you… implying something there?'

'Are you inferring something?'

'I think you're saying Mam was unfaithful.'

Patrick empties his glass, then screws off the cap and refills it, puts more into Lorcan's glass.

'I'm not saying it,' he says. 'But I'll not deny it, either.'

'Did he…? Am I…?'

'Go on. Ask the fucking question.'

'Is he my father?'

'How the fuck should I know? I'm just the man who worked for forty-five fucking years, climbed the greasy pole right to the top, put dinners on the table and, apparently, paid for a fucking gardener. How would I know whether it was him or me?'

Lorcan feels the comment worse than any slap. There had never been any affection or compassion from his father, hell, months might go by in his teens when he didn't actually see the man, but now, not only does Patrick not seem to know whether he even is his father, he doesn't care.

They look alike, though, Lorcan and Patrick. Many people have commented and he can see it increasingly as he gets older.

'No,' he says. 'No, you're lying. You are my father.'

Patrick shrugs.

'Do you actually know they were…? They were sleeping together?'

'She fucking went to leave me.' He shouts this, spumes of spit flying from his teeth and dangling till he wipes his sleeve over his mouth. 'She got in a car with him and fucking left me.'

'What happened?'

Again, there's that motion, that sting of shock as the question hits him. He takes another deep swig.

'I don't know.'

'You don't now?'

'I don't fucking know. I have… I can't explain it. They left. They didn't. I don't know. I've spent years here, sitting, thinking about that night and I still can't figure it.'

'Did you run after them? After us? Did you run at the car?'

'I… I don't fucking know.'

'Do you know anything about the *Book*?' Again, he is able to say it out loud. He has never mentioned it, never been able to mention it with his family before. Something is changing.

'What fucking book?'

'Did it bring you back to life? Did you die and come back again?'

'Get the fuck out. Go on, get the fuck out of my sight.' He stands up and screams, his face scarlet with rage. 'Get out!'

Lorcan has seen him angry but never so riled before. He gets up quickly and pulls the door open. The whiskey glass flies past his head as he runs.

Doircheas is standing at the back door, arms folded. 'What the hell did you say to him?'

Lorcan looks at her face, her features. Surely, she has a look of her father, of Patrick? Or is that just the overlay of years of assumptions. He wonders if he should say something. If one or both of them was the offspring of another man then she would have the right to know. This is not the time.

'Talking about what happened. Back then, when the family went bad.'

'You've no right to be vexing the man.'

'Vexing him? Are you kidding? This man who has denied us any love or affection for near on twenty years? Who is living in a shed so the neighbours won't know there's something wrong here, as if that would hide it?'

'Keep your voice down. I take back what I said about you visiting more often. Get out, go on, get out of here.'

He wants to go back in to his mother, see if he can pull anything more out about Barry, but Doircheas is fuming, and he's none too easy himself after having a glass thrown at his head.

'I'm sorry,' he says, and walks out the front door.

Lorcan, Sunday, 3:15pm

He sits in the car for a while, letting the fire in his blood fuel him. Thirty years of treating his wife and children like dirt, living in the shed like a fool. What a dick, what a total dick. Where is he, now that his son needs him?

But the anger ebbs quickly. Where is Lorcan in his own children's crisis? He may not have moved to the shed when Alice was diagnosed, but he distanced himself all the same. It is not far from the oak tree this acorn has fallen.

How has his Dad dealt with twenty-seven years of spite, of staring at adultery, contemplating the emasculation of somebody else possibly being the father, all of that festering in the dark corner of the garden. Above all of that, the sharp paradox of two days played out against each other, one where he and all his family died, another where they survived. Which was real? Which was hallucination? Was it any wonder, then? The man was a Private Secretary at work, and a confused child at home. Anger was inevitable.

Is there a bridge back? It seems unlikely now, but perhaps Lorcan will return another day. Perhaps he will bring a good Irish and open up a chat. If there's no salvation for this family, perhaps he can be a catalyst to some halfway house.

In the meantime, though, there is Barry. He has the the man's number on his phone. Can he just call him? For that matter, is there any chance the number is still active after such a long time? He has no choice, he has come this far.

He dials the number. It rings; good sign so far. It rings and rings, whining away without the solace of voice mail. Lorcan gives up and presses red, but just as he's pressing he hears something, somebody answering. He redials and this time gets an answer. He waits, but nobody speaks.

'Hello?' he says.

'Wha'?' It's a Dublin voice, thick and throaty even on the phone, like the man has a bad cold.

'I'm looking for Barry.'

'Who is?'

'Sorry, I'm not sure if I've the right number.'

'No, yeh don't, mate.'

'I had this number for Barry, used to do gardens long time back. On Tonlegee Road.'

'He died.'

'Oh, I'm sorry. Are you his… son?'

'Who is this?'

He's losing this battle. He has to take a chance, dive in, throw his hand on the table and see what happens.

'My names Lorcan. My mother was, sorry is, Helen Considine. You knew her back then?'

'Oh.' There's a long silence, broken by heavy breathing, a chesty wheeze. He half expects the phone to click dead, but it doesn't.

'I was wondering if I could come and see you? Just speak to you for a few minutes. I wanted to find out a couple of things, maybe you'd remember?'

Again, only the breathing, rustley, like there's a heavy phlegm on his lungs.

'Alright,' he says at last, and gives Lorcan an address on the North Circular Road.

In the heyday of Georgian Dublin, the North Circular Road was an address to be proud of. In the twentieth century, the houses that might be three stories of glorious red brick over service basements were too big for private individuals so were bought up and divided into far too many tiny flats. Some of the street is still wealthy, though much is mired in drugs and poverty.

Lorcan parks the car off the main road and looks up at the imposing structure he has been directed to. The garden is concrete and bare earth; there are sixteen wheelie bins, two televisions and a fridge to one side. A grand staircase leads up to an arched portico and a massive green door that swings slightly in the wind. The windows are mostly rotten, one smashed and blocked with cardboard. A massive buddleja is growing out of the down-pipe from the gutters.

He walks up the steps to the door. There's a bank of doorbells, none of them labelled, and the disheveled state of them doesn't suggest they are functional. He dials the number again.

'I'm out the front.'

'Right y'are,' says Barry, and hangs up.

Lorcan stands on the top step for a while. A young man in an Adidas tracksuit comes up the steps behind him, pushes open the door, then turns to him.

'Y'alright there, bud?'

'Just waiting for somebody.'

'Grand.'

The door swings shut, and Lorcan is left again. Has he got the wrong house? Might Barry be outside some other house looking for him? He glances around, there's a man five houses up smoking in the garden, staring at him.

'What about yeh?'

Lorcan jumps when he hears the voice. It comes from below in the garden, a man has emerged from the side passage. Lorcan trots down the steps.

'Barry?'

The man standing in front of him is a walking corpse. Gaunt, grizzled, wizzened, dirty. His face, unshaven, has collapsed in on itself, drawing skin over his skull. A small patch of hair clings over his ears. His fingers are buckled and kidney-stained. His tee shirt is advertising the contents of his last meal, by the looks of it, and Lorcan does not want to think about the staining on his sloggy-bottoms.

'How'r'yeh? Is it Lorcan yeh said?'

'Yeah, Lorcan, how are you doing?' He holds his hand out. Barry shakes it with a limp grip, his hand cold and bony.

'Do yeh want to come in or what?'

'I… guess so, yes.'

He leads Lorcan around the back past what might once have been a garden door but is now a crumble of rotting wood. Behind the house is concrete, piled with more abandoned appliances. To one side is a lean-to. He unlocks the door and leads Lorcan in. The space is tiny and cold. There is one sofa with a sleeping bag on it, a toilet in one corner and a sink and microwave in the other. There is an ashtray piled high, a stink of cigarettes. The TV is on showing a soccer match between two unidentifiable foreign teams.

Barry pulls back the sleeping bag.

'Yeh can sit there. D'yeh want tea? I've no milk mind, bleeding fridge is busted. Landlord says he's getting a new one but it's been a month.'

'Eh, no, don't go to any trouble.'

Lorcan looks around. This is blistering poverty; everything smells, everything is stained. There's a firm breeze coming through the window despite it being shut and it's fighting against a gas portable fire. There's signs of water damage in the roof and mold and mildew battling each other for the wall space.

'So,' he wheezes as he sits beside Lorcan. 'Yeh're Helen's son, is it?' He lifts a can from beside the ashtray, cider, half drunk, and takes a swig.

'Yeah, I...' What to say next? Excuse me, are you my father? The thought that this mangy weasel could be blood relation is horrific. 'I'm her son. You did her garden?'

'I did her garden, yeah. I did a few gardens back then. Not a lot of call for it these days, but I keep my phone just in case.' He makes a sound, part choke, part cough, that might be a leery laugh. 'Don't mind me. She was a special woman, yer ould wan. A real lady, yeh know what I mean. Quality.'

The grotesqueness of it grows, becomes nauseating. This man is not his father, he is sure of it, he will not countenance it. The thought of his mother... No, never. In any case, he is here for other things. 'Do you know anything about a *Book*?'

'Ah.' Something approaching a smile insinuates itself onto his plastic cheeks. 'Yeh have it then? I wasn't sure.'

'Did you...?'

'Give it to yeh? Yeah, that was me? Do yeh remember when I gev it yeh?'

'I don't really. I don't remember you.'

'Not surprising. The thing fucks with yer head something rotten, dunnit? I'll tell yeh what, I'm better off without it.'

'How did you get it?'

'Teacher. School I was in had this French fellah, real weird bird he was and all, always into mad stuff. Anyways, he takes us to the beach one day, down to Dollier, like, takes us all in swimming, the gobdaw. So I only goes and drowns. Probably a couple a lads holding me under, if I could remember. So's I wake up and I'm writing the thing in this bleeding book and I'm all: did that really happen? Only it did, and then I have the *Book*.'

'Did you talk to the teacher? Is he still around?'

'Nah, gone. Rumour was he woke up crying and got back on the boat to France. Sent me a letter though.'

'Could I see it?'

The walking corpse holds out his hands, indicating the shithole he calls his flat. 'Now serious, like, do I look like the kind a man keeps bleeding letters?'

'What did it say?'

'Ah, something about be careful, it's powerful but it's dangerous and that kinda shite. Suppose he was right.'

The enormity of this is flattening him. So long he has known nothing, this flood of baffling information is overwhelming.

'So what happened to you?'

'Me? Lived the life of fecking Riley. I could do no wrong, yeh know what I mean. Like, I used to do a bit a breaking in back then, thieving, like. Now don't judge me, I didn't have nothing, fucking nothing, so I stole a bit is all. I could get away with anything. I jumped from one roof to another, I fall and sure then I wake up and I'm writing about it. And of course, now I know which house is worth breaking into and which one to avoid.' He gives a little laugh that turns into a cough.

'Were you able to talk about it? To other people?'

'Never bleeding tried. I mean, I tell one of the lads down the pub about it, next think he'll take it off me, least that's what I thought, not so sure now.'

'How do you mean.'

He takes another deep glut of cider then pulls out a tobacco pouch and starts to roll a thin, mean cigarette. 'Well, I think it's got a mind of its own. I mean, that sounds pure nuts, like, but sure the whole idea of the *Book* and it pulling yeh back to life again and again, I mean that's just plain fucking crazy. Only I think it decides who it wants. When it's ready to move, it finds the next person, yeh know what I mean. I felt it for weeks before I gev it yeh. That's when I started getting me cough from the fags, can't hardly walk up a stair any more. I'm thinking no bother, the *Book* will sort that one of these times, only it didn't.'

'There was an accident?'

He licks the seam on the ciggie, puts the thing in his dry lips and lights it with a match. There's a reek of bitter smoke that starts to rise to the brown stains on the ceiling.

'Yeh remember?'

'I was able to read it. Just today for the first time.'

'What did it say?'

'You were running away with Mam, with Doircheas and me?'

Again that leery smile through the tobacco smog. 'Yeh're thinking what the fuck, like? Yeh're thinking how did yer ma find this fuck-awful thing attractive? I was different then. I'd built me life around the *Book* and I had a bit of flair like. And anyways, I think yer ma was pissed off at yer da, half of it was just a ruse to wind him up, like. Get a bit of a bleeding reaction. Well, she fucking got that and all. C'mere, yeh'll never guess this is me.'

There's a drawer on the little table his ashtray spills onto. He reaches into it and pulls out a photograph. It shows a man, it shows Barry, Lorcan realises, maybe thirty years ago. He was a small man even then, but his face was fine, his chest pressed out with the strength that hard work in the garden can bring. He has a head of hair and yes, a smile that could charm. How did this man become so decayed? Is that the consequence, some kind of reverse Dorian Gray effect?

Lorcan's head is spinning. There must be more he can get from this man but he's barely able to think, the blood pounding in his eyes is pain, he has to get out of this hell.

'I need to go,' he says, standing. 'I... I'll come back again.'

The thing looks up at him, sucking on the scant fag. 'Listen Lorcan, hate to ask and all, only I'm fairly skint. Yeh wouldn't have a few squid in yer pocket?'

He grabs some notes out and hands them over, unsure how much he's giving him, then leaves quickly. He barely makes it to the wheelie bins in the front before vomiting his guts.

Alice, Sunday, 3:20pm

Alice checks her phone again; still nothing. There's the text from Lorcan just after nine this morning: "Have to go to Dublin, talk to my family, back tonight, sorry for running, please trust me. Love you more than life itself."

More than life itself? But not enough to tell her what the he's up to? There are several texts she sent on the theme of "what the hell?" but nothing back from Lorcan.

He's been acting like a dickhead since the diagnosis but this tops it. There have been one or two moments where she thought he was getting it, where he said the right things, but otherwise it's wall to wall drinking and smoking, hasn't spent five minutes with his own children.

She had shouted at him. Hadn't she? Slapped him. Why would she do that? No, it must have been a dream, a fuzzy recollection. The memory slips from her.

She has more to worry about; word has come from Catherine that Pluto is hunting out Eamo. This triggered a panic so deep in her that she realised she was overreacting and had to breathe it out. She will go round to see Eamo later, when he's on shift, let him know.

Alice steps outside and takes long slow breaths. She does not want to react in anger. Words must be had, rules laid down. This cannot be tolerated, but if her temper rules then she will say things she may regret.

Somewhat calmed, but still uneasy, she returns the the buzz of the amusement arcade. Darragh got a cramp from all the chocolate so they had to stop paddle-boarding. Now they have discovered the joys of the *Tipping Point* machines, where you drop a coin into a slot and it falls onto moving tables of coins, trying to tip some of the coins over into the exit chute. It's funny that with all the technology, the flashing screens and screaming sounds, it's the simple fascination of physical mechanics that takes their attention. In that summer that still fascinates her, she had spent plenty of time and money in this same place with the same name on pretty much the same machines, sometimes with Mike, other times with Paul or Simon.

Paul is with them now, Simon has some kind of work call to take so Paul wanted to bring the boys to the amusements along with Adrianne, but Alice insisted on joining them. Frank is here too, feeding them with coins.

She has let too much time go by without making them the centre of her world. This is another reason why Lorcan's sudden excursion is so frustrating, he should damn well be here too.

'You look perplexed,' says Paul, while the two of them stand watching the coins roll into the machine.

Perplexed, she thinks. Where to start on the depth of her perplexity. But one thing is preying on her mind.

'I saw something that has been upsetting me,' she says, taking care not to be overheard by the kids, though the din in the place is prohibitive. 'You know Rhia? She and Jim have a cabin up by the reception, one of the expensive ones.'

'They must be plush.'

'I saw Jim pushing her, grabbing her hair. Like, really violent. I've seen bruises on her before and I've always wondered. I mean, I've never really been a fan of Jim and all but I didn't think he could be abusive, well, not that straight in-your-face abusive. But I saw it. Right in front of me.'

'Shit. Well, you may not have suspected him but I have no problem believing that. Guy's a user, pure and simple, not a good bone in his body. I'm surprised that Lorcan still hangs out with him. But Christ, did you stop him?'

'And I spoke to her, she's all in denial.'

'We have to do something though, right?' says Paul. 'I mean, she can't make the judgement herself. You're the social worker, what's the right path?'

It's upsetting to face but Paul is right. They need to find some kind of intervention. She needs to. Doesn't she? Or does she need to give the focus to her own health?

'Come on, boys,' she says so the kids can hear. 'We've had our fun here, we'll come back tomorrow but right now I think we should get out into the air.'

Cian is reluctant, he is convinced he is on the brink of upsetting a big pile of coins, but she can see the weight of it will take a lot more coins pumped in to topple them.

Soft charcoal clouds with a bluish tinge are rolling from the north making the sea seem like an AI generated scene. The ocean breeze brings the salt smell. This is the seaside like she has always wanted, always known, the slightly chill, fresh feel of a fine Sligo day.

As they walk back, Darragh sidles up to her.

'You know the way Nan's not really our Nan?' he says.

'How do you mean.'

'Well, she's not your mother.'

'Not my birth mother, no, but she adopted me.'

'But your other mother, she died?'

'Yes. Yes, she did.'

'When you were young?'

'Yes. Older than you but young enough to play on the machines in there.'

He is silent for a moment, flicking the cube back and forth in a complex multi-move fast-fingering twist. 'So you had to get used to living without her?'

'Yes, I did.'

She kneels in front of him and looks into his face, his eyes now watching the autonomic actions of his cube hand as he chews his lip with a deliberate intensity. There are waves washing around in that head. *My poor child, my cherub,* she thinks, *you shouldn't have to deal with this.*

She does not say this, at least not with words. She hugs him and he lets himself be consumed, drops the cube unnoticed.

She goes to stand and then: pain! Hard hitting, raw, paralysing, penetrating. It sears from her neck to her legs, burning fiercely. She cries out as she bends double. She cannot straighten, but is brought low, to the sandy clay, to hands and knees, face to face with a half-solved cube. Darragh is screaming. Paul and Frank come running.

She is on her back. Somebody, a stranger, is checking her mouth. What for? He pushes her onto her side. No, no, the agony is intense.

Not in front of my boys, she thinks. *Please God no, not in front of my boys.*

The searing, burning torment becomes a thumping. She starts to breathe again. She tries to sit up.

'No,' says a voice, Paul's she thinks. 'Stay down. I've called the ambulance.'

'Yeh're okay, luv,' she hears Frank's voice. 'I got yer hand now, take it easy.'

She tries to say "not here" but the effort sends darts of pain through her brain.

She wonders where the boys are. Has Frank sent them away, made up some errand so they're not looking at her on the ground? She wishes that Lorcan were here, for all that he's been a shit, she feels a furious need for him. She wants to feel his hand, wants to hear his voice.

The suffering is subsiding. Her sight is restored. Paul is there, and a host of fuzzy faces, none of them her boys, thank God.

'Just wait now,' says Frank. 'Yer Mam is coming.'

For a moment she thinks he said Mammy, and she sees her mother, bright and beautiful, before she was ill, coming to kiss the pain from her.

Lorcan, Sunday, 4:30pm

Lorcan makes himself stop in a garage outside Longford, realising that his focus is drifting. His head is buzzing. The enormity of the things he has heard, coupled with the realisation that he knows almost nothing more than he knew beforehand is overpowering. The image of that homunculus, that hissing Gollum that could have been... No, he can't even think of the biological ramifications, but that his mother...

Of course, Barry had been a different man back then. And his father was certainly no romantic. She had worked as a dancer in the Gaiety Theatre, she would often tell him. Her memories were of happy times, wild times, life in a spotlight. Of course, not proper for a Private Secretary's wife, she had to accept that. He can remember her staring forelorn out the window, longing for her lovely dancing. So she sought something, something to make her whole, to wake her soul? Did she reach for a man in those long empty days? A man with a bit of wildness, a different take altogether from the staid home life? Could that be true?

He buys a sandwich in the shop, ham and cheese, and closes his eyes for ten minutes, the terror of the crash-that-wasn't still sweating inside him.

The images swirl as he restarts his journey. Barry. Mam. Dad in the shed hiding from the horror of crash that wasn't a crash, his wife's betrayal that wasn't a betrayal. He can see her now, sitting in her front room staring at the apple blossom. She was in love with an image of freedom that she could never have achieved.

He stops again at the *Circle K* at Dromore West and asks after his phone. The assistant pulls out a box from under the counter, roots in it and digs out three phones. One is an iPhone. He checks the back, it's inscribed "Lorcan's Phone".

'Thanks, that's mine.'

It won't power on, the battery is flat. He buys a USB charger cable and carries on.

He arrives just before eight into the town, pulls the car into the side of the road just before the campsite, opposite McGinty's. Better check the phone before arriving, he thinks; see what kind of trouble he's in. The phone powers on and begins to ping, message after message, there must be twenty or more. The last one to come in is from Paul.

"Lorcan, please come now. We need to talk to you."

An edge of fear grips his hand as he tries to open the message app, get the context. It was not normal for Paul to message him.

Just then, there is a thunderous altercation from across the road. Several people tumble out of *McGinty's Music Bar*, shouting hysterically, he sees Mike in hid wheelchair follow after. Some drunks being ejected. He wonders idly if it might be Jim.

He recognises one of them: the man who was outside his house this morning. He climbs out of the car. The man has Eamo by the hair, dragging him backwards. There's half a dozen men behind Mike now screaming. There's two other guys around Eamo, tough young fellas, one swinging a baseball bat, the other with a motorbike chain.

Lorcan climbs out of the car.

'Uncle Pluto don't fucking do this,' yells Eamo.

Lorcan starts to cross the road.

'Get the fuck in the car, yeh stupid bollix,' shouts the short man that Lorcan recognises. He realises, to his horror, he has told the brutal drug dealer Pluto where to find Eamo, more or less. Finding him in a small town like this wouldn't have taken too much work once he knew where to start.

'Leave him alone,' says Mike. 'There's too many of us. You're not taking him.'

'Too fucking many? A bleedin' cripple and some culchies?' says Pluto. Lorcan can see a sharp grin on his face. He has to get Eamo out of this. He's done enough damage without betraying the kid.

'Too fucking many for fucking who?' says Pluto.

Pluto pulls something from his pocket just as Lorcan pushes in behind the two young lads and grabs Eamo by the tee shirt. He starts to push him forwards towards Mike.

Time slows, noise ceases. He watches the sedate swing of Pluto's hand like the slow arc of a celestial event. There is a gun, a pistol. He sees one of the guys from the pub, a young man, maybe a bouncer, start to run towards them, his motion languorous. He feels his head pulled gently back; one of Pluto's lads has him by the hair. He sees the sharp smile on Pluto's face, the firm hand and muscular arm that he holds the gun with. He sees the pub guy crashing into Pluto and then there is a light, bright, blinding, almighty.

He sees, or he doesn't see, the crowd shrink back, Eamo bundled into the boot of a waiting car. He sees himself, his body, lying on the ground, head thrown back, face dissolved, blood on the pavement, as the car screeches off.

Lorcan, Sunday, 9:10am

There is a pen in his hand and he is writing. There is no choice in it, no volition. His hand moves, words appear.

I was dead, then alive again, earlier that morning. My head, as ever when this happens, was fucked. I read the stuff that happened when I was ten, or some of it. I spoke to Alice about the Book, even if she didn't listen. Something is changing.

I drove to Dublin. My brutal Dad, God, what a dick, implied - or maybe he just outright said - that some guy called Barry was my mother's lover. Unthinkable, but it appears as if Mam was running away from Dad, and there was a crash, and Barry gave me the Book. I don't know who died that day, me I guess, all of us maybe, but that's why everybody's head is so fucked up, I think.

I went to see Barry. He was a wreck of a man, bitter and consumed by his own self indulgence, his own inability to stand up for himself.

Barry is the "B" who gave me the Book, who left me the note. He told me that the Book chooses when to move on.

I also met Pluto, I didn't know it was him. I guess I told him where Eamo was.

When I drove back to Enniscrone, I saw Pluto outside Mike's. He had found Eamo and was dragging him away.

I intervened. I don't know why. Standing up for myself?

The fucker had a gun. What the hell? He had a gun and he pointed it at me and somebody ran into him and the gun went off and I died. I saw myself, head smashed open. It must have been a big calibre.

The *Book* has brought him back again. Something is changing. The *Book* is beckoning, signalling, saying something to him. Barry said the *Book* will move on, leave him. He will know when it is time. The idea does not scare him.

The *Book* broke Barry. Could Lorcan be like him? Could there be a genetic connection?

Lorcan knows he has been an eejit again. When Alice needed him, he abdicated. Again.

There was something else. From out of the fudge of his half-fried memories he pulls a near forgotten fact: there had been a text from Paul. Lots of texts from Alice, then one from Paul. Why would he have been reaching out? Was it just that Alice was concerned about him, turned to Paul for help? Or could there have been something more serious?

He has to go and see her. His head lurches as he tries to make sense of where he is, when he is. Mike! She's gone to meet him in the cafe down the high street.

He dresses quickly. Outside the door, he pauses. His boys are not up yet. Yesterday - no, today, only the first time, no, second time - he ran off leaving Alice, knowing he should not leave her. Now, he's leaving the boys. Jesus, he can't get this right.

He is wheezing by the time he makes the main street. As he turns the corner, he sees her. The early Sligo sun reflects from a window behind her, wraps itself around her as she walks, transfiguring her momentarily. He is reminded of the moment she kissed him for the first time and his eyes were opened, he had seen her true beauty, no longer in the shadow of Rhia.

She smiles and brushes hair from her face, a natural gesture but one that now seems sprung with splendour.

'Hey,' she says. 'Are you alright?'

He goes to hug her, unsure still if she will accept it or flinch away. She lays her head on his shoulder.

'I'm sorry,' he says.

'What's wrong?'

'I am. I've been an fuckwit.'

'Ooookay. Who's been talking to you?'

'Nobody, I...' Should he try to talk again about the *Book*, share with her the catalyst of whatever change has overcome him? Probably not the right time. 'Listen, your illness. It screwed me over. The things I've been saying, the way I've been behaving. I know it's childish, and pathetic. And it's worse than you think. I've been smoking all the time.'

'Like you think I couldn't smell it off you?'

'And drinking more than you think. I've even been day drinking a lot recently.'

'Okay. Not good.'

'No, way worse than not good.' And again, not perhaps the right time to share his secret liaisons with Rhia. 'I can't hope for you to forgive me but I can tell you I'm sorry. And I can try to do the right thing. Starting now.'

'I don't understand. I mean, this is all very welcome, but really, Lorcan, what the almighty fuck is going on?'

He sees a pink stain on the shoulder of her white tee-shirt. He remembers the mark, ketchup maybe, from that first day, the diagnosis, a harbinger. It has not fully washed out. Nothing really ever washes out. None of those events that the *Book* erased are truly gone, all are trapped in his head like baby wasps in honeycomb, a festering threat. The Leukaemia is a stain that not even the *Book* can wash out.

With all the tenderness that he can attend, he wraps her in his arms and lets his head fall toward her, as he used to when a teenager, dropping his everything into the moment.

'I love you, Alice. I promise you now that I will do everything I can to be here for you, for Cian and Darragh. For me, even. I know I'm a better man than I've been behaving.'

'Jesus, Lorcan, yeh thick eejit.'

'Yes. I know. Do you think you could trust me?'

She lets that question ride, but she does not resist his embrace. 'It's been really hard, Lorcan. I'm getting ill, I know I am, and I don't know what's ahead. The worst part has been feeling alone, while you're out with your beer buddies and coming home stinking of fags and God alone knows what else you might have been up to. I just asked you to be by my side, that's all, and you couldn't do that. You've hurt me.'

'I know. I'm sorry.'

'Do you know, though? It's not you that's sick. It's not you that's dying. What the fuck do you know about any of it?'

'Sorry. I deserve it.'

'Of course you fucking deserve it. You ask me to trust you but how many times have you made promises and yet I still can't expect you to be home with me at night?'

But I can explain, his head says. *The Book. Untime. Once you know then you'll see, you will see it all makes sense.*

It won't though. He cannot expect her to believe and, even if he did, the nature of the *Book* does not excuse his being a complete dick.

He lets her go, steps back. 'You can't forgive and forget and it's unfair of me even to ask, but I can be here. I can show you.'

She shrugs. 'I'm happy that you are saying this, Lorcan, but...' she shakes her head. 'But if you fuck up this time, I can't say what the consequences might be.'

She starts to walk back towards the camp site. There is a real anger in her, he can feel the glow. His heart aches. He wants to get back into that place, the Alice-and-Lorcan place, where they are one person, one entity, but he is locked out. There must be something else he can do, another way forward. He walks beside her, hoping that he can keep his way beside her this time.

'Did you have a nice morning?' he says, trying to stay neutral for now.

'Grand, yeah, I met Mike.'

Lorcan suddenly panics. 'Pluto,' he says. He is dizzy, dazed, alternate truths chase around his head. Is Pluto on his way? Did he tell him about Enniscrone? Was that before he died? Was he shot, really? No, that can't be.

'What? Pluto? As in Eamo's uncle?'

'I...' No. He can be certain, not in this reality. That was *Untime*, it never happened. 'Sorry, I was just... I read something about him. I think there's a real danger.'

'Yes, there is. That's why I have Eamo here.'

'But you're here.'

'I don't follow.'

'Somebody will tell him. Somebody will know. He'll ask one of our neighbours.'

'I think you're being alarmist. He's a dangerous man, but we're safe here. Eamo's safe.'

This is going to be a challenge. Eamo is probably okay today, so long as Lorcan doesn't go to Dublin, but he's seen the consequences if Pluto does get a lead.

Alice, Sunday, 9:50am

Alice is disturbed. Lorcan's apparent change of heart, while welcome, seems sudden. She is not sure she can trust it, he's hurt her too much, though time may tell. She is happy to give him the chance, anything that might take them forward, ease her worries about Cian and Darragh.

Then he mentions Pluto. Why? And why, as they are walking along, does this leave a lingering anxiety, a cold plug of fear, a dig of deja vu? There's something else lingering at the back of her head. Did she have a thundering headache, like, maybe she fell over... But no, she cannot pull that out of her memory, it's purely a floating anxiety.

She feels as if she's searching for something she lost, something that dropped out of her pocket, but was it yesterday or twenty years ago? The sense was just beyond the tip of her fingers.

They pass through the front gate and get to the first junction. The mobile home is straight ahead, but something — deja vu or anxiety again — is impelling her left.

'Can we go this way?'

'Why?' asks Lorcan.

'I... I just fancy it.'

'Okay.'

They start to walk up among the glamorous glamping cabins.

'Rhia and Jim's place is just here, look.'

She looks up and sees Jim and Rhia through the window of an ostentatious cabin. Somehow it's not a surprise, not new even though she has not come this way before. She is about to lift a hand to wave when she sees all is not well. Jim is holding Rhia by he hair, twisting it to the side so her head is bent.

It is a violent scene, vicious. Alice feels a gut fear rising and filling the universe. It floods her eyes. A man, fundamental and masculine. A woman, weak and twisted. She is frozen, wanting to scream, wanting to run in and stop it, wanting to run away.

She steps forward, toward the cabin.

'Alice, no,' says Lorcan. 'It's not our fight.'

'Of course it's our fight.'

Fired by anger, she pushes forward. She dashes open the door with a thundering bang. She sees him with Rhia's hair still cruelly held. Primeval violence is etched in his face. His eyes flare with something like fury and he turns towards her with malice.

Rhia is discarded directly back and hurtles against the breakfast bar, a marble monster in the confines of the cabin. Her chin and neck snap against it, ripping her. Jim's rage is distracted. He turns to watch as a surge of arterial blood drenches him.

'Ohmygod,' he shouts. 'Ohmygodohmygodohmygod.' He reaches down to her, starts to pull her arms. She flops, lifeless. 'Get up. Rhia, get up.'

'Get out of the fucking way,' yells Alice. She tries to push him but he's too big, too heavy.

'What's wrong with Mama?' Forry has emerged from the rooms at the rear in pyjamas.

'Jesus, Jim, go and look after your son, leave her to me.'

He turns to look at her and she can't read him. The viciousness is gone, but what remains is unreadable. There is a carnal spatter of blood on his face. For a moment she thinks he will hit her.

Lorcan grabs Jim's arm and pulls him. Jim concedes, and Alice can get in.

She has first aid but she's missed the last couple of refreshers. Airways are first. No, dammit, the blood loss is first.

Rhia is crumpled in like a sleeping child. Alice leans over, finds the blood is coming from a deep gash under the left ear. She can still see blood pulsing out; good, the heart is still beating. She reaches in and gathers the skin, presses, puts pressure on, keeps pressing.

'An ambulance, quick.'

'On it,' says Lorcan.

'Is Mama okay?'

She glances and sees Forry standing over her. Jim is nowhere to be seen. 'Take Forry outside,' she says. 'And get the police.'

She holds her pressure till her arms are aching wild.

She hears Bob come in, though can't tell how long has passed.

'Jesus, this is not cool,' he says.

'Is the ambulance on the way?'

'Five minutes out, Lorcan says. Can I help?'

She's desperate for a break but can't afford to release the pressure. Rhia groans. She's still breathing, her airways are as good as Alice can manage given the wound. That's as much as she can manage.

She stares at Rhia's face, flaccid in unconsciousness. She could be a sleeping fairy, with that lustrous red hair still bursting from her in a hideous parody of her bleeding. Her skin is pale, even paler than normal, though bruised. Her nose looks soft like a baby's. She does possess an abominable beauty. Little wonder that Lorcan, big fool that he can be, thought himself in love. How many times, she wonders idly, has he looked at that face over the years, and thinks of what might have been? Or how many times has he tasted that face, in those years.

Oh God, she thinks. *I don't want to be here.*

Lorcan, Sunday, 10:10am

Lorcan's head is heaving about inside his skull. He is struggling to hold on to what is really happening. He sees a whirling mix of violence and death: the truck, the gun, the excruciating smack of Rhia's head hitting the breakfast bar. Which one is real. All are real, nothing is real.

It takes all his concentration to call first the ambulance, then the Guards. Bob, whose tent is nearby, turns up and goes in to check on Alice. Lorcan calls Margaret. Within minutes Simon and Paul turn up, and they are only just ahead of the ambulance.

There is a flood of activity then. The paramedics tumble into the cabin, and moments later Alice emerges looking dazed, Rhia's blood spattered on her. The police turn up and he tries to give them the story, Jim's savage abuse and then his disappearance.

'Any idea where he might have headed?'

'Only one place he'd be going,' says Bob. 'True.'

Bob points them to *McGinty's*, they leave their number in case he should return.

'Oh, Jesus,' says Alice, and she starts to run.

'What is it? Alice?' says Lorcan.

'You better get after her,' says Simon. 'We'll stay with Rhia.'

Lorcan catches up with her just before she gets to the mobile home.

'What's wrong?'

'Toilet,' is all she can say.

The boys are sitting at the table with Margaret cooking some food. Lorcan pulls the door open and Alice rushes past, into the bathroom. They can hear sounds of violent retching.

'What happened?'

'Jim attacked Rhia, the ambulance is there, but then suddenly...'

'Maybe you should take the boys down to the beach. Would you like that boys? We can have our burgers in a few minutes.'

Without waiting for an answer, Margaret disappears into the bathroom, bringing towels.

'Come on, lads,' says Lorcan. He's worried, wants to stay, be by her side. He's also a little irritated at being told what to do, but she is right. Alice needs some privacy by the sounds of it.

He takes them both by the hand, surprised that Cian is not pulling away, and leads them out towards the beach.

'Is Mom going to be alright?' says Cian.

'She just needs a bit of time, don't be worrying.'

'Is this because of her sickness?' says Darragh with the perception of innocence.

Lorcan is about to say no, to try to minimise it, but he can't. 'Yes,' he says. 'Probably. We are going to need to come to terms with this. Mom is going to be ill a lot in a while. She will start her chemo and then she'll be out of it. She may be exhausted for months, and we have to be big and strong to help her through it.'

The boys are quiet, depleted. It must be so hard for them, he thinks. The *Book*, if only…

But no. It is time to start facing up to this.

They walk by the sea, sullen. He wants to bring fun but it's hard to ignore the circumstances.

His phone buzzes. It's Simon.

'How is she?'

'Unwell, but Margaret's looking after her, I'm just down at the sea.'

'Grand. Rhia's stable, they were saying, so they've taken her to hospital, but she's still unconscious. Bob followed her on his bike. I've got Forry, maybe I could meet up with you, put the boys together?'

Simon arrives ten minutes later with a football. Simon, Forry and Darragh take on Lorcan and Cian with beach rocks as goal posts.

'Come on, Dad, all I need you to do is pass to me,' says Darragh.

It's a good while since Lorcan has played with Cian and he's surprised at how good he's become. He's a little dynamo when he gets on the ball. Mind you, neither Darragh nor Forry have any hunger to stop him. It is fun though. Lorcan finds himself out of breath from laughing and running.

When Margaret calls them to come back for burgers, Alice is looking better. She has changed and showered.

'What was that?' asks Lorcan when they get a moment alone.

'I don't know. I was, like, ill at both ends. Not pleasant.'

'Has this been happening a lot?'
'No, nothing like this.'
'But you're getting symptoms? It's getting worse.'
'Yes.'
'Should we go to the hospital? Get you checked?'
'Yeah. We should. Tuesday, first thing. We'll pack tomorrow and go back to Dublin Tuesday, just give me a couple more days.'

Lorcan isn't sure. The message that came last night, no, his head spins again; the message that that will come tonight from Paul is nagging at him. But then he's struggling to remember what it was, if it did happen, which series of events led to that point.

They get a message from Bob. Rhia is still stable. They are watching the pressure on her brain and keeping her in an artificial coma for now, but they're not thinking it's life threatening. She's not in ICU.

A little later Alice gets a call from Mike. Again this messes with his head as he struggles to try to put the events in order. Eamo is in danger. Has he already tried to tell Alice that?

Jim had indeed gone to Mike's bar and scrounged a couple of drinks before the Guards turned up and took him to the station.

Alice hangs up before Lorcan can voice his concerns.

'Should we go to see how Jim is doing?' he asks.

'No,' says Alice firmly. She looks around to check Forry isn't in hearing range. 'I think it's time you turned your back on that scumbag. He can't hide behind his false cheeriness any more. He's a wife beater, an abuser, and you have no place with him.'

'Right. What about Rhia, then?'
'Do you think your place is by her side, or by mine?'
'Somebody should be with her.'
'Isn't Bob there.'
'Yes.'
'Right. God, I'm tired.'

She was right. His place was here.

Alice, Sunday, 3:20pm

Alice is unnerved by the violent assault she had witnessed, but she is proud she stood up. It is unfortunate that her actions led to a more serious injury for Rhia, but she is determined not to blame herself, not to let Jim off the hook. Being there, holding closed the wound, should be tearing her up with the trauma, but the fact that she took a stand means everything. It's as if she had that option before and failed, and this time she came through, though she can't put a finger on where that sensation comes from.

Beth and Jackie come back from the hike and join them. They are shocked at the news, but also less than surprised.

'You always did think that Jim was abusing her, didn't you?' says Beth.

'Yes, but this goes well beyond what I thought he was capable of.'

'She has to leave him now, doesn't she?'

'They often blame themselves,' says Jackie.

Alice's phone rings. She pulls it out. 'It's my boss.' She answers. 'Catherine? What's up?'

Catherine explains to her about Pluto turning up at the office looking for her.

'That's weird,' she says after Catherine hangs up. 'You were just talking about Pluto this morning, weren't you Lorcan? And he turned up yesterday looking for Eamo, quite antagonistic.'

Lorcan's eyes dart about as if he's confused. 'I... Yes, I guess I did. Do you think maybe you should get him out of here?'

'I don't know. What made you bring it up?'

'Maybe I had a dream. I'm not sure. Maybe I read something in a paper.'

Lorcan is wavering weirdly. She might reckon he is lying, covering something up, but why would he lie about that. He doesn't seem himself today.

'I'll give Mike a call, see if there's anything he can do, but we need to think about Forry. We can hang on to him, I guess, put him in with the boys or whatever, but what then? I mean, hopefully Rhia's going to be okay, but she's going to be out of it for a few days. And Jim has been arrested.'

'He might not be charged,' says Beth. 'They might need to wait till Rhia recovers. And they won't hold him anyway. He is the father. If he wants the boy back then there's nothing we can do.'

'Just give Jim a few quid and point him towards the pub,' says Lorcan. 'You won't have any problems with him.'

They decide the best thing to do is get the kids out, keep them busy for the afternoon while things work themselves out. Alice wonders how this will fit with her going back to Dublin, to the hospital, like she had said. She probably needs to leave sooner than Tuesday. Can she walk away and leave Forry with the others? They'll do anything for her, of course, and there's no reason she has to take responsibility for Rhia's family, but still she feels it might not be right. Would it be worth going to the local hospital, or is that a waste of time if they don't have her records?

It is a crisp and cooling afternoon, bright but hazy with a sea mist mulling over the strand. Soft charcoal clouds with a bluish tinge are rolling from the north sucking the warmth from her. She bundles the boys up. Forry is silent and brooding, but she's rarely seen him otherwise. She find one of Darragh's hoodies that fits him to keep him warm.

Simon has to take a call for work, so they head towards the amusement arcade. Frank comes with them. Cian tells her there is a really cool chip van that stops in the car park there.

'You have to try the onion rings,' he tells her. 'They're really gear.'

'They're all that,' says Frank. 'We'll be needing a serving each, so we will.'

As they walk with the three boys, she sees Lorcan holding Darragh's hand. It's funny that she notices him being affectionate with his son. It's like a pain that you don't realise is there until it's gone. He has been an absence in the family life since the diagnosis, always off somewhere else. If this is a change it's a good one, but she has to wonder why now?

The amusement arcade is loud and leery, buzzing with boys and girls anxious to pour money into the many machines with flashing lights and loud noises. Lorcan and Frank go to the booth and come back with a small fortune in euro and twenty cent coins that they need. Lorcan watches while Darragh starts pumping them into the push-coin machines.

She has a queer feeling, half nostalgia, half foreboding. This was a powerful place for her, that summer when she was sixteen. It was a place of healing. She had come here often with Paul and Simon at first, then Mike later. But there was pain here also. Was it the echo of her grief at the loss of her mother, or was there something else, a weird deja vu that has taken her?

Simon turns up after a while, but his place has been taken by Lorcan, so they decide to leave the boys to it and grab a coffee from the barista booth outside.

The moment she feels the spritz of damp air outside, the pain whacks her.

Lorcan, Sunday, 3:30pm

It's another nightmare. Another twisted string of the textile woven from strands of conflicting *Untime* and real time.

Lorcan is playing the amusement machines with the boys, having a good time, letting himself loose in the lethargy of childhood. There is a noise from outside, a furore and a shouting. It grips him, knowing at once something is badly wrong, perhaps he knew it already.

He emerges blinking into the light to see Alice lying on the ground, her eyes open, staring blankly, arms quivering in a fit. She wears a mask of death.

Lorcan drops to his knees and takes her hand. He feels it rigid, fierce, but then it eases.

'What...?' The cold pallor has lifted from Alice and her face is coming to itself again. 'What happened?'

Simon is on the phone for an ambulance. Cian is there beside them. 'Mom, Mom, are you okay. Get up.' He is a very scared child. Darragh is silent, lurking.

Alice starts to pull herself onto her elbows.

'Stay still, love, there's an ambulance coming.'

'I don't need an ambulance, I'm fine. I don't want to lie here.'

'Just wait till they're here, it'll only be a minute.'

In the end it is over twenty minutes before the ambulance arrives. Margaret and Paul turn up, Paul takes the three boys back to his mobile home.

Lorcan and Margaret hold Alice's hands. Somebody in the crowd that has gathered produces a blanket and a pillow.

The paramedic sees no major issues when they arrive and do their basic tests. Blood pressure is bullish but other vital signs are fine. She has to go to the hospital, the symptoms are such that a doctor needs to look at her, but a leisurely trip to Sligo hospital should be sufficient.

Alice is talkative, chatty with the paramedic. 'I'm perfectly okay,' she keeps saying. 'I mean, yes, I have Leukaemia but it's early. It's causing me symptoms but it's not fatal, not at this stage.'

The paramedic, a woman probably in her late twenties, does a great job of keeping Alice relaxed. 'We'll just get you to the hospital, get you checked out, okay, Alice?'

It turns out nobody can go in the ambulance with her, that's been the rule since Covid. Everybody is anxious to help out, to follow her, look after the boys and so on. Lorcan insists on going, and wants the others to prioritise the kids if they can, so he ends up following in the car. He runs home to get the car keys. On a whim, he grabs the *Book*.

The journey jars with him, the sense of wrong is strong. Has he been here before? Is this one of the *Untimes* he has lived through?

There is a memory; Paul's text message just before... what? Something to do with Mike, with Eamo? It's just a scramble in his head. And here is his beloved.

She is dying. Of that he is certain. It was written in stone that moment in the panelled office, with the stern but censorious professor staring at them, speaking to them of tumours. It is only time, that conspiratorial commodity, that is all they have left.

When Alice first came to the Gang, Lorcan was still infatuated with Rhia. He knew the truth about Jim by then, but he had made a vow to Rhia, and it was Jim's heady charisma that gave the Gang its energy. He assumed Alice was hanging around to be near Jim, she wouldn't have been the first, but one night she got him on his own and his whole world changed. Realising she was interested in him, he fell in love right there.

It was not the mind-bending, all-possessing love-force that had bound him to Rhia, it was a gentle but much deeper emotion that had defined his life every day since then. It had been a glorious day when she had kissed him, had taken him into her arms and made him into something different.

What had possessed him to remain in Jim's world? It had always been attractive, the singing, the drinking, there had been joyous days. That was the thing. There was a magical updraft in Jim's presence, a rising tide on top of which all boats were buoyant.

Here was his fundament. Nothing mattered to him like Alice, God knew, this was the problem. Of course he would put his faith into the powers of the *Book*. Why wouldn't he. It was real. He knew it was. So the possibility that it would save her, wipe out the nonsense of the Leukaemia, of course he was always going to cling to that. Nobody - at least nobody who had an inkling of *Untime* - could question that.

But the *Book* had failed him. It will still save him from death, it seems, but it will not fix Alice. What value all the *Untime* the *Book* might produce if he has lost the centre of his world. His boys, his beautiful boys, yes, Cian and Darragh would always be there. He would love them, cherish them, and, if it made any difference to her, he would ensure that she knew that, she understood.

The *Book* is in the boot. He does not know why it is there, why he found time to go into the mobile home, with all the other things he should have been seeing to, and pick up the *Book*. His faith in it is shaken. Both despite and because of the experiences of the last few days, *Untime* and real, the *Book* is becoming something alien to him.

He is pointed towards a corridor to look for St Michael's ward. Ten metres along he finds a four bed ward on the left. Alice is in the last bed.

'Hey, took your time,' she says.

'I was only just behind you.'

'Kidding! I'm just embarrassed that I'm wasting their time here. The nurse has decided on a few tests but radiology is closed for the weekend so they won't be able to do them till Tuesday. I said, look, I'll be with my consultant in Dublin by then. They're okay with that but they can't let me out till the doctor has signed off.'

'Really? Is that all? You were… Jesus, Alice, I thought that was it when I saw you there, I thought you were a goner. I was…'

She reaches out for his hand. 'We've got to work on that. You need to be ready.'

'How can you ever be ready for that? Alice, I love you. I love you so fucking much. I'm so sorry I've been a dick.'

'Yeah, you said. Sorry doesn't buy you much in my shop. But facing up to reality,' she smiles, 'that will be a good place to start.'

Lorcan feels a childish reassurance in that smile. There is an inconceivable hope in accepting the hopelessness of Alice's illness. There is a joy in being just here, in not seeking out *Untime* and opportunities to drink and smoke. He must lay down all of that.

He sits for a time, letting her chat cheerfully about her children, about the joy in their play, how Darragh is opening up while Cian is growing more grave.

His mind drifts to Rhia. She must be here somewhere, he should check on her.

'Would you like me to get you a coffee or a tea or something?' he says.

'I'd like to go home. But yes, if you could get me some water. Sparkling if they have it, just cold.'

He finds the canteen easily enough, but goes looking further. The hospital is based on a rectangular layout with most of it on a single floor, so that it's not long before he comes across Bob sitting in a plastic chair.

'How is she?'

'Not cool, man. Still under. I'm giving her family a shout now, her sister's going to come down, though they are thinking of moving her up to Castlebar. Doesn't sound like they are too keen about minding Forry, though.'

'I heard they weren't too keen on Jim.'

'And some. There's a real "well we told her" attitude. Poor Rhia.'

'And poor Forry.'

'You came to see her?'

He quickly explains about Alice, the sudden seizure.

'Woah, man, what a day, all the ladies in your life struck down like a heavenly plague.'

'What?'

'Soz. I'm not just knocked, dude, don't listen to me. Rhia's in there if you want to see.'

She's in a small ward with two nurses and six beds. Lots of scanners and scary machines, maybe this is their intensive care. Rhia is in the bed by the door looking like John Everett Mill's *Ophelia* with her scarlet hair scattered and her slender pallor emerging from the pillow. She looks peaceful, though the heavy bandaging about her chin leaves you in no doubt of the injury. Her eyes are still, motionless.

Eyes that died once, in Burrow beach, the *Book* brought her back. Why her? Why not Alice? Being with Alice was always a joy, since the moment they met. Rhia was a torment, an unattainable target, a panfull of pain. He had been delighted to let her go and run with Alice, except that he had never actually let her go. She had always been there at some part of his head. He knew that, even if he could barely look the truth in the face.

Might the *Book* save Rhia again, from whatever was going on with her now? What if the *Book* was sending him a message?

A steady ladder of remembrances waterfalls over him, deaths and near deaths and traumas, all undone by the *Book*. It is dizzying, lives and un-lives, memories and un-memories. The *Book* has seemed to be salvation, to be a boon, but it has cruelly cursed him. Life must be lived, not un-lived. *Untime*, whether real or remembered, is *Unlife* and Alice is undeserving of such despicable deceit.

Possibilities swirl in his head like a soup thick with vegetables. He cannot see up from down, the awfulness of Rhia lying here, the terror of losing Alice.

He is standing at the edge of the cold sea, feet frozen, shivering as he walks till the water is up to his knees, his thighs, and with one unspoken resolution, dives.

He walks quickly to the car. Bob has gone off, nobody speaks to him. The *Book* is nestled in his boot, in a cloth bag. Had he known this moment was coming when he had taken the time to fetch it?

Then he's back inside. He pulls the *Book* out of the bag. He feels the fine filigree on the cover, the crisp flesh of the pages, then firmly closes it. He places it on the bed, he places it under the sheet where it might not be noticed for a little while, he places it by Rhia's hand, then he turns and walks away from the mysterious miracle.

Has he gifted her, or cursed himself?

Regret rises in him, but is quickly squashed by the noise of nurses calling. He runs to the ward, but Alice is gone. He checks the corridor, sees a bed disappearing. He runs to the door, a nurse blocks him. The world speeds up, slows down, speeds up.

Through a glass porthole he sees a sterile theatre, Alice's trolley, her hand casually thrown to one side, like a painted Adam reaching for God's hand. He sees a nurse pushing, pushing, pushing. What the hell?

He is leaning forward but the nurse at the door is strong, steadfast. Another nurse, a male, joins her, and together they direct Lorcan to a room. He is sat. He is handed water.

CPR. The nurse had been performing CPR. On Alice. A cold craze oozes through Lorcan's legs, a sharpness in the corner of his vision, a heaviness weighing on his heartbeat. He is saying something now, asking questions. Tea is being offered. Or coffee.

The nurse leaves. Lorcan is left sitting. The nurse returns with milky tea in a plastic cup. The nurse leaves.

Bob appears. Bob, the angel of mercy.

'This is not righteous, dude!'

Bob leaves, promising something stiffer than tea.

The nurse appears. A doctor arrives and begins to talk.

What will it take to stop him talking? Weird words. Unwanted here, unneeded. Annheurism, he hears. Risk factors, spinal tumours. Wasted words, for they cannot tell him truth. There is hair sprouting from the doctors nose, grey nasal hair. Shouldn't doctors trim their nasal hair. What will it take to stop him talking?

Lorcan is led to a room, a private ward room. She is lying there. Her body is still warm. Peaceful, there is no evidence of the furious fight the doctor detailed to him. He kisses her mouth. It seems wrong, sinful.

The unreality is oppressive. There she is, the woman he has loved, has always desperately loved whatever his selfish actions, lying motionless, unresponsive. Face pale, mouth lolling, eyes oddly half open. She should burst into life, but she doesn't.

And then she does. Pure white light shines out of her. She glows. She bursts with the glowing. She begins to rise up from the trolley. She turns in the air, head now upwards, feet on the bed. Eyes still closed, her arms flow wide. She is an angel, glorious divinity rising.

'I have loved you always,' he says, his voice a cracked cup. 'I have loved you always. I have loved you always.'

He reaches up to her hand...

...And she is back in the trolley. There are men. Frank. Simon. Paul. A priest. There is a rosary.

'Hail Mary, full of grace, the Lord is with thee...'

'Holy Mary, mother of God...'

'Hail Mary...'

'Holy Mary...'

He is still holding her hand, now starting to cool, when Margaret arrives. She looks overtaken, defeated. She has strength though, Alice often spoke of it, how she dealt with her sister's death.

'Felicia has Cian and Darragh outside,' she says. 'Do you want to bring them in?'

His first instinct is no. No, of course not. The *Book* will fix this. Why subject the boys to trauma, to half memories that will linger in their dreams.

But the *Book* is gone, his solemn sacrifice rewarded so poorly.

She brings them in. He goes to them, poor trembling twigs. He says nothing, but enfolds them each in turn. *Go out, all my love, all the strength that I can summon. Go into these poor children.*

It is too late, but he will follow the promises he has made. He will walk her journey, if now it is a journey only with the boys, so be it. He will take what comes. He will make her proud.

The boys merge under his arms into a soft mess of tears and trembling.

Lorcan, Sunday, 9:10am

There is no pen in his hand. There is no *Book*. Why would there be a book? His head is spinning, pained, battered.

Alice! He leaps up. He is in the mobile home, in bed. Alice is dead. Was that a dream? Did she die, or…

He checks his phone. It's Sunday. Sunday was… Yes, Sunday, she had a fit and… Dammit, his brain is bursting from the barrage. He checks Find-My on his iPhone, it finds her. She's on the main street, in a cafe. She was going to meet Mike.

Okay, she's not dead. How did he think… ? A book! There's something about a book that he can't quite put his finger on. The book can turn time back? No, that has to be nonsense. What kind of dreams was he having? But yes. Multiple layers of Sundays fight for his focus: a crash, a gun. And Alice, dead on a hospital bed. Dead?

Rhia. It all had something to do with Rhia. No, too much information.

He quickly pulls on his clothes. He needs to get to her. As he opens the bedroom, Cian is there. Cian is crying.

'What's wrong?' he says, though he probably already knows.

'I had a dream…'

Lorcan holds him, and Cian doesn't pull back. The boy heaves deep lungfuls of air as Lorcan pulls him tight.

'Dreams can be cruel,' he says, 'but it's only a dream. Don't fret.'

He hears Margaret and Frank coming in the front door, they must have been at mass. Margaret sticks her head in when she sees the bedroom door open.

'Ah, the poor boy,' she says.

'Will you stay with your grandma for a few minutes,' he says to Darragh. 'I just need to run and get Mom, okay?'

Part of him feels he should stay, share his support, but he needs to see Alice. He runs up towards the street, pauses at the turn towards Rhia's cabin. There's something tugging at his head, but he's damned if he can remember.

He's wheezing when he makes the main street. As he turns the corner, he sees her.

She smiles and brushes hair from her face, a natural gesture of her implicit splendour.

'Hey,' she says. 'Are you alright?'

'No. No, I'm not alright. You're not alright.'

'What the hell?'

'I've got all these things. Going on in my head. Going round and round. It's doing me in.'

'Surely it's too early for you to be drinking?'

'I'm not doing that any more.'

'Well, that would be a good start.'

'Do you remember.' He's trying to pull it out of his own —memory but it's like two music tracks played together, neither fully makes sense. 'A hospital, you were in hospital. You fell over. No, not that. There was something first.'

'Lorcan, you're scaring me.'

'You don't remember? Did you dream anything?'

'Yes, I guess.' She shrugs. 'There was a light, I was walking towards it. Mammy was there. It was really peaceful, you know like that dream where you fly.'

'Jesus, Alice, you died.'

'It was a dream, Lorcan.'

'Home. We have to get home, to the mobile home, now.'

He grabs her hand firmly and starts pulling her towards the campsite.

'Stop!'

'Please, Alice. Please, just trust me. I know I've been a prick. I will change. I am changing. But for now, I need you to really trust me.'

For a moment, she could go either way. She accedes, but she's not happy as he pulls her bodily along the track towards the home. He gets her in the door. Margaret has the boys at the table and is pouring cocoa pops.

'Is everything okay?'

'Towels. We need towels and a basin.'

Margaret stands like a fish, mouth bobbing open. Is she

remembering too? Then she starts gathering towels.

'I don't...' says Alice, but she doesn't finish. She runs to the bathroom and Margaret is right behind her.

'Come on, boys. Mom needs a bit of privacy. Let's go see what's happening on the beach.'

Neither Cian nor Darragh is happy with being dragged out. God love them, what a time they've had, if their half-memories match his, and now they see their Mom unwell.

He walks with them over the dune.

'Boys, I want to say something to you. I'm really sorry I haven't been part of this holiday, not properly. I've been off doing my own thing or lying in bed most of the time. I should have been using this as a precious opportunity to spend every minute I could with you.'

'Uncle Simon's been playing with us, when we're not with Mom.'

'I know, and hey, I couldn't teach you to surf like he has, but that's not what it's about. It should be about us being together.'

'Yeah, that's okay, Dad. You can be a bit dull is all.'

'Ah, gee, thanks.'

He tries to draw them out a bit on what they remember but they've lost interest. Darragh is speed-cubing while Cian has found an old burst ball to kick about. Lorcan gets the all clear on his phone.

'So what the hell was that all about?' asks Alice once they have sat the boys to breakfast again.

'I can't explain it to you, Alice. I don't know what's going on, but I knew absolutely that something bad was going to happen to you and we had to get home. And now I know absolutely that we really, really have to get you to hospital.'

'I don't need to go to hospital.'

'You do. Your symptoms...' He stops to pull her a little further out of earshot of the boys. 'Your symptoms have been getting worse and you know it. We can't wait any longer.'

'Tuesday. Tomorrow maybe.'

'No, today. You have to trust me.'

Alice is torn, he can see, and confused. She lacks his certainty but concedes the point about Lorcan getting her home just in time. How did he know?

In the end, she admits to a sense of unease and agrees for Lorcan to take her to a hospital. Margaret agrees, acknowledging she has been worried too, and she'll look after the boys.

Alice pops in to Beth and Jackie in their mobile home to let them know she's heading off.

'You've not been looking great,' says Jackie.

'Hush you,' says Beth. 'You've been looking great, what she means is we've seen signs that you're not well.'

'The sooner the better,' says Jackie.

Lorcan is overwhelmed by anxieties as they get in the car. There's something about Rhia, and then there's Eamo, things he can't put solidity around but a strong sense of doom. Then he gets on the road and it gets worse. He jumps when he sees a truck coming towards him on the main road, and has to stop in a farm gate to get his breath back.

When they arrive at the hospital, there's a sharp familiarity. He recognises the ward with the machines to which they are directed after they've spoken to the triage nurse. He wonders why Rhia is not here, then cannot work out why he had expected her to be.

When the doctor appears, Lorcan feels a cold clamp on his heart. Something brutal has happened somewhere. His feels seasick from the desperate dislocation that washes over him. From the look of him, the doctor may have felt something too.

They explain Alice's illness, the worsening symptoms and the vomiting and diarrhoea. He does the basic tests, sends off some bloods, but isn't seeing anything.

'There's the tumour on her spine,' says Lorcan.

'Yes, you said. I would need to see the charts.'

'But won't that represent more risk? Like in the brain and that?'

'Maybe, but I don't have the equipment here…'

'Wouldn't there be a heightened risk of aneurism?'

'Well, possibly, though that wouldn't explain…'

'Look, doctor.' Lorcan has to pull himself back, get under control. Whatever is getting to him is really taking its toll. 'I just feel… I feel there's something, a risk, we need to check.'

The doctor opens his mouth, takes a breath. He's ready to send this lunatic and his wife away, but then he stops. He shakes his head as if dizzy. 'I…' Again, a look comes over him. Does he remember the conversation they had? But then, what was that conversation? 'Hang on a minute.'

He leaves them there for several minutes. 'Look,' he says when he comes back. 'This is ridiculous, but I agree, I just have this feeling… We don't have an MRI here, but there's one in Castlebar. You know where that is? The Mayo University Hospital? It's about an hour's drive. My friend, Jennifer, she's the chief radiologist. She's nearly finished her shift but she'll hold on a few minutes if you can get there. Listen, this is a big favour I've asked her, you can't just dump people on the MRI without proper diagnosis but...'

Lorcan shakes his hand and thanks him.

'Please don't tell anybody I did this,' says the doctor as they run out the door.

The road from Sligo to Castlebar is much better than the blind back roads that lead to Enniscrone. Lorcan can feel more confident as he drives.

'Are we just fools doing this?' asks Alice. 'I'd rather be home with the kids.'

'No, there's something I can't explain, but I can't let this go.'

'You've been fooling yourself about my illness all along.'

'What do you think? In your heart of hearts. Am I still wrong?'

She doesn't answer. He keeps driving. She calls Margaret, and then Beth, to let them know. Beth tells her she'll follow to Castlebar in case she can be any help.

They are informed at reception that radiology is closed and have to beg and plead the receptionist to call Jennifer. They are grudgingly given directions.

'This is very odd,' says Jennifer, a strong looking woman in her forties with hair forced firmly back from a central parting. 'I wouldn't touch this, you understand, if it was anybody but Ed asking me. No charts, no referral letter, no medical history. I owe him a big favour, he's called it in.'

Lorcan desperately explains it all again, though she remains unconvinced. 'I think it's a mistake,' she says, 'but I've promised Ed, so let's do this.'

Alice has to strip to a hospital gown and remove any metal or jewellery, then she's taken into the room while Lorcan is left sitting outside. He can hear the massive machine moving mechanically from his seat, and the high pitched fussing of fans.

Through an open door, he can see a control room. Jennifer and another woman stare at massive monitors. Images of a head - skull, teeth, eyes, tongue - build themselves into layers. The images spin and dip and dive, fly-throughs on a video game. As one, the two women shift forward in their seats; Jennifer points at the screen. The zoom in madly on something menacing.

Alice is dressed and ready by the time a doctor arrives. Jennifer takes her into the control room, closing the door this time. When she emerges she sits beside them.

'How did you get referred here?' she asks.

'Alice has been unwell... And, we pulled in some favours.'

'Yeah, it's kinda odd, but, yes, there is definitely an aneurysm there, I'm not sure who spotted the symptoms but you may well owe your life to them. It's not ruptured, thank God, but it's very angry looking.'

'Jesus!'

'So, we are going to need to act fast. You're a patient of Professor Bailey?'

'Yes.'

'He's in the Mater? The best thing is if we get you back there, but first I'm going to get some injections lined up, so I'll do that first. Nimodipine and probably, and an ACE inhibitor. That will control your blood pressure, reduce the chance of a rupture.'

She goes through details. The aneurysm can be treated simply, a catheter is used to reach it through an artery and insert a coil or a stent, depending on the surgeon. She'll stay in intensive care until the direct danger is averted. She is going to call the professor but she suspects he'll want to move on that neck tumour as soon as she's stable. She'll also organise an ambulance; Alice will need constant monitoring.

She leaves and they sit in silence. Lorcan sees the Professor's office again, the panelling and padded armchairs. He recalls the way his head pushed out the bad news, drove it back. Why? Why was it he could not be there for her, fully present? Why was he already thinking about drinking?

He kisses her.

'How are you feeling?'

'Scared, but... I knew this was coming, Lorcan. It just came a little sooner than I wanted. Tuesday, I said.'

'Yeah. I'm going to be here for you. I'll be there in the ambulance.'

'No.'

Lorcan is slapped, shocked. He has no right to expect her affection, but a certain rejection is an ice wash.

'No,' she says again. 'Your place is with Cian and Darragh. They need you now.' She grabs his hand, tight, totally certain. 'I have Beth, she's in reception now, her and Jackie. Beth will come with me, if anybody's allowed in the ambulance. You go get the boys, be with them.'

4: Seeing

Alice, Monday, 2:15pm

There is a numb sense of pain, a sore edge of numbness. Alice opens her eyes. She can't tell what day it is. It is daytime, the light tells her that. Is it two, three days since the ambulance brought her here? It has been a whirlwind world since that moment.

Lorcan is beside her, holding her hand. Every time she has come to, there has been somebody with her. Only one, the ICU has strict rules. It has been Margaret, Beth, Jackie, Simon, Frank, and then Lorcan more often than the others. An unending stream of love.

'How are you feeling, love?' he says in a low voice. The ICU is a noisy place twenty-four hours a day, but the clean clinical atmosphere tends to intimidate people, like the echo in a sacred cathedral.

'Woozy,' she says, her throat scratchy. Instinctively, she tries to cough it clear but immediately regrets it as a javelin of pain spikes her neck. She has to shut her eyes and count the heartbeats till is subsides. 'Not great.'

'I love you,' he says.

She nods. He has told her that often on his vigil. Sometimes it has seemed sour; where was he when he could have proven his love? Words are cheap. Perhaps time heals wounds, for now she welcomes his affection. Or maybe he is sincere. She prays that she will come out of this bed, of this hospital, and have time to find out.

'The signs are all still good,' he says. 'They reckon you're out of trouble with the aneurysm, But they'll need to wait a couple of weeks before they work on the spine tumour.'

She nods, or tries to, having little mobility.

The plans are in place. There will be surgery, then radio-therapy followed by chemo. There will be home time, time to be with children and family, as long as they can get the pain under control. It is as good as she could have hoped.

How did her mother deal? Was she faced by these facts? She tried to recall. By rights she was old enough, but she can only remember her own pain. Despite the weeks in Enniscrone, her mother is a ghost, and not a strength.

She squeezes Lorcan's hand, and he smiles.

Lorcan, Tuesday, 10:00am

As soon as Lorcan is relieved in his vigil by Simon, he picks up Cian and Darragh from Margaret.

'I can hold onto them for a while,' she says. 'You need to rest.'

'I'm grand. I'm well rested after a month on the doss from work.'

'It's great to work somewhere that you have that leeway.'

'Yeah, probably more than I've deserved. I'll try and get logged in later, start wading through the emails.'

'Ah, it's a bit early, isn't it. Alice is going to need you.'

'She is, but it's going to be a long journey.'

Margaret nods.

'So,' he says when he gets the boys into the car. 'What'll we do. Your treat.'

'Football,' shouts Cian.

'Ice cream,' shouts Darragh.

So they go to the park and have a kickabout. Cian is really coming on with his skills and can run around Lorcan without Lorcan actually letting him. Darragh is still clumsy and heavy footed, but Cian passes him the ball to take the score every so often.

Afterwards, they go to *Emily's Amazing Ice Cream Emporium*. The boys know exactly what to order. Lorcan spots the *Death By Chocolate* and decides that should be safe enough. A monstrous glass dish stuffed with a dozen shades of brown is handed to him, along with a monstrous bill.

'Just us boys,' he says.

'I prefer it when Mom is here,' says Darragh.

'We all do, buddy. She'll be out of hospital in a couple of days, but she'll be tired. We may have to postpone taking her out for ice cream.'

'I'll look after her.'

'You'll need to go to school.'

'But Mom's ill,' complains Cian.

'And the best thing we can do is get life back to normal. You know Mom is going to be ill for a long time. Us moping around isn't going to do any good for her. I mean, yeah, we're going to have to muck in. You boys will have to do housework, Cian, you're old enough to do your own laundry, and Darragh, you can start by washing your own hair. We'll sort out the hoovering and gardening.'

'Awww,' says Cian.

'Come on, Cian,' says Darragh. 'We can do this for Mom.'

'Yeah,' says Lorcan. 'We've got to be together in this.'

He does his best on the *Death By Chocolate*, then admits defeat and hands the brown mess over the boys. They dig in, the gravitas of the conversation they have had is dispelled in the excitement of the moment. Childhood is such a blessing.

He puts his head in his hands. The weight of being in control, of worrying about little things that Alice once took charge of, is heavy on him. The future hangs over him, it will be exhausting. Somehow, though, he feels more ready for it, the claustrophobic cobwebs in his head have been swept away by the trip to Enniscrone. Whatever is ahead, he is as ready as he will ever be.

Alice, Wednesday, 3:00pm

Alice is out of ICU and in a private ward. The pain in her head and neck is much milder, like the end of a bad headache, without the sharpness that had tortured her at the weekend. She still isn't ready for the main surgery, that is clear, so she has a short reprieve. Tomorrow, all going well she will walk out and have at least a week at home.

Lorcan is with her again, reading a book of Seamus Heaney poems. His long waits in the hospital seem to have brought him back to the world of poetry; it's probably ten years since she saw him reading. Maybe he will start writing again. Calm drifts over her like a warm summer breeze with hints of wheat and salt and basil.

There is a soft knock on the door. Mike enters awkwardly, get's caught as the door swings back on him. Lorcan leaps to help.

'Hey,' says Mike. 'How's the patient? You're looking good.'

'Looking alive,' she smiles. 'You didn't have to come and see me.'

'Are you kidding me? Excuse for a trip to the Big Schmoke?'

She laughs. 'Great to see you.'

'Okay,' says Lorcan, 'I'll maybe wait outside…'

'Ah, don't be jealous, Lorcan. Can't a girl have her ex-boyfriend visit her in bed without her husband being jealous?'

'Um, okay.' He takes the flowers from Mike. 'I'll see if the nurses have another vase.'

'How's Eamo doing?' she asks once Lorcan has left.

'Sorry, bad news on that front. He left, went back to Dublin.'

'What?'

'Yeah, he was loving it, was a natural, crowd all loved him.'

'But?'

'But it isn't far from the tree the acorn falls. We had a couple of lads in one night, they were a bit leery, needed throwing out, nothing bad now, but bothering other customers. Eamo starts to shuffle them to the door but one of them gives him a bit of lip. Next thing, Eamo loses it, by the time we dragged him off the poor lad, we had to call an ambulance.'

'Aw, shit. I'm sorry, Mike.'

'Not as sorry as me. He really was a lovely guy, if you pardon the psychopathic violence. He even rang me to apologise after he scarpered. We had to tell the cops it was him of course, don't know what the follow up will be, but...' He shrugs. 'You can't save them all, Alice.'

'Mike, I'm so gutted over that. Eamo is very dear to me.'

'I know, but there's something in that family. Any road, I made some enquiries and he's firmly ensconced back in his family again. I'm sorry you'll need to move on from that one.'

'Again, sorry to bring that upon you.'

'Not a bit of it, I was delighted. In fact, if you have a chance to talk to your boss, I'm happy to work with other kids, we enjoyed having Eamo so much.'

'Other kids may not be hard workers.'

'Hard work or hard man, you can't have it all. Listen, other news. I'm not sure if it's good or bad news. And maybe now isn't the right time, but anyway, my agent in London found your father.'

'What?'

'Um, yeah.' He pulls out his phone. 'I can call him now, put you onto him. I just spoke to him a moment ago, he's ready. If now isn't good for you... He wants to explain, but I can go through it privately if you would rather.'

'Go through what?'

'Well, why he was absent all those years.'

'He's going to tell me?'

'Only if you feel strong enough.'

She feels woozy, tired and bored at the same time. Now really isn't the time for conversations like this. On the other hand, her father, her actual father, is on the other end of a phone line. Could she let an opportunity like this go? But what the hell can he say that would make this good?

He holds the phone out. 'That's his number, just hit green. I can wait outside.'

'No, you stay.'

Lorcan comes back with a vase. The nurses have loads of them, apparently, gifts from ex-patients. She tells him the news. 'Do I call him?'

'The hell, yes, of course you call him. He's your father.' He looks at Mike. 'You're sure he's her father?'

'Oh, yes, I got a comprehensive history and it all lines up.'

She looks at the iPhone he has put into her hands, a Spanish number displayed. Here, after so many years, is her family. Blood family. She is suddenly scared.

She presses green.

'Hello?' The voice is heavily inflected with Spanish, deep but scratchy.

She moves the call to speakerphone. 'Hi, this is, eh, Alice.'

'Alice. My God, it is so good to hear from you after so many years.'

'I… Daddy?'

'Si. Yes. I am Carlos. I am your father. Although… It's lovely to hear you call me Daddy, but I don't think it is right. I have done nothing to deserve your friendship.'

This is so weird. What do you say to a man who holds the most intimate of relationships with you but is a complete stranger?

'I can barely remember you. I think you took me to the zoo once?'

'I wish I could answer. Most of those years, they are a horrible blur.'

'Okay, so…?'

'So I tell my story. Alice, this is a very bad story. You will think me even more horrible when you hear it. Part of my program is to take responsibility for what I have done, but that does not mean you must listen. Take from it what you need and leave what hurts.'

'Program?'

'I am a recovering addict, Alice. I throw my life away on heroin.'

Lorcan, Wednesday, 3:10pm

Lorcan listens while Alice's father tells a distressing tale. London in the eighties had a fantastic music scene, and Carlos was right in the middle of it. That's where he met Bella, when she was working as a journalist. He had gigged as a bass guitarist, initially doing well. He played on tour and in studio with bands like The Pretenders and the Jam and, yes, he did once stand in for a Bruce Springsteen gig in Manchester.

Of course, success brought the parties, the chaos, the descent into drugs. He was fired from one gig after another once the heroin became his king until he couldn't get work. Bella kept faith in him, but he had time only for his fix.

'I throw my phone away, Alice, you know. Anytime I contact Bella I am looking for money. Once, I steal from her. She has me and feeds me and when she is in the bathroom I take her wallet. I leave you crying.'

He was clean once, for three months — that may have been the zoo visit Alice spoke about — but then he fell again. He was homeless until his brother found him and took him home to Spain.

'I am clean now for twelve years,' he says, his voice echoing a plaintiveness that speaks of exhaustion. 'Of course, when I look for Bella, I look for you, I find nobody. I thought she had found a better life and I was glad. Mike calls me, he tells me she died and I am so so sorry, Alice. The pain I cause her, the neglect of you. I cannot begin to put words around the harm.'

As he listens, Lorcan is reminded of something. A father, neglectful, absent, inebriated. Where does this image come from? He feels it might be real, but it can't be. His own father was absent in a way through his childhood but it would be a long stretch to call him neglectful or inebriated.

Sparkles splash across his inner eye as the thought plays out, his head is light. He has to sit on the edge of the bed. A whole mindscape pours past him, bent around some kind of book. He is falling, he is lying, he is maimed and mutilated in the jungle. Weird worlds swirl and fog about him.

Jesus, he thinks, *is this the alcohol withdrawal? Is this the DTs?* He has not had a drink since Saturday, of course, and his shame at his overindulgence for the previous couple of weeks is a in some ways a mirror of Carlos.

'I can never make anything up to you, Alice,' Carlos is saying. 'But anything I can do, any little thing, I will make it my goal.'

There is a minute of silence. Lorcan looks into Alice's face but cannot tell what is going through her head. Suddenly she laughs, then flinches, perhaps she's reawoken the pain.

'Ow,' she says, still half laughing. 'I thought I would find my mother, you know revisit the time when she died. That's why I went to Sligo. I never thought I'd find my father. You are my father, right?'

'Yes. That is truth, I can be sure.'

'And you remember my mother?'

'I have no right to say this, Alice, but I am still in love with her. She was the only good thing I have done in my life. I am heartbroken.'

'Then you can tell me stories. You can tell me about her, so I can gather her to me.'

Alice, Friday, 4:00pm

Alice is well, at least as well as she has felt for a year. It's frustrating. She's ready. Her head is in the right place. She's going to fight this thing. She's going to take everything they will throw at her, but she has to wait at least another week before they are prepared to start the surgery. She feels all dressed up but without a ball to go to.

Her father's sudden reappearance on the other end of phone and zoom calls, the tales he's told her of when her mother was young, have been a wonderful uplift. She hates him, despises the ground he walks on, that he would leave her Mammy, that he would leave her, what appalling selfishness. But the balm of soft remembered stories is just what she needs, so she will tolerate him for now.

For now, she has a short respite at home, and good friends to keep her company. Beth is making tea and Jackie butters some hot scones she brought with her.

'Guys, you don't need to treat me like an invalid.'

'You are an invalid.'

'Jackie, don't talk to Alice like that.'

'But she is.'

'Alice, I'm so sorry.'

'Yeah but I'm still sitting here doing nothing while you two fuss around. And all the time you put into looking after me in Enniscrone.'

'What the hell did we do in Enniscrone? Eat and drink, and an odd walk on the beach.'

'You were there for me.'

'Well, that's the easy bit. That's just a personal pleasure.'

'So anyway,' says Jackie. 'Did you get what you needed out of the holiday?'

'Hospitalised and rushed under life-threatening conditions back to

Dublin? Yeah, I can tick that one off the bucket list, thanks.'

'Jackie!' says Beth, 'can you not stop saying the wrong thing?'

'Jaysus, everything I say is the wrong thing for you, oh Beth my beautiful and wise old friend. But it's a real question, Alice. You wanted to touch base with your past, find that part of yourself again, wasn't it? How you feeling now about it?'

She stops and thinks. There was certainly a need to explore, to think about her mother. What did she find? A philandering father. Brief memories of her mother. No signposts to salvation, certainly.

'I think,' she says, 'that yes, I did find what I needed. I found what I needed because I took it with me. Mammy will always be the core of my soul, and Daddy, well, let's leave that for now. But it's you too. It's Cian and Darragh. Margaret and Frank. Simon. Paul. That's what I went to find, that is what I was seeking.'

'Well, that's very bleeding philosophical.'

'Jackie! Go on, Alice.'

'That's it. At the end of the day, life is very simple. We live, we die. We touch those around us and they touch us. When I was lying in hospital you guys were there for me. Some day, hopefully years away yet, you'll be the people saying my eulogy. Maybe that's enough.'

'Feck's sake, you're ruining me make up.'

'I notice you didn't mention Lorcan, Alice.'

'Yes, Lorcan too. I'm still sounding him out, but he's changed. The aneurysm gave him a kick in the head, I think. Suddenly he's engaged, he doesn't smell of smoke, hasn't been drinking, and no sign of his eejit buddy Jim, thank the Lord. He's been so bloody remote since the diagnosis. Maybe he needed to go through some stuff, who knows? Maybe. Key thing is he's putting his life and soul into Cian and Darragh now, that's all I ever wanted, to know they'll have him and not some drunken dropout.'

Beth puts an arm around her. 'We'll always keep an eye them, you know that.'

'I do, but it's not the same. They'll always have a father, not like me. That makes all the difference.'

'Come here,' says Jackie. 'What did happen to Jim? And to Rhia? I know Bob was in to see you, but I haven't heard anything about those two.'

'Me neither. They dropped off the face of the earth. I think we can be reasonably sure that Jim's in a boozer somewhere, but we've heard not a word. I hope to God Rhia's okay, but...'

'But you've got other things to take your attention.'
'I do.'
'Well, good riddance.'

Lorcan, Later

Lorcan gets his coffee and sits on one of the sofas at the back of Insomnia. Rhia had asked to meet him. She suggested the *Roundabout* pub, where they had met before, but he is off the booze for a month, so he insisted on a cafe. He's not had a single fag, not since that horrific day when Alice was hospitalised, and he's steering clear of drink, so when Bob suggested they do a month off the gargle together, explore other opportunities, he was all for it. They had gone to a couple of plays, a book fair, all kinds of things he'd never thought was in Bob's repertoire at all. Staying sober has left him with a little halo.

There has been no sign of Jim in that time but this is not unusual. Jim has always been liable to disappear for days or even weeks, and Bob and Lorcan are not going to chase him out only to have him sabotage and undermine their sobriety plan.

He runs through the newspaper on his iPad while he waits. The headline "Gang War in North Dublin" catches his eye. It's a long article, a piece of pure journalism, looking into the escalating violence between two Dublin crime gangs. Sure enough, there's a picture of the arch aggressor, Peter "Pluto" Shortall. He is deviously familiar looking, like the aroma of some past meal he can't place, just the taste on his tongue to tantalise him. Behind, just visible getting out of a car, is Eamo. It's dismaying that he has descended again, after Alice's efforts.

Rhia comes in and sits straight down.

'Hey,' he says. 'Can I get you a coffee?'

'Lorcan,' she smiles. 'You look really good. No, sorry, I don't drink coffee any more. Just water and oat milk smoothies.'

'Sounds delicious.'

'Lorcan, the *Book*, my God, you nearly destroyed me.'

A warm fuzz floods his senses, like the coffee is triple-shot caffeine.

Something about the book, what was it? Had he lent her something to read? It was there at the back of his head, nagging.

There is something about her hair. It's shorter, straighter, but still there's a difference. Is it getting thin, maybe, and are there the start of wrinkles on that perfect face? He wonders if he is noticing something new, or seeing a truth he had missed.

'Sorry,' he says. 'I'm not sure what you mean.'

'Jesus, Lorcan. The *Book*. The *Book*!' She shakes her head. 'You don't remember, do you?'

'I… Sorry. I know I should. I feel like I've forgotten something. It's not your birthday or anything?'

'The *Book*, Lorcan. You gave it to me? You got it when you were ten, or something. Remember the beach, Burrow beach. The *Book* saved me when I tried to drown myself.'

A wave washes over him. He does remember, or did he dream that. He remembers her naked, running into the sea, oh yes, he remembers that, and… And what? She died? Was she really naked?

'I remember you drowning, but you didn't.'

'Right. And other times, you told me there were other times that you died and the *Book* brought you back.'

It's there, and then it isn't, like trying to remember equations when he's crammed too hard for an exam.

'You remember that Jim hit me? In Enniscrone, threw me against a table. I was unconscious. You gave me the *Book*.'

'Okay.'

'And then I woke up, it was that morning again.'

'Yes. I remember, that's how it works, the *Book*. I remember. I gave it to you in hospital.'

'Oh, I didn't know that, I just… It's like you said. I woke up and I was writing in the *Book* and it was before Jim hit me.'

'Yes, yes. And you saved Alice.'

'Did I? What happened?'

'She died? I think? No, she couldn't have. No. We went to the hospital. They found the aneurysm. Fuck, why is this so hard?'

'So I woke up and told Jim, and he hit me again, only harder this time, and I woke up, and he hit me and I woke up. Fuck, fuck, fuck…'

There are tears on her cheeks. She drops her head to her chest and heaves heavy breaths.

'He kept hitting me and hitting me and the *Book* kept bringing me back.'

'I don't understand.'

'I stood up for myself.' She lifts her head and her wet eyes gleam. 'Lorcan, I stood up for myself. I took Forry and we got out of there and we drove to Dublin and left him.'

'Jesus. He must be pissed off.'

'He went ape-shit. My dad got security guards for me, it was the only way I could stay safe, then we got a barring order.'

'Fuck. So you left Jim?'

'Yes. Yes, Lorcan. I've left Jim.'

'Wow. Like fuck wow! Where is he now?'

'England, I believe. Dad gave him a couple of grand and told him to stay away. He'll be back, of course, when he drinks his way through it. He went on the ferry, kept texting me to say he was getting the Gang back together.'

'The Booze Cruise? Hah!'

'Yeah, you remember that? We used to all go. Before you met Alice. And when Jim used to pass out, you and I, well, we'd get it on.' She gives him a bright beaming smile, all trace now of the tears gone.

'Hah,' he laughs. A couple of times they got into some heavy kissing while Jim slept. 'I suppose we did. How I used to wish Jim would just stay passed out.'

'That's why I wanted to meet you.'

'Oh?'

'Well, I'm single now. Jim's gone.'

'Yeah…'

'Look, I hate to be harsh, but, well, how long does Alice have left?'

The penny drops. He gapes at her, unable to believe. He has loved her for so many years, blind to her stupidity, but even so he cannot believe this.

'How long does she have left?' He can't help but laugh out loud. 'She has forever.'

Printed in Great Britain
by Amazon